# FIRST TO GO

*The True Story of Bridget Frisby*

By

# Pam Skelton

*For Esme (RIP) who told me so much about her mother.*

# CONTENTS

"I remember, I remember
The house where I was born…"
- *Thomas Hood, Poet (1799-1845)*

"There is a spot in Tipperary
That's very dear to me,
My heart lies in Tipperary
Which I left so long ago."
- *Old Irish song*

"Give me your tired, your poor, your huddled masses yearning to breathe free, the wretched refuse of your teeming shore. Send these, the homeless, tempest-tossed to me."
*(Inscription on the base of the Statue of Liberty, New York, U.S.A.)*

# CHAPTER 1

Crash!! I was woken by a loud bang! – A booming sound, which frightened the wits out of me. I was on board the ship *Luciana*, a ship of the White Star Line, and we were in the middle of the Atlantic Ocean.

It was August 1898 – I was 18 years old and on my way to a new life in America. I was terrified and turned to John, my companion, saying, "What was that noise?"

John raised himself from his bedroll and we could scarcely see each other in the dark. He put his hand out towards me and held my hand firmly.

"Wait now a minute, Bridget, while I find out." He stood up, pulled on his trousers and made his way towards the steps.

As he left me I said, "Be careful, John!" I realised the ship was no longer sailing steadily.

The ship was tossing and turning on the turbulent Atlantic waves. John was back within a few minutes. "We've sailed right into a storm," he said. It was very dark where we were on the steerage deck but we could hear the bangs and scuffles as other passengers were flung about on their beds. Then a member of the ship's crew arrived to say no one was allowed on deck and all the hatches were being battened down. The ship heaved and pitched and made little headway for many hours. Babies cried and women could be heard praying. The eeriness in that creaking vessel is something I'll never forget. The strange hollow sound and the noise of the crashing waves had replaced the happy, joyous party of the previous evening. Luggage began to slide across the decks and belongings of all sorts came crashing down. We didn't sleep again that night.

Morning was a long time coming but as it grew lighter people began to move about. I got up and noticed how hot and stuffy it was. There was the stench of vomit in the air which I hoped would clear when the hatches were opened up.

The ship was tossed high on the waves. As it ploughed through the water there were loud crashes each time the bows hit a new wave. Many people were suffering from seasickness and lay prostrate, moaning and crying. Some were very ill and unable to stand the confusion. The poor wee children had been sick many times; they hadn't eaten and their stomachs were empty so they were continually retching, making their throats sore. John and I were lucky as, in spite of everything, neither of us was seasick.

Later that day the storm seemed to abate a little and the hatches were opened up to allow fresh air in. What a relief! It was so stuffy in that confined space. John ventured up on deck and returned to say that the ship seemed to be wallowing in the high seas and we didn't seem to be making much headway. At one moment we were in a deep trough of sea with high walls of water all around and then, when the ship rose to the top of the waves, he could see mile upon mile of rough sea and white horses. Water was continually splashing over the decks so he came down below quickly. It wasn't wise to stay up there for long although he was grateful for the fresh air. The skies were heavy and grey. The Atlantic storm was all around us. I prayed we would weather it and reach the end of our journey safely. We had heard terrible stories of people being lost at sea and I was afraid.

Then, thankfully, after about 24 hours we left the storm behind. The sea gradually grew calmer and the ship was able to steam on. We were going to be late arriving in New York.

We were now into the fifth day of our journey. The mood on the ship had changed. Gone were the scenes of merriment, the singing and the dancing. Our fellow travellers were sober and those who had been sick took time to recover. It seemed that our adventure was over and the reality of our situation began to sink in and we had time to think about the past and the future.

Sitting on my bedroll I thought about how I came to be there. After months of preparation I had said goodbye to my native Ireland and to my family and friends at home. I remembered the start of our journey when the ship rolled steadily from side to side as it edged its way out of Cork Harbour and into the Atlantic swell. I realised I would probably never see my family again.

It had been a long struggle to reach this point in my life. Preparations for my journey seemed to have taken months. Sitting there, in that damp, dark hull of a ship my mind went back to my life in Ireland.

# CHAPTER 2

I was born in Ireland in 1878. I lived with my parents and my seven brothers and sisters in a small house in the hamlet of "Islands" in county Tipperary halfway between the small towns of Mullinahone and Ballingarry. My father was the village schoolmaster at nearby Mohober and all the children in the family attended his school. We all joined the school at the very early age of three.

In our early years, our life was dominated by school life. My father was a strict disciplinarian and we knew where we stood with him. In spite of this we loved him dearly and he was the pillar of society. I can see him now, standing at his desk with chalk in one hand and the other hand waving in the air as he expounded on one subject or another. He was deeply religious and like most Irish he was a Catholic and his curriculum contained half an hour of religious instruction every day.

Papa had the advantage of being a scholar in many subjects. There were over a hundred children on the school roll. My father was a slight figure but his long beard and side-whiskers, made him look quite fearsome to some children. He had brown hair and blue eyes but I often noticed that when he was cross his eyes looked a steely grey.

My mother, in her own way, seemed to have a stronger and more enduring faith than Papa's. His was a regimented faith but Mama's faith inspired us. I remember the whole family sitting round the fire on dark winter evenings as she told us stories from the Bible. We listened to her tales of the saints for hours. She knew them all and, as young children, we were fascinated. At the end of the evening she taught us how to pray with our rosary beads. When Grandma Kate was alive she had joined us in this devotion. By this single act alone my mother brought moral control to bear in our home. We loved her dearly and we looked up to her and her values. I shall never forget the picture she had of the Virgin Mary. It hung on the wall above her bed head. It was a true and lasting symbol of her faith.

Our house, when compared with others in the district was quite big, although we only had two bedrooms upstairs. One was over the kitchen and the other over the parlour. They were quite big rooms running from the front of the house to the back. Each had a window in the front overlooking the road and a window in the back overlooking our small farm and the countryside in the distance.

Grandpa Jack told me that when he was a boy the house had a thatched roof but now it had slates. Grandpa Jack looked after our small farm. His father and mother had come to live in Islands in about 1800. His father was a cooper, making wooden casks, barrels, tubs and butter churns. This had been a good living and Grandpa Jack had taken up the trade too but, in recent years, with the coming of the milk co-operatives and the introduction of steel casks the trade had seen a steep decline. So Grandpa Jack had taken to farming.

As youngsters our whole world revolved around our home, the farm and school. We had little idea what the outside world was like. Our only excursions were visits we made to the small market town about 3 miles distant. Normally we walked to town but if we were lucky we might cadge a lift in Papa's cart, pulled by Ned the donkey. Ned was our favourite donkey. Our other donkeys were used around the farm but Ned was kept solely for pulling the cart.

We had five neighbouring houses and with our neighbours we lived close to the earth and close to each other. Grandpa Jack once told me that he remembered the good old days when there were large family gatherings. Family members came from far and wide. It wasn't like that now. We rarely saw our other relations and indeed didn't even know where some of them lived. Grandpa Jack explained to me that in the old days families were much larger and there could be as many as twenty or thirty years separating brothers and sisters and up to 15 or even 20 children in a family. It wasn't unusual for older members of the family to be established with families of their own, whilst their mother was still bearing babies.

One or two relatives lived nearby. Uncle George Frisby and his wife Aunt Mary had lived in the small house next to ours but they died when I was a small child. Their children had all grown up and moved away by the time I was born. Several of them had emigrated to Australia but the two oldest girls had married the Delaney brothers and lived nearby. Then there were the Corcorans who were relatives of Mama. We often met them at Mass. We only saw the wider family, the Frisbys, Corcorans and Walshes when they turned up for weddings, christenings and funeral wakes. These occasions were rare.

As I look back on my life, I am amazed when I remember how many people lived in our house. When I was very young Grandpa John and Grandma Kate slept in the bedroom over the living room. They slept in a large double bed at the far end of the room near the window at the back of the house.

Mama and Papa slept in our bedroom, which was above the kitchen. A curtain divided our room, giving some privacy to Mama and Papa, away from the prying eyes of us children – although now that I know more about life I do wonder how they conceived a total of eight children without us knowing anything about it! We slept well in those days.

I shared a large bed with my sisters Kate and Maggie – eventually joined by the youngest girl in the family Mary-Anne. Thank goodness they were large beds. My brothers John, Richard, Patrick and Thomas slept in the other big bed, two at the top and two at the bottom. So, there were ten of us all squashed together in this one room. I wonder now how on earth we managed in such a small space. But we took these things for granted and I suppose the number of bodies in the room helped to keep us warm in winter.

We had no running water in the house and we fetched this from the pump, which was outside in the lane. My brothers did most of the fetching and carrying using large jars and buckets. Drinking water was always kept in a large white enamel bucket. To save time in the summer the boys fetched water for washing and laundering from the stream which was just across the road. Mama warned us never to drink the stream water.

Candles provided light in our house. There was great excitement one day when Papa purchased an oil lamp. He said that he needed the light for reading and for the schoolwork at his desk in the parlour. This privilege of light wasn't, however, granted to the women of the house who spent many hours sewing and knitting in very poor lighting conditions.

When we bathed ourselves we used a large wooden tub which was kept in the shed, just outside the back door. When we were young the tub was brought into the kitchen and filled with warm water and one by one the children were washed. But as we grew older the tub remained outside in the shed and water was carried out to fill it. Even though we started off with warm water it soon grew cold. We were hardy country folk and didn't mind this even in cold weather. Papa had instilled in us from an early age that "Cleanliness is next to Godliness" and we bore the cold bravely. The worst time was in the early mornings when it was frosty. My young brothers often skimped their washing. But Mama always ensured that we girls were clean. She made sure that on Saturday nights we were all clean ready for Mass the next day.

And so the years passed by and I with my brothers and sisters grew up. Kate was the eldest; Maggie came next, then me and then John. After John Mama had three more boys – Tom, Dick and Patrick. Then her last baby was another girl, Mary-Anne. Mary-Anne was 10 years younger than me.

One of my jobs at home was to help in our small dairy. We only had a few cows and the dairy was only a shed but it served its purpose well. I had learnt to milk the cows when I was quite young but as I grew older I was able to separate the cream from the milk and I became an expert in the art of butter making. This task had been given to me when Grandpa Jack died. That had been a terrible time for the family. Suddenly, overnight, my father became responsible for our small farm which Grandpa Jack had managed this until his death. This was in addition to his school duties. As I look back I realise this event was the first real turning point in all our lives.

I'll never forget the days following Grandpa Jack's death. This was the first time for me that someone in the family had died. My poor grandpa was laid out to rest in his best suit, lying on top of the bed for all the mourners to pay their respects. People who had known Papa in years gone by came from far and wide. This lying in went on for two days and mourners took it in turns to sit beside the bed with him. Prayers were offered by all the mourners. Mama told me that she was thankful that the old custom of keening had died out. She remembered how the keeners used to turn up after the death and start their wailing. She said she found it quite frightening when she was a young girl. The keeners, all dressed in black, looked like witches.

Eventually, grandpa was laid to rest in Modeshill graveyard. The wake followed the lying-in and burial. As a young girl I couldn't understand why everyone was partying, singing and dancing at this sad time. But Mama said they were giving thanks for Grandpa's good life and I wasn't to be sad.

After Grandpa Jack died Papa and Mama arranged for all the family to play their part in the house and on the farm. If we didn't help in this way Papa would have to give up his job at the school and we would lose his small income.

I was given the responsibility of the dairy. My sisters helped with the washing, the cleaning, the cooking, mending and the sewing. Jobs around the farm were given to my brothers. They helped with digging the potato and turnip garden and clearing the stones and thistles from the waste patch at the side of the house ready for the vegetables. They also helped with feeding the chickens and pigs. They picked blackberries in the autumn for Mama to make jam and they searched for nuts in the hedgerows.

So, with all of us pitching in and doing our best to help it meant that Papa was able to concentrate on the school. He was delighted with the arrangements which meant he was still able to support the family with his small salary.

# CHAPTER 3

*1891-1895*

Over these years our lives were very busy and through our efforts the farm and household ran smoothly.

My sister Kate married her old friend John Cleary when she was only 17. She went to live with John and his family. We all missed Kate. Mama missed her help in the house.

A few months after Kate's wedding we were all saddened when Grandma Kate died. She passed away quietly in her sleep one night. She hadn't been ill and just died of old age. She had always complained of "her old bones" which ached and played her up, particularly in the winter. We were unhappy to lose her calming influence in the house. We had all loved her dearly. Mama seemed to miss her most. She had been good company to have around. Now Mama found it very quiet during the day without her when we were all away at school.

About this time I was becoming restless and I confided in Mama that I wanted to leave school. I said, "Mama, I'm sure I've learned all that I'll need in my future life. I can read and write well. What do you think Papa will say about this?"

"Now, don't go getting your hopes up, Bridgie," said Mama. "Papa values your help at school. You're too young to apply for the assistant teacher's job, which is a shame as I think you would be a good teacher. I think you should stay at school and help Papa. Papa wants to make you a monitress in the school. Your small wage will be a great help to us. We have only just been just managing in recent years. Papa does so worry about money."

"Oh, Mama, I can't bear it," I said. "The last thing in the world I want to do is to help at school for the rest of my life. I've had enough of school and lessons. I hate being shut up indoors all the time. I've been going there now for nearly 13 years. Surely, I can be more help to you at home and around the farm?"

"Bridgie, you would be a great help to me but your father needs your help more than I do. Besides, as I've already said, we need the money. If Papa doesn't have your help he will fall behind in everything and that will be the end of all of us. If his standards slip at school he will lose his job and where would we be then? Now, I don't want to hear any more of this silly talk. You mustn't mention this to Papa. It'll only upset him."

"But Mama, surely I can discuss it with him. He might say no but we should be able to discuss it. Surely I am old enough now to put my point of view to him. I wish I had been born a boy. Just look at Jack. Papa has let him leave school much earlier than any of us girls."

"Bridget, that's a different matter. Jack is a strong lad and is born to work on the land and he is a great help on the farm. I wish you could just be good and do as you are told like Maggie does."

"Like Maggie does! For sure, I'm glad I'm not like Maggie. She has no spirit. I'm going to lead my life as I like and do what I want to do. Maggie will probably stay at home and will never say boo to a goose. I'm glad I have a mind of my own!"

"Bridget, I don't want to hear another word of this. You must consider the family."

"All right, I won't mention it again," I said and I flounced out of the back door. I made my way up the field at the back of the house to my favourite place. I always went there when I had time to myself. I spent some time in the quiet of the countryside thinking about my problems. What would happen to me if I did leave school? I couldn't think of a way in which I could earn my keep. I would have to find employment somewhere. Living out in the wilds of the country I had no idea of what jobs were available elsewhere. It wasn't often we heard of jobs for girls even in our locality. Most girls left school, got married and started a family. Others went to be nuns. If I wanted to find work I would have to move away. Well, perhaps it might come to that one day. I really was quite upset, but I was sorry I had spoken so rudely to Mama. When I returned home I would have to apologise.

I made my way over to the old oak tree and sat on a fallen branch. Grey storm clouds were gathering in the west. My mood matched the weather. I wished I could be transported back a few years when life had been so carefree and happy. Suddenly, I heard a whistling noise behind me. I turned to see my old friend Danny Murphy. "Danny, how wonderful to see you. We only seem to meet on Sundays at chapel nowadays."

"It's good to see you too, Bridget. What are you doing up here all by yourself?"

I explained what had happened and Danny listened sympathetically. Danny had left school and had started a job in the village. He was helping the blacksmith and was enjoying his new-found freedom.

He was sorry to see me so unhappy and his heart went out to me. "Bridgie, I know how hard it must be for you, but don't forget it's hard for the rest of the family, too."

"I know that, Danny. But I feel different from the others. Jack is happy working the land and Maggie is content to stay indoors. Tom always has his nose in a book and the youngsters don't seem to have a care in the world. I seem to be betwixt and between them all. When I am not at school I am working in the dairy by myself. I enjoy that, but sometimes I am quite lonely. I often wonder what life will be like in future. 'Tis for sure, I don't think I'm cut out to be a dairymaid or a teacher for the rest of my life. I don't know what the answer is but I suppose things will work out eventually."

"Bridgie, I think you need some fun in your life. Why don't you ask your parents if you can have a day off on Saturday and come with me to the fair? It'll do you good to have a change and it'll be a great day. There's to be a market and everyone will be there. Please come with me."

"Danny, I wish I could but by the time I finish my dairy work, half the day has gone and that will make you late. I'll wait until I'm a little older. Then you can be sure I'll be doing the things I want to. I don't want to upset Mama and Papa at the moment. They both have a hard life and I don't want to give them trouble now. Danny, I hope your offer will still be there when I am ready to come with you."

"Bridgie, we've been friends for many years – ever since I can remember. Something draws us together. We've always enjoyed each other's company. I can't think of anyone else I would rather have with me. So I'll wait till you are ready."

"Thanks, Danny. I feel much better now. It's time I was getting home. Look, it's starting to rain. Let's run down the hill to the house. Come in and say hello to Mama and stay for a cup of tea."

So we got up and, holding hands as we had done so many times, we ran down the hill towards the house.

On the following Saturday I found myself going into town. I wasn't going to the fair but had another reason to go. Kate was due to give birth to her first child and we had received a message from John Cleary early on Saturday that Kate had gone into labour. We were all very excited. This would be Mama and Papa's first grandchild and I would be an aunt. All morning we talked about Kate, wondering how she was and unsure when we would get more news about her. We wondered whether it would be a boy or a girl and what name they would choose for it.

Mama and I walked into town and arrived at the Clearys' in late afternoon. John was glad to see us and welcomed us. "Come in, come in," he said. "I'm so glad you've come." We could tell by the smile on his face that all was well. It didn't take long for him to tell us that he was now the proud father of a little boy.

"Oh, John, sure that's grand," said Mama.

He led us into the living room where his parents greeted us and we sat down and they offered us the usual cup of tea. We wanted to know how Kate was and John assured us all was well and the nurse was with her. Mama was anxious to see her first grandchild and I wanted to see my first nephew.

We didn't have long to wait. The nurse came downstairs. She said, "Well, mother and baby are both fine. Kate has been very lucky. She had a very easy first birth. She is a strong young lass. She wants to sleep now, but I think she would love to see you for a few minutes before she does."

Mrs Cleary looked across at Mama and said, "Mary, come on, let's go and see our first grandson. Come with us, Bridget."

We climbed the stairs to the bedroom. Kate was sitting up in bed looking a little tired but very well. The new baby was in the bed beside her. She picked him up and we all crowded round to look at him. The baby was a little darling. He had a lovely pink complexion, blue eyes and his head was covered in fair, downy hair. I held his tiny hand and wondered at this little miracle. We hadn't had a baby in the family since Mary-Ann was born. Mama and Mrs Cleary were delighted with their new grandson and we could all see how happy Kate and John were.

Mama said, "No matter how many times you see a new-born babe it always seems to be a miracle that's never happened before. He's grand and I'm so pleased for you both."

I asked them if they had decided on a name and they said that it was to be John – after Grandpa Jack. Grandma Kate would have been so pleased.

Kate was beginning to look tired so we left her to rest and promised to visit her again in a few days. Mama and I made our way home before darkness fell.

On our way home we walked through the town and passed near

the fairground. Mama remarked on the noise! Young men, women, girls and boys were making their way there. Mama said, "Have you ever thought of going to the fair, Bridget? You are young and would enjoy it."

I told her about Danny's offer and explained that I didn't think I could spare the time. "Oh, Bridget, you know what they say, 'all work and no play make Jack a dull boy'. Sure, it's time you started to enjoy life. We all have to work hard but that doesn't mean you can't go out occasionally and enjoy yourself."

"But, Mama," I replied, "I'm sure Papa won't give his approval. He probably thinks a fair is the last place his daughters should visit."

"Well you leave him to me, Bridget. I think you should go. Besides, we would be very happy if you were with Danny. Times are changing and Papa must realise you should be free to do these things. All those young people we saw making their way towards the fair this evening were decent folk. He might have something to say about spending money – but that's another matter. It's hard enough to earn money and even easier to spend it."

I linked arms with Mama as we walked home and thanked her for agreeing to speak to Papa. Maybe next time the fair came to town Papa would let me go with Danny. I decided to wait and see.

As we walked home it grew darker and it was very quiet in the countryside. Mama and I didn't speak much but I hadn't felt so close to her for a long time. The quietness of the countryside brought a peace and solitude, which matched our relaxed mood. It had been a good day.

# CHAPTER 4

*1896-7*

The summer of 1896 was busy and we had to finish the haymaking before the weather turned. The farm kept us all occupied through those summer months. The weather remained good and each morning we rose early. Maggie and I helped Mama to prepare a lunch for everyone. The whole family went out into the fields to help with the harvest, except Mama who joined us at lunchtime. Towards noon Jack and Tom went home to help Mama carry the food and the jugs of milk and water out to the field. I'll never forget those long, warm and sunny days in the happy company of my family.

One Sunday on the way home from Mass, Danny suggested we take a shortcut through the fields to see how the harvest was going. No one was working in the hay field as it was Sunday. As we approached the field Danny caught my hand and started to run. We came to the old oak tree and sat and talked for a while. Then Danny got up and ran to the nearest haystack. It was only three feet high and not completed. He climbed up on top. He said, "Come on, Bridgie, climb up here with me."

I was always happy when we fooled around like this but I wondered how I could possibly get up there with him. Undaunted, I picked up my long skirts and, with him holding my forearms. I pulled myself up. We sat down on top and surveyed the view. It was a beautiful, clear day, with not a cloud in the sky. We could see for miles. Danny asked me, "Have you ever been over there, Bridgie, to the mount Slievenamon?"

"No, I haven't. But I've often wondered what it's like. It looks beautiful."

"It is beautiful, Bridgie. We must go there one day for a long walk. Slievenamon means 'Mountain of the Woman'. Come with me one day and I'll tell you the tale of the mountain as we walk."

I agreed to go at the next possible opportunity and I laughed at the thought of the adventure that lay ahead. Danny turned to me and pushed me back so I was lying on top of the hayrick. He knelt beside me and looked at my face. "Bridgie, I wonder if you will ever realise how much I love you," he said. I was surprised at this sudden admission. I laughed again. "Bridgie, don't laugh. I'm serious. Bridgie, can I kiss you?" He leant forward and delicately kissed me on my forehead. My hair was falling across my face and he carefully pushed my hair back from my temples. Then he kissed me gently on the cheek. I could hear his heart beating. I was a little frightened. This was the first time I had been kissed by a boy. Mama had warned me that kisses led to other things so I was very wary. I'll never forget how tender and loving Danny was that day. Before long our lips met and I didn't resist his embrace. In fact, I enjoyed it and I couldn't explain the feeling I had within my breast as we held each other close. I had never felt like this before.

We climbed down from the hayrick and we walked down the field towards the house. We were both quiet but just before we reached the house Danny turned to me and said, "Bridgie, you are so quiet. You're not cross with me, are you?"

I looked at Danny and laughed. "Danny, I think I love you too. No, of course I'm not cross."

Danny almost whooped with joy as I said this and he ran circles round me in delight. Then he picked me up and carried me the last few yards back to the house. "Put me down!" I shouted. We reached the kitchen door and Danny put me down. We said goodbye and he turned and went on his way. I stood at the door waving until he was out of sight.

Summer turned to autumn and I continued to help Papa at school. I had made up my mind to tell Papa I didn't want to spend the rest of my life at his school. But I was soon to realise that my religion was a bar to me taking up a responsible job. It seemed that I was doomed to stay at the school forever, or be locked away in a convent as a nun. I couldn't believe that being a Catholic was a bar to progress. But it was and I realised that my country was still in the dark ages and my future was at stake.

Disaster came soon when, following a school inspector's visit, Papa was instructed by the Education Board to strike my name off the school roll. I hadn't been officially appointed as monitress by the Board. Papa was ordered to return all the money I had earned. It was so unfair. This was to be the turning point in my life.

# CHAPTER 5

On a crisp winter's afternoon in late December I was strolling home from Mass, on my own and deep in thought. My world had been turned upside down and I found myself without work. I really didn't know what I was going to do. My mind was in turmoil as I tried to think of a way out of what to me was an alarming situation. Not only was I out of work but I was no longer contributing to the family income. I was at my wits' end and couldn't see a way forward.

Suddenly, my thoughts were broken by the sound of footsteps behind me. I turned to see who it was. It was Danny Murphy. "Oh, Danny, how good to see you," I said.

"Same here," said Danny, "and what's this I hear about you leaving school and being a lady of leisure with nothing to do?"

"Oh, Danny I wish I did feel like a lady of leisure. You really don't know how bad things are. I just wish I knew how to occupy myself. You see, one minute I was helping Papa at school and now, suddenly, I find myself thrown out of school. It's ironic because I had been nagging Mama to let me leave school. But now I've left I have nothing to do, except the usual old chores around the farm. I get up early and finish the dairy work by 11 o'clock and then I have nothing to do for the rest of the day. To be sure, after only two days at home I'm already so bored!"

"Bridgie, this isn't like you – you've always been so bright and happy. I don't like to see you like this. How did this happen? Why did you have to leave school? I thought your father needed your help and you enjoyed being a monitress. What's brought about the sudden change?"

I told Danny about the School Inspector's report and explained that I had never officially been appointed to the school and Papa had given me the job without the permission of the Board of Education. Now, Papa had no option other than to do as the Inspector instructed. If he didn't he would be in great trouble. I told Danny I was upset but it was worse for Papa and he was devastated as he was left with no help at school.

Danny understood the situation immediately and realised why Papa was so worried. He was staggered when I told him that we had to repay my wages. I said, "There's very little I can do to help Papa now. I am doing as much as I can at home and on the farm but I am so bored. I think I'll soon be forced to leave the comfort of home. Sooner, rather than later, I'll have to start earning my living in some way. I really don't know what I will do."

"Oh, Bridgie, sure you mustn't worry like this. Think about it. You are young, attractive, and well educated. You should have no trouble finding a job and I know you will be good in whatever you choose to do. Come on now, you don't have to make a decision immediately. Take your time and think about it. In the meantime we can enjoy ourselves. Come to town to market with me next Saturday. You promised me a long time ago you would come one day. I know you will enjoy it. Come on, Bridgie, you are too young to be worrying like this. You have your whole life ahead of you. We don't enjoy ourselves enough. Here we are stuck out in the country and our lives are very restricted. The only people we meet are our families and neighbours and the Priest on Sundays. We ought to get out and see life a bit more. Come on! What do you think? Will you come with me?"

"All right, Danny. I'll come. I think you're right. It will do me good to have a change of scenery. I'm sure Mama and Papa won't mind me coming with you. I'll look forward to it."

Danny's attitude did a lot to cheer me up but I still had niggling worries at the back of my mind.

The next Saturday we went to town together and had a wonderful time. All the young lasses and lads were there and I met many old friends. Some lived away from our district and I hadn't seen them for some time. Danny and I walked home that night along the country lanes, holding hands and I felt happier than I had for years. When I thanked Danny for a good time I don't think he realised how much I meant it.

After that day Danny and I spent many good times together. On Sundays we walked to and from chapel together. One day, Danny told me it was his greatest wish to see the world. "Oh Danny, that is my wish too. I don't want to be stuck at home for the rest of my life. I've this yearning inside me to see something of the world and I'm determined that I'll do it, one day."

I had always liked Danny. He was intelligent and we were able to have good conversations together. Danny caught hold of my hand and said, "Bridgie, you and I are so alike. You know I often think I would like to spend the rest of my life with you."

"Danny Murphy, what do you think you are saying?" I said, pulling my hand away from his. As I let go of him I felt a slight regret in my heart. "I like you, Danny," I said. "But I know, if I let our friendship develop too far it wouldn't be long before we were spending the rest of our lives together. You can be sure if that happened we would stay here in this neck of the woods for the rest of our lives. Then we would never see the world!"

"Bridgie, we've known each other for many years now. Do you know you are the only girl I can really talk to? We've never fallen out or quarrelled. I'm sure there is a future for us together." I was wary of becoming too close to Danny. Something always held me back.

Education had changed the hopes and aspirations of young people. Life certainly was changing and it seemed quickly too. As we neared the end of the century it seemed that more and more people I knew were leaving home and travelling away. Papa often wondered whether this change was for the better, for he never ceased to mention it. I knew my friendship with Danny had brought me much happiness and this had helped me through a difficult time.

# CHAPTER 6

Mama and Papa were pleased that Danny and I were friends and probably hoped we would one day marry. One day I opened my heart to Mama. "Mama," I said, "you and Papa really don't know how I feel. You just don't understand. I have a great empty feeling inside me. I'm not fulfilled in any way and to be sure getting married isn't going to solve the problem. I've a yearning inside me to help people. The trouble is that stuck out here in the wilds of Tipperary there is no one I can help, except my family, and I've been doing that all my life. Things can't go on like this. I'll have to find a way to support myself and I hope you and Papa will support me in whatever I decide to do."

Mama was saddened by my unhappiness. She wished there was something she could do to help but, in her simple country way, marriage seemed to be the only answer.

The answer to my troubles didn't come quickly but in time Papa was to be the one to provide the lifeline to take me out of my predicament.

Although things didn't seem to be going well for me we had good news for young Tom. He was doing very well at school and Papa entered him for the examination to go to the De La Salle College in Waterford which was nearly 40 miles away. If he was successful he would go away to stay at the school in September as a boarder. We were all pleased for him – but I know he was very uncertain about leaving home and going to boarding school. I talked to him and told him about the advantages of going away to school and getting a good education and meeting other people. Eventually he agreed to go. So, unexpectedly, Tom went away to school. Mama and Papa were very proud of his success. I had never thought Tom was the cleverest of the family, but he worked the hardest and now it had paid off for him. I hoped he would be happy at school and not find it too difficult.

# CHAPTER 7

My future was still unresolved and my despair led to an unusual and uncharacteristic depression. I moped about the house for days and the only time I left the house was to go to chapel on Sundays. Mama and Papa were concerned for me and often talked late into the night about my future. I didn't see Danny so often now and when we did meet he found it difficult to enjoy my company in my mood of despondency.

Our New Year celebrations at the end of 1897 and the start of 1898 were great fun and my mood seemed to improve. I had planned many games for the family to play together. Papa and Tom played well-known folk tunes on the violin and we all sang along to them. The party went on until after midnight when we all saw the New Year in together.

Although this was a time of celebration it was also a time that we were to remember for many years to come. It marked the turning point in all our lives, particularly mine.

Apart from playing his fiddle Papa had been quiet during the party. But after midnight, when we had seen the New Year in, he called me to one side in the sitting room and said he wanted to have a talk with me.

I realised he must have something important to tell me as he rarely took me aside like that. So it was that Papa put a suggestion to me. He said, "For some time now I have been corresponding with my sister, Catherine, in America. As you know, she went to New York about twenty years ago with Mama's sister. Their first employment in America was in the clothing industry. They worked hard and saved their money. Then, together, they managed to buy their own sewing machine. As you know the sewing machine is a marvellous invention. It is powered by the foot working a treadle. It is a wondrous thing and makes sewing much quicker and easier."

"Are you thinking of buying one for us Papa?" I asked.

"Well, now, that's not the point of my story," said Papa, looking knowingly towards Mama who had just joined us. "Your aunts worked very hard and they started their own dressmaking business. According to the letters I've received they are doing very well. Business is pouring in and they have more work than they can cope with." He paused for a few seconds, and then he continued. "They have asked me if you would like to go out there and join them in their enterprise. They have offered to pay your fare and they will send you enough spare money for a new outfit for the journey and for pocket money to see you through until you get to New York. Of course if you do choose to work for them you will be paid a wage."

There were gasps all round the room at this news for by now everyone was listening. The room went quiet and everyone waited for my reaction.

I was stunned by this news. But, I had a lump in my throat. Was this the opportunity I had been waiting for?

"Papa," I said, "this has come like a bolt out of the blue. I don't know what to say. I'll have to think about it."

"I understand," replied Papa. "You must take time to think about it. I'm not getting any younger and it won't be long before I have to retire from the school. I could go on for another year or two. Nothing is decided yet. I don't need to tell you that if I give up my work we will have no income. My priorities in future will lie on the farm and I'll have to make sure that this change in circumstances will sustain us. As a result of your hard work, Bridget, we've been able to sell butter and milk and we can build on this in future. We can also sell honey and jam and the wool always fetches a good price."

Papa continued: "I know you'll understand that, whatever happens, whether you stay here or travel overseas, you must start earning your own living. As you know it's very difficult for you to get meaningful employment here in Ireland. You might get a servant's job at one of the big houses but you are educated and I don't want to see you wasted like that. I know you have no desire to become a nun. I think you should accept this offer. But think about this for a while. Try and make up your mind within a week or two so I can reply to your aunt's letter."

Maggie had been very quiet. She was visibly shaken by the news and she wasn't slow to make her feelings known. "Well, when my turn comes you can count me out," she said. "I'm not leaving here to go off to foreign parts where I don't know anybody. If you want to go, Bridget, don't be expecting me to join you. I'll be staying here with the family."

"Well, nothing is finally decided yet," said Papa. "We've only just received this offer. It's for Bridget to make up her own mind. I know she will do what is best for her. I'll discuss it with you again, Bridgie, in a few days' time. Try and imagine the wonderful opportunity this will be for you."

It was then that I noticed how old and tired Papa was looking. His long beard was now turning from grey to white and he was fast losing the hair on his head. He looked worn out and I realised he was doing the best he could for me. From that moment I knew I was going to accept the offer and I was determined to make a success of my life.

# CHAPTER 8

New Year's Day 1898 started off quietly. There was a sober mood in the house. Mama was busy in the kitchen but she didn't talk about the previous night. She didn't have to say anything. It was clear to everyone she was sad at the prospect of losing another daughter. But, as usual, she didn't discuss this with Papa who seemed to have dominion over the household – particularly us women!

Even though I had made up my mind to go to America I still had worries about leaving Mama. I needed some fresh air to clear my thoughts. It was time to go for a long walk and sort out my mind to make sure I really knew what I was doing. I had to be absolutely positive that I really did want to go away. I told Mama I was going out and I quickly collected my cloak to shield me from the cold air. I set off across the fields at the back of the house, where I knew I could be alone with my thoughts.

Walking quickly, I soon felt warm in the sunshine. I was about 3 miles from the house when I stopped for a few minutes. I realised I was quite high up in the hills and I was now on open common land. I sat on a rock. Looking down to the valley below I could see our house, which looked like a small white doll's house. Smoke rose from the chimney in a long tall column. There was no wind to blow it away.

As I sat still on the hillside I was aware of the beauty of nature all around me. I started to think through what this momentous step meant for me. I tried to envisage some of the good things it might bring for me. I knew I wanted to go to America more than anything.

One thing did trouble me though. I hadn't mentioned this to anyone yet. The aunts in America were dressmakers and there was one thing I wasn't good at. That was sewing! I felt it would be wrong to go all that way, with my fare paid by my aunts, only for them to find I was no good at the job. I decided to tell Papa about my worries. America was supposed to be the land of opportunity and I was sure that if I didn't like dressmaking I could turn my hand to something else.

I had been away from the house for most of the morning. On my way home I made a decision. Whatever happened, this was an opportunity I must not miss. It was what I had been waiting for – a chance in a lifetime. It was not quite what I had expected but it was my opportunity to see something of the world. I wasn't going to miss it. There were some things I needed to talk to Papa about, but those could wait until I had talked with Danny. I decided to talk to him after chapel on Sunday.

As usual, on Sunday the whole family went to chapel. After the service I met Danny outside.

"Will you walk home with me?" I asked.

We set off in the direction of home ahead of the rest of the family who were standing around talking to friends and neighbours. We walked quickly down the little hill leading away from the chapel. As soon as we were out of sight of the family I said, "Danny, I have something very important I want to talk to you about."

And so I poured out my news to Danny. I told him about Papa's letter from the aunts. I gave him the plain facts and didn't indicate to him what my feelings were about the proposal.

"Well, Bridgie, that's marvellous. It's just what you've been waiting for. You must grab this opportunity and go. Sure, I'll miss you. But we must keep in touch and who knows; I may even come over there myself one day. They say America is the land of opportunity. Oh, I wish I could come with you."

"Danny, I agree with you but there are complications." I told him I worried about Mama coping without much help. I also told him that I probably wasn't suited to taking a dressmaking job.

"Well, that seems quite straightforward to me," said Danny. "Your mother will have to have help in the house. There must be someone in the village willing to come in for a few hours every day. I'm sure your father could be persuaded to pay this small wage. You could even agree to send some money home to help out. In fact, I know just the person. Mrs Tobin has been looking for something to do. She needs the money now that her husband has passed on. She's a very good cook and by the state of her house it seems she is good at housework too. Things have been very hard for her over the last few months since her husband died. I know her children don't do much to support her. There you are now. Already, that's one of your problems solved."

"I knew it was going to help talking to you, Danny. Two heads are better than one, as they say. You always seem to be more objective than I am. I seem to have too many problems swimming around in my head."

"Well, I don't know if I can help with your other problem," said Danny. "I can't help you to sew. But I do think you were meant for better things than that."

"I've made up my mind that I am definitely going, Danny. But as Papa arranged all this without even consulting me I think the time has come for some bargaining. I'll insist that Mama has help in the house and I'll tell him he must let the aunts know I am only a mediocre seamstress. If he doesn't do that, he is deceiving them. I'm sure he will agree. Then, when I get there I'll do my best to please them but if I fail I'll be free to look around for other opportunities."

"Bridgie, when do you think you will be going?"

"Well, it will take a few months to sort everything out. I have to decide what I am taking with me and I have to book my passage. There must be a thousand and one jobs to take care of before I go."

"Then, we must make the most of the next few months and really enjoy ourselves. I'll try and get over to see you more often. We mustn't forget we promised ourselves a trip to the Slievenamon Mountain."

We were now approaching the house and even though we had walked the long way round we still arrived before the rest of the family.

"Danny, I don't know what I would do without you as a friend," I said.

"Sure, I don't know either. And what will I do without you when you go? Before you go I know one thing is for sure, I'll be having the best goodbye kiss that any Irish man ever had from his girl!"

"There you go again, Danny Murphy. But, Danny, you know I couldn't go without saying goodbye properly to you. Let's wait and see what happens, shall we? It's a few months away yet."

We held hands for a few minutes and looked into each other's eyes. I felt that old surge of tenderness in my heart for Danny. When Danny smiled his eyes smiled too. He put his arm round me and gently kissed me. We held each other tight for a few moments.

The silence was broken by the arrival of Pat and Dick who had run ahead of the rest of the family. As usual, they were full of energy and entered into a mock boxing match with Danny. Then the rest of the family appeared and it was time for Sunday lunch. So Danny and I said goodbye. As he left Danny said, "Don't forget, I'll be round to see you when I can get away."

The next day we were up early and Maggie was already pounding away at the washtub when I arrived downstairs. It was strange how everyone was carrying on with his or her work as though nothing unusual had happened. Mama was pegging out the washing on the line. After breakfast I took the washing in and Mama set to work with the ironing.

After lunch I said to Maggie, "Why don't we go for a walk? It's a lovely day and we've finished most of the work. I'm sure Mama won't mind if we go out. I think there are things we both want to talk about."

"All right," replied Maggie. "Let's get our cloaks on and go now while the weather is good."

And so we walked out at the back of the house, across the fields and up the hill until we were so warm that we had to stop for a rest. We sat on the same rock I had sat on two days previously.

Maggie was the first to speak. "Bridget, I know you want to talk about America. Well, so do I. When my turn comes to join you I don't want to go and I'll dig my heels in and they will have to carry me all the way to the boat!"

I laughed. "That would be funny, Maggie. I can imagine it now – Papa getting the boys to help bundle you up on the cart and then tying you down so you can't escape."

We both laughed at the thought of this. Then I said, "What is your greatest fear, Maggie? Is it the journey, or the dread of what lies ahead, or is it just that you don't want to leave home."

"Well, to tell you the truth, Bridget, it's a bit of all of those things. But the thing I hate most is the thought of Mama at home on her own trying to cope with all the family. I lay awake in bed last night thinking about it and it troubled me so much I couldn't sleep. It's all right for Papa; he has the boys to help him on the farm."

"Well, Maggie, I've been doing a lot of thinking. This is the way I see things. Papa has been writing to the aunts without even involving me. And he is contemplating sending me to be a seamstress!! Have you ever heard of anything so crazy? You know the needle and me. We just don't get on. So, I have an idea. I think I'll do some bargaining with Papa. I'll insist that Mama has extra help in the house. And then I'll tell him that he must let the aunts know that I am not very good at sewing. I'll only go if he agrees to these two proposals."

"Rather you than me, Bridgie," said Maggie.

I continued: "He will surely say he can't afford help in the house and then I'll tell him I'll be sending money home to help. Also, he must impress on the aunts that if things don't work out I must be free to look for work elsewhere in New York. What do you think about that?"

"I think it's a marvellous plan, Bridget. We'll both be happy knowing that Mama isn't overworked. But do you really think you have the nerve to tackle Papa in this way?"

"Well, Maggie, just wait and see. If Papa thinks I am old enough to travel to the other side of the world on my own then a bit of straight talking won't go amiss. I'm not afraid of him."

We made our way home. We were both quiet as we walked. I realised that of the two of us I was the stronger character. In the past Maggie had resented me for this. But now things were different. This plan of Papa's had thrown us together. I knew that in future if Maggie did eventually join me she was going to rely on me to help her in so many ways.

The next day I tackled Papa on the subject and I outlined my worries to him. To my surprise he thought it was a good idea for Mama to have help in the house, particularly when he knew I was going to send money home for this. He also agreed to tell the aunts about my standard of sewing and he agreed to write to them that evening.

I felt as if a great load had been lifted off my shoulders. As soon as I had finished my work I ran up the back garden and into the field and raced across it. When I was far enough away from the house where no one could hear me I cried out in delight, "Whoopee! I'm going to America. Whoopee. Whoopee! I'm going to America."

I sat down under a tree and tears fell down my cheeks. I was crying with joy and excitement, but both of these emotions were tinged with sadness. I realised that once I had left this comfortable home I might never see my parents again.

# CHAPTER 9

It didn't take long for Papa to pen his next letter to America. As agreed, he outlined to the aunts all the suggestions I had made. To my amazement, when he had finished he said to me, "Read what I've written, Bridget. You'll see I've included all your ideas and thoughts."

Whilst I cast my eyes over the letter, Papa went and sat beside Mama. He said, "Bridgie has been holding me to ransom. She has persuaded me you will need help in the house if she goes to America. I agree with her and she has promised to send money home out of her wages to help pay for this. How do you feel about that, my dear?"

"Well now, doesn't that sound an excellent idea? I must admit, I've been wondering how I was going to manage. But don't forget Maggie will still be here. It surely is a grand idea."

Mama got up from her chair. She came across the room and put her arm around me. "Thank you," she said. "I'll miss you so much when you go. The money will in no way make up for your absence but it will make things much easier for me to bear. Thank you."

I hugged Mama. "I'll miss you too, Mama." By now tears were running down our cheeks. I promised to write home frequently. "Papa will read my letters to the family, Mama, and you will have all my news."

But that wasn't the end of it. Papa said he wanted to have a talk with me and we sat down together near the fire. "Bridget," he said, "this is a long journey you are undertaking and I don't want you to go alone. It's usual in such circumstances for a young person to have a travelling companion and I'll have to arrange this."

"Who will it be, Papa? Surely you won't send me in the care of someone I don't know!"

He replied that he was making enquiries in the parish hoping to find someone travelling to America soon. I really hoped Papa would be able to find someone I knew. He agreed to do his best but it might not be easy.

In the middle of the next week I had a visitor. Mama answered a knock at the back door. "Why if it isn't Danny Murphy? Come on in, lad. Bridget will be pleased to see you."

"Thank you, Mrs Frisby. I don't often get time off during the evenings but today I had help on our small farm. One of the lads from the village came in to help me. So, here I am, making the most of the opportunity to see Bridget while she is still here."

I was surprised to see Danny. "Danny, you said you were going to try and get some time away. But I didn't think it would be so soon."

"Sure, haven't I just been telling your mother? One of the lads from the village came and helped me so I've finished early. I decided to stroll over and make the most of the time that's left before you go."

We decided to go out for a walk.

Danny said, "It's a clear bright night out there. We won't go far. Just to the bridge and back. Shall we see how many stars we can recognise?"

I put on my cloak and out we went.

As soon as we were away from the house Danny asked, "Do you have any more news about America?"

I told him all that had happened and he was surprised that things had progressed so smoothly.

As we reached the bridge Danny said, "Just look at that lovely clear sky. The stars are twinkling so bright. Do you see that one there? That's the North Star."

"How do you know that?"

"I read about it. That group there is called the Great Bear. See, those there, follow my finger. It's shaped like a saucepan. When we get indoors I'll draw it out for you. Then, in future you will be able to recognise it. And do you realise, Bridgie, that the North Star points towards the North Pole? When you are in America, you will be able to see it from there too. When you've gone and I am lonely and missing you I shall look up in the sky. Whenever I see that star shining brightly, I'll think of you in America, on the other side of the world, and I hope you will be looking at it too, and thinking of me."

"Oh, Danny, you are an incurable romantic. But I will do that. Whenever I think of home and you and whenever I am lonely, I'll look up at that star. It will hold us together across the miles."

I shivered. Danny took hold of my hand and looked into my eyes. "You're getting cold. It's time we went in. Bridget Frisby, you know you are beautiful and I love you. When I look into your eyes I can see the stars reflected from the skies above."

Danny pulled me round and kissed me on the cheek. And then he kissed me on the lips – a soft gentle kiss and I responded as I felt the warmth of his face against mine. Once again, I felt that warm feeling in my breast as he held me close.

We stood together with our arms around each other for a few minutes more and then Danny said, "Come on. It's getting cold. Let's get you home or your parents will think I've kidnapped you."

Two weeks later a letter arrived from America.

After supper the whole family gathered round the fireside. It was a Saturday and we were all in a happy mood and ready for a singsong. Mary-Anne asked Papa to play his fiddle so we could have some musical accompaniment.

"Not just yet," Papa replied. "I had this letter this morning from New York. I'm sure that you all want to know what it says."

He sat back in his chair and started to read the letter quietly to himself. As he did so we all watched him, waiting for some sign that it was good news.

Then he announced, "It's good news. Let me read part of the letter to you. First of all, they thank me for my letter. Then they say they are grateful to me for being so forthright in telling them Bridget isn't brilliant at sewing! That's putting it bluntly, isn't it? They appreciate the situation and they say they hope Bridget will learn quickly when she starts work. However, they agree she will be free to take up other work if she doesn't make the grade with them."

"Oh, thank goodness," I said. And all the family agreed.

Papa continued, "They set out here the whole plan. Here now, let me read it to you."

*Richard, you must obtain all the necessary paperwork in Ireland. For instance, Bridget will have to have a medical examination before she comes. She must carry the medical certificate with her as it will confirm a clean bill of health. You must get this done and ensure nothing goes wrong at the last moment.*

*We enclose some money to purchase a new travelling outfit for Bridget. Any leftover cash can be used for other necessary things like shoes or a travelling case. Please spend it wisely. Also, you should make sure she has sufficient pocket money for the journey. The authorities will ask her how much money she has on her person when she boards the ship. This is important as they won't let paupers on board!*

*When Bridget is ready to travel please let us know. When we came to America we sailed from Queenstown harbour in Cork. Bridget will have to go to Cork by train.*

*Finally, we hope Bridget will be with us by the summer. As you know our business is growing fast and we have so much work and we are finding it difficult to cope.*

*Please write again when you have made all the arrangements. By the way, we forgot to mention it goes without saying that we will provide accommodation for Bridget in New York and of course we will meet her when she arrives.*

Papa then continued, "They send their love to you, Mary, and to the rest of the family. And here is a $10 note! The boys crowded round Papa. They had never seen American money before or indeed such a large amount. Papa held out the banknote for them to look at. Maggie, Mama and I were all very quiet. For us, the moment of truth had almost arrived.

I smiled at Mama and went and sat beside her. I put my arm round her shoulder and gave her a kiss. "Thank you, Mama, for all you've done for me. You and Papa have given me a very good start in life." Maggie sat with us but was very quiet.

I said, "Maggie, I have a few months before I go. We must enjoy every minute of our time before the day arrives."

# CHAPTER 10

After our New Year celebrations I went with Mama and Papa to visit Kate. I was going to miss her when I went away so every minute I could have with her now was important.

We set off in our old cart pulled by Ned the donkey and we were soon on our way along the lanes. The familiar "clip-clop" of hooves rang out as we made our way. I thought how different life would be in New York. I decided I should try and remember every little detail, every moment – every sound, every sight and even every smell of my homeland. The sound of old Ned's clip-clop would be difficult to forget.

I looked into the distance at Slievenamon Mountain, beautiful in its ruggedness. It had a strange way of changing colour every moment as the clouds passed over it. Sometimes it looked warm and inviting. At other times it looked cold and dark. Today it was warm and the sun shone down on it. The clouds were few and far between – small white puffs, very high, scudding across the deep blue sky. I remembered that Danny had promised to take me walking up on that hill.

We arrived in town and I left Mama and Papa to go about their business and made my way to Kate's home. She wasn't expecting me and was surprised and delighted when I arrived.

Kate's husband John worked for the Royal Irish Constabulary and was rarely there when I visited. He worked shifts and often worked at night.

"Bridgie, come in," Kate said. "How lovely to see you." We

embraced each other. Kate was alone so we were able to catch up on all our news and have a good gossip. We sat in the large kitchen where the Cleary family spent most of their time. It was very homely.

Young John Cleary, Kate's first child, was playing out in the back yard with two young neighbours. He heard voices inside and ran in calling out, "Aunty Bridgie, Aunty Bridgie, hello!" He ran towards me and leapt up into my arms, flinging his arms around my neck and kissing me with such affection. He was a lovely boy. Soon Kate would be giving birth to her second child.

I thought to myself how well suited Kate and John were and I was pleased that Kate was so happy. It was as if they had always known one another. I wondered if I would ever find such happiness. Even though I was off to America I envied Kate.

I told Kate I was to have a travelling companion and she was intrigued to hear about this. "Who will it be?" she wondered. I told her that I had no idea but I wasn't going to think about it until later when I knew who it was.

Kate laughed. "I can imagine you will give someone a hard time if you don't like him or her," she said.

We both laughed and I asked Kate how long it was before the baby was due.

"Just five weeks now," said Kate.

"Well, I must see you more often in the next few weeks," I said. "I'll see you every time we come into town. And we'll meet up as usual at chapel on Sundays. I'm so glad I'll be able to get to know the baby before I go."

Mama and Papa arrived earlier than expected and Kate made us some soup with newly baked bread. Then, the talk was all about babies. We wondered whether it was going to be a boy or a girl.

Papa then said, "Bridget, do you remember John Breen?"

"Yes," I said. "He was one of the big boys at school."

"Well," said Papa, "I just bumped into him in town. He's just finished his apprenticeship as a carpenter and he's planning to go to

New York this year. I think he'll be an ideal travelling companion for you. He must be about six or seven years older than you. What do you think of that idea?"

Secretly, I was relieved and pleased as I had always liked John but my reply was guarded. "If you think it's a good idea, Papa, I'll go along with it. What happens now?"

"Leave it to me," he said. "I'll go and visit him in the next day or so and put the proposition to him."

We said goodbye to Kate and were soon on our way home. On the way, Papa told me he had made enquiries about sailings to New York. There was a ship sailing at the end of August. He said he had wanted to take me all the way to the ship but if I was travelling with John Breen he was happy for us to go by train on our own. He would take us to the train station.

Three weeks later John Cleary's young brother Paddy arrived at our door. He had hurried all the way to see us and breathlessly he said, "John sent me with a message. It's your Kate; she has had her baby early. It all happened very quickly. Her pains came this morning and it was a bad time for her because everyone was out and she was on her own. My ma and pa came home just in time and they called John back from the Garda station. He arrived just before the baby was born. John said to tell you Kate and the baby are both doing fine. It's a girl and I think they are calling her Margaret after my ma."

Soon we were all sitting round the kitchen table asking Paddy what the baby looked like, and when could we visit. Mama and Papa decided to go the next day to see their second grandchild.

Papa then went to his cupboard in the sitting room and opened a new bottle of whiskey, which was indeed a rare thing for him to do. He poured himself a tot and then offered some to Mama. Mama never drank spirits but said, much to everyone's surprise, "Well, there's a first time for everything. Sure, I'll have a wee drop. We must wet the baby's head." Papa offered Paddy a drink and he wasn't slow in accepting. Jack looked at Papa with raised eyebrows. Normally,

Papa wouldn't let Jack drink spirits as he was too young but as Paddy had accepted he poured a small tot for him too. Maggie had made a pot of tea. She and I drank a cup of tea and we all celebrated the baby's birth.

# CHAPTER 11

I was so pleased Kate's baby had arrived early. It meant I could get to know my new little niece before I went away. The next family event was the christening of "Baby Margaret".

Both the Cleary and Frisby families gathered at the chapel and it was a very happy occasion. Mama had lent Kate the christening gown, which had been worn by all the Frisbys. It was a clear, fine day. After the service we all made our way back to the house for the celebrations that followed. The party was held at our house as we had more room than the Clearys.

The party went on late into the evening. Once again the fiddle came out and there was much singing and dancing. Eventually, the Clearys made their way back to town and peace returned to our household.

A week later, I decided it was time to buy my new outfit for the journey. We had always made our own clothes so it was with excitement that I went with Papa and Mama to Kilkenny. Maggie decided to come with us. Papa carried out other business in the city while we were in the dress shops.

I enjoyed looking at all the dresses in the shops and eventually I had two favourites. The first was a dark green three-piece. It had a long skirt and a hip-length jacket fitted at the waist. It also had a pretty white blouse. The other was a dark navy colour.

Mama thought the colour of the green outfit suited me best as it went well with my auburn hair. So that is what I chose.

As the day drew to a close, we made our way home, through the lanes that led us from county Kilkenny and over the border into County Tipperary. We rode into the sunset and the beautiful sky cast a warm glow on the hedgerows. I listened to the sound of Ned's hooves along the country lanes. All was peaceful. It had been a happy day.

The next Sunday at chapel, Kate was anxious to talk with me. "Bridgie, I have something to tell you. Please don't tell Mama and Papa yet. Keep this news to yourself for a while. As you know John works for the Garda. Now that he has finished his training he is to become a constable."

"Oh, that's wonderful news," I said. "You must be so proud of him. The extra money will be helpful."

"Well, yes, it is good news and I am proud and glad," replied Kate. "But there is something else. The Constabulary don't like their men working in the county in which their family lives. It's likely John will be posted out of Tipperary to another county. I have always known this might happen but I am worried that we won't be near at hand for Mama and Papa if anything goes wrong. So I'm not looking forward to telling them about this."

"Sure, you mustn't worry yourself," I said. "I know they will be pleased for you. Mama and Papa want more than anything to see their children happy and successful. They will be glad for you as this means you and John have a better chance in life and will be earning more money. When do you think you will move and where do you think you will go?"

"John says his new rank will be confirmed next Wednesday when the County Chief Inspector visits the area. We'll have to wait and see where they are sending us. The only good thing is that we were here when baby Margaret was born. I wouldn't have been very happy having a baby amongst strangers. What do you think I should do, Bridgie? Shall I tell Mama and Papa today or shall I wait until we know more?"

"You must tell them today. There's no time like the present and now you've told me there's a chance I might let the cat out of the bag. It will give them time to get used to the idea before you have to move. If you leave it until nearer the time it might hit them hard. Anyway, you might be posted into County Kilkenny and that's only a few miles away. I am so pleased for you both, Kate."

"All right," said Kate. "I'll come home with you now and tell them then. John is working this morning. I told him if he doesn't find me at home then I'll be with you."

After lunch, Kate told Mama and Papa her news about the pending move. Whilst they were pleased about John's promotion and glad that Kate was happy, they were sad to be losing another daughter. They would miss Kate and her little family.

The following week we heard that John Cleary had been posted to Limerick County and he was to report immediately at the start of the following week to his new Garda station. His posting was to a small town called Galbally, which was close to the Tipperary border. There was scarcely time for goodbyes. John went on ahead of Kate so he could take up his new post and came back to fetch his family a week later. Kate soon wrote home and told us they had moved into a police house, which was small but plenty big enough for the four of them. To start with all they had was a bed, two chairs, a kitchen table, the baby's cradle and some bed linen which Mama had given them. So Kate had become a homemaker, purchasing items for the house to make it comfortable. The money they had saved soon went so Kate set about making things for the home such as curtains and even making rugs for the floor. They settled in well and made friends with their neighbours.

Meanwhile, Papa had been sorting out the paperwork for me. He had written to America and we were waiting for the ticket to arrive from the aunts. The ticket finally arrived a month after Papa's letter. At last I knew the date of my departure. The boat was to sail on the 21st August 1898. My passage was booked on the SS *Lucania* departing from Queenstown Harbour. It was leaving on the afternoon tide and the expected date of arrival in New York was the 28th August.

A few days later Papa announced that he and Mama wanted to talk to me. Papa said that whilst I was out they had a visit from Danny. "He wants to take you up to the Slievenamon Mountain before you go to America."

"He mentioned this to me a few weeks ago," I said. "What is your concern?"

"Well, you haven't been out with a boy on your own before so I am anxious at the idea. There's no telling what can happen to a young girl if she isn't forewarned."

I looked across at Maggie and she winked at me. We both knew a sermon was coming now. I restrained myself from smiling and said, "Don't you want me to go, Papa?"

"Well, your mother and I would be happier if more than two of you were going, but young Danny has given me his word that you will come to no harm. I must say I like the lad and always have. I trust him but I want you to promise me you'll behave yourself."

"Papa, if I'm old enough to go to America – I think I can be trusted here in Ireland! After all, it's only a few miles away."

Now it was Mama's turn to have her say. "Bridget, you'll spoil your chances of going to America if anything immoral happens. You must take us seriously now. We want you to go with Danny and to have a good time but we want you to be aware of the dangers that can happen between a young girl and a boy."

Then I think I shocked everyone by saying, "Mama, I've heard about young Mary Connolly and how she went with a boy and committed a mortal sin. I know this behaviour outside marriage is objectionable in the eyes of the church. There is no way I want to be ostracised and labelled a 'fallen woman' like poor Mary. Besides, if that happened you would disown me like Mary's parents have. Did you know she's been sent to a convent? And when her baby is born she will lose it because it will be sent to an orphanage. No, that isn't the life I choose, so you have no cause to worry."

There was silence in the kitchen for a few minutes. Both Mama and Papa looked shocked at my outburst and Maggie's head was bent over her sewing. I think she was amused but she kept her head down.

Then Papa said, "Bridget, we'll leave this subject now and I'll talk to you again tomorrow. That's enough about it for now."

Whatever Papa intended to say to me I was determined to go and I wouldn't let him stop me To be sure, I thought, if they can trust me to behave myself in America, on the other side of the world, surely to goodness a day on the mountain isn't going to hurt.

The next day I was up early. Mama was in the kitchen and we had breakfast together. Whilst we were eating Mama said, "Bridget, you shouldn't have talked to your father like you did yesterday. But I think he is reassured now. I had a long talk with him last night and I hope you won't let us down. You must apologise to him for your outburst. He is reluctant to let you go off to the mountain but I think he is resigned to the idea now. If you really want to go you shouldn't upset him again."

"All right," I said. "But I find it hard to believe that you and Papa trust me to go to the other side of the world and you can't trust me to behave myself on a day out with Danny."

"Bridget, I think you know the answer to that one. When you've left home you will have to take responsibility for your own moral behaviour but while you are still living under this roof, your father and I are responsible for you. Besides, if anything bad were to happen it would spoil your chances for the future. Now, we don't want that, do we?"

I got up and went round the table to Mama and put my arm round her shoulder and kissed her on the cheek. "Mama, you always have the knack of putting things in perspective. I'm going to miss you. But I won't do anything to spoil my chances for the future. And I know Danny wouldn't want to spoil things for me either."

"Well, that's as may be. But men are strange creatures, Bridget. The mountain can be a romantic place and nature has a way of stirring up passions so strong that they overcome all sense of reasonableness. This is what we want you to be aware of."

Later that day Papa called me to one side to talk to me. What he said to me was short and sweet. He said, "Bridget, about our talk last night. I think you are aware of the dangers of being out alone with a young man. I am not going to spell them out. You are a responsible young woman now and Mama and I trust you. So go ahead and arrange this outing with Danny. It's a long time since I was up on Slievenamon Mountain. It's very beautiful and I think it will leave you with a lasting memory of your homeland. I know you will enjoy it."

"Thank you," I said. Then I kissed him and since this was an unusual occurrence in our household he looked slightly embarrassed. "Och, away with you now," he said. "I'll always ask myself why you are the only one who can get your own way with me."

It didn't take long for me to find Danny. He was at work in the blacksmith's and he was surprised to see me. He wasn't able to stop work and talk but I asked him to call at our house on his way home. He winked at me, saying as he did so, "It's all right then, is it?"

I nodded, "Yes," and went on my way.

Danny called in that evening and we went for a walk to discuss our outing. We agreed to go on the following Saturday. We made arrangements about the things we were to take with us; and also what to wear. "You should wear strong boots, Bridgie," he said. "And it could rain on the upper slopes so you must bring a cloak with you." So we were all set for our outing.

When Friday night came I was very excited at the thought of our expedition. I had never been very far from home and certainly had never been on a mountain before.

# CHAPTER 12

As arranged, we were up bright and early on the day of our trip. Mama had packed food for us and when Danny came he put the food in his backpack. We also had bottles of milk and water. It was just 6 o'clock and Mama and Papa were there to see us off. Mama said, "Now, have good time the both of you."

Papa added, "Danny, mind you look after her."

"I will, Mr. Frisby, you can be sure. We'll have a good day and you can expect us back before it gets dark. But if we're later than that please don't worry. I'll make sure whatever happens Bridget is safe. I promise you, you have no need to worry."

And so Danny and I set off down the road, turning occasionally to see Mama and Papa. We waved to them as they grew faint in the distance. We turned the corner at the end of the lane by the bridge crossing the King's River and set off towards Mullinahone.

Danny was striding along beside me and I felt proud to be with him. We were holding hands and it was a beautiful morning. We hadn't talked since we left the house. Suddenly he turned to me and said, "We're going to have a wonderful time, Bridgie. It's a long jaunt so we'll have to keep up a good pace otherwise we won't be back before sunset. I can't wait to see your expression when you see the view from the top of the mountain."

Then I told Danny about the fuss Mama and Papa had made about the expedition. He laughed and said, "Well now, Bridgie, just as if I would have my evil way wit' you. Don't you think I've tried this many times; but you've always brushed me off? I can count on the fingers of one hand how many times we've kissed. If your parents knew what a strong-minded daughter they had, they would have no need to worry. I know you're determined to keep yourself for the man you marry. My only regret is that it won't be me."

"Danny, you are so kind and understanding," I said. "You make me feel humble, yes – almost guilty because I have withheld myself from you. I know you understand and I'm very lucky to have a friend who is so sympathetic and considerate."

An hour later we passed through Mullinahone. It was so early very few people were up and about. We made our way south out of the town and headed on the road that led towards the mountain. I could see it looming up in the distance. Soon we came to Ballyduggan Bridge.

At the cross in the road Danny asked me if I wanted to stop for a short rest and maybe a drink but I preferred to continue. "Are you sure now?" he said. "The next stretch of the road is quite long and takes us to the foot of the mountain."

"Yes, let's keep going," I said. "Maybe we can stop when we get to the end of this road."

It was turning out to be a lovely day and we soon came near the foot of the mountain. We stopped for a while and had a drink. I took off my cloak, which was very heavy, and Danny strapped it to his backpack. Then I did something which would have had eyes turning at home and the 'tut-tutting' going. I picked up the hem of my skirt and tucked it at intervals into my waistband. Danny laughed as he watched me and asked why I was doing that. I explained to him that when we left the road and the ground became rough I didn't want to trip up on my skirts, nor did I want it to be covered in mud. He laughed and said that I looked like a gypsy – all I needed was a headscarf and a bag of pegs to complete the picture.

"Sure, Bridgie, if only your parents could see you now. They would march you straight back home. You look like a real Romany."

"I don't mind what other people think," I said. "In any case, I don't think we'll be seeing many people, do you?"

"No," said Danny and moved towards me, tenderly picking a strand of my hair off my face and placing it behind my ear. "Just let me look at you, Bridgie, will you? Can I have just one little kiss before we start our climb?"

So, once more, Danny took me in his arms and our lips met. I don't know how long we stood there with our arms entwined. I felt safe and relaxed in Danny's company.

So, we climbed the mountain, stopping occasionally to look back at the view. When we were about halfway up we could see a few houses in the distance, tiny white dots. We thought we could pick out our houses. But this was fanciful and it was unlikely we had pinpointed the correct ones.

The ferns grew tall on the mountain and sometimes we had to forge a pathway through them. Fortunately, Danny had brought a long stick with him and he beat down the ferns so I could walk through without them catching on my skirt. Occasionally we came across a large bare patch of springy turf, with clumps of purple heather and gorse bushes scattered about. The colours were beautiful – the brown of the bracken, the purple of the heather, the gold of the gorse, the green of the turf and the blue of the sky.

At the halfway point we sat down and had a rest. We were hungry and decided it was time for lunch. I spread my cloak on the ground and we unpacked our sandwiches. It was so peaceful up there. Occasionally, we heard the call of a bird and the rustle of the wind. The world just seemed perfect. I turned to Danny and said, "At times like this I really and truly believe there is a God up there."

"Yes," said Danny. "There's some truth in the saying that this is 'God's own country'. I can feel the power of Him. The scale of nature makes me feel small and insignificant – just a speck on the surface of his world. Sure, it makes you think, doesn't it?"

We were quiet for a while and we watched in wonder all that lay around us.

"Time to be on our way, again," said Danny. "I remember a tale of some lads who were caught up here in the mist. It can be a terrible thing when the mist comes down. I want us to reach the top before the middle of the afternoon, before any mist arrives so we can start our way down in good time. Come on, let's get moving."

We continued our climb. On our way we came across some large granite stones. When we explored them further we realised this was the entrance to a cutting in the hillside. Danny explained to me it was a place of shelter, sometimes for the sheep in bad weather and sometimes for people who had gone astray and were lost. It smelt horrible inside and we didn't stay there long.

"Not far now," said Danny. "Just about another 100 paces or so and we'll be at the top."

And then we arrived. I couldn't believe what I saw before me. There in the distance to the south of us lay the town of Carrick-on-Suir and away to the left Waterford town and further on in the far distance were the Comeragh Mountains. I stared in disbelief at the wonderful view. "Let's sit down," said Danny. We sat on my cloak and I leaned against Danny and we held hands. He pointed to the Comeraghs and said, "The sea is beyond those hills. If the sea was visible from here I would be up here on the day you sail. It would be my last chance to see my love sailing away to a new life."

We were silent for a while. I felt guilty to be leaving Danny but I knew he didn't blame me for going. I rested my head on his shoulder and shed a few tears. "Danny, you are so dear to me. I am so sorry I have to go. But I must do this."

"I know, I know," he said. "Hush now, hush." He took out a kerchief from his pocket and he gently wiped the tears from my face. And we kissed again. The warm summer breeze blew in our faces and the sun shone down on us. It was restful there and we lay down in each other's arms. My head was on Danny's chest and his arms were round me. It felt so good and we were both tired after our walk. And so we fell asleep on the mountain.

# CHAPTER 13

I don't know how long we rested but I awakened as Danny moved and sat up. He looked down at me and said, "Wake up. I'm afraid we're in a wee bit of trouble."

"Why?" I asked, rubbing my eyes and then looked in horror as I saw the mist swirling round us. I shivered as it now felt quite cold.

"Sure, the mist came down quickly while we slept," said Danny. "But don't worry, Bridgie. It usually only hangs around on the top of the mountain and we just need to go down twenty or thirty feet or so to get out of it. We'd better be quick now, and try to find the path we came up on."

Danny was very calm but I was a little worried. I hurriedly stood up and picked up my cloak, which was damp from the turf, and gave it a good shake. I threw it round my shoulders and tied the necktie strings. Danny was packing the remains of our food into his backpack and we were soon on our way.

Danny led me down the mountain path. It was a strange feeling but in the mist I had lost all sense of direction. We came to a place where the path divided. Danny stopped for a few moments and decided to take the left fork. I wasn't sure this was the right way but I followed. There was no point in arguing as Danny had been here before and I trusted him to get me back home safely. We stumbled on and gradually the ferns grew higher till they were up to our shoulders and we were beating a path in front of us again.

"It's no good, Bridgie. We must have taken the wrong turning.

This wasn't the path we came up. I think we're going in the wrong direction. We'll have to go back to the fork in the track." We turned round and climbed back up. When we reached the fork the mist seemed to have worsened. It was very quiet and the eeriness was quite unnerving. I shivered from the cold air. I was glad I was with Danny. I felt safe with him and I was sure we wouldn't come to any harm.

After about half an hour, we still didn't seem to be making progress. "Do you think we are going in the right direction, Danny? You said it was only twenty or thirty feet down the mountain to get out of the mist. We must have covered that amount of ground by now. It's so confusing."

"Let's rest a minute and listen for the noise of sheep. Do you remember we passed them on the way up and they bleated if we went near them?"

So we stopped and listened. We could hear nothing. Danny looked worried. Suddenly, I started to laugh. I couldn't help it and I couldn't stop. "What is it, Bridgie?" said Danny with a smile on his face. "It's not really funny, you know. What's making you laugh?"

I stopped laughing and said, "I was just thinking of Mama and Papa and wondering what they will say if we don't arrive home tonight. They will think we have been up to all sorts of wicked things. I shouldn't laugh really, but sometimes I think Papa brings this sort of thing on the family because he's so concerned about us all." I was laughing again and said, "Don't take any notice of me, Danny. I think my laughter is a nervous reaction." Danny, although worried about our predicament, could also see the funny side of things.

"Now look, Bridgie, we have to make a plan. We're wasting time at the moment and who knows, we might be going round and round in circles, even going down on the wrong side of the mountain. If we don't come out of the mist soon, I think we will have to settle for a night up here. And if we do that, we'll have to have a shelter. Let's build one now and make it our base. We can still try and get down but if we don't make any headway we can return to our shelter."

54

"Do you really think it will come to that? Mama and Papa won't sleep all night with worry. They may even send out a search party for us."

"Don't worry about them now, Bridgie. Let's concentrate on our predicament."

As always, Danny was right. I was completely in his hands and decided to do exactly what he told me. Eventually we came to some large rocks and there we made a makeshift shelter. The rocks were in a V formation and we made a roof of ferns. There were some dead branches lying nearby and we used these as the foundation for the roof and we placed the ferns on top of them. If it came to rain or if a storm blew up we would be out of harm's way. I worried that we might have to spend the whole night there. Danny told me not to worry and said, "I wish a wind would blow up, it would blow this mist away."

When the shelter was complete I saw Danny collecting small stones and putting them in his pocket. "What are those for?" I asked.

"Well, we'll continue down that other path and we'll tread down the ferns as we go. Then, whenever we reach a fork in the path we'll lay a little pile of stones. Then, if we do have to retrace our steps we'll be able to find our way back to the shelter." So, I joined Danny and collected as many small stones as I could find. My pockets were bulging with them as we set out again.

We made our way down the mountain again and kept going for about half an hour. It had started to get dark and it was difficult to see the path ahead. Danny stopped and stood facing me. He placed his hands on my shoulders and looked into my face. "Bridget, I'm so sorry," he said. "I wouldn't have suggested this expedition today if I knew the weather was going to turn bad. Sure 'tis bad luck, that's what it is. And we were having such a good time, too. I don't think we can go any further. I think we must go back to the shelter and stay there out of harm's way."

He led me back up the mountain. I knew Danny had made the

right decision. But deep inside I really worried about Mama and Papa. They would be beside themselves.

We sat down in our shelter on a heap of dead ferns. I took my cloak and put it round both our shoulders. Danny put his arm round me and we sat there, leaning against each other. We were quiet for a long while for there didn't seem to be anything to talk about. The day had been spoilt. Then I decided not to let this upset leave bad memories.

Eventually I said, "Danny, in spite of what has happened I really have enjoyed today. It's been a wonderful experience for me and I shall never forget the view from the top. When I am away from here it will be a memory I will often recall."

We must have fallen asleep then and I woke to the voice of Danny telling me the mist had lifted. He said, "It's very dark out there, but fortunately, the skies have cleared and there is a full moon which gives plenty of light. I think we should make tracks now, Bridget, even though it's still dark."

I yawned and said, "Yes, we should try to get back as soon as we can."

We gradually descended the mountain and were soon on the road again. We arrived home at 4.30 in the morning. As we approached the house I saw the candles were still alight. We were nearly at the house when I said to Danny, "Are you prepared for Papa's tongue?"

"Yes," he said. "Don't you worry, Bridgie. I won't argue with him. I'll give him the opportunity to let off steam. Then I'll tell him we've done nothing shameful and I'll defend your good name to the end!"

So we entered the kitchen and Mama and Papa rushed towards us. "Oh, thank goodness, you're safe," said Mama.

"Yes," I said, hugging her as she clung to me. "Thanks to Danny."

Papa was relieved to see we had come to no harm. He said, "We saw the clouds rolling in from the west during the afternoon. I started to worry then and then we saw the mist come down. But Danny, I knew Bridget was going to be safe with you." Mama, true to form, was busying herself at the fire and making a pot of tea for us.

And so we recounted our tale. I told them I wouldn't have missed the excursion for anything. I described the wonderful view to them. Mama had never been on the mountain and was interested to hear all about it. I apologised for having worried them but I was glad they understood our predicament. When we'd told them all about our adventures Mama said, "Well now, for sure, I think we should try and get some sleep in what remains of the night." We all agreed and I walked to the door with Danny and bade him farewell, thanking him for the day and when he had gone the three of us made our way to bed.

# CHAPTER 14

The day after our trip to Slievenamon the rest of the family wanted to hear all about our adventure. It was the most exciting thing that had happened in the family for ages. They didn't stop talking about it for days. Maggie confided in me she was surprised Mama and Papa hadn't been cross with me for being out so long. We both realised they were relieved to see me home safe and soon forgot their worries.

The next Sunday at chapel I met up with John Breen and we discussed the arrangements for our journey to America. We quickly renewed our old friendship and I was happy to have him as an escort.

August soon arrived. We had a big "farewell" party at the house. Many of our friends and relatives arrived at Islands for the chance to say goodbye to me.

It was a happy occasion with much merriment, dancing and singing and party games throughout the evening and past midnight.

At about eleven o'clock in the evening I felt a hand on my arm. I looked round and saw Danny standing by my side. "Bridgie, come outside for a short while. I have something to tell you." We left the party, unnoticed by anyone.

When outside, I said, "What is it, Danny?"

"Sure, let's walk a while into your back field. I have something I want to say to you."

It was a clear night and the sky was full of stars. We walked up the field and approached the old oak tree, which had the remnants of our old swing dangling from its main branch – a piece of frayed rope.

"Do you remember the happy times we had as youngsters climbing this tree and swinging from the rope?" said Danny.

"Yes, I do. That was a long time ago. I'll never forget the carefree days of our childhood. Those were good times."

"Bridgie, the time has come to say goodbye. I wanted to say this to you away from the crowd. Do you remember what I asked of you a few months ago? Do you remember how I said I wanted to say goodbye to you?"

"Yes," I replied, "I remember," and I laid my arms around Danny's neck and looked up into his face. "Danny Murphy, I have valued your friendship since we were very young. I am saddened I have to say goodbye to you. But, truly, I do hope it won't be forever. I love you in a way that I can't describe. 'Tis the hardest thing for me to leave you. But we both know I must go."

"I know, Bridgie, and I respect you and love you for your strength of character. I just wanted these minutes together out here in this place which we know so well, so our last time alone will be one we both always cherish."

We looked into each other's eyes. A great feeling of love welled up in my chest and I could see in Danny's eyes, the love he had for me.

Danny held me in his arms. Our lips came together. It was a long, tender, loving kiss. We experienced great affection at that moment and I knew we really loved each other. I wondered why we had to part. Life seemed very cruel, but I knew I had no alternative and had to go away.

I didn't know how long we stood there enfolded in each other's arms. All I knew was this man had given me more friendship and love than anyone else in my short life. I was sorry to be going away without him and I wondered if we would ever meet again. It was a sad moment.

We made our way over to a fallen branch and sat there together, cherishing these last moments together. We didn't need to speak. We were both thinking the same thoughts. Danny put his arm around my shoulder. Time passed and it grew darker.

Soon, it was time to re-join the party and we walked back towards the house. We were happy and at the same time sad. It was a strange feeling. Danny told me he felt he was losing his only love, but he would always cherish those last moments together. He said he would never forget me.

The party continued into the early hours. The most unexpected thing of all was when Danny got up and sang a solo. He asked Papa to accompany him on the violin. He sang the old Irish ballad "I'll Be Your Sweetheart".

*I'll be your sweetheart if you will be mine*
*All my life, I'll be your valentine…*

Danny sang with great feeling, looking at me all the time. No-one at the party could have doubted the depth of his love for me. Everyone was quiet while he sang. It was very moving. When he finished they all applauded and everyone joined in the chorus which they sang a second time. I had tears in my eyes as they sang. For sure, I thought, whenever I hear that tune I'll think of Danny.

Eventually the party came to an end and there were the goodbyes and the farewells from all the relatives and friends as they left. Everyone wished me good luck, good fortune and happiness in my future life. Soon the family were alone in the house, with only one week remaining to prepare for my great journey.

The following day Mrs Tobin arrived to start helping Mama in the house. Maggie spent time showing Mrs. Tobin round and made sure she knew what she had to do.

The days flew by in that last week and I packed my few belongings into my new travelling case. Papa ensured I had all the paperwork. He told me what every single piece of paper was for and I put them all away safely in my new carrying bag.

In that last week Maggie and I became very close as we realised the time was near when we might not see each other again. Little did Maggie realise that as the oldest child in the family she would now have more responsibilities heaped upon her.

# CHAPTER 15

So, the day of departure arrived. Papa was taking us to Laffans Bridge railway junction early in the morning. The train was the Dublin to Cork express. It would take us to Cork, where we would embark on our ship at Queenstown Harbour. My brothers and sisters and neighbours were outside the house to wave us goodbye and I came out of the house in my new outfit. Papa said I made a very pretty picture. Rather uncharacteristically for him he told me I was "a bonny lass" and he was proud to see me looking so fine in my new clothes.

Then the moment came when I kissed each in turn goodbye. Mary-Anne was tearful but I said to her, "Don't forget, Mary-Anne, I want you to help Maggie and take care of Mama for me. As soon as I arrive I'll write and send you all my news." So Mary-Anne wiped the tears away from her face and tried hard to smile. Tom comforted her by putting his arm round her shoulder. Maggie was quite distressed and stood quietly with Pat and Dick while Jack helped to load my luggage.

We clambered aboard the cart and Papa took up the reins. So, I left home, waving to my family until they were mere specks in the distance. Mama and Papa were very quiet. After a mile we stopped at John Breen's house to collect him. John and I chatted all the way to the station. Even though I was sad, I was very excited. I was leaving with very mixed feelings.

We passed through the village and friends and relatives came out to wave us on our way. They were shouting "goodbye" and cheering and we heard calls of, "Good luck," and, "Take care of yourselves."

An hour after leaving home we arrived at the station. John Breen and Papa unloaded the luggage and made their way through the station entrance. Mama linked arms with me. She took me aside before going into the station. "'Tis with a very sad heart that I'm saying goodbye to you, Bridgie. But I want you to know that at the same time I'm very happy for you. This is a wonderful opportunity and you must make the best of all your opportunities in life. Remember the things we have taught you and keep up your chapel going and be a good girl. If you want to come home at any time you know you will have to save the money for your fare. But I'll never turn you away from your rightful home if you decide not to stay in America. Just one final thing, remember what I've always said to you – when in doubt, always follow your heart!" Then she kissed me. I'll never forget my feeling of sadness as I hugged Mama at that moment. I wondered if I would ever see her again.

Papa and John finished unloading the luggage and then, to my surprise, Papa took me to one side and said, "Well now, Bridget, this is the last chance I have to talk to you before you go. I want to give you some advice. Your mother and I have done the best we can in raising you and teaching you your manners. And I've made sure you are well educated and able to read and write. But you are sensible enough to know those are only superficial things. The most important things for you to remember are God's teachings. Remember to say your rosary every day. Keep up your chapel going and attend Mass and confession regularly. If you do these things you will have a good life. I know you will work hard and I have every faith you will succeed. That is all I have to say, except that you go with my love and with the love of all the family. Keep in touch with us and write and tell us all your news. You are the first of my children to go to America and I am proud of you."

Then he embraced me and, unusually for him, he kissed me goodbye. Papa wasn't given to displays of affection and I was surprised at this outward expression of his love. I responded by kissing him and throwing my arms around him and I gave him one last hug.

A few minutes later Papa took his pocket watch out and said, "The train is due soon." Then the train came into sight, clanking and puffing and blowing steam as it entered the station. This was the first time I had seen a steam train and I was amazed at the size of it and at the loud noise it made as it rumbled towards us. It slowed to a halt and John found an empty compartment and he bundled the luggage on board. John threw his cap on the luggage rack and jumped back onto the platform with us. We were all quiet for a few minutes. Then we saw the guard take up his position at the rear of the train, with his green flag in his hand ready to blow his whistle. Papa said, "I think it's time to be going on board." This was the moment I had dreaded most. I flung my arms round Mama and kissed her goodbye yet again. "Take care of yourself, Mama," I said. "And don't let them work you too hard. I'll write to you with all my news. I think you know that a large part of my heart remains here with you."

Mama managed a brave smile and returned my embraces. "Aye," she said, wiping a tear from her cheek.

I hugged Papa again as he said, "We'll all look forward to your letters. God be with you, Bridgie. Goodbye, John."

In next to no time we were on the train and we heard the guard blowing his whistle. The huge steam engine whistled and started to move away from the station. Slowly the carriages followed it. Papa and Mama stood together on the platform, waving us off. I leaned out of the window and waved until I could see them no more. The train turned round a bend and they disappeared from sight. It was time to join John in the carriage. We sat in silence for a long while. John tried to make conversation. But it was no use. Nothing could take the place of my family and I felt a great loss.

The parting had been so final. I remembered Papa saying I was the first to go in the family and I wondered who would follow me. Nothing could take the place of my family and I felt a great loss – the parting had been so final.

# CHAPTER 16

Our journey to Cork took almost three hours. Mama had provided us with a packed lunch – the usual bread and cheese. John tucked into his but I wasn't hungry and only picked at mine. I decided to keep it for later.

While John was eating I thought with fondness about the send-off my family and friends had given me. I was going to miss them all. I looked at John and realised that he hadn't received a farewell as I had. I wondered about this. Perhaps, I thought, it was different for young men. He was after all several years older than me and maybe he didn't like outward displays of affection.

We arrived at Cork on time and we couldn't believe our eyes. The train station was crowded with people, some arriving and some departing. The hustle and bustle was something I had never seen before. There were so many people, all going about their business. John took care of the luggage and I clung to my bag containing my papers, frightened that in the hubbub it might be stolen. It was a long walk to Queenstown quay so John suggested we hire a cab. I wasn't sure we could afford it but we hailed one and John asked, "How much to the quay?"

The driver replied, "Which ship are you heading for, sir?"

"The Lucania," said John.

"Fine, fine, sure we'll be there in two shakes – she's berthed on the West Quay. It'll only cost you two or three pence. She's sailing on the midday tide, isn't she?"

"Yes," said John. "I hope she sails on time. But can you make that two pence? We're a bit short."

"All right, hop in," said the driver. I smiled at John's art of haggling.

I was enthralled by all I saw. Neither of us had been in a place like this before. It was an adventure for us both. Cork was so big and there were crowds of people everywhere. The whole scene was new and exciting.

The cab soon arrived at the quay and we alighted quickly. John paid the driver who pointed out our ship to us. For the first time in our lives we saw the sea. Until now I had only seen the sea and ships in picture books. I was amazed at the large variety of boats tied up along the quay.

The dockside at Cork was like something never imagined. Such a wide variety of people, all crammed on the side of the dock – what a mixture. There were passengers, their relatives who had come to see them off, the ticket brokers looking for those who had not yet purchased their tickets. Then there were the vendors of all sorts of things from fruit to ribbons, from sweetmeats to soap. Before we left home Papa had instructed me, "Keep clear of the vendors. You should have everything you need and these people charge exorbitant prices."

We had to go to the port medical officer. "There's the Medical Office, over there," I said. So, we pushed our way through the crowds and joined the queue outside the office of the port doctor. This was going to be a long wait as some passengers hadn't brought certificates from their own doctor. Even though we had our medical certificates we were still subject to medical inspection by the doctor.

Just in front of us was a large family with mother, father and eight children. They wore ill-fitting clothes and it had obviously been a struggle for them to collect the money for the passage. The youngest child was only a few months old and didn't look at all well. The mother shielded the baby in her shawl as they made their way forward. They entered the office ahead of us and we waited outside. Before long, loud voices could be heard from inside. It hadn't taken long for the medical officer to discover that the baby wasn't well. Then when he found that one of the young boys had a hacking cough the whole family were declared unfit for the journey. In the opinion of the doctor it was likely that at least one of them was suffering from tuberculosis and they were forbidden to travel. The angry and dejected family left the office. I was upset by this sad scene and expressed my sadness to John. "It is very sad, Bridget, I agree. But it's good they aren't allowed to travel, since who knows how many of them might be infected? They might pass the illness to others."

"Yes, John, you're right, but I'm thinking of the hours of planning and scrimping and saving they must have done – all for nothing. It is a sorry sight and one I wish I'd never witnessed. Where will they go now? They must have sold all their belongings and left their home."

"Aye, that's true I heard that many people just leave their homes and take the last two or three months' rent with them to pay for their passage. Look, it's your turn now to see the doctor. In you go, Bridget."

Two minutes later I emerged from the office with a smile on my face. "He didn't even inspect me," I said. "He took one look at me and said, 'Are you quite well? Show me your tongue,' and then he stamped my ticket."

"Well, that's because you are a healthy bonny lass," said John.

John was equally quick and laughingly I said, "What a bonny lad you are!" We both laughed. That was the first hurdle over.

Our ship had anchored out in the bay and there was a small boat ferrying the passengers out to her. We joined the queue.

I watched the other people in the queue. Some were families with several children. Others were young married couples. There were a few single young men but no unaccompanied girls. I could now see the need for me to have a travelling companion. On the whole the queue was orderly and we slowly moved forward.

Our turn came and we were soon on board and being whisked out to the *Lucania*. A member of the ship's crew said, "Have your ticket ready, lass." Soon the ship was towering over us and it was our turn to go on board.

We clambered up the gangway and I had to be careful not to trip on my long skirt. We stepped on deck and a sailor told us to follow a green sign that pointed in the direction of the steerage deck. We were travelling "steerage" class with hundreds of others and it was good that we had arrived early so we could find a space for ourselves.

We made our way below deck and discovered that there were already a number of passengers on board. These people had boarded the ship in Liverpool and had made themselves at home, taking up most of the good places. But we found a good corner where we were able to spread ourselves out before the rest of the passengers descended on us. "Well, this is it," said John. "This is our home for the next few days. Let's hope we have a good voyage and arrive safely in New York. Most of all let's look forward to health and wealth in the future."

Gradually, within the next hour, we became accustomed to our new surroundings. We each had a crude bunkbed onto which we piled our belongings. It was quite dark below decks but there were one or two portholes dotted around. From these we could see other ships bobbing on the water. Our ship would soon be leaving Cork, bound for America.

We decided to go on deck and watch the scene as the ship sailed. As we stood on deck we could see in the distance the crowd lining the quay. Many hundreds of friends and relations had gathered to wave their loved ones off. This brought a tear to my eye, as there was no-one there for us. Surprisingly, John put his arm around my shoulder. He was thinking the same thoughts as me. We waved to the crowds. My memory is of a sea of hands, some people waving handkerchiefs, others waving with their caps. As we moved away we could hear the loud shouts of farewell from the quay.

We both had tears on our cheeks as we saw the land of our birth disappearing into the distance. We realised this might be the last time we saw the old country, the country of our parents and the country of our childhood. This last look at our homeland was sorrowful but we had to admit we were looking forward to the new life that lay ahead of us.

We went below and settled in for a quiet few hours. But it was far from quiet. We were tired after the train journey and slept sporadically on our bunks which were piled up with our coats and luggage.

After two hours of patchy sleep I sat up. John had disappeared so I guessed that he was away exploring the ship. I looked around at the hundreds of other groups of Irish men, women and children on their way to a new life in America. They were busying themselves – making themselves comfortable for the long voyage. They had already fought over their positions. The amount of space allocated to each person was small. It was difficult for some of the big families to find a place where they could all be together. But things were beginning to settle down. Many of the passengers looked tired and weary. This was life changing for everyone.

# CHAPTER 17

The coming of steam ships had reduced the time taken to cross the Atlantic Ocean to about seven days, but sometimes less with fair weather conditions. Before, in times of sail, it had been known for a ship to take 35 days or more. My aunts and uncles who had sailed before us in days gone by had written home to tell of the terrible crossings they endured. The ships then were smaller and conditions more cramped. The new steamships were bigger and could carry more passengers. Accommodation was now much better than it had been in the days of the sailing barque. We were fortunate as the *Lucania* was the quickest oceangoing liner, with the proud reputation of having won the Blue Ribband for the fastest Atlantic crossing.

By law all ships with more than 300 passengers had to carry a ship's surgeon. Stringent laws ensured no overcrowding and basic food was provided for travellers. Inspectors made sure all was in order. In the old days people had to supply their own food for the journey. Things had changed a great deal since then.

My thoughts were interrupted by the arrival of John at my side.

"Hello, John, where have you been?"

"Bridget, I've been up on deck again. It's wonderful up there. The air is fresh and cool. Every now and then we meet a wave and up at the front you can feel the salty water on your face. Will you come up on deck with me?"

"Not now, John. I'm just getting acclimatised to the atmosphere down here and all these people – our new neighbours!"

John was surprised at my reaction and sat down beside me. Concerned, he asked, "Are you all right?" In the past I had always been adventurous and game for anything and this solitary and quiet person wasn't the girl he had known back home.

I whispered to him, "John – I think we have to make sure of our places here. We've only just set sail. You remember what a scrabble there was when we came on board. There seems to be a lot of jostling going on and we must hang on to this space. Also, we must keep an eye on our belongings. You go ahead now and go up on deck. I don't mind keeping our place. I can go up when you get back."

"I think I'll stay with you. I think you're right. This is a good little corner here. We don't want to lose it. This baggage here is the sum total of our worldly possessions. We must look after it carefully. Anyway, it'll soon be time for us to have a hot drink before we settle down for the night."

Normally I would have been keen to join John on deck and I felt mean for not going with him. Already, since leaving home, I felt different. I was becoming aware of the enormity of what we were doing. These thoughts weighed heavily on my mind and I realised I must take responsibility for myself in future.

John stayed below decks with me and we tidied our bedrolls ready for the time when we settled down to sleep. It was comfortable sitting on the bedrolls and I made myself a backrest from the rest of our luggage. The berths were small and there was hardly enough room for luggage and it was good that we weren't carrying much. The light was poor so reading was difficult. We sat there talking quietly. Inevitably our conversation turned to home and to the time we had first met.

We were both at Papa's school and I was in the juniors and John was in the seniors. I always looked on John as one of the "big boys". He was good looking and had a cheery smile and twinkling blue eyes. He had a mop of brown hair with a lock, which always fell forward on his brow. I had always enjoyed his company because he talked to me as an equal in spite of the difference in our ages. Our paths parted when John left school so it was amazing that we were making this journey together. When John left school he became apprenticed to a carpenter in the nearby town so our paths had never crossed.

Now, here we were, on our way to a new life in America. John's future was planned out. He had served his apprenticeship and was now a fully-fledged carpenter. My future was less certain. I was going to live with my aunts, Maggie O'Connell and Catherine Frisby in New York. They had emigrated several years ago and were doing well for themselves. They ran a small dressmaking business and employed half a dozen girls. They wanted me to join their work force. I was going to do this but, unbeknown to them or to anyone else at home, I had other ideas. I saw this as my passport to America and I hoped to do other things in future. At that moment I had no idea what those things were. I just knew that my future didn't lie with them forever.

John sat down next to me and handed me a mug of cocoa. I thanked him and smiled. The cocoa tasted good. It was some hours since our last meal and we wouldn't eat again until breakfast. I warmed my hands on the mug.

It had been a long day and we were both exhausted. At the other end of the steerage deck a group of youngsters were dancing and singing, accompanied by a fiddle and a squeezebox. They were good tunes – songs we had known all our lives and they reminded us of home. Soon, many of the passengers had joined in.

In all, the scene was one of great activity and enjoyment. I remarked to John that our fellow passengers didn't seem to be sad at leaving the old country. In fact, once out on the open ocean the scene was one of hustle, bustle, commotion and gaiety. Everyone was looking forward to the great adventure which lay ahead of them.

Eventually, I fell asleep wondering what lay ahead for us. What would life in America be like, I wondered?

# CHAPTER 18

I woke just two hours later and looked around me. Most of our fellow passengers had settled for the night and many were asleep. I looked at John and he opened his eyes. "Aren't you asleep yet?" I asked.

"No, I couldn't – I've been thinking of the folks back home and thinking about the future."

I whispered back to him, "Yes, I've been doing that all day. Do you think we've done the right thing?"

"Only time will tell, Bridgie. It's too late now for second thoughts. But whatever happens to us I hope we'll always be close friends." We lay there for a while not speaking and lost in our own thoughts. As the ship gathered speed it started to rock, battling its way against the Atlantic swell. It was a comfort to have John with me when we were so many miles from home.

We didn't sleep much on that first night. We tossed and turned in these new and strange surroundings. It was hot and there was very little air on the steerage deck. The swell of the sea was strange to us. Many of our fellow passengers found it hard to bear. At midnight I decided I needed to go up on deck for fresh air. I whispered to John, "Are you awake?"

He replied, "Yes, what is it?"

I said, "Let's go up on deck and get some fresh air." I put on my cloak and we made our way up to the deck.

The wind was blowing strong and it was difficult to walk on the deck. We swayed from side to side, hanging on to each other lest we should fall. I suddenly started to laugh. John said, "What is it, Bridgie? What are you laughing at?"

I replied, "We must look so funny. If anyone sees us they will think we are the worse for drink. We must look like two drunken sailors!"

John laughed with me and we made our way to the starboard side of the ship. It was a bright moonlit night and we could still see the coast of Ireland with one or two twinkling lights in the distance, across the water. We would soon be leaving it behind. I had tears in my eyes, despite the laughter a few minutes before.

A young man and his lady friend came and stood with us. "Sure 'tis a sad sight, to be sure," the man said. "Just to think this might be the last time we see our dear old country."

John realised this might upset me and tried to change the conversation. He looked ahead and could see a light in the distance. "Is that another ship?" he asked.

"No, to be sure that's the Mizzen Head light. 'Tis told there's been a light on those rocks for many a year. In fact, they have plans to build a proper lighthouse on the headland," said the young man. "That will be the last sight you see of Ireland – I've heard it said they call the Mizzen 'the teardrop of Ireland'. So shed your tears now for once we're past it there will be no looking back for us."

It was a sobering moment as we passed the light. We were all very quiet. After a while we decided it was time to go below and settle down again so we made our way back below deck.

The partying below deck, which had started when we left Cork, was continuing into the night and I longed to join in the dancing. John said, "Come on, Bridget, let's dance. It might be the last chance we have for merrymaking for some time. Let's make the most of our time on board."

After the first dance I said, "You're right, John. There's no need for us to be grieving because we've left home. Our lives lie ahead of us and we should enjoy the voyage."

It certainly did feel strange to have no work to do and only have time for enjoyment. I had never travelled far from home nor had I known what it was to have a holiday. I looked back on my life and I realised it had been a round of hard work and drudgery. The only relief we had was on birthdays, weddings or funerals when we really let our hair down.

On the third night of the crossing a storm blew up. We were woken in the middle of the night by a loud crash. The ship was tossing and turning on the Atlantic waves. A member of the crew arrived to say no-one was allowed out on the open deck and all the hatches were battened down. The ship heaved and pitched and made little headway for many hours. It was tossed high on the waves as it ploughed through the water. There were loud crashes each time the bow hit a new wave.

Many people were seasick and lay prostrate, moaning and crying. The whole place was beginning to smell of sour sick, sweat and perspiration. I don't think any of the passengers had washed since they had come on board and some probably had fleas or nits. I longed for a breath of fresh air.

Next morning the storm abated slightly and the hatches were opened up to allow fresh air in. What a relief! John ventured up on deck.

When he came back he said the ship seemed to be wallowing in the high seas and we didn't seem to be making any headway. He said that one moment we appeared to be in a deep trough of sea with high walls of water all around and when the ship rose to the top of the waves he could see mile upon mile of rough sea and white horses. The decks were awash with water so he came back down below quickly. The Atlantic storm was all around us. The skies were grey and heavy. I prayed we would weather it and reach the end of our journey. Thankfully after a further 12 hours we left the storm behind. The sea gradually grew calmer and the ship was able to steam on. However, we would be late arriving in New York.

The storm had changed the mood on the ship. Gone were the scenes of merriment. Now the spirits of the travellers were sober. Those who had been sick took time to recover.

The ship picked up speed after the storm and we were surprised when we reached New York only half a day late. The captain had a timetable to stick to but he would make up lost time on the return journey.

# CHAPTER 19

The day dawned bright on the 28th August 1898; the sea was calm on the morning of our arrival in New York. As soon as land was sighted all passengers were up on deck to see the landscape of America unfolding in front of us. There was a buzz of excitement amongst us as we realised we were nearly there. Before long we were steaming close to the city of New York and the vista of Manhattan's buildings stretched out in front of us. We had heard tales of tall buildings but nothing had prepared us for this view. Nowhere in Ireland was there a city like this. We were entering a new world.

And then, over to our left, we saw the Lady of Liberty. The Statue of Lady Liberty had arrived in New York a few years earlier and was a gift of friendship from the people of France to the people of the United States. The statue was huge and was made of copper. It had been transported to America in several hundred pieces and had to be reassembled when it was placed on its island.

Lady Liberty was a welcoming sight as we steamed closer to our point of disembarkation. A few years later I was to read on the statue's pedestal words reflecting the hope for freedom and opportunity shared by the millions who see Miss Liberty after a long ocean journey.

Close to the statue stood the burnt out remains of the Ellis Island Immigration Centre. The immigrant reception centre at Ellis Island which was only about 5 or 6 years old had burnt down the previous year and now incoming immigrant ships were redirected to a makeshift immigration centre at the Barge Office on the southern tip of Manhattan Island. As soon as the ship docked we trundled ashore with our belongings. We were eager to be near the front of the queue and everyone was jostling for a place. There was a sense of relief to be on dry land again. This was the dawn of our future life. We had arrived in America.

We were fortunate to be the first ship to arrive that day – passing through the Barge Office was not going to take too much time as we didn't have passengers from other ships holding us up. We waited patiently for our examination by the American authorities. The authorities were worried about illnesses like tuberculosis and never let anyone in with the slightest suspicion of fever. Some travellers were sent home if they were unwell and others were detained in quarantine.

We joined the queue at the medical office. Again we had to undergo medical examinations. As we were young and healthy it was for us a mere formality. Our papers were checked and we passed the medical check quickly. But others, who hadn't withstood the journey well, were subjected to longer examinations. With our papers stamped and given the "all-clear" we passed quickly through the hall and we were soon on our way to find our waiting relatives.

Crowds of relatives and friends lined the pavements waiting for new arrivals. Gradually, one by one, a waving handkerchief or a familiar face or a name shouted out was recognised. John and I were looking for our respective aunts. We hadn't seen them since we were young children and neither of us could remember what they looked like. The crowd was so big that it was like looking for a needle in a haystack. I was surprised to see police officers mingling with the crowd to keep order. I was anxious and a little frightened by the crush of people. "I hope they've come to meet us," I said to John.

"Yes, come on," John said. "They must be here. Don't forget your Aunt Catherine paid your passage. She's not going to lose you that easily." I laughed. We seemed to be getting our sense of humour back. It was good to have our feet on dry land again. But the strange thing was that we both could still feel the rise and fall of the waves, even though we were now several hundred yards away from the sea.

Then we spotted them. John's Aunt Ellen and my Aunt Catherine were standing together, scanning the crowds and didn't see us approaching. John and I were both very apprehensive. We wanted to make a good impression. The aunts looked severe and John said to me, "They haven't seen us yet. We can escape now if you want to." I laughed when John said, "Just think, we could be off to the Wild West and make a new life for ourselves, away from the busy city."

Just a few more steps and the four of us were reunited. The aunts were delighted to see us and told us it was almost fifteen years since they had last seen us, before they left Ireland when we were tiny children.

"Welcome, welcome," said Aunt Ellen.

"Yes, come along now," said Aunt Catherine. "We must organise your luggage and get you both home as soon as possible."

So Aunt Catherine summoned a porter and instructed him to carry the luggage. I was glad John was there to help.

The porter found us a horse-cab and soon we were settled inside it. The aunts tipped the porter and we were on our way towards our new homes.

The aunts chatted away, asking us about the voyage. We told them about the storm and about how frightened some of the passengers had been. "Sure, I nearly brought my stomach up," I said.

The aunts laughed. "Well, I'm sure it was better than when we came," said Aunt Ellen. "The ships are so much better now and cross the Atlantic quickly. When we came we didn't know how long the journey would take. The sailing ships in those days were at the mercy of the winds. The crossing is much faster now with the new steam ships."

As we rode along we were enthralled by all that we saw. New York was a thriving city and I was astounded by the difference between this city and the rural surroundings we had left behind.

There were large apartment blocks, five or even six or seven storeys high. "Why do they build them so high?" I asked. Aunt Catherine explained that the population of New York was about three and a half million people. The population of the city was the same as the whole of Ireland. New York was the gateway to the American continent. Land prices in New York were high because land was scarce. Living accommodation and land to build on was in great demand. So the property developers built their buildings high. We were very quiet as we took in the scene around us. This was a remarkable place and we could hardly believe our eyes.

Soon Aunt Catherine and I arrived at our destination. John and his aunt said goodbye to us and continued on their journey to New Jersey. I was sad to leave John and hoped we would meet again soon.. We'd exchanged addresses so we could keep in touch by letter.

We arrived at my new home in east 38$^{th}$ Street in midtown Manhattan where my aunts had their apartment. I was later to learn more about the layout of the New York streets. The other half of the street was west 38$^{th}$ Street and led up to a long street called 5$^{th}$ Avenue. When we had waved John off I turned to look at my new home. It was a large apartment block, five storeys high, built of red brick. The ground floor appeared to be a shop. My aunts' apartment was on the third floor. They had 2 bedrooms, a living room and a kitchen. I wondered what the sleeping arrangements would be.

My other aunt, Aunt Maggie, had returned from work and I was introduced to her. After the introductions we settled down for supper and as we ate, I told them more about our journey and the storm. After the meal I was very tired and ready for bed. The day had been long and exciting. However, I wasn't allowed to rest so quickly. The aunts wanted to talk more. They wanted news of the family back home. Many questions followed and they were pleased with all I told them. I didn't tell them about Papa's trouble with the school authorities. But they were concerned to know if the house and farm were well looked after since the death of Grandpa Jack. I reassured them that all the jobs on the farm had been allocated to my brothers and sisters. They also wanted to hear news of the neighbours who they remembered from long ago.

Then it was time for bed and I was taken aback when they told me that I would not be sleeping in their apartment! There was an apartment next door where several of their girl workers lived and space had been made for me there. I was astonished at this news, coming so late in the day as it did. My surprise must have shown on my face and the aunts were a little uncomfortable. I had expected to be living with them. But this wasn't the case. I was taken next door with all my baggage and, after the introductions, the aunts left quickly.

I was welcomed by my new roommates. There were three of them – Brenda, Eileen, and Magda. Brenda and Eileen were Irish and Magda was Italian. We all shared one bedroom. They had anticipated my arrival and showed me my bed. I must have been very quiet and said, "I think I'll have an early night. It's been a long day and I'm exhausted. Let's talk in the morning."

As I lay in my bed I cried quietly to myself. I had expected to be living with my aunts. Nothing had prepared me for this. The girls seemed nice but the shock of my situation had hit me hard. I was so tired I soon fell asleep. This had been the longest day in my life.

# CHAPTER 20

The day after my arrival was a Sunday and I slept late and woke refreshed. The other girls were already up and Brenda made me some breakfast. She told me they all contributed to food and rent. Money was put in a pot once a week for this. The aunts had put my share in for the first week but after that I was expected to contribute. Brenda was a quiet girl and I liked her immediately. She was several years older than me and took me under her wing. Brenda said I could go with the girls to chapel. I was glad of this invitation.

After breakfast we all set out for Mass. It was a beautiful day and after church Brenda suggested a walk in Central Park. This park had only been opened for about 20 years and before this Manhattan didn't have any recreational space. The area where the park stood had been marshland and thousands of tons of topsoil were brought in from New Jersey, across the river and millions of trees and bushes were planted. It was wonderful to be able to step into the park and walk away from the noise of New York City. It was a place of beauty where one could enjoy the scenery – an oasis in the city – the first green landscape I had seen since leaving Ireland.

I was amazed at how many people were out walking after church. Sunday seemed to be a time for leisure. We strolled through the tree-lined pathways and watched families enjoying their day off. We came across a band playing popular marches. I was intrigued to see people relaxing and enjoying the sunshine. It was very hot and Brenda said there were fewer people here than usual. In hot weather many people flocked to the beaches at Coney Island to bathe in the sea and ride on the roller coaster. This was a new world.

After our walk we returned to the apartment and spent the rest of the day sitting together and talking. Later, I decided I must let the family know I had arrived safely and I wrote my first letter home:

*My dearest Mama and Papa, Maggie, Jack, Dick, Pat, Tom and Mary-Anne,*

*Well, here I am at last in New York. We had a splendid voyage apart from two rough and stormy days. Many passengers were seasick. John and I felt queasy at times, mainly through lack of fresh air. When the storm blew up all the hatches were battened down and we were not allowed on deck.*

*Aunt Catherine met me from the ship and I was soon whisked away by cab through the streets of New York. This is a fascinating place. Just imagine buildings five or sometimes even six or seven storeys high! Here in the apartment we are on the third floor. It is so strange not to be able to step outside into the garden. I am living in an apartment next door to the aunts! I share it with three other girls who all work for the aunts.*

*This morning I went to Mass with the girls and after church we walked in Central Park along tree-lined pathways. Everybody seemed to be on holiday to-day. Bands played in the park. Sunday here is a day for relaxation.*

*I send you much love and affection. My thoughts are always with you. I will write again soon. Aunt Catherine and Aunt Maggie send you their love.*

*As always I remain your affectionate daughter,*

*Bridget Frisby.*

That evening my aunts explained to me what I was to do at work the next day. They lost no time in telling me how different things had been when they came to New York. "When we arrived," they said, "we were among thousands of immigrants arriving daily and nearly everyone wanted to live in New York City. We were amongst Irish and others from European countries such as Germany, Italy, and Poland. Most of us when we arrived were very poor. At first we lived on the lower east side of Manhattan. Rents were lower there and we lived in a crowded tenement building. Our building housed three or four families on each floor. We lived in one room and shared washing facilities with many people. It was very cold in winter."

They had to find work quickly in order to pay the rent. They worked in the textile industry in the "garment district" of the city. They worked hard and took work home in the evenings to earn extra money. They sewed on buttons, made buttonholes and made cuffs and sleeves for shirts and blouses. This homework earned them a few additional dollars each week and they were able to save. After three years they had saved enough to buy their own sewing machine. So then they were able to bring more work home and the extra dollars trebled. Soon, their savings grew to a sizeable sum. This gave them independence and it wasn't long before they set up their own dressmaking concern. They now supplied "made-to-measure garments" and served a different market from their former masters at the factory. They now had a thriving business and were able to send money home. When things got better they moved out of the tenement building further uptown to the present apartment in midtown Manhattan.

As they grew busier and the order books filled up it occurred to them that some of the family in Ireland might come and join them in their enterprise. So they had written to Papa with this idea. I was glad Papa had kept in touch with them because this had been my salvation.

As I left them that evening they told me to be ready to go to work next morning at 7.30 sharp. After hearing about the conditions in which they lived when they had arrived I didn't feel quite so bad about being pushed in with the other girls.

Before going to sleep, I looked out of the bedroom window at the bright lights of New York. I wonder if I'll ever get used to living three storeys up above the street, I thought. I was finding it difficult to get used to the idea that there was no back door and no garden.

I looked up into the sky. The stars shone brightly. I could see the North Star. I thought of Danny back at home and wondered whether he was looking out too! I whispered, "Goodnight, Danny," and climbed into bed and fell asleep.

# CHAPTER 21

Next morning we were up at half past six ready for my first day at work in America! I was soon washed and dressed. I wore my work clothes, which I had brought with me from home. These consisted of undergarments of a chemise, dark cotton stockings, knee-length drawers with a corset and a petticoat. Over these I wore a navy floor-length skirt and white blouse with long sleeves.

After breakfast we set off for work. We travelled in one of the electric "street cars". These vehicles were crammed with people all going to their work and before long the tram was full to overflowing. The streets were crowded too. In addition to these streetcars there were other forms of transport – there were horses pulling delivery wagons and others hauling loads of coal. I watched the loads of coal being shovelled through openings in the pavements into the basements of the buildings. Then I caught my first sight of an elevated railway that rumbled noisily overhead at first floor level. I could hardly believe what I saw.

I watched with interest our fellow passengers. Women chatted together – some were talking in strange languages which I didn't recognise. New York was full of immigrants.

Soon we reached our destination in the "garment district" where many tailors worked. Aunt Catherine opened the heavy door of the building. We entered it to find several workers already at their workbenches. Some were cutting out garments; others were working at sewing machines.

A large matronly lady appeared to be the overseer and was organising the work. The aunts said good morning to everyone and made their way to the back of the building. I was aware of many eyes staring at me as I followed my aunts. The workers were wondering who I was. I hadn't expected to see so many people in the works. There were at least a dozen employees there.

I followed the aunts to the back of the workshop to two small offices. We sat down and they explained to me they had a loyal and hardworking workforce. The pay was good and the aunts said this was the way to keep good staff. Apparently, their competitors paid poor wages and staff moved about amongst all the workshops to find better pay and conditions. But these women and girls were satisfied with their pay and they were even paid extra if they achieved more work than that which was set for them. But it had to be of good quality. It was eerily quiet in the workshop and I realised that the women were all working hard to earn extra pay. This was quite different from the "chattering" school room I was so used to.

"It's very warm in here," I said.

"Oh, you'll get used to it," said Aunt Catherine.

I didn't really like what I saw. It seemed the workers were prepared to accept anything so long as they were paid well. I couldn't help thinking the atmosphere would be better if there was more talk amongst the employees. Also, there were no windows. There was a skylight but it was dusty and looked as if it had never been open. I hoped it wouldn't take long to get used to this environment. It seemed very strange. I felt stifled. It was all so different from the clean fresh air I had left behind in Ireland.

I was introduced to the overseer and she set about teaching me the ins and outs of the sewing machine. I was fascinated by the speed at which garments could be made. My first job was "button-holing". By the end of the day I hadn't managed to master this job and I felt quite despondent.

At the end of my first week Aunt Catherine took me into the back office. "Now, Bridget," she said, "what are we going to do with you? I knew from your father's letter that sewing is not your strong point. Your work this week certainly bears this out." My stomach took a lunge when she said, "I really don't think you will be of use to us in the workshop. It's such a shame. But here in the office we've many things that need attention. You could be most helpful here. How does work in the office appeal to you?"

"Well, it's not what I expected to be doing," I said, "but I prefer to work with pen and paper rather than needle and thread. So I think that's a grand idea."

I was relieved to be out of the claustrophobic workroom. The office wasn't much better but there was a small window there. I opened this and felt a slight breeze, so much better than the heat in the workroom.

Soon I was learning all about the office work. There was much to do. Letters had to be written to our suppliers of cloths, silks and threads. I also wrote to customers telling them when their garments were ready for a first fitting or had been completed.

The aunts spent a lot of their time talking to customers who seemed to be calling in all day either with new orders or collecting finished orders. A telephone had recently been installed. It hadn't rung all day. I was anxiously waiting for it to ring. Although I was intrigued by it I hoped it wouldn't be my job to answer it. There was a glass partition between the office and the workshop. Through this I could see the girls at their machines and I marvelled at the speed at which they worked. I was pleased with my situation now and glad I was working in the office. This was better than making buttonholes all day. It was a beginning and I counted myself lucky to have a new start in a new country. There was no way I could have a job like this at home in Ireland. After these brief thoughts of home I turned back to my work. At the end of the week in the office I returned home tired, yet happy that I had been able to help my aunts. I felt I had earned my pay.

We were always hungry when we returned home after a busy day.

Our evening meal usually consisted of meat and potatoes with vegetables followed by a generous supply of fresh fruit. This meal was a luxury for me but at least I felt I had earned it after my long day.

On the way home from work we often stopped at the market to buy food. The market contained fresh food, such as vegetables and fruit. Brenda explained that other foods such as cereals, custard and canned meat, tinned fruit were becoming common and could be bought from the grocer's shop. This was such a change from home where we had never bought tinned food and had grown all our own fruit and vegetables. At weekends Brenda took me to some large food stores. One was the Great Atlantic and the other the Pacific Tea Company.

A great benefit of working in the office was that I managed to complete my work in five days and I didn't have to work on Saturdays. So, on my first free day I went out to explore more of New York City. I wished I could contact John. I hadn't heard from him since our arrival. Like me, he had probably started working straight away and hadn't time to think about anything else. When I went out on my own I had strict instructions not to go far, nor to get lost and not to talk to strangers.

I wandered to uptown Manhattan and found a large store called Wanamaker's. It was in a building several storeys high with large plate glass windows such as I had never seen before. Inside the store, the upper floors seemed to be supported on large stone pillars, which were placed at regular intervals. This left plenty of space for the counters and shelves on which were displayed a large variety of goods. Many people were doing their shopping. I was intrigued by what happened when a customer made a purchase. The shop assistant put the money into a small metal container and put it into a metal tube. Then he pulled a handle over his head. The money was being sent over to the accounts office in the middle. I was surprised when I saw the container flying over my head. Eventually the container came hurtling back and the customer was handed the receipt for his purchases and change from his money. Later when I was back at home the aunts explained to me that these were pneumatic tubes and used in all the large stores.

I looked at all the wonderful things on sale and realised you needed plenty of money to live comfortably in New York. I began to understand now why the workers at our place worked so hard. On this first foray into the city I didn't buy anything as I had very little money with me but I was thrilled with all that I saw.

One morning we were about to leave the apartment for work when the post-boy arrived. He had a letter for me. Brenda handed it to me, saying, "Here you are, Bridget. Here's a letter for you. Look, it has an American stamp and a New York postmark. Who do you know who lives here?"

I immediately thought of John. I knew the letter must be from him as I knew no-one else in New York. I think I coloured up when Brenda handed the letter to me. But I looked surprised, saying, "Thank you," and muttered, "it may be from John Breen. I haven't time to read it now." I stuffed it into one of my pockets. I was intrigued, but quietly delighted.

I was bursting to know the contents of the letter. Apart from Danny back at home, John was the only man whose company I enjoyed.

I waited until lunchtime to open my letter.


*Dear Bridget,*

*I promised to write as soon as I had settled in New York. I am living with my aunt, my uncle and my six cousins. Aunt Ellen is very good to me.*

*I spent the first few days in America looking around and meeting old friends who had come here before me. Then, I set about finding a job and I have secured a position as a porter in one of the big hotels in Fifth Avenue. At the moment I'm on cloud 9 as they are paying me a wage, supplying me with a uniform and I have a room at the top of the hotel. And all my meals are free. The pay is not terrific but 'tis easy to increase it with tips.*

*So, I am a happy man. I hope to find a position as a carpenter when I have saved some money. How are you Bridget? I hope you are well and enjoying yourself.*

*Do you think you will be able to come out with me? I enjoyed your company on the ship. T'would be a shame if we did not meet again. On Sundays, after church we go to Central Park to relax. Will you walk with me in the park one Sunday?*

*I hope you will write back with an agreeable reply.*

*Your friend, John Breen.*

I sighed when I finished reading the letter. Here was a voice from home in this new land. People here were good to me but I missed my family and friends. Here was someone I really knew and I felt comforted knowing John wanted to renew our friendship.

That evening I sat with the girls and told them about the letter. They were pleased for me and when next I had the opportunity I told the aunts of the letter. They suggested John should collect me from their apartment. They thought John must be a good, decent young man as Papa had entrusted me to travel with him and this friendship would have their blessing. I felt slightly aggrieved that they thought they had such control over me. Now that I was in America and trying to make my way I thought I should have more freedom to do as I wanted but I know they meant well.

The following Sunday John came to the apartment and I re-introduced him to my aunts.

I started to go out regularly with John. This brought me a new freedom. There were no restraints on my actions, as there had been at home. Now it was my conscience that dictated what I should or shouldn't do.

My newly found independence turned out to be both stimulating and fulfilling. I enjoyed my friendship with John but I didn't think it would be a long-lasting relationship. I wasn't like my sister Kate and I wasn't going to marry the first man who came my way.

# CHAPTER 22

I soon realised there were two faces to New York. The face seen by the outside world was the bright lights and glitter in the shops, the theatres and smart hotels. In Manhattan the streets were crowded and noisy, especially at road junctions where carts and trams jammed the streets. The drivers impatiently clanged their bells and shouted with frustration. At lunchtime, it became even busier with the office workers rushing out to find the quick-service or takeaway restaurants. One Saturday I took a tram ride to the outlying districts of New York. By contrast these industrial areas were dismal and some of the people lived in slums – really terrible conditions. This was the other side of New York. It reminded me of the tales I had heard back home about the slums in Dublin. I suppose all big cities had their bad sides. I heard there were street gangs and prostitutes in New York. Corruption and crime was unrestrained. I didn't dare venture into the worst parts of the city. I soon realised there were many poor people who didn't have jobs. I felt quite uneasy.

It was difficult to come to terms with the comparatively affluent environment in which I lived and the poverty I saw in the slum areas. The aunts didn't know I had been to these places. They would be horrified if they found out. I knew they had endured harsh conditions when they first arrived and indeed for several years but they seemed to have forgotten that some people still lived like this. In one way, I was glad the aunts had set up their workshop in a reasonably favourable district but the things I had seen humbled me. I wished I could find a way to help these poor creatures. But I could see no way to do this. My upbringing and faith made me very aware of the plight of others.

After my first three months in New York I began to realise I wasn't totally happy. I had tried hard at work and made few errors. But the aunts just seemed to take me for granted in the office. I knew my work was good but they never praised or complimented me. I learnt quickly how to keep the ledgers in order and I was now well acquainted with the various suppliers and the costs of the materials. I decided I would have to stick it out. But I couldn't see me staying with them forever. I continued to work hard but I longed for my days off when I had time to myself.

Since I had been in New York I had received two letters from home. Papa had written them both. There wasn't much news from home about the family. Mrs Tobin was still helping in the house and the money I sent had arrived safely. The boys were helping on the farm and Mary-Anne had started to learn to cook. I had written back and given them all my news. I told them about my meetings with John on Sundays, but I omitted to tell them about my other excursions on Saturdays.

# CHAPTER 23

One day I received a letter from Ireland from my dear old friend Danny Murphy.

It was obvious he still missed me and, after reading the letter, I sat wondering about my future. If only Danny had been able to come to America with me. That would have been perfect. If Danny was here maybe I would have been able to put up with this life with the aunts. But would I? What did I really want from life? I thought about the poor people I had seen in the slums. I realised from that moment what I really wanted to do – I wanted to help people. But I didn't know how I was going to achieve this.

Winter was now coming fast. New Yorkers had experienced bad weather the previous year when the city had the worst winter in living memory. Apparently, it snowed for many hours and there were fierce gales and blizzards. One day, in the worst snowstorm of all, the mesh of telephone and telegraph wires hanging over the streets of New York collapsed. When winter was over and spring came the wires and cables were laid underground to avoid another catastrophe.

A similar bad winter was predicted for the coming months. It turned out to be correct and we had a very bad time. Many people were ill with 'flu, bronchitis and pneumonia and the hospitals were full to overflowing.

The doctors and the hospitals were finding it difficult to cope. One day, on my day off, I saw a queue of people outside a hospital. I could not believe that so many people could be ill. My curiosity got the better of me and I went into the hospital to see what was happening. All around me were sick people and nurses and doctors rushed off their feet. I felt inadequate and wanted to help. I stopped a nurse and asked if there was anything I could do. "Sorry, dear," came the reply, "we need qualified people. Are you a nurse?"

"No," I said. I left the hospital and went home feeling quite despondent and useless.

That night I tossed and turned in my bed. I couldn't sleep. I couldn't discuss my concerns with my aunts – they would never understand. They thought they had improved my life by giving me a job and paying me a good wage. They didn't know I was so unhappy.

I missed my home and my family and most of all Danny. I wanted to work where I was appreciated. I needed more satisfaction from life. If only I could have worked for just a few hours in that hospital. That would have been marvellous. I would have come home satisfied and I wouldn't be troubled now. I wondered if I could train to be a nurse. I decided there and then to find out more about it and see if it was possible. My heart told me I should be helping people. I thought about Mama's words to me before I left home: "Follow your heart." In America I had a better chance of making my dream come true than back home in Ireland. These thoughts led to the second turning point in my life.

Exhausted, at last I fell asleep. The following day I set about enquiring about becoming a nurse. I found out about hospitals in New York and managed to obtain a list of half a dozen. I wrote to all of them and enquired if they had vacancies for trainee nurses. I sat back and waited for a reply.

Two weeks later an official-looking letter arrived addressed to me with a New York postmark. It was from one of the hospitals. They told me they had vacancies for trainee nurses and they were prepared to consider my application. I would have to sit a written examination in literacy and numbers. If successful, I would have to go before the Board of the Hospital for an interview. They also sent me details of the training programme, which took two years to complete. They enclosed details of the pay which was less than I was earning now but board and food were free and they supplied everyone with uniforms. I could barely contain myself but I had no-one to share this with.

I kept my news to myself and decided to discuss this with John the next weekend. When I told him of my decision and showed him my letter he said, "Bridget Frisby, you are a one. If anyone gets what she wants out of life I think it will be you." He was keen to read my letter in full. After he had seen the contents he said, "Are you going to go ahead with this?"

"Yes," I said, "I will. But first, I'll wait a few days to see if any of the other hospitals reply. Also, I think I should write home to my parents and tell them what I intend to do."

"Good for you," said John. "Bridget, I'm glad you've done this. I'd noticed you getting quieter and I wondered what was wrong. Also, I have something to tell you. I've been given the chance to get back into carpentry and I have a job interview next week."

"John, that's wonderful," I said. "I'm so happy for you. So, it looks as if we'll be making a move at the same time," I said.

"Yes," said John. "It looks that way, doesn't it?"

# CHAPTER 24

As soon as I could I wrote home to my parents. I had great difficulty in writing the letter. I didn't want to upset them and I didn't want them to feel I had broken my contract with the aunts. Most of all I wanted them to understand that I was determined to achieve my ambitions, but I wanted to do it with their approval.

I wrote:

*My dearest Mama and Papa,*

*I am writing to seek your blessing on a decision I have made about my future. Since I have been in New York I have seen so many different sides of this great City. I have seen great opulence but I have also seen much suffering and poverty. I feel a great need to do what I can to help those poor people who are worse off than me. I want to train to be a nurse.*

*I haven't told the aunts of my ambition as I want your approval first. Please let me know what you think of this idea. I do hope you will approve. I won't proceed without your blessing. I truly believe this is my vocation.*

*I will await your reply. In the meantime, I hope you are all well.*

*With love to you all, as always,*

*Your loving daughter Bridget.*

A few weeks later I received Papa's reply to my letter.

*Dear Bridget,*

*Thank you for your letter. I read it to Mama and told her you wanted to help others and she wondered at first if you wanted to be a nun. She was delighted when she heard you wanted to train as a nurse. We are both very happy about this, but we must point out that you are taking a big step in a foreign country and you must be sure of what you are doing. We will not stand in your way and we wish you well and you have our blessing.*

*You must tell the aunts what you intend to do. They will not be pleased but as Mama always says "Follow your heart".*

*From your loving parents.*

*Richard and Mary Frisby*


I was delighted with my parents' good wishes but I wasn't looking forward to telling the aunts about my intentions. I decided to tell them straight away. I was a little worried that they might want me to move out of the apartment completely when I moved to the hospital. I wanted to keep in touch with them so I hoped I could keep some of my possessions in their apartment. When I had time off from the hospital it would be good to have a base in the City. I decided to give them my news on Friday evening.

Friday evening came all too soon. I was invited in for the evening meal with my aunts. I knew my news might be taken badly. By now, I knew enough about my aunts to know they could get very cross. I couldn't pluck up courage during the meal to start a conversation. After supper, we sat down in the sitting room. Aunt Catherine was reading and Aunt Maggie was completing some embroidery. I had brought Papa's letter with me and it was in my lap. As I sat there I reminded myself that Mama and Papa thought I was well suited to be a nurse and they had given the idea their blessing.

"Did you have good news from home in your letter yesterday?" asked Aunt Maggie.

"Yes," I said. "Well, actually, I have something to tell you."

"What's this? Not bad news, I hope," said Aunt Maggie.

I took a deep breath and then I began. "I wrote to Mama and Papa a few weeks ago because I had something to ask them. I wanted their blessing." When they heard this they sat up, eager to hear what I had to say. I came straight out with it. "For you see, I want to train to be a nurse."

The aunts looked at me in a stunned silence. My words were like a bolt from the blue and something they had never anticipated. A few seconds passed and Aunt Maggie asked, "What did your parents have to say about this, Bridget?"

"They say they think I'll be most suited and they are pleased that I might have found my vocation. They have sent me best wishes for the future. They agree that I should go ahead."

A stony silence followed. "You realise that you are breaking your contract with us, don't you?" said Aunt Catherine. I expected her to be the one to object.

"Yes," I said. "I realise that but you will recall Papa wrote to you before I came here telling you he wasn't sure if I was suited to the type of work you were offering me. And I haven't been able to help you in the workshop. Please try and understand. I feel a great need to take care of sick people. As you know there is a great shortage of nurses and I want to help if I can. I am so sorry if you think I've let you down."

"Well, actually, life has been easier since you arrived as we didn't have clerical help before you came. Clerks are two a penny in New York so it won't be difficult to find someone to replace you. When do you intend to start this nursing?"

"Well, I haven't even applied yet," I said. "I hope you won't throw me out before I'm offered a position. I wanted to tell you of my intentions before applying. I hope I can continue working with you until I'm accepted at the hospital."

"Well," said Aunt Maggie, "I think you've done things correctly, but you'll have to give us a chance to talk together about this. Catherine and I must discuss the matter together." They appeared to have closed ranks and this worried me. It was unusual for Aunt Maggie to speak up like this.

"When do you think you will be able to let me know?" I asked.

"We'll have an answer for you by tomorrow," said Aunt Maggie.

I thanked them and then said, "Well, I think I'll go to bed now so you can talk this over. I'll see you in the morning." And so I made my way back to our apartment.

When I reached the bedroom I sat on my bed and many thoughts crossed my mind. My aunts were the most difficult people I had ever come across but I hoped they were going to agree to my proposal. I felt frustrated and I was glad I wasn't going to be working for them for much longer. With these worries on my mind I had difficulty falling asleep that night but after a few hours I drifted off – probably from mental exhaustion!

When I woke in the morning it was early and I lay in bed thinking about my position. Here I was in a strange country working for two strange women. They might be my aunts but they were so different from my relatives at home. I felt very lonely. I couldn't wait to apply to the hospital. I wanted so much to make a success of this.

I couldn't wait to see John Breen again. As I lay there I thought about John and also about Danny back at home. They were my two props who had always supported me when I needed a shoulder to cry on. I hoped I would be laughing, not crying the following day when I met John.

I decided it was time to get up and to face my future, whatever that was going to be.

# CHAPTER 25

The next day the aunts announced their decision. They said they were glad I had chosen to be a nurse and they wished me every success. They also told me I must look upon their apartment as my home in America. They knew I would be living in the hospital but they wanted me to feel free to stay with them when I was off duty. I was pleased and relieved by their response and thanked them.

Events progressed very quickly from that day on. I completed the application form for the hospital and wrote a letter to go with it. I wanted the covering letter to be just right and I took some time writing it. I had to provide the name of two references. I put the name of Father O'Brien the Parish Priest and asked John Breen to vouch for me. Soon my application was in the post.

I decided to forget all about the application and I made up my mind to approach other hospitals in New York if I didn't get a reply.

Three weeks later, on the 11th November 1898, I received a reply from the hospital. I read it out to my aunts:

*Dear Miss Frisby,*

*Thank you for your application to become a trainee nurse. Please attend for a written examination on the 29th November. You should bring your own pen but paper will be provided for your use.*

*Please come to the main hospital entrance and report to reception. You will be directed to the examination room.*

*We will notify you the result of your examination within one week and if you are successful we will invite you to come for an interview with the Matron and the Hospital Bard.*

I went for my examination and within a week I heard I had been successful and I was to attend for interview on the 14<sup>th</sup> December. The aunts were delighted with this news. I immediately wrote home to tell Mama and Papa. It was up to me now to make a good impression at the interview.

On the 14<sup>th</sup> December I attended at St. Joseph's Hospital in the town of Yonkers, New York State, for my interview. I arrived at the hospital fifteen minutes early and I was ushered into a waiting room. I sat nervously on a red leather upright chair. I looked round the room. There were oil paintings on the walls of men in dark suits who I assumed had been connected with the hospital in the past. Some wore spectacles and they all had side whiskers or beards and looked dour and stern. I was very nervous. I was neatly dressed and wore gloves, but the palms of my hands felt damp. It was unbearably quiet in that room. The minutes ticked by.

Then, the door opened and a lady dressed in a blue uniform entered. She said, "Miss Frisby?"

I replied, "Yes."

"Please come with me. Matron and the Board are ready for you." We walked along three long corridors, not saying a word. Then just before we reached the room the lady turned to me and said, "Have you had an interview like this before?" I said that I hadn't.

"Well now, don't be nervous. They might look old-fashioned and like stuffed dummies, but they're quite human really. Just imagine that you're talking to your father or your brothers and act naturally – you'll be fine, I'm sure."

I was relieved at her kindness and thanked her and smiled. Then I said, "I recognise your accent, are you from Ireland?"

"Yes, from County Cork, many years ago."

"I thought so," I said. Then I was shown into the room. I was instructed to sit on one side of a long table. On the other side sat the Matron, in the middle, with four governors on each side of her. There was a clerk at the end of table taking notes.

One man started the interview. "Miss Frisby. I believe you have only been in America for a short while. Who are you living with?"

I explained I lived with and worked for my aunts in Manhattan. Then they asked me why I wanted to be a nurse. My reply was simple. "I want to help others who are worse off than myself. My present job gives me no satisfaction. This is something I must do."

Several more questions followed and I think I answered them well. They seemed satisfied with my answers and they impressed on me how hard the training was. They said I must be prepared to get up early every morning and be prepared to do menial tasks such as cleaning out the sluices, and feeding and washing the patients amongst many other jobs.

How did I feel about this, they asked? I replied, "I'm not a stranger to hard work or to rising early in the morning. I lived on a farm in Ireland and we were always up at the crack of dawn. It will be wonderful to be doing something really helpful."

Then the Matron explained to me that the training lasted for two years. If the Board accepted me I was expected to live in the nurses' home. After the two years it was normal to work and live at the hospital for a further period of at least one year. This final year was the pre-registration year and if I completed the full three years I would then be a fully-fledged and qualified nurse.

Finally, they asked me if I had any questions. I only had one. "Will there be any class work and will there be any examinations?" I asked. They replied that class work was on one day a week, with an examination at the end of every year.

"Well, Miss Frisby, we have several other applicants to interview. We have places for 30 trainees and 52 young women have applied. Your interview is finished now. We will let you know the result before the end of the month."

I thanked them and smiled as I left the room, saying, "Good-day. Thank you for your time."

As I travelled back home, I had no way of knowing whether I had done well or badly. I didn't think I had made any mistakes so I decided to be patient and wait for the result. When I arrived home the aunts were keen to know how I'd got on. All I could say was, "I did my best but I have no idea if I'll be accepted. I'll just have to be patient and wait and see." I described the hospital to them and told them about the Board of Governors and the Matron.

"Were you nervous?" asked Aunt Maggie.

"Yes, I was when I first went in. My nerves disappeared as soon as I started to talk. There was a lady there from Ireland who put me at my ease before I went in."

"Well, good luck to you, Bridget. We hope you are successful."

Two days before Christmas a letter arrived from the hospital. I opened it with a trembling hand, realising that in it lay my future.

*Dear Miss Frisby,*

*Thank you for attending for interview with our Board. We are pleased to tell you that your application has been successful and we are writing to offer you a place as a trainee nurse in this hospital, commencing on the 1ˢᵗ February 1899.*

*As mentioned to you at your interview, the training will cover a period of two years, terminating with a third and final pre-registration year. On completion of three successful years, you will become a fully trained nurse.*

*If you accept this offer you should make arrangements to move into our Nurses' Home on the last day of January, in order to start your work with us on the following day. Please report to the Home no later than 12 noon on that day. When you arrive you will be allocated to a bedroom which you will share with three other trainees. Lunch will be provided for you. After lunch you will measured for your uniform and you will receive this before the end of the day. From that time on, whilst on duty your uniform must be worn at all times. Please read the Rules and Regulations of the Nurses' Home, which are enclosed with this letter.*

*Your salary will be $6 a month. You will be provided with all your meals. After two years your salary will rise to $14 a month.*

*Please write to us informing us that you intend to accept this offer. We take this opportunity to welcome you to St. Joseph's if you decide to proceed.*

On the 31st January 1899 I arrived at St. Joseph's Hospital, Yonkers, in Westchester County, New York, ready to train for my career as a nurse.

# CHAPTER 26

On my first day at the hospital my fellow trainees and I were taken to the linen store to get our new uniforms. We were given 3 starched white muslin caps, 3 long, floor-length, pale blue uniform dresses with starched white collars and cuffs. The pale blue differentiated us from qualified nurses who wore dark blue uniforms. We also had a white-bibbed apron which we wore on top of our dress and we had starched white belts, which we wore over the aprons. Before our arrival we had been instructed to purchase strong black shoes with low heels and black stockings. I had saved my wages to buy my shoes and stockings. Also I bought myself a watch, which I wore on a chain attached to my belt. I soon learnt that I didn't need this watch during the first few months so I wore it tucked into my belt so it wouldn't be damaged.

After our clothes had been issued we were ushered into changing rooms and we proceeded to don our new uniforms. I felt grand in mine. There were lots of laughs and giggles as we struggled with unfamiliar collars and cuffs. Then even more laughter when we tried to put on our caps. During the last few months I had grown my hair longer so I could wear it in a chignon. I was glad of this as the cap sat neatly on top of it and I had little need for pins, as did many of the other girls. One of the girls commented it was a good job there was a hospital laundry, as she didn't fancy starching her uniform every week. Then it was time for inspection. The sister in charge was a stickler for tidiness and cleanliness and many of the girls were pulled up for not wearing their uniforms correctly. Two others were sent away to clean their fingernails.

Sister told us that during our first month in training we would be inspected each day as we arrived on duty. After that, the inspections would reduce to one a week and then in time to one a month. We soon realised that looking right was just as important as doing a good job!

The next morning, all neatly dressed in our new uniforms, we were taken on a tour of the hospital. I was in awe of everything I saw. We saw young children, confined to bed, with faces as white as the sheets they lay in and old men and old women with many different illnesses.

After the tour it was time for lunch. The food was only just passable. However, when you are hungry you'll eat anything. We soon learnt that if we didn't eat at the prescribed times it was a long time before the next meal. After lunch we were given our timetables and we had to read the rules of the nurses' home and then we were allocated to our wards. I was to work on the same ward as three other girls – Ellen, Ivy and Mary.

I hadn't realised how hard the work would be. After one week I recognised what a relatively easy time I had been having in New York, living near the aunts and working in their office. That, together with the long sea voyage, had been a restful time for me compared with this new regime. I had forgotten how hard I had worked back home in Ireland. I was grateful I'd worked hard at home as I found it easier to cope with the new routine than many of my contemporaries. When we returned at night to the nurses' home I went to our sitting room and read a book. But most of my fellow trainees retired to bed exhausted.

We were up early each morning for breakfast at 6.30 a.m. After breakfast we reported to our wards. I had become friendly with Ellen and we were on the women's medical ward. There were so many poor souls there. I had thought that I was going to tend to their needs… not so at this early stage in my career! From the moment I entered the ward I was at the beck and call of my superiors. "Nurse Frisby, empty this bed pan!" Or, "Nurse Frisby, it's time to clean out the sluices."

Then it was, "Nurse Frisby, sweep the floor," and, "Nurse Frisby, take these plates to the kitchen." I began to wonder if I would ever help the patients. But somebody had to do these menial tasks and the senior nurses had been through this same routine when they were juniors. I came into my own on Mondays when we went to the classroom. Our teacher was called "Sister Tutor". This was her official title. She taught us anatomy and physiology and practical nursing. We were given written exercises which we had to complete by Friday. I took copious notes and always enjoyed my homework. I had little difficulty in keeping up with the class work. Only time and the final examinations would tell if I was any good.

After my first week at the hospital I wrote home to Mama and Papa and told them of my experiences. I told them about the jobs I had to do on the ward. I told them about our studies and about the things we were learning. I told them how I longed for the day when I could progress to the things the older nurses were doing.

# CHAPTER 27

My first month at the hospital passed very quickly and my first day off soon arrived. Surprisingly, I couldn't wait to see the aunts again and I was up early that day. I suppose this wasn't strange as they were my only relatives in America. I arrived at their front door just before 9 a.m., much to their surprise! Aunt Maggie opened the door, exclaiming as she did so, "Why Bridget, how lovely to see you so early. I wasn't expecting you until later. Come on in." It was Saturday and Aunt Maggie had taken the day off so that we could have time to together.

We embraced as if we had been apart for years. I hadn't realised how fond I had become of Aunt Maggie until that moment. I suppose this was natural as I was so far away from home. I missed my family at home but was so busy at the hospital I didn't have time to be homesick.

We were soon chatting away and I had so much to tell her. I told her all about my work and she was amazed to hear about all the unskilled tasks I had to perform. She thought I'd been better off working for her as a clerk. I tried to make her understand that I was a junior first-year student nurse and I didn't expect to be doing any real nursing until the second year.

When we'd exchanged all our news we went out on the town. I had no money to spend but I enjoyed going round the large department stores. We had lunch in a small café and the sandwiches and mug of tea were such a change from the hospital food.

The rest of the afternoon we spent in the park before returning to the apartment for our evening meal. It had been a good day and after supper I returned to the hospital.

When I arrived back at the nurses' home I discovered that very few students had gone out. They were all too tired and most of them had spent the day resting and catching up with letter writing. They were surprised to hear how much I'd achieved and they wondered where my energy came from. The following day things were back to normal. On Monday we went to our classroom for more lectures. At last we started to do some practical nursing. Although it was only teaching us how to make beds it was a step in the right direction and I enjoyed the class. Soon we were to move on to things like simple bandaging and how to treat awful things like bedsores. All this was better than bedpans and sluices.

# CHAPTER 28

Throughout the summer I continued to enjoy my work. I visited my aunts whenever I could. They had given me a key to the apartment and told me to make it my base. I only saw them if my day off was on a Sunday. Occasionally I met up with John Breen. We managed to see each other about once every three months. I always looked forward to these meetings. It was good to have a friend nearer my age. He was a sensible lad and we always managed to have fun together.

Spending time with John didn't stop me thinking about Danny Murphy and wondering from time to time how he was getting on. In the early months of my time in New York he had written to me quite often but lately I didn't hear from him so often. Then one day a letter arrived. He told me he had been walking out with a girl called Joanna and they were getting on well. At first I was disappointed to hear this but I knew this was selfish of me. After all, I'd gone off and made a life for myself and I couldn't expect him to wait for me forever. In spite of Joanna, I was very fond of him and I knew he was still fond of me. Circumstances beyond our control had sent us in different directions and our ways had parted. I was a great believer in fate and if it wasn't meant to be then so be it.

I told my friend Ellen about Danny's letter and said I thought he was soon to marry Joanna. She understood how I felt. Ellen was a good friend and I knew I could always confide in her. From time to time things were reversed and she found me to be a good listener to her problems. We were both lucky to have someone to confide in.

# CHAPTER 29

My first year at hospital went quickly and in December I was pleased that I passed my first-year exams. Now, I was ready to start my second year's training. All was going according to plan when one day, just before Christmas, I received a letter from my sister Maggie. It disturbed me greatly.

*Dear Bridgie,*

*I hope this letter finds you well. I am writing because I want to come to America. Things in the school have gone from bad to worse. I am sorry to trouble you but Papa seems to have little interest in his work now. The other day he didn't go to school at all. I was left to look after all the children on my own. Papa seems to have 'mood swings' and Mama and I worry about him.*

*Mama wants Papa to give up teaching to concentrate on the farm. She thinks he is struggling with the responsibilities of school and farm. We all do what we can to help but this never seems to be enough.*

*Do you think it's possible for me to come to America? I always said I would never leave home but now I want to get away.*

*Mama is well and sends her love. She suggests that you are careful in your reply; as Papa doesn't t know I've written to you.*

*With fondest love*

*From, your loving sister Maggie.*

This was like a bolt from the blue! I couldn't take it in. I read the letter several times over before the gravity of the situation started to sink in. I knew Mama had a hand in that letter. Maggie was never very good at letter writing and I sensed Mama's involvement in this. Here I was, thousands of miles from home, and I felt utterly helpless. What could I do? It was time for me to go on duty so I hurriedly pushed the letter into my uniform pocket and rushed to the ward.

Later I shared my news from home with Ellen. She said, "I really don't know what to suggest. But you should take time to think this over. It's your day off next Sunday. Why don't you discuss this with your aunts?" I was glad of Ellen's friendship and agreed to talk to my aunts.

For the rest of that week I felt very low and I wasn't sleeping well. I had to be so careful not to let it affect my work. Sunday came at last and I arrived at my aunts' early in time to have breakfast with them. I shared my news with them and they were very concerned. They knew Papa still had a family to support and they realised he wasn't getting any younger. They understood how difficult it must be for all the family.

"Thank you for sharing this with us, Bridget," said Aunt Catherine. "This is a family matter and we'll give it a lot of thought. Let's go to Mass now and when we come back we'll put our heads together and see if we can come up with a solution." I was very relieved and felt much better when we went out. But the letter had cast a shadow over all of us.

When we returned from church we sat in the sitting room and Aunt Catherine began by asking me a question. "Bridget, can you tell us what you think of Maggie's needlework?"

This was a difficult question to answer. I knew Maggie wasn't particularly good at sewing. In fact she was rather slapdash. But I could see why they were asking this and I had to be careful what I replied. After some thought, I replied, "As you know, Maggie has been helping Papa in the school as an Assistant Teacher. She had to pass an exam in needlework and she has had quite a lot of experience although I don't know how good she is. She has never complained about her job so she must enjoy it."

I thought this reply was tactful. I hoped it was what they wanted to hear. It wasn't like me to be dishonest, but I was trying my best to be diplomatic. I had to find a solution to the problem.

"That sounds good," said Aunt Catherine. Aunt Maggie nodded in agreement. "Well, we have a suggestion. As you know we are always on the lookout for good workers and Maggie seems to fit the bill adequately. The good basic knowledge she has is most important but she will have to learn how to work the machines. If you agree we'll write to your father and ask if Maggie can come and work for us. That way, he won't know Maggie has contacted you. What do you think?"

"Oh, that's wonderful. I can't thank you enough. Mama and Maggie will know your letter is in response to Maggie's plea to me."

"Well, let's hope it works out well this time," said Aunt Maggie.

"I hope so too for all our sakes," I replied.

I went back to the hospital that evening with a load taken off my mind. The next day I was happier than I had been for a long time when it dawned on me that my sister might be coming to America. I hoped Papa would allow her to travel.

# CHAPTER 30

Life at the hospital continued as before. At last I was learning more and gaining experience. Life on the ward was very busy. I soon learnt that it was silly to get too attached to patients as they didn't stay with us for long. As soon as the doctors felt they could look after themselves they were discharged. Most patients could not afford to stay long in hospital and were glad to be sent home.

When my next day off arrived I hurried, early in the day, to see my aunts. As soon as I saw Aunt Catherine's face I knew she had good news. "Come in, Bridget dear. We have excellent news for you," she said as she ushered me in. Aunt Maggie was there too and told me they had received a letter from Papa.

I was anxious to know the contents and they lost no time in telling me. "We're delighted," they chimed in unison. "Your father has agreed that Maggie should come and work for us. So it won't be long before she is with us." I was so relieved.

After lunch I met John and told him about Papa's letter. He was pleased to hear the news but he realised I would have to share my precious time off between him, the aunts and Maggie. "I hope you won't stop seeing me now that Maggie is coming," he said.

"Of course not, John, I promise you." But I realised that in the first few months Maggie was going to take up a lot of my time. I would have to show her around New York and help her get her bearings. I suggested to John he could help me with this.

That evening, when I returned to the nurses' home, I wrote to Maggie telling her how much I was looking forward to her arrival.

# CHAPTER 31

Time passed quickly in the next few months. The day soon came when Maggie was due to arrive. Many letters had passed back and fore across the Atlantic making all the arrangements. I couldn't believe the day of her arrival was nearly here. I was due a few days' vacation so I arranged to stay with the aunts for 3 days.

Maggie arrived on the 28th April 1900. Like me, she had sailed on the *Lucania* from Cork. Aunt Catherine came with me to meet her. The scene was similar to when we arrived two years earlier. I was excited and could hardly contain my joy when I saw Maggie's face at the barrier. She was soon with us and looked so well. As she came towards us I ran to her and we flung our arms round each other. Aunt Catherine was clearly surprised at this outward display of emotion. I cannot describe my joy at seeing my sister again. I felt that I was no longer alone in New York – my family had joined me.

We took a horse-drawn cab home to the apartment. Maggie chatted all the way, telling us about her voyage across the ocean. I laughed at her and reminded her she had once told me she never intended to leave home and now here she was in New York. Aunt Catherine listened quietly while we talked nineteen to the dozen.

News from home came over dinner that first night. I had the feeling Maggie wasn't telling us everything. Later, when we retired to bed I heard it all. Maggie told me that Papa had fallen foul of the school inspector again. The previous October he had been, in the words of the Inspector, 'admonished on the neglect of written exercises for his pupils'. Then in November he was rebuked on the 'untidiness in the schoolhouse and on carelessness in the accounts'. I was shocked to hear these things. Only then did I realise the enormity of the problem and the reason Maggie wanted to get away.

"Oh, Maggie," I said. "You poor thing. However did you put up with it? You had to work in the school when all this was going on and I suppose the atmosphere at home was bad too."

"It was a terrible time," said Maggie. Things had deteriorated rapidly in the two years since I left home.

Before we settled for the night Maggie told me things had started to improve since the decision was made for her to come to New York. Papa had taken on a full-time assistant to replace her and he was running the school and Papa was concentrating on putting the account books right and the Inspector now seemed happier. Also, Papa was able to spend more time at home so the farm wasn't suffering. Before we finally settled for the night Maggie made me laugh at all the pranks the boys had been getting up to. It was late when we went to sleep and we slept late the next day.

When we woke the following day we discovered the aunts had already gone to work. They had left us a note telling us to make ourselves at home and help ourselves to food.

I spent the rest of my leave showing Maggie around New York. She told me she had made friends with a boy on the boat. His name was John Casey and she had taken his address. He was living nearby with his uncle, Michael Casey, and they had agreed to meet. Maggie was looking forward to meeting up with him at Mass at the weekend.

Maggie had never shown interest in boys at home and I was surprised to hear this news. She seemed to be a different person now. She had grown in confidence and was much happier. The moody, sulky Maggie I remembered from days gone by had disappeared. I hoped and prayed for her success in America.

Maggie was looking forward to starting work with the aunts. She now had the right frame of mind and I knew she would work hard. At the end of my time off I made my way back to the hospital feeling happy about my sister.

# CHAPTER 32

Maggie met up with John Casey again and soon they were spending most of their time together. They were inseparable. I wasn't surprised when Maggie told me that she and John wanted to get married. I thought this was excellent. John had found a job working at one of the top hotels and he hoped to progress from liftboy to porter and he said, "The sky's the limit if you are prepared to work hard in America." He had great ambitions to climb the ladder. Maggie was happier than she had ever been. I suggested to her that she write and ask for Mama and Papa's permission to marry. Together we penned a letter home.

Maggie soon received a letter in which they sent their love and blessings for the future. They were delighted with the news. She was glad to receive our parents' good wishes. She couldn't wait to see John to give him the good news but she decided to tell the aunts first.

When Maggie announced her news Aunt Catherine said, "Well I never – this is a surprise." Aunt Maggie just looked taken aback and said nothing. She let her sister do the talking.

"When is this to be, Maggie?" asked Aunt Catherine.

"John wants us to get married as soon as possible."

"Well, what does he mean by as soon as possible? For one thing, you have nowhere to live. Unfortunately, there isn't room for the two of you here."

"Please don't worry, Aunt Catherine. John says we can live with his uncle. My main concern is that I want to continue working for you. John won't be able to support us both as he is only a junior liftboy at a hotel. His Uncle Michael lives nearer to work so there is no problem with the travelling. What do you think?"

Aunt Maggie spoke for the first time. "Well now, Maggie, I think that's fine. We don't want lose you so soon. It would be a shame if you left us now after we've spent time training you. Yes, I think you can continue to work for us. Do you agree, Catherine?"

"Yes," said Aunt Catherine. "I quite agree." Maggie thanked them and couldn't wait to tell John the news.

The next time I saw Maggie we had much to talk about. She and John had seen the Parish Priest and they had set a date for the wedding. The aunts had agreed that Maggie's wedding dress could be made in the works. So Maggie was able to play a great part in designing and making her own wedding dress.

# CHAPTER 33

Maggie and John were married in September just five months after Maggie arrived in New York. It was a wonderful church service and I was the bridesmaid. After church we went back to the aunts' apartment for the wedding breakfast. Aunt Catherine said it was a pleasure to be doing something to help the family from "back home". In spite of the aunts' rather stern exterior they actually had hearts of gold. As they had no children of their own they treated us like daughters. Many old friends and relatives were invited and most of them were Irish. It reminded us of the parties we had at home. There was much singing and dancing. I often wondered what Mama and Papa really thought of Maggie getting hitched so quickly!

After the wedding I saw Maggie less frequently and I was surprised how much I missed her. But I knew she was happy and I was pleased for her.

I wrote home to tell the family all about the wedding. I described it in great detail and told them about the aunts' kindness.

A week after the wedding a letter arrived from home to say Kate was expecting her third child. Kate and John were still living in Limerick and didn't get home to Islands very often. I owed Kate a letter so decided to write to her with all our news.

I had neglected writing to Kate but I never forgot Mama and Papa. They received a letter at least once a month from me, sometimes more often. I always sent home the promised money and Maggie added to this from time to time. Maggie wasn't so fond of writing and she always asked me to tag a paragraph on the end of letters for her. I did this willingly, for I knew Mama and Papa always wanted news of her.

# CHAPTER 34

Several months later I received a letter from Papa and was dismayed to hear that once again things weren't well at home. The boys were growing up and, although they still helped on the farm, as they grew older they had distractions. They were spending more time out and about away from home. They often went into the town to the fairs and markets and they were beginning to be interested in girls! Papa said in his letter, '*Would you believe it Bridgie they now stop at the public house on their way home and I am a' feared this might become a habit. Jack is old enough to do this but I am alarmed that he is leading Dick and Pat astray.*' He went on to tell me not to worry and asked for my advice. He said, '*Do you think it would be a good idea for the boys to come to America? How easy will it be for them to find jobs over there?*' I decided to give this matter some thought before writing back. Papa also mentioned things weren't going well at school. He was spending more and more time on the farm and he regretted he often neglected his school duties.

I was saddened by this letter. Poor Papa – ever since Grandpa Jack died he seemed to have the weight of the world on his shoulders. There was a postscript to his letter. It concerned Kate. She was nearly at the end of her term with her third child and it was due to arrive in the next few weeks.

There was nothing I could do to help in his predicament. I decided to talk to Maggie next time I saw her and we might even mention the problem to the aunts. They might have some good ideas about where the boys could find work.

It was several weeks since I had seen Maggie. When my day off arrived I went to see her. We embraced as if we had been apart for years. I realised how fond I had become of her. I suppose this was natural as we were both in a strange and distant land. Maggie said she was often homesick and if I wasn't so busy at the hospital I knew I would be quite homesick too.

We were soon chatting away and had so much to tell each other. I noticed Maggie looked tired and had grey shadows under her eyes. I asked her if she was well. She replied, "Yes, sure I'm fine," but I couldn't help wondering what the problem was. It wasn't long before she told me John was spending more and more of his time at work. There was a lot of pressure on him to work long hours and they didn't have much time together. She said, "All I seem to do is go to work, come home and wash his clothes and cook for him. Then, when he comes in, he eats his supper and falls asleep in the chair." I sympathised with her but there was little I could do to help. Maggie wasn't happy with her life and this saddened me.

After a while I told her about Papa's letter. She was disappointed to hear the news. Her first thought, as usual, was about Mama. She asked, "Does Papa mention how Mama is managing? Does he say how she is?"

I replied, "No. He doesn't, but I'm sure she has to work hard and I hope she isn't looking as tired as you. I'm quite worried about you. I think you need a rest. Why don't you ask the aunts if you can have a few days' holiday and then persuade John to do the same?" Maggie shrugged her shoulders and said she didn't think it would be possible but she would think about it.

We talked at length about our brothers and wondered if they would get jobs in New York. Then there would be the problem of where they would live. Maggie had already decided there was room for them at Uncle Michael's; she said, "I know they're a problem for Papa but if they are away from home Papa will stop worrying about them. They're young and I know for sure if they want to get on in life they couldn't do better than come to America. There's no future back home in Ireland for them. I'll ask Michael if they can have the spare room. Yes, I'll do that, Bridgie, and then when I have an answer I'll let you know."

I had the feeling Maggie would welcome the boys with open arms. She seemed so lonely. I told her she was taking on a big responsibility by offering them a home. But as much as I tried to make her change her mind she wouldn't hear of it. She said, "Bridgie, it's the answer to so many problems. It can only be for the good." Maggie had made her mind up and it wasn't for me to change it. I decided to wait to hear what John's uncle Michael thought about the idea.

Later that day we went out and when we were sitting drinking our tea in a small café at lunchtime, Maggie confided in me that John was rather too fond of his drink. She said, "Between you and me, Bridgie, I know he goes out after work drinking with his work-mates. I'm sure that's why he falls asleep in the evenings." Then she said something that surprised me. "Bridgie, sometimes I wish I was single like you. I really envy you your freedom. I feel so tied down and wonder what the rest of my life will bring."

I was troubled to hear Maggie talking like this. Things had been so good between her and John when they first married and it hadn't taken long for things to go wrong. I put it down to the stresses and strains of working long hours. But there was nothing I could do. I felt so hopeless. My words of sympathy sounded empty and I couldn't begin to imagine what torment Maggie was going through.

In the evening we went to see the aunts. We told them about Papa's letter and they agreed the boys couldn't do better than come to America. "Well," said Aunt Catherine, "if they do come there will be five of you here. That will leave only two at home, in fact only Mary-Anne as Thomas is away in school most of the time. Things will be easier for your mother and father if the boys come here. Quite apart from the worry of bringing up a large family, it will ease their financial burden."

So that was it. As soon as John's uncle had agreed to the plan I wrote to Papa and told him that if the boys decided to come to America there was a home for them with Maggie. I finished the letter, saying, 'If you decide to go ahead with this plan, let us know and we'll look forward with great excitement to welcoming Jack, Pat and Dick.'

Christmas 1900 passed without incident. We were soon into the very cold weather of January and February and we had many snowstorms. The streets were icy. Many people fell and broke bones and the accident department at the hospital was inundated with casualties. Some of these unfortunate people were admitted to the general medical wards to recuperate and we were rushed off our feet.

I was lucky to live in the nurses' home where it was warm and comfortable but even so, I was looking forward to the spring and warmer weather.

# CHAPTER 35

One day when we had finished our duties for the day we were relaxing in the nurses' home. I had received a letter from home that morning and I had stuffed it into my pocket intending to read it in the evening. Papa hadn't taken long to reply to my letter about the boys. I opened the letter and started to read.

My heart took a leap as I read the first sentence: *'This is probably the most difficult letter I will ever have to write to you.'* It continued, *'Mama and I have the saddest news to impart.'* I couldn't think what was coming next. I thought it was obviously not about the boys. Then as I read the next sentence I gave a gasp, holding my hand over my mouth. *'Your sister Kate has died in childbirth.'* The enormity of this news engulfed me completely and my eyes filled with tears. How could this be? Kate was such a fine and fit person and she was only 3 years older than me. She had never had any medical problems. My mind raced ahead and I started to worry for poor John Cleary who would have to care for the new baby, not to mention the other two children.

By now, the others in the room realised something was wrong and Ellen asked, "Are you all right, Bridget?" I started to cry and was unable to tell her what had happened. I just sobbed and sobbed. The other girls in the room were all very concerned and didn't know what to do.

Brenda came and sat next to me and put her arm round my shoulder, saying, "Don't take on so, Bridget. What's happened?"

After a long while I was able to blurt out the news and all I said was, "My dear sister Kate has died."

It was at that moment that I realised how far away from home I was. I felt desperate. There was nothing I could do. I couldn't even go and tell Maggie or the aunts. This would have to wait until my next day off which was three weeks away. Worst of all, Kate had died without me saying goodbye to her. I was unable to read the rest of the letter and it fell into my lap.

The girls were concerned about the way I had taken the news and one of them went to fetch Sister Tutor. When she came, she said, "Come with me, Bridget. Let's go to my office and you can tell me what's upsetting you." I told her about my letter and she was very sympathetic. She listened to me and told me I must take a few days off to be with my family in New York. I hadn't even thought about that. She said it was normal to allow staff compassionate leave. Even though it had happened so far away and I was not able to attend the funeral I was still allowed time off. So, she granted me four days' leave. She suggested I should have a hot drink and go to bed early and go to the aunts' the following morning. I was so grateful to her and her kind words helped me to cope. However, before going to bed I went to the hospital's chapel as I felt in me a great need to pray. I knew Mama and Papa would be praying for Kate back at home and I drew comfort knowing I was doing the same. I knelt and prayed, remembering all the good times we had with Kate when we were children back in Ireland. I also prayed for John Cleary and the other two poor little souls who had lost their mother at such a young age and of course for the new baby. This was the first real tragedy to hit me in my life. It was different from the time when I lost my grandparents. Old people were expected to die, but not young people – this seemed so cruel. This was the most sobering thing that had ever happened to me.

I drew great strength from my prayers and I left the chapel feeling a little better. I hadn't read the rest of Papa's letter but my thoughts now reflected on what Mama had always told us in times of trouble.

She always said, "Sure, 'tis God's will. It must be for the best." When Mama said this she was just rationalising the situation. It helped her through troubled times. I couldn't see how this could be for the best. I wasn't able to rationalise as Mama did. I realised I had to be strong to convey this sad news to Maggie. I was unsure how Maggie would take the news. In her present state of mind, I expected her to be devastated. I wasn't looking forward to this.

On my way back to the nurses' home from the chapel I looked up at the sky. It was a clear night and the stars were shining brightly. I traced out the Great Bear with my finger and then found the Pole Star. I thought of Danny and I was in no doubt he was thinking of me for he had surely heard the news.

As suggested, I went to bed early – ready for the next day. That night I had difficulty sleeping. I kept drifting in and out of sleep. I couldn't erase from my mind the image of Kate's lovely face and young Johnnie and baby Margaret. I wept many times and when I woke in the morning, feeling wretched, my pillow was quite wet from my tears.

I was up early and had breakfast with the other girls. I told them Sister Tutor had given me a few days' leave. I was soon on my way to see Maggie. When I arrived at the works I hesitated before going in. They would be surprised to see me at this time of day. I composed myself and thought about how to tell them the news. I went in and made my way to the office. Sure enough, the aunts were there and thankfully they were alone. "Well, look who's arrived," said Aunt Maggie.

Aunt Catherine came towards me and could see from my face that something was wrong. Together, they both said, "Bridget, whatever has happened?"

I stuttered my reply. "I've had a letter from home. It's bad news," I said.

"Come into the office and sit down," they said in unison.

At last I managed to get the words out. "It's Kate. She's died in childbirth," I said. "Papa didn't tell me the full details but the baby has survived. That's all I can tell you. The hospital has granted me four days' leave to be with you and Maggie while we grieve."

"Oh dear, oh dear!" they said in unison and Aunt Catherine started to make a cup of tea which was her panacea for all ills.

"We must call Maggie in and tell her," said Aunt Maggie. "But let's calm ourselves before we do."

And so I had the terrible task of conveying this news to my sister. She reacted as I had the previous day and burst into tears. It was an automatic reaction to fling our arms about each other and I don't know how long we stood there like that. Neither of us could really believe the news and we were very distressed. The aunts were equally upset and it was obvious not much work would be done that day.

The worst part about it was that we all felt so helpless. At times like this you realised the need of having your family around you. We sat together in the office and for a long time we were quiet. Then the aunts decided Maggie and I should go home. I said, "Maggie, why don't you come to church with me?" I told her I had gone to the hospital chapel the previous evening. I told her that praying for Kate and the family at home had given me strength.

"That's a good idea, Bridget," said Aunt Catherine. "Now, here's the key to the apartment. After church go there and think of it as your home. You can use the sitting room and make yourselves some food when you're hungry. We'll shut up the works earlier than usual and come home to you as soon as possible."

"Yes," agreed Aunt Maggie. "It will be good for you to have some time together and talk this through. I expect you will want to show Maggie your father's letter, Bridget."

We left the aunts and made our way to church. As we entered we saw Canon O'Brien. He came over to us and bid us a cheery, "Hello." Then he said, "What's the problem, my dears? You don't look very happy."

We told him our sad news. He was a good listener. "Sure, you've done the right thing in coming here now," he said. He talked away in that soft Irish brogue, explaining to us, "God works in mysterious ways!" Then we prayed for Kate with him. We each lit a candle before leaving. We felt so much better and made our way back to the apartment.

We were soon brewing a pot of tea. Neither of us felt like eating. Our hearts were at home in Ireland. We were both devastated. As we sat sipping our tea I reached in my pocket and brought out Papa's letter. Maggie asked me to read it to her. I read the first part about Kate, followed by the good news that the baby had survived. It was a baby girl. We wondered about the rest of Kate's young family. Baby John was now five years old and Margaret just two. John Cleary would have to look after his young family as well as holding down his job in the Constabulary. We could tell from the letter that Papa and Mama were devastated.

I wrote back immediately to Mama and Papa. It was all very well for us to wallow in our own grief but they must be feeling ten times worse than we were. They would have to support John and the children for a while and then there was the funeral to arrange. So I sat down and penned our letter.

*Dearest Mama and Papa,*

*Your news has been such a shock to us. We feel so helpless here in New York as there is little we can do to support you. But we have been to church and prayed for Kate with Canon O'Brien who was very kind to us.*

*As your letter was brief we do not know what the funeral arrangements are. We hope and pray you are able to bring Kate back to Tipperary and give her the burial she deserves. We hope she can be buried at Modeshill with Grandpa Jack and Grandma Kate.*

*Our thoughts and prayers are with you all, especially John and the three children. We would be with you if we could at this terrible time.*

*With love to you all*

*Bridget and Maggie.*

I slipped some dollar notes into the envelope and sealed it. We went out to post it and felt much better when the letter was on its way to Ireland.

The next three days were terrible. Maggie and I both stayed at the apartment. Maggie managed to get a message to John to tell him what had happened. I was surprised he didn't come to see us. It was at times like this that Maggie needed his support and it was evident this was lacking. I worried about Maggie and John but this wasn't the best time to tackle Maggie about her problems. It seemed that Maggie was pleased to have a few days away from John.

Things were soon back to normal, or as normal as they could be. As time went on, even though we were still grieving, the pain of our loss grew less. The worst thing of all was being so far away and not being able to help. Four weeks later we received another letter from Papa.

He told us that Kate had been buried in the small churchyard at Modeshill with our grandparents. I was so pleased to hear this. I remembered this little churchyard on the little hill and now I had something to hold on to, knowing where Kate was. The beauty of the graveyard was its solitude and position. Being on a small hillock it provided a wonderful view of the surrounding countryside. On fine days the view towards Mount Slievenamon was magnificent. Kate would be at peace in that place.

Papa told us that John Cleary and his children were staying with them. John Cleary had compassionate leave and had put in for a transfer back to Tipperary. The young Cleary children found things strange at first and of course they missed their mother but they were settling in well. Mama was pleased to have the sound of young voices about the place again. Papa confided in us that he was worried that Mama was finding it difficult to manage, as she wasn't getting any younger. Most of her time was spent cooking and making meals for the large family.

Papa said the boys and Mary-Anne had, like the rest of the family, been broken hearted by the loss of Kate and the boys were, for the time being at least, behaving themselves. For the moment all was well at home and Papa had put off the decision about the boys coming to America.

# CHAPTER 36

I was still very busy at the hospital and it was some time before I saw Maggie again. When I did, I was very upset. It was my day off – a Saturday. She didn't work on Saturdays so I went to call on her. John opened the door and said rather gruffly, "Sure, you'd better be coming in, now. I'll give Maggie a call." So I went in and sat in the kitchen waiting while he called her from their bedroom. John seemed tense and was not his usual cheerful self.

Then Maggie appeared. Imagine my horror when I saw she had a split lip and a black eye! "Maggie, whatever has happened to you?" I asked.

"I had a fall," she said.

"Yes," said John. "She slipped outside on the sidewalk. I'd best be off now or I'll be late for work," he said. "Cheerio, Bridget." I said goodbye to him and when he had gone I turned to Maggie.

"Come over here and sit down," I said. "However did this happen?" Maggie started to cry. I could see immediately something was wrong and questioned her further. "Maggie, did you really fall? Come on now, you can tell me. I must say it's a funny place to hurt yourself. Usually, a fall results in bruises to the legs or knees and maybe a hurt back. I can't imagine how you split your lip and blackened your eye!"

Maggie threw her arms around me and wept. At last she managed to get some words out, "It's John. He's been hitting me about," she said.

I exclaimed, "John did this to you – why ever did he do that?"

She calmed down a little and said, "Bridgie, John made me lie to you about falling down. Did you see how he stayed here to make sure I gave his version of the story? The truth of the matter is he's drinking too much and coming in late at night very drunk. If I so much as ask him where he's been, he thinks I'm criticising him and he starts to hit out. Oh, Bridgie, the drink is a terrible thing when it affects a man like that! You have no idea of the rage John gets in and how hard he hits. Sure, I don't know how much longer I can take this."

"Well," I said, "something has to be done. I don't think you should stay here. Does Uncle Michael know about this?"

"No, he's usually in bed asleep when John gets home. I don't think he has any idea how bad things are."

"Well now," I said, "I think you should leave him. I know it's against our religion and all we have been taught but I can't stand by and see you being hurt. I've heard of men like this before and once they start there's no stopping them. I think you should move in with the aunts immediately. Do they know this is going on?"

"I think they suspect all is not well. But they haven't asked me. Bridget, I can't leave him. We haven't been married long. I dread to think what other people will think. Perhaps I'll give him one more chance. If I threaten to leave him maybe he'll change his ways. Believe it or not I still love him. It's a funny thing to be able to love and hate someone all at the same time."

I replied, "Well, from what I've heard, once a man like this gets the drink in him there's no stopping him. Things just go from bad to worse. I think you are deluding yourself if you think things will get better. I can't go and leave you here with a monster like that. Mama and Papa would never forgive me if anything worse happened to you. Maggie, I implore you to come with me to the aunts. Please!"

But Maggie wouldn't give in. So I did the next best thing. We talked the whole matter over and I asked her to promise me that if John as much as lifted a finger to her again she would leave him and go straight to the aunts. She promised to give this some thought. I was beside myself. How could she be so stupid? There were men like this back home in Ireland and their women always stood by them. I had never understood this but I hoped Maggie had the courage to make the break. She didn't promise me anything but she was really frightened and it wouldn't take much for her to leave. I decided not to say any more but I was worried as it would be another month before I saw her again.

Although it was a lovely day, with a clear blue sky and bright sunshine, it was marred by the sadness I felt for Maggie.

Encouraging Maggie to leave John was against our faith but I was enraged that a man could treat her so badly. I had already lost one sister and I didn't want to lose another. I was determined that either John should behave himself or Maggie should get out of that house. Mama and Papa would be very unhappy, whichever way things went, but I believed Maggie's happiness and well-being were more important than our parents' feelings.

Several weeks later I was surprised to receive a letter from Ireland. I didn't recognise the handwriting. I quickly tore open the envelope and read the contents. It was from my brother Jack. He wrote:

*Dear Bridgie,*

*I have never been much good at writing but I must write to you now. Since we lost Kate, Papa has not been himself and he has been letting many things slide. He doesn't go to school til halfway through the day and when he comes home he just eats his meal then sits in his chair moping. He does very little on the farm and I have been left to sort things out.*

*Now the School Inspector seems to have it in for Papa. Mama is worried about Papa's state of mind. I don't want to burden you with worries but I need your advice. The Education Authorities in Dublin have threatened Papa with dismissal and they urged him "to exert himself strenuously to raise the proficiency of the school".*

*Mama and I are both of the opinion that Papa should retire from school and concentrate on the farm and the home. Do you agree?*

*Bridgie, I am sorry to trouble you but Mama and I decided to ask for your advice.*

*I will close now, Bridgie. When you reply please send your letter "care of the Post Office" in Mullinahone. I will pick it up from there and Papa will not know I have written to you.*

*Mama sends you her love and I send mine.*

*From your brother Jack.*

This was another worry but I decided not to reply immediately. It was difficult for me but I knew the ultimate solution was for Papa to retire.

I threw myself into my nursing for the next few weeks. My most enjoyable spell was on the children's ward. These were such poor mites. Some of the children had problems with their ears, some had tuberculosis and others had broken legs or arms. They were all so loveable and they missed their parents. It was our job to get them fit and well and make them feel at home. I enjoyed reading to them and there was a regular spot each afternoon when I did this. The ward sister locked herself away in her office during that hour. We joked that she put her feet up and had forty winks. In reality I knew she was doing important things, like catching up on paperwork, ready to report to the doctors when they made their next rounds.

One of the most important things I learnt was never to become too friendly with any one child as they all deserved our love, care and attention. Most of them were well enough to go home quite quickly. So the acquaintances we made, although warm and intense at the time, didn't last for long. This was a blessing in disguise as it helped us not to become emotionally attached to them. Those were happy times and I was sorry when I was moved to another ward.

Our lives had gradually returned to normal after the loss of Kate. I was still worried about Maggie and John but it was a month between our meetings and I had to be patient to find out how she was faring.

The next time we met she was looking much better. "Well," I said, "you look pleased with yourself! What's been happening since I last saw you?"

"Bridgie, I do believe my prayers have been answered," she replied. "Not long after you were here, John came home one day and announced that his job was changing. There have been several developments at his hotel. They decided the only way he could do his job effectively was to live in. So, a few days later he packed his bags and moved to the hotel."

"Well, I suppose that's good for you. How often does he come home?"

"Bridgie, he's only come home twice since then. The first time he came to pick up some more of his belongings and he stayed for just two hours. He was stone-cold sober so I thought living in must be good for him. The second time he came it was his day off and he had been drinking a little during the day and he came for an evening meal. I was pleased to see him and as I was already cooking for Uncle Michael and myself, it was no trouble to give him a meal too. He stayed and ate with us. Even though he had been at the drink he was reasonably sober and he was more like his old self."

So, things seemed to have settled down for a while. I just hoped things really were improving.

I was anxious to be careful about what I said at this difficult time so I just said, "Well, Maggie, you are certainly looking better and that pleases me."

Later I told Maggie about Jack's letter. I had brought it with me to show her. We had a long discussion and we both thought the school was getting too much for Papa and we agreed that it was best if he retired and concentrated on the farm. We also thought it was a good time for the boys to come to America.

It was soon time to leave and I made my way back to the nurses' home feeling much better about Maggie. I slept well that night.

# CHAPTER 37

A week later I received a letter from Maggie. It was typically Maggie, written on a scrap of paper and very short. She said Uncle Michael had agreed to have the boys provided they find jobs as soon as possible after they arrive. She ended by saying all was well with her and she sent her love.

So, the following evening I replied to Jack. I told him I was writing to Papa and would suggest to him that now was a good time for the boys to come to America. Also, I would suggest that he retired from school as he would be losing the boys' help on the farm. I couldn't do any more I hoped all would go well. I knew that Mama would do all that she could to persuade Papa that this was a good idea.

After writing to Papa I sat back and waited for a reply.

Papa's letter came soon. He told me things were gradually returning to normal after Kate's funeral. Things had been very quiet for a few months and the boys had behaved themselves but of late they seemed to be returning to their old ways. But at last Papa had decided to pack the boys off to America. He was pleased they were to stay with Maggie and he asked me to thank John's uncle for offering them lodgings. He asked me for his full name and address so he could write to him. He said the boys had too much time on their hands and he thought the only way they could become more responsible and sensible was if they had to earn their own livings. Papa made no mention of school problems so I assumed things had quietened down on that front. I wondered if he was going to retire.

My first year's training was now nearly at an end and I was due to take my first examinations. We were all very nervous. If we didn't pass we would have to leave the hospital and all our hard work would have been a waste of time. The day of the exam arrived and we all stood outside the examination room waiting to be let in. Many of us had never sat an exam before and this added to our anxiety. Five minutes before the exam was due to start Sister Tutor opened the door and asked us to come in. "Sit wherever you like," she said. "In a few minutes I'll give you your papers. You must answer two questions from each section. You have two hours to complete your paper."

I studied the exam paper. I was glad to see I had revised the topics covered by most of the questions. I felt quite relieved. I looked round the room and saw that most of my contemporaries appeared to be pleased with the paper.

The next two hours passed quickly and Sister Tutor collected in our papers. She told us to come and do our practical exam the next day. The exam results would be posted on the notice board in ten days' time.

We went back to the nurses' home and relaxed together, discussing the answers we had given. Most of us were quietly confident. The rest of the evening was spent in practicing bandaging, arm slings and taking temperatures and pulses amongst many other things, in readiness for the practical exam. I slept well that night knowing I had done well in my written exam and I was looking forward to the next day.

In ten days our exam results were posted on the notice board and we all rushed to see what our fate was. I was pleased to see my name in fifth place for the theory paper. I had achieved a mark of 86 out of a possible 100 marks. Then to my amazement I saw I had come top in the practical exam. We had all passed and we were very relieved.

That evening I wrote home to Mama and Papa to tell them my good news. I knew they would be delighted.

I had a lot to tell Maggie the next time I saw her. When I arrived she told me that Uncle Michael had received a letter of thanks from Papa so she knew the boys would be coming. Then I told her all about the exams and my results. She was pleased to hear my news.

I asked Maggie how things were between her and John. She seemed much happier and more relaxed. She told me that she saw little of John. When he wasn't working he was out with his mates drinking and after that he always went home to his quarters at the hotel to sleep. "You know, Bridget, I sometimes wonder whether I really am married. I am leading a very solitary life. I'm glad I have a job to go to and the aunts have just made me a supervisor. I quite like the responsibility and my pay has increased. If it weren't for the aunts and Uncle Michael I don't know how I would cope. But I mustn't complain, sure, when you think of it, it's a lot better than being at home standing at the washtub all day and cooking and cleaning."

"Yes," I replied, "I sometimes wonder what would have happened to us if we had stayed at home. I think we both really miss the family and our friends. Another thing I miss is the fresh air and green fields. It's so dirty here in the city."

"Wouldn't it be wonderful if we could just go back for a holiday to see everybody?" said Maggie.

"Yes, we're growing up and Mama and Papa are getting older. I've made up my mind, Maggie, that as soon as I am qualified and earning a proper wage I will save enough to go home for a holiday. Who knows, I may even stay – that's if I can get a job over there as a nurse. It shouldn't be too difficult."

"You're not thinking of leaving me here alone, are you Bridget?"

"No, of course not, you must save your money and come with me. Anyway I'm just dreaming. I don't think we'll ever see our homeland again. That's why I'm so keen for the boys to come over here. I am longing to see them again."

Our conversation soon drifted onto our plans for the rest of the day. The weather was particularly good so we decided to go to the park for some fresh air and a walk. I had plenty of exercise in my job but the exercise was good for Maggie as she was sitting down all day. After our walk we went to see the aunts.

We showed Papa's letter to the aunts and they were interested to hear that the boys would be coming and asked us to keep them informed of any news of this.

It was not long before another letter arrived from home. Papa was delighted with my news of my exam results and said, *'To be sure, at last we have someone in the family who is making a name for herself!'* I laughed when I read this. But I knew I had to take my final exams and qualify before I could celebrate properly. Yes, that would be my moment of satisfaction. Papa went on to say that they had all had a party to celebrate my success. I could imagine it now.

The neighbours and relations would have all been singing and dancing until late at night. As I read the letter, I realised again that I really did miss my home. But I could do nothing about that.

In his letter Papa told me he had stressed on the boys that when they arrived in New York they mustn't be idle. They had to look for work as neither Maggie nor I had the money to support them. They had to take responsibility for themselves and it would be a strange new world for them. He hoped they would face up to the challenge.

# CHAPTER 38

The next few years proved to be very hectic. I was busy at the hospital, learning new things and taking exams and we had a continual flow of correspondence from home. My brothers were determined to make the move to America as they realised there was no future for them in Ireland.

I was surprised that Patrick, my youngest brother, arrived before his brothers in 1902. He had always been a wilful lad and was determined to make his way in the world. Maggie and I arranged to have a time off so we could meet him from the ship and then show him around and help him to acclimatise to his new surroundings.

Despite his young age – he was only just 17 – Pat quickly found a job as a barman and was living with people he worked with and didn't take up the offer of staying with Maggie. He seemed to settle well and we rarely saw him. He had left home without Papa's permission. Papa wanted Jack, the oldest, to go before him. But Pat was keen to get on in the world and said, "Leaving sleepy old Ireland was the best thing I've ever done." I worried for him and hoped he would not get into the wrong company. He thought he was now a man and could do what he liked but underneath I could see he was quite vulnerable. Living at the hospital it was impossible for me to keep an eye on him.

Then in 1903 our brother John (or Jack as we called him) arrived. Maggie and I went to meet him and we spent time introducing him to New York. It was a fine, warm day and Maggie and I stood on the quayside looking out towards Ellis Island. The old Barge Office which I had travelled through was no longer in use and the Ellis Island building, which had been burnt down, had been rebuilt. Now all immigrants came through this building. Jack was coming on the *Saxonia* and it was expected on time. After what seemed like hours, the ship approached and we waited a long time while he went through the immigration process. We waited anxiously. Suddenly we saw him. "There he is," said Maggie excitedly. We waved our arms, calling out his name. When he saw us he broke into a run. We threw our arms around each other and I was nearly in tears to see him looking so fit and well. He had certainly grown up since I last saw him.

It was a very emotional time for the three of us. So much so, that at first we could think of nothing to talk about. All the questions we had wanted to ask about home had been forgotten. Before long we were on our way back to Maggie's house. Jack was looking forward to seeing his new home.

It was not long before Jack was spilling out all their news from home. He told us about Papa and the problems he had at school. He told us that at last Papa had now retired and was spending all his time on the farm. Jack said, "We haven't really been very helpful. But you see, we had no jobs to go to and we were very bored. Whenever we did manage to find some work we wanted to spend our hard-earned money. We went to the pub with our friends and you can imagine what Mama and Papa thought about that. They told us we were irresponsible and needed to settle down. But you see, Bridgie, we had could see no future in Ireland and no stability and life seemed hopeless. We couldn't really see what we had to be responsible about."

Sometimes they arrived home from the pub the worse for wear and Mama was always there waiting up for them. She chided them and threatened that if they continued to drink she would send them to Mount Mellory. We all knew about this place. It was a monastery in the hills where drunks were sent to dry out. "Of course," said Jack, "we were never truly drunk, just a little merry!" We all laughed at this picture which he painted so vividly and which brought back so many memories of dear Mama.

Our talk wasn't all about the future and work. Jack hadn't lost his sense of fun and there were many laughs and jokes. He told us about his experiences on the ship and had us roaring with laughter. Maggie and I hadn't laughed so much for a long time.

The following day Maggie and I took Jack out and showed him the sights of the city. Jack was amazed at the size of the buildings and at the number of people. He hadn't realised how busy this city was. He had learnt a lot from the letters we had written home, but nothing really prepared him for the enormity of the place. We asked him if he had any idea what sort of work he intended to do and we bought newspapers with job advertisements and we spent the evening poring over them.

By the end of the week Jack had found himself work in a hotel kitchen and we were all relieved things had worked out so well. This was a start and he could move on to a better job later. I wrote home to Mama and Papa with the good news.

During that first week, Jack was keen to meet John and was surprised that Maggie saw so little of her husband. Maggie told me that John came home towards the end of Jack's first week and fortunately he wasn't the worse for drink. They all got on well and I hoped things were going to continue in that way. I was glad Maggie had Jack living with her – it might stop John treating her so badly. However, I hoped that John wouldn't lead Jack astray. I decided not to get involved. Jack was old enough now to make his own decisions. His mind had certainly been focussed since he left home and he seemed keen to succeed.

I wrote home regularly that year and I was pleased to hear from Papa that since Pat and Jack had left, life had been much easier with not so many mouths to feed. Papa was spending all his time on the farm. He had reduced the number of cattle and sheep and they were now relying on the pigs and chickens for meat and eggs. A new creamery had been opened locally so he was sending all his milk there so there was no more butter making. Mama was coping well in the house, even with the Cleary children to look after. John Cleary was contributing to the family budget and Papa said this was a great help. But he thought John would soon move on to make a new home for his small family. I was intrigued to know if there was another woman in his life but Papa didn't mention that.

The next year passed quickly. Maggie was still having a bad time with John. His drinking was worse and it was not long before he lost his job and he was moping about at home for most of the day. It was good that Maggie had a job to go to. When she arrived home in the evening John was usually asleep in a chair and the place was in a mess. There was nothing I could do. I told her if it was me I wouldn't put up with it, but Maggie was stubborn and very loyal.

# CHAPTER 39

It was not long before I was taking my final exams. I finally qualified as a nurse in 1903. I was so happy and wrote home immediately to tell Mama and Papa. My proudest day was when I received my nurses' medal at the prize giving. I wished Mama and Papa could have been there. I now had to do my final year at St. Joseph's and after that I would be free to find work anywhere in the world. I couldn't believe my good fortune.

Shortly after I qualified I took a short holiday and spent it with Maggie. It didn't take me long to realise how unhappy she was. John continued to hit her about when he was drunk. We talked for many long hours about her problem. Finally I agreed with her that she would be better off without John and should leave him. He was no good for her and she deserved better. We talked about her financial situation and she told me she had saved up some money of her own. After much heartache she decided to leave the aunts' employ and look for a live-in post in a hotel. She was dreading telling the aunts. She just wanted to get away to a place where John couldn't find her.

Several weeks later Maggie wrote to tell me that she had been appointed housekeeper/linen manageress at one of the big hotels. The job was a good one and she was able to make use of her sewing skills. It was a "live in" job and the money was good too. She had all her meals provided and didn't have to pay rent. I was glad things appeared to be working out well for her.

My own life was working out well too. As always, I enjoyed my work and I had built up a group of close friends. I went to church regularly and joined the church Youth Group that met socially on Friday and Saturday evenings. We did all sorts of things. We played cards, had a singing group, a sewing circle for the girls and there were regular dances on Saturday evenings. St. Joseph's hospital was attached to St. Joseph's church and it was natural that most of the nurses who were originally from Ireland worshipped there. The boys who came to the club were from similar backgrounds and it wasn't unusual for us to take part in Irish folk dancing. Several of the boys played instruments – two on the violin, a drummer, a bagpipe player and another lad who played the Celtic pipes. These parties reminded me of the good times we used to have at home. It also reminded me of the fun we had on the boat. Put a few Irish people together and it didn't take long before merriment ensued.

My final year at St. Joseph's passed quickly and I was now free to look elsewhere for work. At first I was undecided about which way my career should go. I didn't want to leave New York. I wanted to keep in touch with Maggie and the boys. They were all doing well apart from Pat who seemed to drift from one job to another.

One day I received a letter from Papa. The folks at home weren't getting any younger and I sensed that things were difficult for them. Most of us sent home money regularly and I was glad we were able to help.

*My dear Bridget,*

*I need not say how happy I was on receiving your very kind letter this morning. Oh! How delighted we are to hear that you are all well and doing well. Patrick, I have to say, did not write to me for the past year and a half. He said he wrote but he did not – I do mind telling lies – he was always stubborn and self-willed. Strange to say he would not converse with his father who bred him decently and well. I never denied him anything that I could afford. In one way when he was here he was very good to lend me money when I was in need. Is he a practising Catholic? Find out this and impress on his mind the value of adhering to his religious duties. I am praying for him and for all of you.*

*I know you would be rejoiced when you hear that Tom was in Callan. Yes, he won the victory; he is a star in literature. Well, if you were to see him, a perfect gentleman in manners and appearance.*

*Your mother is working hard as usual. She now has Dick, Tom and Mary Anne to care for. We are pretty fair in health. I am suffering from stiffness in the legs but no pains of any harm. The little one, baby Cleary, is going to school. John Cleary and family are well. How is poor Maggie?*

*All friends are well. I hope all friends over there are well too. Allow me to tell you to be sparing in sending money to Mary Anne. She does not know how money is obtained in America. She is fond of finery, perhaps to spend it in new gowns. She has no reason to complain. I gave her an outfit when she started. She has to live cheap while serving her time. Please write often for I have a great wish to be talking to you frequently.*

*Your affectionate father, Richard Frisby.*

After reading this letter I was more than ever convinced that in a few years I must take a trip home to see Mama and Papa. I had already started saving towards the fare home but I was only halfway there. Never seeing them again was out of the question. Papa's handwriting had deteriorated lately. In the letter he seemed to wander from one member of the family to another. He had never rambled like this in previous letters.

I noticed his worries about Pat. The letter confirmed what I thought about him as he hadn't settled as well as Jack. He was five years younger than Jack so there was a difference in their maturity. It wasn't my place to lecture Pat as Papa suggested. There was little I could do to help. He would have to stand on his own feet in this new life.

I was glad that Papa had one son to be proud of. At least Tom was doing well and Mama and Papa were enjoying his successes.

I wondered about Mary-Anne. She had recently left school and started a job. I didn't think I was sending her too much money – I only sent it on her birthday and at Christmas. Papa was living in the past. He had never had much money himself and didn't really understand the need for it. It was different for the younger generation. I had a feeling that Mary-Anne might soon be in America with us.

I was now more than ever convinced that my next move should be to a well-paid job to enable me to visit my parents. I kept my eyes open for suitable nursing positions. One day, my friend Ellen pointed out an advertisement to me. It was for a position in a nursing home in Manhattan. The salary quoted appeared to be very good and I decided to apply for it.

I was delighted when I received a reply to my letter. I was invited for interview and duly arrived at Dr. Bull's Nursing Home in Manhattan, taking with me my nursing certificate and wearing my nurse's badge. On the day of my interview I travelled by train to Manhattan and found my way to the imposing building. It wasn't far from my aunts' apartment and I made a mental note that if necessary I might be able to live with them.

I was shown into a waiting room and was surprised at the opulence. This was so different from St. Joseph's. For a start, there was carpet on the floor. It all looked very plush and was quite new. There was a table with a vase of fresh flowers in the middle of the room and a pile of magazines. I picked up a brochure describing the nursing home. I glanced through it and was able to read it before my interview. I discovered that this establishment was far removed from the hospital in which I trained.

It appeared that all the patients had individual rooms. There were no large wards. Visiting was allowed at all times during the day. In fact, visitors were made welcome and encouraged to come as often as they liked. The nursing home specialised in recuperation, rest, and convalescence for its patients. I realised that there would be no really sick people. I wondered if I could cope with this sort of nursing. But I put these thoughts to the back of my mind when my name was called. My interview was with the Director of the nursing home, the Matron and two other gentlemen who I supposed to be either doctors or maybe owners of the home.

I was ushered into a room and sat in front of the panel and waited for their questions. At first they asked me about my training and then they wanted to know how long I had been in New York.

My answers seemed to satisfy them and then the Director said, "Do you know what we do here, Nurse Frisby?"

I was so glad I had read their brochure. "Yes," I replied. "I believe patients come here for recuperation after surgery or other illnesses. You are a convalescent home with fully qualified medical staff and nurses."

The Director looked at me across the desk and said, "Very good. But, tell me, why do you want to leave St. Joseph's and come here?"

I decided that honesty was the best policy and replied that I had three reasons. The first was that I wanted a change after St. Joseph's and I wanted to gain experience in a different environment. Also, I wanted better wages than the hospital paid and the third reason was that I would be nearer my family, some of whom were now living in Manhattan.

They seemed pleased with my reply and then the other two gentlemen asked me one or two medical questions that I was able to answer easily. Then, the Matron asked the nursing questions. Here, again, I seemed to give good answers. I was asked when I could start with them if I was successful in my interview. I told them I had to give one month's notice at St. Joseph's. They gave me a piece of paper with details of the pay structure and said I would have to live out as accommodation for nurses was very limited. The Director said they had several more interviews to do but I would receive a letter by the end of the week if I was successful.

When I left the home I made my way straight to the aunts' apartment. I arrived as they were coming in from work. They were pleased to see me and I told them all about the interview. They asked me if I thought I would like this change of job. I told them I was surprised at the affluence of the home and I thought it might take some getting used to. But, yes, I thought it would be good for me to see another side of life!

When I was back at the nurses' home Ellen was keen to know how the interview had gone. I told her all about it. I impressed on her that she was the only one who knew I was saving up to take a trip home to Ireland. I told her, "The extra money will come in very handy if I get the job. I intend to save as much as I can so I can make that trip. It will be strange working for a different class of people and I'll miss the wards and the friends I've made, but it's a means to an end." Ellen wished me good luck.

Ten days later the letter I had been waiting for arrived. To my delight I was offered a place on the staff of Dr. Bull's Nursing Home at a salary which was more than I expected. It was nearly twice as much as I was earning now. I couldn't wait to accept this offer.

I handed in my notice at St. Joseph's and was sorry to be leaving all my friends behind. But when the day of my departure came I was given a wonderful send off and received many presents from my friends. I was sad to leave them but many of us exchanged addresses and I hoped to meet up with some of them again in future.

It was now 1905 and it was seven years since I had arrived in America. My brother Richard had finally decided that he too would come to America. Maggie and I were at the dockside to meet him when he arrived. Richard was now nearly 20 years old. He told us he had wanted to come to America for a long time but Papa had persuaded him to stay at home to help on the farm. He was very relieved at last to be away and was looking forward to the future. I asked him what he wanted to do when he had settled and he told me he had heard that a very good job was working for the New York Fire Brigade. I worried about this as I knew vacancies were few and far apart and I was pleased when a few days later he announced that he had found a job as a clerk in an office and he was happy to do this until he joined the fire brigade. He settled in well and he and Jack were now boarding at a house in Columbus Avenue with cousins we had never met. I was glad my two brothers were living together.

Later, I helped Dick write to the New York Fire Brigade to enquire about the possibility of working for them. He had a short reply telling him it was necessary for him to become a naturalised American citizen before he could apply for that job. You had to live in America for 5 years before you could apply for naturalisation so he would wait before applying again. He continued to work at his office while his brother Jack had changed his job and was working in the market with a butcher. They had both settled well in New York.

# CHAPTER 40

On a fine sunny day I reported for my first day's work at Dr. Bull's Nursing Home. I was now living with my aunts which was very convenient as it was only a short walk from the home.

On arrival I was given a tour and then issued with my uniform. I changed into this at the first opportunity. I was then shown to the Matron's office. She issued me with a timetable showing my duty times for the coming month and introduced me to my supervisor senior nurse Brennan. Together we were responsible for rooms 1 to 6. I noticed that Nurse Brennan had an Irish accent. We hit it off immediately and I looked forward to working with her. We had the same sense of humour and that first day at work was fun.

I worked hard at Dr. Bull's but found it difficult to come to terms with the affluent patients we looked after. Their standard of living was so much higher than anything I had ever experienced. I couldn't help comparing them with my poor old Mama and Papa. Not for them the luxury of fully carpeted floors and flowers in vases. I remembered the stone floor in our kitchen at home and the rush matting that cut into my knees when we knelt to say our rosaries. I couldn't let these feelings get in the way of my work so I put them to the back of my mind. I was now building up a nice little nest egg towards my journey home and this was my objective.

After six months at the nursing home I was promoted to Senior Nurse in charge of my own staff. This involved a pay increase so I was delighted.

While I was working at Dr. Bull's I nursed some very interesting patients and it was surprising how much they were prepared to divulge about their lives. We heard some fascinating stories.

One day I was called to the Director's office and I wondered what I had done wrong. I knocked on the door and heard his voice boom out, "Enter." I went in and he indicated to me to sit on the chair in front of his desk. This was unusual. I wondered what was coming next. Normally we stood when being given our orders! I sat down, as indicated, and he started by saying, "Nurse Frisby, we have been very pleased with your work since you joined us." I breathed a sigh of relief. He continued, "We have a very special patient coming in tomorrow and I want you to look after her. She is an American lady from a very well-to-do family – the Vanderbilt family. This family is rich and famous. They are millionaires with vast money invested in shipping, engineering and railroads. This lady, who is a daughter of Cornelius Vanderbilt, went to England a few years ago and married the Duke of Marlborough so she is the Duchess of Marlborough by virtue of her marriage. She won't be bringing her own staff with her but I want you to pay full attention to all her needs. Nothing must be too much trouble. I don't think I have to tell you that if we treat her well she may recommend us to her wealthy friends. It's important she is pleased with all aspects of her stay with us. I want you to take full charge of her. If you have any problems with any of her requests please come and see me and I'll help you. Are you happy about this?"

I thought for a moment and replied, "Yes, of course and thank you for choosing me. May I ask what the Duchess' condition is?"

He told me she had suffered a nervous breakdown and her doctors had suggested a few weeks with us to help her recuperate. He laughed and said, "I don't know what caused the breakdown, but no doubt in due course she will confide in you, as they all seem to!"

The Duchess of Marlborough arrived at the home the next day. We had prepared her room and it was spotless. Matron brought her to me and introduced her. I curtsied and we took her to her room.

Matron said, "Well I'll leave you with Nurse Frisby now," and she left the room.

Consuela Vanderbilt, the Duchess, was a very attractive young woman about the same age as me. I helped her unpack her small travelling case and put her clothes away for her. She sighed and said, "I am so tired. I think I'll go to bed now and rest. You may leave now."

I was surprised at her curt attitude but I indicated the bell push and told her to ring if she needed anything. So I left her.

Outside the other nurses were keen to know all about her but I told them I knew nothing as she had been very abrupt with me. It didn't take long for the Duchess to soften. After the first week I nearly knew her life history. She told me she had a very unhappy marriage. She had left her husband, the Duke of Marlborough, at home in England with their two sons. I asked her if she minded leaving the children and she replied, "I love them dearly but even my love for them couldn't keep me there. We lived in a beautiful palace – Blenheim Palace in Oxfordshire – I had all a girl could wish for except, that is, the love of the man I married. He only married me for my family's money and it has made me very sad. I was desperate to leave him but he wouldn't let me take my sons with me." I then knew what had made her so ill. She was sick with worry and obviously suffering from nervous exhaustion. I felt sorry for her.

She told me she wanted to divorce her husband and return to America but a divorce wasn't possible as she was Catholic. She confided in me that in the future she might apply for an annulment of her marriage. This shocked me.

I continued to nurse the Duchess while she was with us. Even though she had softened with me she didn't do so with any of my staff. She was very strict with them and told me to instruct them to address her as "Your Grace" at all times. I had to make sure the day and night staff knew of her wishes. Every morning when I arrived at work and went to see how she was she said, "Thank goodness you're back. I can't get used to those awful night nurses!" After a few weeks

I was able to laugh when she said this and before long she was laughing with me. She seemed to be well on the road to recovery and I though the day of her discharge was not far off.

The Duchess told me many tales of the grandeur of the palace in which she had lived in England. I could hardly believe the size of it. So many rooms and all lavishly furnished and decorated. The entrance hall on its own probably took up more space than our whole house back home in Ireland. There was a sweeping staircase with portraits of all the ancestors of the Duke of Marlborough on the walls. She told me, "I hated looking at those pictures every time I went upstairs. They were a lot of bellicose old men and I wished for prettier pictures." She said she often used the servants' staircase rather than see these old portraits. But she was able to decorate her boudoir as she liked. Here, she had silk curtains at the windows and pretty pastel colours that suited her better.

Most of all, the Duchess disliked the shooting parties she was forced to attend. She told me she had once been a guest at Warwick Castle with other important guests, such as the Prince of Wales, the son of Queen Victoria, and several prominent politicians.

All the tales I heard about the grandeur of these moneyed classes astounded me. I found it difficult to reconcile this with the poverty I had witnessed in my short life. I had to keep reminding myself of the reason I was working here.

As the Duchess' health improved and the colour returned to her cheeks she told me more about her life. She had married when she was only 17 years old. She told me how different aristocratic life in England was from life in America. She was a democrat by nature and found it difficult to accept that the aristocracy in England were superior to others, as they believed they were. She said they truly believed their birthright put them above all others. Women had little freedom and were expected to be ornamental, and were not credited with any brains. It was a man's world. With a life so strange to her it was not difficult to see what had made her so ill.

She told me of her first visit to Europe with her parents, before her marriage. They had visited many places – Egypt, Turkey, Italy and France. She adored France. It was after that trip that her marriage was arranged. Her parents were keen for a close connection with the English aristocracy and were able to buy this by arranging to pay a large dowry. She was too young to realise the mistake she was making and she didn't want to go against her parents' wishes. She shared with me her belief that the English aristocracy were a sham and had little money. They knew that rich Americans were queuing up to buy a title and the price for this was high. They needed this money so they could continue their rich life style and maintain their mansions and palaces. She said her husband's main aim was to promulgate his dynasty. The aristocracy had great dynastic ambitions. She said, "As soon as I had provided an heir my usefulness ended. I felt unloved."

I was so sorry for her.

One day the Duchess talked to me about religion. She was a Catholic like me and she remembered the day she was confirmed. She said, "I knelt in the church and promised to worship God for the rest of my life. I found this very difficult because my parents' marriage was falling apart at the time and I believed my father intended seeking an annulment and hoped to marry again. And now, I have reached the same crossroads. You are so lucky not to have had these problems!"

After several weeks the Duchess was well enough to leave the home. I was happy she was better but I would miss her. When she left she handed me an envelope and said, "This is for you. You have helped me bounce back and I am so grateful. Put it away in your pocket before Matron sees it."

I helped her with her packing and Matron and I escorted her to the door where her father was waiting to take her to his home. After she left Matron tuned to me and said, "Well done, Nurse Frisby. You certainly made a hit there."

When I returned home that evening I remembered the envelope I had stuffed in my pocket. I tore it open and imagine my delight when I took out a $5 note. A short note, which read "Thank you – Consuela Vanderbilt", accompanied it. I noticed she had reverted to her maiden name. I smiled to myself as I tucked the note away in my purse ready to bank it with my savings.

I had been so busy at work that I had missed several notable events in New York City. At the end of 1903 a new suspension bridge called the Williamsburg Bridge had opened. It spanned the East River and connected Manhattan to Brooklyn. It was said to be the world's longest suspension bridge, longer even than the Brooklyn Bridge.

Another exciting innovation was the New York subway which opened in 1904. Maggie told me that she and some friends had taken a ride through the underground tunnels a few days after it opened. The subway filled a desperate need as it eased the congestion caused by horses, wagons and carriages in the streets above. The subway had taken 4 years to build but it was a wonderful solution to the city's traffic problem.

Life returned to normal for several weeks at the nursing home after the Duchess left us but she was a talking point amongst the nurses for some time. It was not long before another notable person was admitted to the home for nursing care. Fortunately, she wasn't on my section. I only knew about her when I heard the nurses in their break time gossiping about their charge. She was a young chorus girl called Evelyn Nesbit. Apparently there were many stories circulating in the home and it was difficult to know which was true.

The gossip surrounding Evelyn soon grew out of all proportion and Matron told me one day she had decided to move Evelyn into my care. She said, "I know you'll be the soul of discretion and won't divulge any of Evelyn's secrets to the other nurses." I wondered whatever these "secrets" could be. I was soon to find out. But I was surprised by what I did hear from Evelyn. I was amazed that this young girl had seen so much of life in such a short time. She was just nineteen years old.

From the day Evelyn came into my care her youth and beauty struck me. She looked so young, much less than her nineteen years. She reminded me of my younger sister Mary-Anne at home. She had a beautiful face and long auburn hair.

After a week Evelyn was telling me her life story. She told me her father, a lawyer, had died when she was only eight and the family was thrown into dreadful poverty. Their debts mounted, and they had to sell nearly all their furniture. Evelyn's mother had tried to run a boarding house but that didn't work out. She then resorted to taking in washing and sewing to make ends meet.

Evelyn with her mother and her young brother Howard, moved from place to place in desperation and despair. Howard and Evelyn stopped going to school at an early age. Evelyn recalled, "I often found my mother weeping as the bills piled up."

I asked Evelyn about her work. She told me she had always wanted to become an actress and this was difficult in Pennsylvania. She said, "One day a friend introduced me to an artist and I was soon posing as a model for him. I was only fifteen at the time. He was pleased with the results of his work and he recommended me to other artist friends of his. Not long after that my picture started to appear in magazines and books."

I was a little surprised when she told me that some of the poses were quite revealing. I asked her, "Did your mother allow this?"

Her reply was, "She didn't really approve and told me it was a bad profession but she couldn't really object. After all, I was by then the main source of my family's income."

Evelyn could certainly chatter and I remember thinking how self-centred she was. Whenever I grew tired of hearing about her life I told her I thought she should get some rest. I hoped that when she woke she would be more rested and less chatty. But it seemed to be that she needed to recount her life story. When she did wake up from her sleep she had more energy. She continued with her story and told me she had insisted that her family move with her to New York where she knew she could earn ten times more money for modelling.

Once she arrived in New York, Evelyn immediately found work as an artist's model. She soon discovered real money could be earned by posing for fashion artists.

To Evelyn, New York was a glittering city. It wasn't long before she was famous as a fashion model. She appeared in newspapers and magazines and was one of the most beautiful models in America. She came to the notice the well-known artist Charles Dana Gibson, probably the most popular artist in the States. As one of his models she became one of the famous "Gibson Girls".

Within days of posing for Gibson, Evelyn landed a role in the chorus of the big hit musical Floradora. For Evelyn, her time in Florodora's chorus was a dream come true. Talent was secondary to beauty in the theatre. Rich and powerful men wanted to be seen with the chorus girls. The newspapers followed the girls' social lives, and many of them married far above their station. For the first time in many years, Evelyn's future looked bright. Evelyn said, "My mother's objections to my lifestyle became few and far between as my fame grew and the money poured in."

Evelyn seemed to live in a fantasy world. When she wasn't sleeping or talking she was reading cheap love stories in magazines.

Evelyn's stage name was Evelyn Nesbit. But only a few months before coming to us she had married one of her persistent suitors, the Pittsburgh millionaire Harry Thaw. On her medical notes her name was Evelyn Thaw.

Harry Thaw, her husband, visited her often and showered her with flowers and presents. He even arranged for her food to be cooked by the head chef at a nearby five-star hotel. This was most unusual but it was allowed because of the wealth of the Thaws.

I had my own opinion of Evelyn. I thought she was empty-headed and spoilt. But she must have had a lot of common sense or she wouldn't have managed to get where she was. Her poverty had driven her but I did wonder about her morals.

Evelyn had been with us for four weeks and I noticed that apart from Harry she had another, less frequent, but nonetheless fairly constant visitor. He was old enough to be her father and I thought maybe he was an elderly relative. One day I went into Evelyn's room not knowing Mr. White was visiting and I apologised for interrupting and as I left I heard Evelyn call him "Stanny". I thought this odd for a young girl to be calling a 50-year-old man by a pet name. Later Evelyn told me her visitor was none other than the famous architect Stanford White. She told me he was a millionaire and had designed many of the new buildings in the city. She said he had designed the Grand Central Station and Madison Square Gardens. He had placed the gilded statue of Diana in plain view of the city on the top of Madison Square Gardens. Although married to Harry, Evelyn seemed to be infatuated by this older man.

Evelyn told me she first met Stanford White before she was married when she was sitting for Mr. Gibson. When she was in the cast of Florodora he went to see the show every night. I could not believe a man of this age, who was apparently happily married, could be so besotted with a young girl. I was surprised by what I heard.

Mr. White regularly sent Evelyn flowers while she was in the nursing home. Before she married Harry, Mr. White had kept himself in favour with her mother by taking her out to lunches. He had paid the rent on better living quarters for the family and he had paid for Evelyn's brother's education. Evelyn told me that for a long time "Stanny" had been the only man in her life. She raved about him. He was the most charming, charismatic, smartest man she'd ever known. She was infatuated by him. But she realised he wasn't going to leave his wife for her so she chose to marry Harry Thaw, another millionaire who was also paying her much attention.

Harry Thaw was more Evelyn's age but seemed a little eccentric. Mr. White always avoided Mr. Thaw and managed to visit Evelyn when he wasn't around. Evelyn told me that Harry was jealous of Mr. White. He hated him because of his conquests with the showgirls. Harry tried to compete with Mr. White.

I found it difficult to follow the rest of the story. Evelyn was still rambling. She and Harry had travelled to Europe together. Something had happened in Europe and that had a lasting effect on Evelyn and I believed this had some bearing on her present condition. She was vague about what had occurred in Europe.

When they returned from Europe she suffered an attack of appendicitis. This, together with a nervous condition led to her stay in hospital. The first week was in one of New York's main hospitals where she had her appendix removed and she came to us for the remainder of her hospitalisation and recuperation.

Evelyn eventually left us and life returned to normal. I wondered who my next patient would be. Life was certainly fascinating at Dr. Bull's.

# CHAPTER 41

As my savings grew I decided to tell Maggie about my plans to have a holiday at home in Ireland. It was difficult to broach this subject and I hesitated before speaking. I said, "Do you ever wish you could go home, Maggie?"

Her reply astounded me. "Yes," she said, "I yearn for the simple life back home in Ireland. T'would be a dream come true to go home and stay home."

Her reply made it even more difficult for me to tell her my plans. I hesitated, before saying, "I've been saving my wages so I can make a trip home. I want so much to see Mama and Papa again. They are not getting any younger and I sense that things aren't easy for them."

Maggie looked very surprised. "You're so lucky, Bridget. My wages are so low I could never save up the fare."

I paused before I said, "It'll be strange going on my own but I can't save your fare as well as mine. I'll hate leaving you behind. I really want to go this year before Mama and Papa get any older." Maggie agreed that I should go. I was very relieved at her reaction.

The next patient to come into my care was an older gentleman called George Owen, who had been ill for a long time. I nursed him for some time and his health gradually improved. He was racked with arthritis and was often in great pain.

One day the doctors suggested to Mr. Owen that he should take a holiday in the sunshine. He liked this idea and pondered over it for a while. One of Mr. Owen's frequent visitors was his grandson

Nicholas. He was fond of his grandfather and spent some time discussing with him possible holiday ideas. They talked of Florida and the southern states. Nicholas asked me if I thought a sea cruise would be good for his grandfather. I said that provided the sun shone and it wasn't too windy it was a good idea. Certainly the fresh air would do him good. But I emphasised that he should consult the doctors before making any decision.

A week later Nicholas came to me, very excited, "What do you think, Nurse Frisby? I have just seen the doctors with details of a proposed trip. There is a boat leaving for Europe in three weeks and there are vacancies on it. The destination is Naples in Italy. They think it is an ideal destination and grandfather has asked me to accompany him."

Once again, I would be sorry to lose my patient. That was the part of nursing I disliked. As soon as you got to know a patient he was well enough to move on. Mr. Owen was a kindly old man and suffered his pain with great fortitude. I was going to miss him.

I was leaving work one evening when the Director called me into his office. He said, "I'll come straight to the point, Nurse Frisby. Mr. Owen is planning a trip to Europe. The doctors recommended he should have a nurse with him on his journey." My heart leapt. He smiled at me and continued, "Mr. Owen has asked us if we could let you accompany him."

I couldn't believe what I was hearing. He continued, "Of course your fare will be paid and you will have all your food provided. There will also be a small wage." He went on to give me details and ended by saying, "Well, what do you think?"

I replied, "I never in my wildest dreams expected this to happen. I'm so pleased I have been chosen but I need time to take this in. May I think about it and let you know later?"

He agreed but impressed on me that time was of the essence. Mr. Owen wanted a fairly quick response. The boat was sailing in just 17 days' time and my passage had to be booked. I agreed to give him my decision the next day. He said he was sorry to be losing me but emphasised that my job would be waiting for me on my return.

It didn't take me long to make up my mind. In fact my thoughts raced ahead. Europe – I might be able to have a few days in Ireland. On my way home from work I was already planning what to take with me on the journey.

I told my aunts my plans that evening and made a hurried visit to Maggie to tell her the news. I asked her to tell the boys for me in case I didn't have the opportunity to see them before I left. Poor Maggie, I could see that she was envious of me but she bore the news well.

The following day I was at work early and was waiting for the Director when he arrived. He was pleased with my decision and told me I could give the news to Mr. Owen myself. Before I left his office he said, "As I told you yesterday, there will be a place for you here when you return. We will miss you when you go."

When I went into Mr. Owen's room a few minutes later he was sitting up in a chair by the bed and looked at me apprehensively. I smiled at him as I said, "Good morning." Then I thanked him for the offer and told him I was very pleased to accept. He was delighted with my decision and for the rest of the day was in very high spirits.

The next few days passed by quickly. The other nurses at Dr. Bull's were excited by my news and I knew they all wished they had been chosen.

Nicholas came to see me when the arrangements had been finalised and told me he had ordered my ticket. He gave me the date and time of departure and suggested I leave work a couple of days before then. Our destination was Naples in Italy and we were sailing from New York.

When I left the nursing home the nurses gave me a wonderful send off. They had collected together and had bought me a present. I would treasure this always. It was a small make-up case ideal for my toiletries on my journey. I was very happy as I waved them goodbye.

Before leaving New York I wrote home to Mama and Papa to tell them my plans. I wondered how they would react to my news. I told them it might be difficult for them to write to me for some time as I wouldn't have a permanent address, but I would write regularly.

# CHAPTER 42

The day of our departure soon arrived. Maggie, Jack and two friends from the hospital came to see me off. I waved when I saw them but I was too busy to spend any time with them. I rushed over to them and after a few quick kisses and hugs I was back helping the Owens. I was sad to be leaving Maggie in New York but I knew she had the aunts and the boys if she had any problems.

At the dockside I had much to do. Not only did I have my own luggage and belongings to take care of but I had to make sure that Mr. Owen and all his goods were safely checked in. I soon realised that Nicholas, or Nick as I eventually called him, was so excited he was not much use to me. Fortunately, Charles, the family's cab driver had driven us to the docks and he helped with the wheelchair. I watched Charles' every move and learnt much from him. I was impressed by his intelligent anticipation of his master's needs. Charles knew what every groan meant. Soon all the cases were loaded on trolleys and trundled away.

Our tickets were stamped and we made our way up the gangplank. Nicholas helped with his grandfather and a porter was assigned to assist with the wheelchair. These ships didn't really cater for invalids and I was worried that we might have problems on the voyage.

We were soon on deck. Among the crowds lining the quay I could see Maggie, Jack and my friends waiting patiently to wave me off. I waved to them and could hear their calls of, "Goodbye – safe voyage!" I could feel my tears welling up. I was waving to them with a handkerchief and now I wiped my tears and blew my nose. I waved again, blowing a kiss to Maggie and then made my way in the direction of our quarters. It was a short, sharp farewell with my family. I wondered if I would see them again.

I was very surprised at the elegance of our quarters. This ship was much smaller than the one on which we had sailed across the Atlantic to America some years before. It was designed for the rich Americans who cruised to Europe, not for the poor Irish immigrant. We had the luxury of sailing first class. Mr. Owen was quite pleased with the arrangements. He had a large suite with a veranda for his wheelchair. The suite comprised a sleeping area, a lounge area and a separate bathroom. Nick had a separate cabin down the corridor and my cabin adjoined Mr. Owen's. This was necessary as I was on call during the night. Mr. Owen had a bell to call me which he could ring at any time of night or day. I had to work hard but I was thrilled to be going back across the Atlantic. I was aware of the heavy responsibility my duties placed on me, but my heart was light at the thought of returning nearer to home. I didn't know what lay ahead and, even though our destination was Italy, I felt as if I was going home. It was a strange feeling.

I examined our quarters and settled Mr. Owen on the veranda with a travelling rug over his legs to keep him warm. The veranda had large sliding windows which could be closed if it was windy. Mr. Owen could take in the view without getting cold. He seemed pleased so far and asked me to order a pot of tea for him and he lay back in his chair and relaxed.

I unpacked Mr. Owen's luggage and moved my own luggage into my cabin. I noticed that my cabin had two doors, the one that led into Mr. Owen's cabin and the second which led into the corridor.

I decided to go back on deck to give a final wave to my family and friends. As I arrived back on deck I realised we were ready to sail. The captain blew three short sharp blasts on his funnel and the men on the dockside untied the ropes. The ropes trailed in the water and the ship slid gracefully away towards the Lady of Liberty. I waved again to Maggie and Jack and watched until they were small specks in the distance.

I returned to our quarters where tea had arrived and I served it to Mr. Owen. He said, "Stay with me for a while, Nurse Bridget. I want to have a talk with you." I sat down next to him and he motioned me to pour myself a cup of tea. I wondered what he was going to say.

We sat for a while in silence, watching as the tall buildings of Manhattan slide away from us. The ship then headed out into the Atlantic. Then Mr. Owen said, "Nurse Bridget, I want you to know that my condition is worse than I have given you to believe. In fact, this may be the last trip I'll ever make. As I told you when I appointed you it has always been my wish to see Europe and I fear I might not return to America. Nicholas doesn't know this. I asked him to accompany me so that I had a member of my family with me if I don't survive the journey. Also, as you know, he is my eldest grandson and will inherit all that is mine. I don't want him to know my illness is terminal. So I am confiding in you. When the time comes, and it could be in a week, a month or perhaps in a year's time, he'll need your help and support. I want you to know that if I die whilst we are abroad, I don't want my body returned to America. I'll be buried in a foreign land. I don't want to cause you any trouble."

He continued, "I know Nick will be devastated if this should happen and he'll need you to guide him. Can I rely on you to support him in this way?"

I was shocked by Mr. Owen's frankness and his obvious acceptance of his fate. It was a few minutes before I replied; "Mr. Owen, of course I'll respect your wishes. I'll give Nick all the support he needs. But, may I ask you one or two questions?"

"Thank you, my dear. I am so grateful to you. Yes, of course you may."

I expressed to him my surprise that neither he nor the doctors had told me of this situation before. I asked what was to happen if he did pass away while we were in Europe. For instance, what did he want me to do with his belongings, had he written a Will and would my employment terminate immediately?

"Nurse Bridget, I was worried that if I told you my predicament before we set sail, then you might not have come with us. I didn't want to run the risk of you walking out on me before we set sail. Had I known you then, as I have come to know you in the last week or two, I need not have worried. I hope you understand this was a risk I had to take. Some young ladies, you know, wouldn't have been so tolerant and understanding as you have been. As for my belongings, yes, I have made a Will and it is lodged with my lawyers in New York. In a few days' time I shall give you their name and address. You need have no worries about sorting these things out. My lawyers will take care of everything. Nick is the main beneficiary in my Will and most things will be left to him. I'll shortly be writing a letter for Nick, which I want you to give to him when I am gone. In it I'll tell him that you are to remain on the family payroll until you have found other suitable employment. Also, I'll arrange for him to pay for your passage back to America, or to Ireland or wherever else in the world you choose. I will of course let you have a copy of this letter for your own reassurance. Does that satisfy you?"

"Yes. Yes. Thank you," I said.

I was then quiet for a long while.

Then I said, "Mr. Owen, I'll do all I can to ensure that this journey is comfortable and enjoyable for you. You must tell me if there is anything you need at any time. I'll do my best for you."

"Thank you, Nurse Bridget. You are a good girl and I am pleased I chose you. Goodness, you should have seen some of the others! I wouldn't have started this madcap journey without you! I think we're going to have an enjoyable time. Well, I'm sure there are things you need to do now. So, my dear, leave me and I'll be happy for the next hour or two. When Nick comes back, ask him to come and see me, will you? And, by the way, things may not be as dire as I have suggested. Who knows? I may make it back to the States."

"I'll keep a lookout for Nick," I said. I looked at him and smiled. He had a kindly face and I thought how brave he was. "I'll go and finish my unpacking," I said. I went to my own little cabin. I didn't have many belongings with me. I was wearing my nurses' uniform and had only one change of this for the voyage. But I did have some of my own clothes to wear if I needed them. I discovered there was a ship's laundry and I decided to arrange for my uniform to be laundered when I needed a change.

The sea journey to Italy was scheduled to take about ten or eleven days. I couldn't believe it was only 6 years since I had come to America. So much had happened in that time. We were not yet out in the open sea and it felt as if we were still on dry land. The ship thus far was excellent and I was very pleased with the arrangements.

The cabin staff were very attentive and I only had to ring a bell for one of them to be at the door in seconds. Anything I wanted I could ring for and I began to enjoy myself. When I had unpacked my own belongings I finished tidying away Mr. Owen's clothes. Soon his cabin looked very respectable.

When Nick arrived back I told him his grandfather wanted to see him. Before he went in he told me about all he had done since coming on board. He had investigated every nook and cranny of the ship. He was enjoying himself and this was a nicer, more pleasant young man than the one I had first met in New York. Now, he was more relaxed and I began to look forward to our adventure, in spite of the unpleasant news Mr. Owen had given me. Nick told me he had made friends with some young ladies from Pennsylvania and there was to be dancing that evening. I was pleased for him and pushed him in the direction of his grandfather. "Go and tell your grandfather what good luck you've had," I laughed.

We spent a very relaxing time on our ship across the Atlantic and the Mediterranean and we were soon approaching Italy.

# CHAPTER 43

I was thrilled with the view of Italy as we steamed towards Naples. It was a fine, clear day and in the distance we could see Mount Vesuvius. The weather was warm, the sea was azure blue and there wasn't a cloud in the sky. Two hours after docking we were on the dockside and Nick had a carriage standing by to take us to our hotel. We were staying at the Grand Hotel. Mr. Owen and Nick had very pleasant rooms with harbour views. My room was on the top floor, where there were single rooms for the servants of the tourists. Mr. Owen was able to contact me at any time as our rooms were connected by bell. It took us two or three days to settle in our hotel. Then, on the fourth day Mr. Owen decided we should go out and see the sights. Nick called for a carriage and instructed the driver to show us the sites of the town.

After our trip round Naples we were tired and relaxed for the next two days. Nick went out occasionally and visited all the wonderful shops. He told his grandfather he had found some amazing shops. They were full of curios and works of art, and specialised in items for the foreign traveller.

We visited the shops the next day. Mr. Owen was intrigued by all he saw. This was to be the start of many similar excursions over the next few months. Mr. Owen bought trinkets for his relatives at home. There were necklaces for his nieces, brooches for his sisters, and elegant perfume bottles for his friends. For himself he purchased works of art, small items of furniture, porcelain ornaments and small bronze sculptures. Soon, the hotel room was full of these items and I began to worry about how we would transport them if we moved on. I talked to Nick about this and he arranged for the presents to be sent back home. He found a company that specialised in packing and sending items to the States.

Then we made a trip to Mount Vesuvius. The carrier we engaged brought with him a local guide, Guido, who stayed with us all day. We made our way towards Propriano in the southern suburbs of Naples. We passed through vineyards and acacia groves on our way and, as we drew nearer the mountain loomed up ahead of us.

Guido spoke good English and sat in the carriage with us. He told us there was a funicular railway going up the mountain nearly as far as the crater. The railway had inspired the Italian song "Funiculi, funicula" and then, without being asked, he gave us a rendition of the song. We laughed and clapped. Mr. Owen and Nick had taken to this guide and were enjoying the trip. Guido told us that the first railway had not held many people. When the little train started off on its journey a bugle sounded. This could be heard in all the surrounding valleys. The train travelled at a steep angle. The car was pulled by a wire rope that was driven by an engine. At the height of the tourist season several hundred people could be carried up the mountain each day. The cost of running the railway was high. The engine was fuelled with coal, which had to be carried on horseback up to the first station. It wasn't long before the railway company was in money trouble.

Then in the late 1890s an Englishman – Thomas Cook – offered financial help to the funicular. Thomas Cook had a company, which arranged travel for English tourists in Europe and worldwide.

Mount Vesuvius, Naples and the surrounding area were popular tourist regions and Thomas Cook believed this was a good investment. Guido told us that short-sighted locals opposed the purchase. A group of local guides had even tried to blackmail Mr. Cook. When he refused to pay the blackmail money they burnt the station down, cut up the track and threw one of the cars into the crater. It was rebuilt but was attacked again. This led to closure for six months. But this time the local guides realised they had acted stupidly and they decided that their opposition wasn't helping anyone, least of all themselves. Guido was very well informed about the region and it was fascinating listening to him. We were lucky to have found him.

As we reached Propriano we entered the lava fields. All around us were extraordinary dark brown shapes, the old lava flows. As we climbed higher we gained a superb view of the Bay of Naples with the islands of Ischia and Capri and the Sorrento headland. We stopped at the Hermitage Hotel that had also been built by Thomas Cook. We had lunch there and afterwards, in the afternoon, we ascended the mountain on the funicular.

As we rose up into the clouds Guido told us that this was the only railway in the world that ascended an active volcano. At the top we left the train and walked towards the edge of the crater. We were in awe of the potential danger. Smoke was billowing out of the crater and we could see fire bubbling down below. It had been difficult to negotiate all the different forms of transport with Mr. Owen in his wheelchair – but we succeeded. I hoped the volcano didn't erupt while we were there as moving quickly was difficult. I told Nick of my worries and he agreed we should try to return to Naples as soon as possible. We were both quite frightened by the rumblings that were taking place under our feet. Nevertheless, the whole experience was breathtaking.

When we arrived back at our hotel Mr. Owen was exhausted and Nick helped me get him to bed. It had been a long day and we decided not to go far in the next few days. Nick and I agreed the day had been an experience not to be missed.

It was a wonderful time of year to be in Italy and it was now early summer in the year 1906. We had been in Italy for nearly six weeks. No plans had been discussed for moving on to another place. Mr. Owen was happy here but decided that when the weather became too hot we should move north and visit other popular tourist attractions.

One evening I made sure that Mr. Owen was settled in his bed and, when I was free, I intended to go out for a short walk to get some fresh air. Before I ventured out I went to my room and changed my clothes. I stood in front of the mirror, brushing my hair and, as I tidied myself, I wondered what the future held for me. So far I had achieved quite a few of my ambitions but I didn't know how long we were to stay in Europe. Mr. Owen talked of going to London eventually before returning to New York. I had asked him if I might have a few days to go home to Ireland to see Mama and Papa when we were in London. He said I was entitled to a break and if Nick was prepared to look after him he was quite willing for me to do this. I had this to look forward to.

As I stood by the mirror, I heard a knock on my door. Nick was calling my name. I went to the door and saw a worried young man standing there. Other people were hurrying about the hotel corridor and I asked what was causing the commotion. "Bridget, you must come quickly," said Nick.

"Whatever's happened?" I asked.

"Well, it's only a rumour at the moment, but I think it's true," he said. "They say Mount Vesuvius is erupting. I think it's a bad one and we may have to leave town immediately."

We discussed what we should do. Nick decided to go and find out more about this and I went to tell Mr. Owen what was happening. We might have to move on and this would entail packing all our belongings. Nick ran off and I made my way to Mr. Owen's room to find him in a state of some consternation. Apparently, he could hear the rumble of the eruption and he guessed what was happening. "Bridget," he said. "Thank goodness you've come. If Vesuvius is erupting we must flee this town and get away from the danger as quickly as possible."

I told him Nick had gone to see if he could find out the extent of the danger. I suggested he sit quietly whilst I packed his belongings.

As I did so I thought to myself how glad I was that we had sent all Mr. Owen's purchases home. I worked as quickly as I could. I calmed Mr. Owen who was very worried. I knew he felt useless at being unable to help.

Soon Nick arrived back. "It's not good news," he said. "The volcano is erupting and they are saying it looks as if it's going to be the worst eruption in living memory. There was no way of telling how it was going to affect us but the general view of all visitors was that it was a good idea to move on."

It was now quite late in the evening and I asked him how we could travel so late in the day. "I've been quite lucky," he replied. "I went to the marketplace and found a carrier who is prepared to take us wherever we want to go. He is waiting outside and I need to go and tell him where we are going. What shall I tell him, Grandfather?"

Mr. Owen looked thoughtful and it was a few minutes before he spoke. "Well, there is no point in going south," he said, "all the roads will be congested, but I think we should go north and try and make our way to Rome. That is far enough away to be safe. I'm sure the carrier will realise such a long trip will be worth his while financially. Nick, go back and tell him we want to go to Rome. Bargain with him and obtain the best deal you can."

"Right," said Nick. "I'll go straight down to him now. But Grandfather, I mustn't beat the price too low in case someone else offers him a better deal. Carriers are hard to come by and I must ensure we don't lose him."

Mr. Owen said, "Off you go then and do your best," but Nick had already left the room before he got to the end of the sentence.

I finished the packing and turned my attention to Mr. Owen. He needed to be wearing warm clothes for the journey and this was my next task. Thirty minutes later he was ready and Nick had returned. "All's well," he said. He had arranged for the hotel porters to start taking our luggage down to the carrier. Nick had also settled the hotel bill.

At ten o'clock that night we fled the town of Naples and we started on our journey to Rome. As we left the hotel I was amazed by what I saw in the distance. Great plumes of red smoke spiralled into the sky and every now and again there were loud rumblings. This was a large eruption. People were running in all directions and the hotel was emptying fast. The Italians were an excitable race and even though we couldn't understand what they were saying we could hear the anxious tones as they shouted to each other.

Our carriage set off at a slow pace. It was going to be a difficult journey on the crowded roads but Nick had done well as the carriage had a large interior. I settled Mr. Owen and made sure he had plenty of travelling rugs to keep him warm. Nick sat next to him and I sat opposite. Our luggage had been packed in the rear section including the wheelchair.

Two horses pulled the carriage. In fact, the "carriage" was more like a wagon. It reminded me of the pictures of wagons I had seen, years earlier, making their way out west in America. The driver sat up aloft on a bench.

We made our way towards the northern outskirts of Naples. The roads became more and more congested. The journey was going to take a long time. I didn't know what price Nick had negotiated for the trip but I was sure it was expensive. From time to time we had a view of the turmoil behind us. The sky looked an angry pink and grey colour and the light from the plumes of fire lit up the night. It was the best firework display I had ever seen but quite frightening!

Two hours later we were still not far beyond the outskirts of the town. We were so lucky to get away from this awful catastrophe. I prayed we would soon be safe and out of danger.

Crowds of people were seeking refuge from the impending disaster. On our way we passed the railway station that was teeming with people. I thought to myself what a good thing it was that Nick had suggested we travel by road. It wasn't the comfiest way to travel but at least it meant we didn't have to wait around in cold, draughty train stations. The trains would be very crowded.

I looked over at Mr. Owen. Like me he was looking out of the wagon and taking in all that he saw. "If I had known this was going to happen, Bridget, we wouldn't have made this journey. Quite apart from exposing myself to danger, I have involved both you and Nick and I'm very sorry."

I knew Mr. Owen wasn't a religious man but I said, "I'm praying that with God's help we'll get through this."

He looked over at me and said, "I wish I had your faith. I've noticed what great strength it gives you. Who knows, maybe one day I'll come to believe too." I told him I was lucky. I had never known any other way and had lived with religion since the day I was born.

After about three hours we were well on our way out of Naples and heading towards Rome. Our wagon was making good progress and I asked Mr. Owen how far we had to go. He said, "If we pick up speed we should be there a few hours after daybreak."

Our hotel in Naples had packed some food and drink for us and I thought it was time to have a snack. I opened the box and poured a drink of milk for the three of us. We then ate bread rolls with cheese and olives. I felt much better after this; food always comforted me. When he had finished his food Mr. Owen settled down to try and sleep. "Try and get some sleep yourself, Bridget," he said. "The worst is over now and our next hurdle will be to find somewhere to stay in Rome. Judging by the crowds on the roads this journey might take longer than we imagined." So, after I had passed some food and drink to our driver, I settled back and tried to sleep.

All sorts of things were going through my mind as we jostled along the road. I thought of Mama and Papa. If they knew where I was and what was happening they would be very worried. Then I thought of Maggie and the boys back in New York and of my friends at the hospital. They would all be amazed to hear of this adventure. I was glad I had come on this trip and was thankful that, so far, we had not come to harm.

# CHAPTER 44

We arrived in Rome at midday. The journey had taken longer than anticipated because of the large number of travellers on the road. This didn't bode well for our chances of finding somewhere to stay, but at least we were out of danger. We decided if we didn't find a good hotel we might have to travel on beyond Rome.

Our driver knew his way around and took us right into the centre of the city. When there he asked other cab drivers where we could find accommodation. They directed him to several hotels and we were lucky to find rooms at the second one, the Hotel Venezia.

Once again I unpacked Mr. Owen's multitude of cases. I had already settled him in his bed and he was sleeping like a baby. The journey had tired him out and I was thankful I could now grab a few hours' rest myself.

The following day all talk was about Mount Vesuvius. The news was that the top of the mountain had destroyed the top half of the funicular railway. Much of the surrounding area was covered with ash. There were rumours of deaths and injuries but no official figures had been announced. I was glad we had moved on. Naples was like a ghost town as so many people had left.

It took us a while to recover from our experience. But nothing was going to stop Nick who was soon up and about. He spent several days out and about round the beautiful city of Rome. He drew up a list of the places he thought his grandfather should visit and was looking forward to showing him round the city.

I was surprised at Nick's enthusiasm for ancient monuments. He was a true 'American' interested in all things old.

Nick suggested we should visit the Via del Corso, moving on to the Piazza del Popolo and then visit the Pincio Gardens. His favourite monument was the Pantheon – a beautiful temple. He also wanted to take us to the Coliseum, a huge amphitheatre in which the ancient gladiators of the Holy Roman Empire had performed. Then he planned to take us to the ancient city walls and the Forum then the Catacombs, which were ancient tunnels under the city where the early Christians practised their religion and where they were buried.

After those places we visited a square containing four fountains. One of these was the Trevi fountain, which had been built in the 18th century and into which tourists threw coins and made wishes. The most popular wish was to return to Rome again one day.

I wanted to visit the Vatican. I decided to raise this later – knowing that after a few days Mr. Owen would be tired and need to rest. While he was resting I might be able to have a few hours off and achieve my ambition. I could imagine the excitement at home when I wrote to tell them of my experiences!

My visit to the Vatican was the crowning glory of my stay in Rome. I stood in St. Peter's square on a Sunday morning and the Pope himself came out onto the balcony and addressed the crowds. The atmosphere was electric. It didn't take me long to write home about my experience.

It took us three weeks to complete our tour of the sights of the Holy City of Rome. Sometimes, as I lay in my bed at night, I thought about the places we had visited and was amazed at all that happened to me in my short life. From a quiet start in Ireland I had travelled to the hustle and bustle of New York and now I was seeing the culture of ancient Europe. I wouldn't have missed this for anything. Fortunately, Mr. Owen's health seemed to have improved since leaving America and the climate here in Italy suited him well. There had been no more talk from him of the possibility that he might not live to return to America. I think he thought his doctors at home might have been wrong. My job was easier than expected and my work was more as a companion than a nurse.

Now that we had seen all the sights of Rome our thoughts turned to where the next stage of our journey would take us.

# CHAPTER 45

We soon moved on to the district of Umbria and the town of Assisi. The countryside was beautiful and wonderful wild flowers abounded. Everything was lush and green. Apparently this was the best time of year to visit the area. Later in summer it was very hot and the grass dried out and turned from green to brown.

Assisi is a tourist and religious centre, famous as the ancient home of St. Francis of Assisi. Whilst there we visited the Basilica of San Francesco, I was amazed to find that the actual tomb of St. Francis was in the crypt of the Basilica.

We didn't stay long in Assisi. Nick was keen to move on and our next stop was Florence.

It was now June and very hot in the summer sun so we didn't stay long in Florence. The city is in the middle of Tuscany and is capital of the region. In the few days we were there we visited the Ponte Vecchio and all the jewellers' shops. Mr. Owen was entranced by the gold, the silver and the cameos. He could not resist more presents for his family!

A day or two later we moved on to Pisa and saw its famous leaning tower. Mr. Owen had met some American travellers who had journeyed south from France and they told him they had a lovely time in Nice on the French Riviera. So, he decided that would be our next destination. Before long we were on our way again. I was getting used to this itinerant life and I was glad I hadn't brought much luggage with me. But having to pack Mr. Owen's possessions was always a mammoth task.

# CHAPTER 46

We made our way by train to Genoa in northern Italy and then on to the seaside resort of Nice in France. On the train Nick chatted to an old chap who told him that in days gone by there was no railway link from Italy to Nice and the roads over the mountains had been treacherous. In those days travellers travelled by boats that operated along the coast, carrying passengers from Italy to France, thereby avoiding the hazardous mountains. The boats, called feluccas, were open to the element and were rowed by up to a dozen men. They were large enough to carry a post chaise with all its passengers and luggage. In winter this mode of transport was preferred even if the seas were rough. It was better than the perilous journey over the Maritime Alps. Since those days a railway had been constructed through the mountains. We crossed the Maritime Alps by railway.

We arrived at Nice in the evening and the first thing I noticed was a wonderful cool breeze blowing from the sea. The town of Nice is on the Cote d'Azur on the French Riviera, overlooking the Mediterranean Sea. Those who first discovered Nice called it "La Paradis" – paradise. My first impression of the town was the contrast between the blue sky and the red terracotta tiles on the rooftops and the azure blue sea. It looked a very attractive place. We left the train station and Nick made enquiries about hotels. We were soon settled in our hotel which was near the Promenade des Anglais, a long boulevard on the seafront.

In the following few days Mr. Owen made a miraculous recovery from the tiring journey. He insisted we should take a walk along the promenade. The mildness of the climate suited him well. He benefited from the sea air from the first day. On the promenade I noticed how smart and well-dressed the tourists were. This was quite a change from Italy. The ladies wore hats to protect them from the sun and carried parasols.

Back at the hotel I chatted with one of the waiters who told me many English aristocrats spent winters in Nice, staying in a hotel or taking a villa in nearby Cimiez. He said English royalty, princes and princesses and even Queen Victoria had visited the town. Nice had only been a part of France for less than 50 years. Before this the town was under the control of Italy or Sardinia and had even, at one time, been occupied by the Spanish. In spite of its history, the town had settled into a sort of Franco-English town. The natives, or Niçois as they were called, depended on the English tourists for their livelihoods.

One day on my day off I went for a stroll on my own. I came to a small group of shops, mostly selling souvenirs and I started to browse. I noticed one of the shops sold newspapers, Italian, French and English. There was even a copy of an American newspaper. The headline caught my eye:

'MURDER TRIAL TO START SOON IN NEW YORK'.

I couldn't contain my curiosity and peered closer at the paper. I scanned the article quickly, gasping as I read the words, *The Murder of Stanford White, architect of reputation, murdered by Harry Thaw.'* I knew then the meaning of the expression 'blood running cold' for that was how I felt. These were the men who had been associated with Evelyn Nesbit who I had nursed at Dr. Bull's Nursing Home. I had to buy the paper and my hand was trembling as I handed over the money. I folded the paper and hurried back to the hotel.

I let myself into my room and threw my bag and my purchases on the bed. Then I sat and read the paper. I couldn't believe what I was reading. Harry Thaw, Evelyn's husband, was in prison accused of shooting Evelyn's lover, the architect Stanford White (the visitor

Evelyn called Stanny). The paper wrote that Harry Thaw had been tormented by jealousy of his wife's earlier lover, Stanford White and had shot and killed him point blank on the roof of Madison Square Garden. The paper called it "The Crime of the Century". The paper went on to describe Evelyn's earlier life and I realised this was just the beginning. Much more would be revealed at the forthcoming trial. I decided to keep in touch with these goings-on and buy the American papers regularly. Later, I found Nick and showed him the newspaper. He was intrigued and we agreed to follow the story as the trial unfolded.

# CHAPTER 47

A few days later Nick found a copy of the Washington Times. Pictures of Mr. White, Mr. Thaw and Evelyn were splashed across the front page. This paper contained more details of the forthcoming murder trial in New York. I thought about the nurses in the nursing home and I was sure they were also glued to the papers. Harry Thaw was in custody and the trial was due to start soon.

For several days Mr. Owen was content to sun himself in the hotel garden. I was a little worried about Nick as this town was much quieter than other places we had visited. I suggested he should arrange some trips out into the countryside for his grandfather.

On my first day off I decided to explore the back streets of the town. It happened to be market day and I lost no time in purchasing a straw hat and a beautiful parasol. I felt quite grand and looked forward to our next stroll on the promenade. Life in Nice seemed to run at a slow pace; quite different from the other places we had visited. It was wonderful to mingle in the market and look at the produce on sale. As well as beef and lamb, there were rabbits, hare and wild boar on sale. Then there were the cheeses, fruit and vegetable stalls and fish. I noticed that a favourite fish was the anchovy and I learned later that one of the local delicacies was anchovy served in olive oil.

I ventured further into the narrow alleyways, past old buildings and was drawn on by the wonderful smell coming from the local bakery. Most of the shops in the old town were frequented by local people with few tourists. Here I found bargains in leatherwork and other souvenirs and bought one or two presents for Mama and Mary-Anne. I bought a small leather purse for Mama and a tortoiseshell hand mirror for Mary-Anne.

As a result of my suggestion Nick quickly arranged a few trips for us. Mr. Owen didn't seem to want to go far but he was soon enjoying himself when we visited places like Menton further along the coast and inland to the Maritime Alps. Here we found a village inn where we stopped for our lunch. The mountain scenery was beautiful and the air fresh and invigorating. We were amazed by the gardens full of beautiful flowers and by the fields containing fruit trees, mainly citrus fruits. Abundant flowers and fruits scented the air. At times we had problems with the wheelchair but Nick managed to overcome this difficulty.

# CHAPTER 48

Summer passed and autumn soon came. Towards the end of October we became aware of the mosquitoes. The hotel supplied us with mosquito netting but we still suffered with occasional insect bites. I wondered when we would be moving on again. One night, in the early hours of the morning, I was awoken by the anxious voice of Nick outside my door. "Nurse Bridget, Nurse Bridget," he called, tapping the door. I hastily put on my slippers and pulled my dressing gown on and went to the door. "I'm sorry to disturb you," he said, "but can you come? Grandfather is not at all well."

I replied, "Of course, just wait a minute."

Nick waited outside the door while I pinned up my hair. Whatever the problem was I couldn't appear with my hair down around my shoulders! I threw on some clothes and went to see what the problem was. I found Mr. Owen lying on his bed, very red in the face and covered with beads of perspiration. I felt his forehead, which was very hot. I don't think he was even aware of my presence. I took stock of the situation and noticed his breathing was laboured. I asked Nick to open a window to let some fresh air in, as it was very stuffy in the room. Then I took his pulse. It was very slow. By now I realised he was indeed very ill and I turned to Nick and said, "Nick, your grandfather needs a doctor. I don't know what is causing his condition but we must get help quickly. Can you do that?"

Nick mumbled, "Of course," and disappeared from the room.

Ten minutes later Nick arrived back, saying, "The doctor's on his way. He'll be about twenty minutes or so. How is Grandfather?" I told him there was no change in his condition.

The doctor soon arrived and placed his bag beside the bed. Fortunately he spoke English and as he moved towards Mr. Owen he said, "How long has he been like this?" Nick replied that he had found him about an hour previously. The presence of the doctor seemed to have a calming effect on us. He spoke in measured tones and before long seemed to be in full control of the situation. After a cursory examination he looked across at me and said, "Are you a relative?" I explained to him that I was the family's travelling nurse. He said, "Good. Can you tell me anything about the patient's medical history? Is there anything you think could have brought this on?"

I explained that Mr. Owen had been ill in America but that he had recovered and was now convalescing. I was anxious not to alarm Nick more than necessary about his grandfather's condition so my replies were guarded. I said, "Do you think maybe his fever is caused by something he's eaten?"

"It's possible," replied the doctor who reached in his bag for his stethoscope. "Nurse," he said, "can you get to the other side of the bed? I need the patient in a sitting position, if possible." So we linked arms under Mr. Owen and manoeuvred him into an upright position. I made him more comfortable with extra pillows. Then I bathed his face again to cool him down. Meanwhile, the doctor continued his examination. "Can you hear me, Mr. Owen?" he said. "I want you to take some deep breaths." He listened to Mr. Owen's chest. This done and saying nothing, he continued the examination. There was an eerie silence in the room whilst he looked into his eyes, pulling down his lower eyelids. He placed a spatula on his tongue and examined his mouth and throat. He looked into his ears and looked for any signs of a rash on his torso. Then he examined his extremities, looking at his fingers and finally his feet and toes. In all he carried out a very thorough examination.

At this point I had no idea what Mr. Owen was suffering from.

Finally, the doctor indicated that I could make Mr. Owen comfortable. He suggested he should have some water to drink and there should be a plentiful supply for him to drink during the night. He also asked me if his stomach had been upset in any way. "Was there any vomiting or diarrhoea?" I said I hadn't noticed any of these symptoms.

The doctor asked Nick to go outside with him. Nick said, "Come with us, Nurse Bridget. I think you should hear whatever the doctor has to tell us."

So we left the room and made our way downstairs to the foyer where we sat down. The doctor said he had been a little bewildered at first but he had a fairly good idea of the cause of the problem. We waited anxiously to hear what he had to say. Looking at Nick, he said, "I'm sorry to say that your grandfather may have suffered a slight stroke or even a mild heart attack. However, the fever is making the diagnosis difficult. The next 24 hours will be critical. You should arrange for someone to sit with your grandfather all the time. I'll come back tomorrow afternoon and I'll be in a better position to give you a diagnosis."

He continued: "I must tell you, however, that there has been an outbreak of typhoid fever in the town in the last few days. I very much hope this isn't another case."

He turned to me and said, "Nurse, if Mr. Owen feels sick or vomits or if you think his condition has worsened please send for me. In the morning please take this prescription to the chemist and ask for it urgently. There are two items, the medicine must be taken immediately and then twice a day. The second item is a powder. This should be added to water and drunk twice a day."

He handed the prescription to me and I asked where the nearest chemist was situated. He replied, "Oh, that's easy. There's a new British Medical Hall, recently established. It is in the Avenue de la Gare. They have English-speaking pharmacists so you should have no difficulty." I thanked him. He shook Nicholas by the hand and bade us goodnight and left the hotel.

Nick and I were quiet for a few minutes and then Nick said, "I'm so glad you are with us." I was surprised at Nick's frankness. He wasn't given to showing his emotions.

I looked at him and smiled, saying, "Sure, we get on well, so we do. We must work together now and make sure your grandfather is soon back to good health."

Nick agreed with me and said, "Will you be all right to go to the chemist in the morning?" I told him it was not a problem.

We then agreed that I should sit with Mr. Owen for the next 3 hours while Nick tried to get some sleep and Nick would do the following 3 hours, allowing me to have a short rest. I didn't think I was going to get much relaxation that night.

I was up early in the morning and had a quick breakfast. I looked in on my charge and told Nick I was going to the chemist. Mr. Owen was sitting up in bed but not looking well. He managed to smile at me as I left the room.

I hurried out, found the pharmacy and went in. It was a large shop and had quite an affluent air to it. At one end it stocked perfumes, make-up, face creams and other toiletries. I saw the dispensary at the other end of the shop and made my way there.

A tall good-looking young man in a white coat approached me on the other side of the counter. He addressed me in a strange language, which I took to be Italian.

I looked at him with a puzzled expression and noticed the twinkle in his eyes. Was he making fun of me, I thought? No, he didn't realise I spoke English. I thought he must be Italian. I reached inside my bag and handed the prescription to him. Hesitatingly, I said, "Could you make up this for me please?"

He smiled and took the prescription from me and read it carefully. Then he said, "This will take about 30 minutes to prepare. Will you wait for it?" I said I would and he showed me to a seating area and asked if I would like a cup of coffee while I was waiting. I was rather taken aback at this but quite pleased as I had hurried my breakfast and not eaten much. In due course another young man arrived with the coffee for me. I relaxed in the green leather chair. It was very plush and whilst I waited I looked around and noticed that the staff were all very smart in their clean white, starched coats. This was obviously a well-to-do establishment. The smell of perfume from the other end of the shop permeated the air. It was quite a grand place. Later in the day the shop would be full of wealthy tourists buying perfumes and make-up.

The young man returned and I went over to the counter. He told me the medications were well labelled with instructions and handed me the packet. I paid for it and he returned with the change, saying, "I hope Mr. Owen will soon be returned to good health, Mrs. Owen." I was surprised he had taken the trouble to memorise the name on the prescription but somewhat taken aback that he thought I was Mrs. Owen.

"Oh," I said. "Thank you, but I am not Mrs. Owen. I am Mr. Owen's nurse." I had to correct him straight away but he looked startled at my frankness and apologised for his mistake.

"I'm so sorry," he said. "Please forgive me."

I lost no time in returning to the hotel and administered Mr. Owen's first dose of medicine. He seemed much better during the day but it was at night that he worsened. And then the vomiting started. I was quite worried and discussed the situation with Nick. We both agreed that we should call the doctor again.

I was shocked when the doctor eventually pronounced that Mr. Owen was suffering from typhoid fever. The doctor told us he had been concerned the previous evening and was hoping that Mr. Owen would improve overnight. He had hoped this had been a false alarm. But it was not.

The doctor said that under normal circumstances he would transfer Mr. Owen to the local hospital. But there were no beds available and the hospital was full. He asked me if I was happy to nurse my patient in the hotel. I had no option but to agree. I don't think Nick was happy with the situation but there didn't seem to be an alternative. I agreed to do this but only if he was available at any time if Mr. Owen's condition worsened. He agreed to this.

So began a very worrying time. I spent most of my day with Mr. Owen. There was little I could do to help him except make sure that he was comfortable. So I took to reading a book whilst he slept. At the end of the first day Nick suggested I have a few hours to myself. He took over from me and I was relieved to have a break. After I had eaten I decided to get some fresh air and went for a walk on the seafront.

I was strolling along when I saw the figure of a young man walking towards me. As he approached I realised it was the young man from the chemist shop. He came up to me and took off his hat saying, "Good evening, this is a surprise. What is a nice young lady like you doing out on your own like this?"

I explained to him that I was just grabbing a breath of fresh air before returning to my patient. He asked if he could walk with me. I was somewhat surprised at this but agreed. As we walked we talked. It was amazing how easy he was to talk to. We seemed to have much in common.

He told me about his home in Wales. He had been brought up in a small Welsh village in a valley. The only industry there was coalmining and his father worked in the pit. He had an elder brother who worked in the local grocer's shop. As a young boy he had only spoken the Welsh language and at the age of sixteen his father had apprenticed him to a chemist in a nearby town.

He had served his apprenticeship for five years and then at the age of 21 he decided to make his way in the world. His mother was sad when he left Wales. He obtained a job in London with a large company. Then the company sent him to their new outlet in Nice so that he could learn the French language. His mother was unhappy at this move. It was two years since he had come to Nice and he longed to go home to see his family. He didn't talk much about his father. I was comfortable in his company and I told him about my childhood and why I had gone to America.

He walked me back to the hotel and I was sorry to say goodbye to him. Then, as he was leaving he said, "Thank you for your company. I have enjoyed the evening. May I walk out with you again?"

I had no hesitation in saying, "Yes," but told him it would depend on my duty hours. We agreed to keep in touch.

For the next two days Nick and I took it in turns to look after Mr. Owen. We were both feeling the strain. I continued my evening walks on the promenade but didn't see "my chemist friend" again.

Mr. Owen was not improving and I noticed red spots had appeared on his body and he was complaining of a bad headache. We called the doctor again. He was unhappy with Mr. Owen's condition and prescribed more medicines for him. I talked to the doctor about the fever. He told me it was usual for outbreaks of this illness to occur in the height of summer when it was very hot. It was normally caused by poor hygiene conditions so he was surprised to find it in this hotel. It was unusual to have an outbreak in autumn and this might be due to the fact that we were enjoying an Indian summer. He told me if Mr. Owen's condition didn't improve in the next 48 hours he would be very concerned. He didn't want to worry Nicholas about this.

I went to the chemist again with the new prescription. There was a new young man on duty and I was sorry not to see my new friend.

But, just as I was leaving the shop, I almost collided with him. He had finished work for the day and was on his way home. After the usual pleasantries he asked if he might walk me back to the hotel and I was secretly very pleased. I liked this young man and his fresh open manner. There was no side to him and we seemed to hit it off from the very start. In a very short time he felt like an old friend and our conversation took up where it had left off a few days ago. To passers-by it looked as if we were on holiday together. It was a strange feeling but I felt I had known him for a very long time.

The next day was to bring more worry. Nick contacted me to tell me he wasn't feeling well and he had called the doctor. He returned to his bed.

The doctor came and pronounced that Nick, too, was suffering from the fever. At that moment I felt utterly alone with two sick patients to look after. It had been so different in the nursing home and the hospital. I had always worked with a team of nurses and the doctors were on hand at a minute's notice. But now, here I was in a strange land with no colleagues. I had to be strong to get through the next few days.

Now, with both my charges ill, it was difficult to have any time to myself. I talked to the doctor about this and he said I needed help. He mentioned it to Mr. Owen and a night nurse was engaged. Her name was Annette. She was a little older than me and had lived in Nice all her life. Fortunately, she spoke English and was familiar with typhoid fever and had nursed many cases in her time. I was glad of her help. She came to the hotel at 6 o'clock every evening and stayed until morning.

So, in the evenings, I had some time to myself and I started my walks on the seafront again. It wasn't long before I met Philip again. He was very interesting to be with and told me all about the history of Nice and as he talked I forget about my worries back at the hotel.

I asked him why the boulevard on the seafront was called the Promenade d'Anglais. He said that back in the 1820s during a hard winter a severe frost occurred which killed a large number of orange trees in the Nice area. The people in the surrounding countryside relied on the citrus fruits for a living. After the frost many men were thrown out of work. The British residents arranged to provide relief work for these men in the construction of a coastal road. As a result the road became known as the Promenade des Anglais. The new road transformed the town. There were many fine English shops on the Promenade together with fashionable lounges, ballrooms, a theatre and billiard halls. Smartly dressed ladies and gentlemen frequented these.

Philip, or Phil as I now called him, told me the coming of the railway had transformed the town. It had even brought the Russian Emperor Alexander II and his Empress to the town on holiday. Some Russian families who followed decided to take up permanent residence. As a result Phil's employees had taken on a chemist who spoke Russian. It was becoming a very cosmopolitan town.

Phil and I continued to meet on most evenings and I was happy in his company. One day he asked me if I was able to join him for an evening meal at one of the little inns in old Nice. I accepted without hesitation. We had an excellent evening. The company was good and so was the food. The Nice district relies on the products of its farms for food and so we dined on fine meats, salads and fruits. The local custom was to drink white wine with the meal but this was always diluted with water. It seemed a strange habit but we decided, "When in Nice we should do as the Niçois do."

Parts of Nice were lit up by electric lights and this drew large crowds in the evenings. Phil told me this was nothing compared to the crowds who turned up for the Mardi Gras Carnival on Shrove Tuesday each year. He said it was a flamboyant and expensive affair. All local society turned out in their carriages. He also told me about the Battle of Flowers that took place annually on the promenade.

We had a lovely evening and as we walked back to the hotel Phil caught hold of my hand. I couldn't remember how long it was since I had held hands with a man. My mind went back to Danny at home but that seemed a lifetime away. This was something new and I felt there was something very special in our relationship.

I thanked Phil for a lovely evening and, like the gentleman he always was, he took off his hat to me and wished me goodnight at the door of the hotel.

My happiness, however, was to be short-lived.

During the night I received a call from Annette. I rushed to Mr. Owen's room. She told me how worried she was. Mr. Owen was lying on the bed and his breathing was very laboured. She said, "He has been like this for about an hour now. He is refusing water and didn't eat his supper this evening. His pulse has slowed even more and I'm worried. I think we should send for the doctor." I agreed and we called down to reception and asked them to arrange this.

Half an hour later the doctor arrived. He examined Mr. Owen and his face was grave. "I'm sorry, my dear, but he doesn't seem to be responding to treatment. There's only one thing I can suggest and that is that we take him into hospital. I don't think you should have the responsibility of looking after him now he is in such a delicate state."

I didn't answer immediately. Then I said, "I must talk to Nicholas before agreeing."

I went to Nick's room and knocked on the door. He was feeling much better but I told him the unwelcome news of his grandfather. He was very upset and asked me for my advice. Hesitatingly I said, "Nick, I have been trained to take the advice of doctors. Dr. Roget has vast experience with this fever and I don't think he would make this suggestion unless he thought it absolutely necessary." I could see that Nicholas was not convinced. I asked him if he could manage to come to his grandfather's room to talk to the doctor. When Nick saw his grandfather he immediately agreed that he should go into hospital. So, Mr. Owen was transferred to the local fever hospital.

# CHAPTER 49

Life was becoming very difficult. With Nick ill in bed in the hotel and Mr. Owen in hospital I didn't know where to start. I wasn't sure what to do about Annette. She wasn't needed now to sit with Mr. Owen at night.

Dr. Roget suggested that Annette should look after Nicholas. He said her workload would be very light but he thought it important I was relieved of some of my duties. I was pleased to hear this and I went to tell Nick what was happening. Nick was worried about his grandfather and asked me to visit him in hospital. I agreed to visit Mr. Owen every afternoon.

I told Nick that Annette had to be on hand to make sure he was all right. He laughed at me, saying, "Come on, Nurse Bridget, I'm not a baby. I just need to rest and regain my strength. I'll soon be back to normal." This cheered me up slightly.

After my first visit to Mr. Owen I took a circuitous route home, hoping to see Phil at the chemist shop. I was lucky as I bumped into him just as he was leaving the shop. His first words were, "Hello. How are you, Bridget?" So I poured out my story to him. He was very understanding. "You must take care of yourself," he said. "With two patients to care for in different places you will get very tired if you're not careful. Also take care not to catch the fever yourself."

I laughed at his concern and told him not to worry about me. My life in Ireland and my time in New York had toughened me and I was very resilient. I said, "It'll take a lot to wear me down."

Phil smiled and asked if I was still able to walk out with him in the evenings. We agreed to meet later.

Our walks continued and I became very fond of this new and very dear friend. We had a lot in common. We were both from rural Celtic backgrounds and had the same sense of humour. Wherever we went on our long walks Philip always had a tale to tell me.

October was a lovely time to be in Nice. The air was full of the fragrance of herbs such as thyme and rosemary. We even saw cacti growing in some gardens, alongside brightly coloured geraniums. Phil told me the geraniums were often still flowering at Christmas time.

Phil introduced me to the local newspaper printed specially for the English tourists. It was called the Menton & Monte Carlo News. It contained information and news for British residents and visitors. It provided details of social life, sport and entertainment on the Riviera. I was intrigued to read this. It made me realise that the British were quite a large contingent in the South of France. Although I was from Ireland, where we were still fighting for Home Rule, my travels had widened my horizons and I almost felt British. My Papa would be horrified to hear me say this, but travel certainly broadens the mind.

I regularly visited Mr. Owen in hospital. One day I bumped into Dr. Roget who told me he wasn't happy with Mr. Owen's progress and he was uncertain what more he could do to help. I then told him about Mr. Owen's confession to me about his health when we left New York. He was not surprised to hear what I had to tell him and said, "It's almost as if he doesn't want to go on. I believe he thinks he may have reached the end of his journey!"

I suggested we should try to encourage him to eat more so he would gain his strength. I had never really thought it would come to this, as Mr. Owen had become invigorated during our journey. This was such bad luck. I asked if there were any tonics available that might help. "My dear," said Dr. Roget, "I think you should face up to the possibility that he won't be with us much longer. I have seen this happen before. The fever has debilitated an already unwell and unfit man."

I still couldn't believe we had done all we could and said, "Well, I shall pray you are wrong." We both left the hospital together and I didn't know what I was going to tell Nick when I returned to the hotel.

Luckily Nick decided he felt well enough to get up and dress for dinner that day. He asked me how his grandfather was and I told him I wasn't happy with his condition. I also told him Dr. Roget didn't hold out any hopes for a quick return to health. I couldn't bring myself to tell him exactly what Dr. Roget had said. He said, "Don't worry, Nurse Bridget. He's as strong as an ox. He'll pull through." But I had my misgivings.

Nick knew about my friendship with Phil and he was pleased for me. He told me that now he was feeling so much better I could have a day off. He suggested I coincide this with the time when Phil wasn't working.

That evening I unburdened my worries to Phil as we walked. He understood my problem and said he knew of Dr. Roget's reputation. He said it was unlikely he had made an incorrect diagnosis. I told him I hadn't told Nick the full facts. He suggested I should ask Dr. Roget to talk with Nick. I thought this was a good idea.

Phil asked me if there was any likelihood of me having any time off. "Well," I said, "it's funny you should mention that but Nick said I should take a day off whenever I like!"

"Well, fancy that," said Phil. "I'm free on Saturday, shall I arrange a trip and show you some more sights? Would you like that?"

I was delighted and quite without thinking I took hold of Phil's hand. He showed no surprise even though most people would think this very forward of me. We held hands as we walked. It seemed the most natural thing to do.

When I returned to the hotel that evening I was met by Nick who told me he didn't need Nurse Annette anymore and asked me to relay this news to her. I was sorry to see Annette go but I still held out hope for Mr. Owen's recovery and I asked her if she was available for night duty if he was released from hospital. She said that provided she had no other work she would be pleased to help. We parted on good terms and I hoped to see her again but not under the same circumstances.

# CHAPTER 50

On Saturday Phil organised a trip to the mountains. It was a lovely autumn day. We set off in a coach Phil had hired for the whole day with a driver. As we travelled into the country, with the sound of the horses' hooves on the road, I was reminded of home and the regular trips we had made at home by donkey cart into town. But this was much grander.

That day I realised once more how fond I was of Phil. As we sat in the coach we held hands. We went along the dusty roads and Phil pointed out the interesting sights. We saw old churches, old monasteries and vineyards. We stopped at an inn for lunch.

Over lunch Phil asked me what would happen if Mr. Owen didn't recover. "How are you placed?" he said. "Will this mean that you are out of work and will have to leave Nice?"

I looked at him and realised he was being very serious and asked, "Why do you want to know, Phil?"

He looked at me for what seemed like several minutes and surprised me by saying, "I don't want to lose you. I think we have a lot in common. I have never been happier in the company of a young woman than I am now. You are the first girl to make me feel like this."

I was surprised at how forthright he was and tried to lighten the tone of the conversation. I laughed and said, "Why ever should you worry about me? You have a good job here and I am sure you meet lots of young ladies in your job."

"Bridget, listen to me please," he said. "I've had sleepless nights thinking about this. To tell you the truth I know I love you and I can think of nothing better than spending the rest of my life with you. I miss you so much when we are apart."

I could not have been more surprised. I sat there looking at him and realised my laughter had been out of place and rather cruel. I gathered my thoughts together and said, "Have you really thought this through? There will be many insurmountable problems in our way. Do you really mean what you are saying?"

"Yes," he said. "Will you marry me, Bridget?"

I was completely taken aback. As we sat there holding hands I smiled at him. I realised then what a wonderful person he was and what a rock he had been for me in those troubled days. I said, "I never thought our relationship was serious, Phil. You have surprised me. My life has been so wrapped up looking after my patients and wondering where our travels will take us next that I have never thought of marriage." Phil looked very disappointed.

I hastened to add, "But I'm very flattered that you've asked me. I have grown very fond of you, but there's a lot to consider."

When he heard this he smiled and said, "So it's not a 'no', then?"

"No, it's not," I said.

We returned to Nice that evening and I promised to give a lot of thought to Phil's proposal.

As I lay in bed that night I couldn't sleep. My mind went over and over the lovely day I had with Phil and, of course, his proposal. I wondered where we would live if we did marry. I was concerned that I would have to leave Mr. Owen and Nick if I married. But I knew one thing over everything else, I now realised how much I loved Phil and I loved him more than Danny Murphy, John Breen or any other man.

I had written to Mama and Papa a while back to tell them our stay in Nice was to be prolonged due to the illnesses. I hinted to them that I might be able to visit Ireland if we eventually travelled on to London. I had told them that I was feeling a little depressed with both my charges ill.

Now, the uncertainty of everything depressed me again. My euphoria on our day out was short lived. I was down in the dumps and I wasn't sure what lay ahead if I married Phil. I started to worry about the future when I should have been very happy!

It wasn't long before I had a letter back from Papa.

*My dear Bridget,*

*Your letter reached me yesterday morning. So you are to time on the Continent longer than you anticipated. However, cheer up and be contented and try and be at home and make hay while the sun shines. All I have to say is that I hope we shall see you soon. I could not write to you lately, as I did not know your destination. Now I shall write oftener.*

*I shall surprise you with news when you come home which would be too long for me to write here. I know you have not heard any of this news.*

*This world is grave. Mind your religious duties wherever you are located and you will be God's child. I pray for you often. May the Blessed Virgin be your guardian angel.*

*Do you think you will be allowed to come over here from London at the time the old gentleman and family will be returning to New York?*

*I had a letter from Maggie not many days ago – poor thing is lonely after you but said she was in hope of seeing you home soon.*

*I hope you are enjoying yourself in every possible way. Again, cheer up! You and I shall have a jolly drive from the train station here.*

*All the family are well, so are all friends.*

*I am my dear Bridget your very fond father*

*Richard Frisby.*

It was good to hear from Papa and his letter helped me realise how lucky I was. Once again, though, I sensed my father was getting older. This letter was even more rambling than the last one. It was covered in ink blotches and crossings out and was written on an old piece of lined paper from an exercise book. I needed to go home to

Ireland soon. I wondered how I was going to manage this. I also worried about Maggie missing me if I married Phil and stayed in Europe. I had many problems on my mind.

# CHAPTER 51

The next time Phil and I met he was expecting a reply from me. I hesitated before bringing up the subject. At first I told him about my wish to go home to Ireland to visit my parents. He understood this and said he wanted to go home to Wales to see his mother and father. He had been away for over two years and missed his family.

Then I broached the subject of his proposal. I said I was happy he wanted to marry me but I thought there were things we should discuss before I gave him my reply. He asked me what these were and I said, "The thing that worries me most, Phil, is that we haven't discussed where we will live and how we are going to manage in the future." He said he had never intended staying in France and it was his wish to go home to Wales and, if possible, to run his own pharmacy business and he was now hoping I could go with him. I was pleased to hear this but replied, "That sounds lovely, Phil, but it does mean I have to end my employment with the Owens. On the other hand, if Mr. Owen doesn't recover I'll be out of work anyway."

Phil realised that with Mr. Owen's illness everything seemed to be up in the air and understood my difficulty. He told me he intended soon to ask his employers for a transfer back to London. He said, "If they don't agree to this I'll give them my notice and we might both be out of work." We laughed at this but it wasn't really funny. I only had enough money saved to make a trip home with not much spare but I remembered Mr. Owen's promise to continue paying me if anything happened to him. Phil told me he could manage for a while without a job but he would have to get his business up and running soon. He had been saving for a long time in order to buy a shop and he would have to be careful with his money.

"So," said Phil, "do I take it that you are accepting me?"

I was guarded with my reply. "There is one thing we haven't discussed, Phil." I hesitated before saying, "It's about our religions."

"That shouldn't be a problem," he said. "I'm a Welsh Baptist and you're an Irish Catholic. We won't worship together but I see no difficulty in that."

To Phil it was just a matter of going to different chapels to worship but I worried that religion could lead to a gulf between us. My church decreed that all our children should be brought up in my faith. As far as I was concerned, our home would have to embrace the Catholic faith from the very start if it were to succeed. From the bottom of my heart I wished Phil was a Catholic. The Church might insist he convert to Catholicism. He wasn't aware of this.

Phil noticed I had become quiet. He said, "Penny for your thoughts!"

I smiled at him and asked, "Do you know what the Catholic religion says about marriage?" Although he was in France where most people are Catholic he had no idea what I was talking about. Nice was a cosmopolitan town catering for most races and most religions. It had Catholic churches, Anglican churches and even Russian orthodox, to name but a few. We were facing a problem which Phil didn't seem to understand. I did my best to explain to him the doctrines of my church. I told him the best thing was for him to convert to Catholicism so that our children could be brought up in my faith but I was surprised at his reply. He said he would never do that. He was adamant. I was astonished at his inflexibility as he rarely went to church whereas I went regularly.

So, we came to an impasse in our relationship. I couldn't see things going any further and I was desperately upset. I could see that Phil was too. But we were both stubborn people and believed in our own faiths.

Phil walked me back to my hotel that night and we were both very quiet. When we reached the hotel I turned to him and said, "Do you really love me, Phil?"

He replied, "Of course I do. I would not be asking you to share my life if I didn't."

"So will you give this problem some thought?" I asked.

He replied that he didn't think it was a stumbling block. As we said goodbye I realised things were not going to be easy for us. Phil kissed me gently on the cheek and said, "Let's both sleep on it and we'll talk again tomorrow."

I went to bed feeling uneasy. I had met the man of my dreams. I loved him deeply but I had never thought my faith would bring me such difficulties. I didn't sleep well that night.

# CHAPTER 52

The next day, before meeting Phil I went to see the local Priest. I told him my problems. He said no-one could stop me marrying Phil if I found a Priest prepared to officiate, although he stressed this might be difficult. He said, "The marriage will only be recognised by the church if all your children are brought up as Catholics." I explained to him that Philip had no intention of converting to Catholicism. He said it would be in the best interests of all if he did. He told me I should encourage Phil to do this. He was firm in his advice and I left him feeling very depressed.

I met Phil later and told him what had happened. He couldn't believe what I was telling him. He was angry at first. "Why is your religion more important than mine?" he asked. "Why do my children have to follow your faith? Surely there is some way we can compromise?" I told him that my religion didn't allow for compromise.

We were both devastated. Two stubborn people!

I couldn't believe things had come to this. My faith had meant so much to me all my life and now it appeared to be denying me the one thing I really wanted.

Phil and I agreed not to see each other for a few days. This would give us time to think about our predicament. We agreed to meet again in a week's time.

I returned to the hotel, feeling desperately unhappy. When I entered the foyer the concierge told me there was a message on the reception desk. I hurried across and was handed a note. It was from Nick. It was short and to the point:

*Dear Nurse Bridget,*
*Grandfather has taken a turn for the worse and I've been called to the hospital. Dr. Roget is with him. Please come over to the hospital.*
*Nick.*

I hurriedly stuffed the note in my coat pocket and rushed out. I was breathless when I arrived at the hospital. I went straight to Mr. Owen's ward.

As I entered the ward I noticed the curtains had been pulled round his bed. I hesitated before joining Nick at his grandfather's bedside. Nick was looking distraught. "Thank you for coming so quickly," he said. "I've been here for 2 or 3 hours now. Dr. Roget sent for me."

I looked at Mr. Owen and could see that he was very unwell. His breathing was laboured and he was very hot. Dr. Roget arrived and asked to speak with me outside. He told me he feared the worst. A sudden rise in temperature like this was alarming for someone already in a frail state. He didn't hold out much hope for Mr. Owen lasting the night. He asked me if I was prepared for this. I replied that I wasn't and in fact I had thought he was on the mend. Dr. Roget admitted he had thought that too, but he had seen cases like this before and the prognosis was not good. "You'll have to prepare young Nicholas for the worst," he said. "It'll be hard on him for he is obviously very fond of his grandfather. Do you think you can cope?" I told him not to worry and said I would do my best. He then departed as he had other patients to visit.

I went back to Mr. Owen's bedside and sat quietly with Nick. There wasn't much we could do. Occasionally, I was able to wipe the perspiration from Mr. Owen's forehead but I couldn't ease his condition. I made him comfortable in the bed but for once in my life I felt quite useless. Strangely, since I had started nursing I had never come across a death and I hoped I would cope. I also had the burden of telling Nick what Dr. Roget had told me.

Nick asked me what Dr. Roget had wanted. I decided I had to tell him the facts. There was no point in beating about the bush. He would have to know sooner or later. We went outside the ward and when he heard the news he was distraught. "Do you really think the doctor is right?" he said. I told him I had no reason to doubt him and told him he should prepare for the worst. I asked him if he had ever lost a relative before. He thought for a few minutes and replied, "No, not anyone as close as this. I remember when I was young, an aunt and then an uncle died. But that didn't mean much to me. I was too young to understand the real meaning of it." He was quiet for some time and I decided to leave him to his thoughts.

I returned to Mr. Owen who was sleeping fitfully. After a while, Nick returned and said, "Nurse Bridget, have you ever lost a loved one?"

I remembered the terrible time I had when my dear sister Kate died. I told him about this and how terrible it was not to be with the family in Ireland and not being able to mourn with them.

He said, "I suppose I should be grateful for small mercies. At least, if the old man does die, I'll be with him. But I wish the rest of the family were here with me."

We sat for some time without speaking and I left Nick to his thoughts. There was little I could do for Mr. Owen. From time to time one of the hospital nurses asked if we needed anything.

Mr. Owen died peacefully in his sleep that night.

Nick and I were both sitting with him. It was very calm and I don't think we even knew when it happened. He just didn't wake up. Nick was very upset. He had never witnessed anything like this before. I suggested he should go back to the hotel and try to get some sleep. There was nothing more we could do for the moment. "Will you take care of things here for me?" he asked.

I replied, "Of course, off you go now and get some sleep. You are going to need it for there will be much to do now. I'll come and see you in the morning."

The next day Nick said he hadn't slept much. He was very worried. He had been turning over in his mind all the things that needed to be done. He had to let the folks at home know the sad news and then he had to arrange the funeral. He asked me to help him.

I recalled what Mr. Owen had told me when we had first boarded our ship in New York. Somewhere I had the name and address of his solicitor. I found this and gave it to Nick who took it with him to a local solicitor recommended by the hotel.

Nick returned later that day and looked a much happier person. He had spoken with the solicitor who had been very helpful. Together they had wired the States with the news. They had contacted the family and Mr. Owen's solicitor. Replies were expected in a few days. In the meantime Nick and I visited a funeral director and made arrangements for the funeral.

That evening I decided to tell Nick what his grandfather had told me when we left New York. I said, "Nick, I must tell you that your grandfather was very ill when we set off on this trip. He told me he would be surprised if he lasted the journey. I think he has done wonderfully well to come this far. He died a happy man and he'd almost completed the trip of a lifetime. You should hold on to that thought. He was a contented man at the end." Nick was grateful to me for telling him this. It helped him come to terms with his loss which was so sudden and unexpected.

The next few days were very busy and I hadn't seen Phil for nearly a week. At the first opportunity I went along to see him and told him what had happened. He was most concerned. He asked me to convey his sympathy to Nick and offered to escort me to the funeral. I was pleased at this offer of support. I hadn't expected this. Phil didn't ask me if I had thought any more about his proposal. That would have to wait now.

The day after the funeral Phil and I met again. He was pleased to see me and said I looked much happier. I told him I was relieved that all had gone to plan and now I had time to consider the future. "Will you be including me in your plans?" he said hesitatingly.

I knew this subject would come up and I was prepared for his question. I told him I was now free to go home to Ireland to see my family and Nick was returning straight away to America. I looked at him and smiled as I said, "As you know, I went to see my Priest. We must have a talk about the future and decide how we are going to manage, as I want to spend the rest of my life with you! We'll have to compromise in some way. I can't imagine life without you now."

"Does that mean you are saying yes?" he said.

I replied, "Yes, I think it does. We'll find an arrangement to suit us both but I don't think it will suit my church!" Phil laughed and said he had never been happier.

In true style Phil wanted to go out and buy an engagement ring immediately. I told him we must decide about religion first. And so it was that we decided to compromise. We would both continue to worship at our own churches, but if we had children the boys would be baptised in his church and the girls would be Catholics like me. I knew the church would frown on this, but I didn't want to miss this one chance of happiness. It was the first time in my life I had questioned my religion. Compromise seemed to be the only way to be with the man I loved so much.

I had written to Maggie earlier and told her about my problems with Phil. The day after I had accepted Phil's proposal I received a letter from Maggie in New York. It was just like Maggie. She didn't like writing letters and it was short and to the point. She wrote:

*Do what your heart tells you. Life is too short to be bound by the things our parents and church have taught us. We've always lived according to the faith and have done nothing wrong. I married John because he was a Catholic and it was the worst thing I could have done. Go ahead and marry your Baptist and be*

*happy. As Mama always said, "Follow your heart". You have my blessing.*
  *With fondest love, Maggie.*

Dear Maggie, I knew she understood my quandary better than anyone. I soon replied to her with the good news that Phil and I had decided to marry.

# CHAPTER 53

Phil was still waiting to see if his firm would transfer him back to England. He anticipated a reply soon. We had to wait for this before we could make any further plans.

In the meantime, after the funeral, Nick tied up all his loose ends in Nice and decided not to continue his journey through Europe. He was trying to arrange his passage home. He had received a reply from his grandfather's solicitor and told me my services were no longer required, which of course I expected. He told me my fare would be paid to wherever I wanted to go and I would receive another month's salary to help me on my way. I was delighted with this and told him I wanted to go home to see my parents. I also told him about Phil and about our plans for the future. He was pleased for me and I think rather relieved that I had something to look forward to. He didn't feel he had let me down. I was another problem off his mind! All he had to do now was to arrange his journey home. The solicitor in New York would tie up all the unfinished business for him.

He wished me well and told me to enjoy myself until Phil and I could make arrangements to travel back home. So I had a wonderful time of leisure waiting until Phil and I could leave Nice together.

During the following days when I was on my own I spent many hours wandering the back streets of Nice and exploring the town. I loved the market and bought some more small presents to take home to my family. The weather was kind and I enjoyed this enforced holiday. I liked being on my own after the hectic days since leaving

New York when I always seemed to be at the beck and call of Mr. Owen. At last I felt I had some freedom.

Phil and I met most evenings and one day he came with the news we had been waiting for. His employers were arranging a transfer back to London for him so he would continue to work for them. He was entitled to a few days' holiday so we decided to travel back via Paris and have a few days there. Phil made all the necessary arrangements.

Phil loved to travel and see different places. When he first came to Nice he had, during his holidays, spent time in Switzerland at Lake Lucerne. He had also spent a few days in Italy. So, I was not surprised when he told me what our itinerary was to be. We were going to travel by train first to Lyon and spend a day there.

Then we were to go on to Paris by train and have two days there. The final leg of our journey was by train to Calais then boat to Dover and onward by train to London. I was looking forward to this journey.

I told Nick about our arrangements and he had news for me. He was leaving in two days' time. He had to take the train to Marseilles to catch his ship for New York. We were both pleased things had fallen into place so easily. I would be sorry to say goodbye to Nick. We had never had a cross word and I had become quite fond of him, in a motherly sort of way, although he was only a few years younger than me.

So, it was with some sadness that I waved Nick off when he left Nice. I wondered if I would ever see him again.

# CHAPTER 54

Things progressed rapidly after Nick left. In no time at all Phil and I were boarding the train for Lyon. I loved being in Phil's company. We had the same sense of humour and the same interests. We arrived in Lyon and spent the day looking round the town. In the evening we boarded the train for Paris.

I wanted to attend Mass at Notre Dame in Paris and asked Phil to come with me. I hoped he would but I was surprised at his reaction. He was quite cross. "We agreed to follow our religions independently," he said. I realised then how serious he was about this. This was the only thing to come between us. I knew I must not suggest this again. Deep inside me I had forebodings and I was secretly worried about the future. I still hoped that one day we might see eye to eye on this.

I bought a newspaper in Paris and it was full of the news of the trial of Harry Thaw in New York for the murder of Stanford White. Harry was described as a millionaire playboy. The sex triangle was described in great detail and was a shock to the American nation. The newspapers carried all the lurid details; things which Evelyn herself had never mentioned to me while I was nursing her. But now I understood why that poor young girl was so unwell and distraught. She had been forced to face so much unnatural behaviour.

My heart went out to poor Evelyn who was cross-questioned by the defence and prosecution lawyers. She had to divulge so much of this sordid story to the public. On the instructions of her lawyer she had dressed conservatively and the papers said that she didn't look a day over sixteen. She was questioned about her relationship with White. She told of his initial kindness and she described in detail her lunchtime visits and romps on a velvet swing. She said that White had forced her to sit on the swing naked and he had pushed her till her feet were above his head. Then, Evelyn spoke of her ruin.

She told the courtroom about the drugged champagne he'd given her and he'd made her wear a yellow kimono. She described her tears and screams in vivid detail. The courtroom was hushed, and some jurors displayed visible outrage.

The lawyer defending Harry Thaw emphasised that Evelyn had told Harry about White, in the same awful detail. Evelyn herself told the court of her husband's tears and sobs when she'd related her tale to him. Yet, despite her ruin, Thaw loved her enough to marry her. But he had shot White in a jealous rage. And now he was facing the court and jury.

The prosecution cross-examined Evelyn and did their best to highlight Evelyn's unsavoury past. Their questions implied that Evelyn knew very well what White's intentions were, even though he was married. She had gone along with it for "fame and fortune". They questioned whether the champagne had been drugged at all, as she had implied. She appeared scandalised by these suggestions.

She was asked, "Did you love Stanford White?"

She replied, "No."

Then they asked her, "Did you hate him?"

"Yes," was her reply.

She was pressed even harder with questions like, "Why, then, did you continue to meet Mr. White?" Evelyn tearfully claimed to have resisted his caresses, but said that she and her family depended on his support. She said that White had forcefully insisted on seeing her. The prosecution's attempt to portray Evelyn as a promiscuous liar backfired. Public sympathy remained with her as she pleaded for her husband.

The jury, surprisingly, returned without a verdict. They could not agree. Evelyn's testimony at her husband's trial helped save her husband from being found guilty of murder. The newspapers believed it was her greatest acting performance! I wondered what the final verdict would be.

I was to learn later that there was a second trial and Harry Thaw pleaded guilty to murder by temporary insanity. He was committed to a state hospital for the criminally insane. I often wondered what happened to Evelyn.

After our stay in Paris we continued on to London where I found a live-in job at a nursing home in Putney. Phil moved into lodgings nearby in Fulham. He had a few days off before returning to work but we were only able to meet in the evenings as I was working during the day. Living in tied me to my job and for the first time in my life I didn't want to be so involved.

One weekend Phil told me how anxious he was for us to get married. He had sensed that I wasn't very happy in London. He wanted us to marry and live together. I told him I desperately wanted to marry in a Catholic church. To my surprise Phil agreed to this. He said, "If I don't do this for you now you might never marry me." I was very relieved.

I wanted to pay a visit home to Ireland before we married and asked Phil to come with me. He wanted to but he wasn't able to have more time off. I was disappointed at this, as I wanted to introduce him to my parents and I wanted him to see my home. So I had to take this trip on my own.

I'd made a good friend at the nursing home, Miriam Murphy, who was Irish and a Catholic like me. I discussed with her the problems of marriage. She understood the difficulties and said she thought the church might insist that Phil converted to Catholicism. I was devastated when I heard this and decided I couldn't go home to Ireland until this had been sorted out. Miriam asked around her Irish friends to see if they had any ideas. I was delighted a few days later when she told me about a Catholic church nearby in Putney that might marry us without insisting that Phil convert to Catholicism. The church had only been built two years ago and the Priest was anxious to swell his congregation so he was willing to overlook Phil's religion. Phil and I lost no time in visiting the church and talking to the Priest. He agreed to marry us. We were delighted.

I decided to go home to Ireland to give the good news to Mama and Papa. I travelled on a Friday night so Phil joined me and as far as Bridgend in South Wales so he could spend the weekend with his parents. Like me, he wanted to tell his family the good news. He hoped they could come to London for the wedding but he was doubtful about this.

# CHAPTER 55

It was January 1907 when we left London from Paddington Station. A long journey lay ahead. Phil put our luggage on the rack above us and we settled down in our compartment. The train engine started up and the guard took up his position with his green flag and whistle. The carriage doors had all been closed and we leaned out of the window as the train drew away from the platform. Then we quickly shut the window as, in the confines of the station, the smoke was surrounding the train and entering the carriage. We settled down for the journey. I had a good book with me and intended to spend most of the time reading. But Phil had other ideas and as we sped through the countryside we talked about the past, the present and the future. Phil told me all about his childhood in the Welsh valleys. He told me about his brother, Tom, who was six years older than him, and his half-sister, Kate, who was younger than him. Phil's parents had adopted Kate when her parents died. She was a distant cousin but he had always thought of her as a sister. When Kate came to live with them his father had not been keen on the idea but his mother was very fond of the girl. I told Phil all about my childhood in Ireland and we realised that we both had good parents who had done all they could for us in difficult times. We respected our parents and were glad of the values they had instilled in us from an early age.

We sped on through the English countryside and in the dark winter evening couldn't see much. Phil knew all the stations along the line – Reading, Swindon, Didcot, and Bath. He told me that not long after Bath we would be going through the Severn Tunnel. The tunnel ran under the River Severn and linked England to Wales. It shortened the journey between the two countries. Before it was built the journey went north through Gloucester before heading for South Wales. We entered the tunnel and I was surprised at its length.

The train came out of the tunnel and into Wales. Phil said he always felt he was nearly home at this stage of the journey. He was very proud of his nationality in the same way that I was. He was a little upset that the darkness made it impossible for him to point out landmarks to me. It was not long before we approached Cardiff.

We changed trains in Cardiff. While waiting for our next train we went to the station buffet and had a welcome cup of tea. We weren't hungry but Phil persuaded me to have an iced bun. He said, "Come on, let me treat you. You've a long journey ahead and you'll be very hungry by morning." We sat and drank our tea and munched our buns.

We were soon winging our way westwards again. Phil left the train at Bridgend. His parents lived in a Welsh valley – the Ogmore valley, in a small place called Nantymoel. His father was fireman in the local coalmine. Phil joked with me and told me it was just as well I wasn't going with him as his parents only spoke Welsh. I couldn't believe that they didn't speak English and I wondered how I could converse with them when we did meet. Phil said, "Don't worry. I'll be your interpreter!"

We laughed when I replied, "That's a good idea and if I say anything you think might offend them you can change it. In that way I should never fall out with my new in-laws!"

As we neared Bridgend Phil prepared to leave the train. He surprised me when he said, "Have a good journey and make sure you come back again. Don't let them persuade you to stay at home and marry a good Irish Catholic! I'll expect you back in a week's time."

I laughed at this and replied, "Do you really think that of me? Sure, I'm not going to lose you now that I've found you!" We both laughed again and we kissed goodbye. Phil asked me to give his regards to Mama and Papa and to apologise for not accompanying me. We agreed to go to Ireland together in a year or two when we had settled into married life and when we could afford the two fares. So I waved goodbye to Phil and settled back in the train.

I was looking forward to the voyage across the Irish Sea. I had written to Papa and asked him to meet me at the station in Kilkenny.

Fishguard was at the end of the line and I awoke when the train jolted to a stop. Fishguard Harbour had only recently been built and the ferries had only just started using this harbour. A few years earlier the journey was much more circuitous from London to Liverpool then to Dublin and finally Kilkenny. I left the train and made my way to the night boat. I was so tired I slept for most of the journey and when I woke we were just coming into Rosslare harbour. It was early morning and I had to catch another train. I was now wide awake and even though it was winter I enjoyed the journey through the lovely Irish countryside to Kilkenny. It was wonderful to be back in my own country and I felt at home as the train made its way towards my destination. I began to feel nervous and I had butterflies in my tummy as the train drew nearer to Kilkenny. It was nine years since I had left Ireland.

Sure enough when I reached Kilkenny there was Papa on the platform patiently waiting for me. The train was nearly an hour late but I could see he was as excited as I was. He looked much older and frailer but there was no mistaking him with his long white beard. He looked much shorter than I remembered. He had on his best Sunday suit – just for the occasion! As we hugged one another I realised there were tears running down his face. "Oh, Bridgie, Bridgie," he said, "I never thought to see you again. And you look wonderful. It's so good to have you back."

Outside the station Papa had the donkey and cart waiting and when my case had been loaded he helped me up. Then he climbed aboard himself, took up the reins, said, "Giddy up!" and we moved away.

"Mama is at home waiting for us with Mary-Anne and Bab-Ann Cleary. They can't wait to see you. And Tom will be coming home sometime this week." I couldn't wait to be reunited with the rest of my family.

The journey home through the lanes of Ireland brought back many memories. The hedgerows were strangely bleak in winter but the hawthorn bushes didn't bloom until April or May so I was a little early for these. Those were the sights I remembered. Papa wanted to hear all my news. We didn't stop chatting all the way home. As we approached the house I saw Mama and Mary-Anne and little Bab-Ann coming out to meet us.

It was almost ten years since I had left home. Now, as we drew near, everything seemed much smaller than I remembered it. But the greeting I received was not small! We were all so happy to be together again. Mama came towards me with arms outstretched and we embraced each other with tears in our eyes. It was a joyous occasion. Mary-Anne and I embraced and then I turned and bent down to Bab-Ann. I put my arm around her and gave her a kiss. To me she looked like a little Kate and I loved her from the moment I saw her. She clung to Mama's hand and was quite shy.

We eventually made our way inside. I had forgotten how basic everything was. The house had become somewhat worn and dilapidated since I had left. It didn't look cared for but I knew Mama worked hard to keep things in order. The lack of money really showed and I was sad for Mama and Papa. But the love and kindness I had known as a child were still there and this gave warmth to the house. We were soon ensconced in the kitchen round the familiar table by the fireside with a mug of tea to warm us up.

I had forgotten that water came from the pump and that there was no electricity. This really was back to basics. Time had erased so much of my memory of home. When I was young I hadn't taken as much notice of my surroundings as I did now. My priorities had changed and I wondered if this was for the good.

Mama busied herself preparing our mid-day meal while Mary-Anne and I caught up with all our news. After lunch I decided to take a rest as I was tired after 18 hours travelling. Mama took me upstairs to her room. She had prepared a bed for me in her room, where she and Mary-Anne and Bab-Ann slept. It was bitterly cold. We sat together on the bed for a while, chattering away. She was anxious to know how Maggie was but I wasn't able to give her much news. I had to approach the subject carefully. I didn't know if they knew Maggie and John were living separate lives. It soon became apparent that Maggie had written and told them this. Mama was sad about Maggie's circumstances but she had more up-to-date news than I had. After a while she left me to rest.

I looked around at the room. The bare floorboards were clean and there was a rug at the side of my bed. I went over to the back window and looked out. There in the distance I saw on the hill our old oak tree. I wondered if the neighbouring children still climbed it as we did. I climbed into bed and slept soundly for two hours. When I woke I felt refreshed and I re-joined the family downstairs.

It was late afternoon and getting dark. Mama greeted me and said, "Bridgie, we have a surprise for you this evening. We have invited all the friends and relatives in for a party. They are all anxious to see you."

There was nothing I wanted less than this as I was so tired. I tried hard not to show my feelings and said, "That will be grand."

We sat down again in the kitchen and Mama was making another cup of tea for me. Suddenly, Papa burst in through the back door followed by the wind which I remembered so well. He struggled to shut the door against the wind and came over and joined us. "Have you told Bridgie about tonight?" he asked. Mama said she had.

I was about to tell them about Phil when Papa burst out with, "Bridgie, there is someone coming tonight who I want you to meet. He has taken over the Ryan's farm. As you know it's a large farm so he must have plenty of money. His name is William Huggins and I think he is looking for a wife!" I was astounded at this and looked across at Mary-Anne who realised this was a bolt from the blue. She winked at me and I think she understood my astonishment. Papa continued, "If he takes a shine to you, Bridgie, he might ask you to marry him and you could settle back here in Ireland."

I was stunned by Papa's remarks. I gulped before replying, "I don't think I could marry him without knowing a lot more about him."

"Well now," said Papa. "He has plenty of money. For sure he has that big farm. I know you and he will get on like a house on fire."

I decided it was now or never so I said, "Actually, I've got something to tell you all. Mama, come and join us at the table." Mama looked surprised but wiped her hands on her apron and did as I asked.

Then I began. I told them I had met Phil in Nice and we had become very good friends and he had asked me to marry him. I had my engagement ring in a small box in my pocket and I took it out to show them. "Here," I said. "Look at this. This is the engagement ring Phil bought for me."

Mary-Anne peered across the table and said, "Well, now. Look at that. It's lovely, Bridgie. For sure, he must love you a lot to buy you such an expensive ring. Is it a real diamond?"

I said it was and looked at Mama and Papa. They both sat quietly and said nothing.

Then Mama said, "Will we be meeting Philip soon?" I explained that we couldn't afford the fares for two of us to come to Ireland and it would take us a year or two to save up enough money for this. She said, "Surely you're not going to marry him before we meet him?"

I said, "Mama, I love him so much. I know you will love him when you meet him. He is a wonderful person. I wish you could come to London for the wedding. Just think, if I had stayed in America and married there you would never have met my new husband."

Papa was very quiet and then asked, "When do you propose to get married?" I told him we were to marry soon after I returned to London.

As far as Papa was concerned I really had put the cat among the pigeons! He had been quite sure I would fall into the arms of this William Huggins and marry him and stay in Ireland. I knew he was upset.

I hadn't told them about our religious problem. I decided they had enough news for one day and resolved to tackle this later. But this was not to be. Papa lost no time in asking me, "Is Phil a good Catholic, Bridgie?" I had to tell him the truth and when I did you would have thought he had been struck by lightning. "But, Bridgie, you can't marry outside the faith. It's against all you have ever learnt. It's not possible. If you have any children what will you teach them?" There was a bewildered silence in the kitchen.

Mama, as always, was the one to pour oil on troubled water. She turned to Papa, saying, "Richard, we must realise that Bridgie is a grown woman now and she has been travelling the world. We shouldn't be surprised that she's met a man who is not a Catholic. She must have met plenty of men since she has been away from home. Here in Ireland most of us are Catholics. But it is not like that in the wider world." Papa was still uneasy with the situation and didn't reply. Mary-Anne excused herself and said she was going to get ready for the evening. I decided to join her. We went upstairs together.

When the bedroom door was shut Mary-Anne, still only 17 years old, came over to me and gave me a big hug. "Bridget, I'm so pleased for you. I hope you and Phil will be very happy. Don't be upset about Papa's reaction. He can't help it. He doesn't know anything about life in the big wide world."

I replied, "I know. I know. You are a good girl, Mary-Anne. You have had to put up with him on your own since we all left home. How on earth have you managed?"

It was then that Mary-Anne told me that she, too, planned to go to America. She had written to Maggie and intended to go towards the end of the year. But I was sworn to secrecy as Mama and Papa didn't know about this. She said, "I'll have to wait a while to tell them. They will have to get over today's shock first." We both laughed. But I was troubled. I dreaded the evening that was to come. I had to meet this William Huggins. I was sure Papa had almost promised me to him.

We changed our clothes and went downstairs to meet our guests. It wasn't long before they arrived. There were many familiar faces. It was wonderful to be amongst them all again. Then William Huggins arrived. I had deliberately worn my engagement ring for the evening. If he had any sense at all he might notice this!

To my surprise William Huggins was about twice my age. His hair had started to go grey and I think he was even losing hair on top! I wondered whatever Papa was thinking about. There was no way I could marry an old man like him. I expressed my thoughts to Mama. She understood and was not surprised by my reaction. She told me she had warned Papa before I came home that he shouldn't be making plans for me. She took me on one side and said, "Bridget, I am so happy for you. Now that you have travelled so much, I don't think it is right for you to settle back in Ireland. It would be difficult for you to find happiness here after all your travels." I kissed her. Mama always seemed to understand me. I was so glad of her support.

During the evening I got to know little Bab-Ann who was a real treasure. She was very fond of Mama and spent most of her time here with her grandparents. Soon, her father John Cleary and his other two children turned up. John had now moved back to his parents' house with son John and daughter Margaret. John told me that when Kate had died they had all come home and stayed with Mama and Papa. Then he was transferred to the Garda station in Callan which was just over the border in Kilkenny. They had moved back with his parents so he didn't have so much travelling to do. He was sorry to leave Islands. He said that little Bab-Ann had refused to go with him. From time to time he took her back to see her other grandparents but she still preferred to be with Mama and Papa. I knew Mama loved having her about the house and John agreed that it was probably for the best. We both agreed she was like another little Kate.

Imagine my surprise when Danny Murphy turned up that night. He brought with him his wife Joanna and their two young children. The children were put to bed upstairs and I sat with Danny and Joanna and reminisced over old times. Danny was very happy in his marriage and I was glad for him. I told him about Phil and he was pleased for me. Joanna was very quick to invite me to their house for tea on Monday and I gladly accepted. I looked forward to talking to them in their own surroundings.

As the evening drew on I felt like an outsider and realised I had grown away from my roots. I was saddened by this but knew that my future lay elsewhere.

The party took its usual course. Neighbours and relatives were coming and going and music and dancing kept everyone amused. Mama had laid on food for all and the drinks flowed too. I was surprised Papa had provided so much but he was obviously proud of me and glad to have me home. I think he hoped to persuade me to stay. He also wanted to impress William Huggins!

Halfway through the evening my younger brother Tom turned up. Both he and I were well dressed and looked quite out of place among the others. I was surprised at how shabby everyone seemed. The lack of money was evident but this didn't stop them having a good time. We were enjoying ourselves in the good old Irish way.

Tom and I had a long conversation and he told me about his teaching post. He was doing well and was thinking of applying for a position in a bigger school. I wished him luck. Then our conversation turned to my travels. Tom said he had followed details of my travels through Italy and finally France with interest. He asked me what I was going to do now I was back in England so I told him all about Phil. He was sorry to hear of Papa's reaction to my news but he wished me luck, saying, "You deserve to settle down now, Bridgie, and have a happy life. You have worked hard to get where you are and you should remember Mama's old saying, 'Follow your heart'!"

After the first night at home, I began to wonder how I was going to spend my time with a whole week in the country and nothing to do. It was so strange to be back in such a quiet location; I didn't know how I was going to fill my days. But I need not have worried. As promised I visited Danny and Joanna and spent a lovely time with them and their young children. They had settled down in Danny's mother's little cottage. Danny was now in charge of the blacksmith shop. They were very happy and although I envied them a little I was looking forward to going back to London to marry Phil. I would not have had it any other way.

As the week drew on I realised what a sheltered existence we had lived as children. I relaxed in the quiet of the countryside but missed the hustle and bustle of the wider world. I was also missing Phil. In the evenings we all gathered round the fire in the kitchen. It was then that I realised how much I had grown away from my family. I told them many tales of life in New York and they listened with rapt attention. I also gave them as much news as I could of the boys and Maggie. Once we had exhausted family news there was little else to talk about. I was glad when bedtime came.

Nothing more had been said about William Huggins but Papa had been very quiet. I missed the conversations we used to have. I didn't like to see him so morose. I so much wanted him to agree to our marriage and decided to talk to him again.

The next morning I came downstairs for breakfast with some photos I had brought from London with me. There was a very nice studio photo of Phil.

When we had finished breakfast I brought the photos out onto the table. Mama and Mary-Anne were very interested. Mama said, "He's a handsome young man, isn't he?" I smiled and nodded in agreement.

Papa on the other hand didn't look at the photos and started to get ready to go out on the farm. Mama had other ideas and called him back to the table. "Look at these, Richard. Bridget's brought some photos to show us." So Papa painstakingly searched for his glasses and came over to the table.

He looked at the photos and I could see he approved of Phil. "Well," he said, "we haven't met him, but I must admit he looks to be a very pleasant young man. I think you have made a good choice, Bridget. When I come in this evening we will discuss this matter further," and he turned away and made his way to the back door.

As he went out Mama called out, "Have a good day, Richard."

When he was gone Mama, Mary-Anne and I all sat down round the table. I heaved a sigh of relief. I thought I could see a chink in Papa's armour. Mama laughed and said, "Don't you be worrying yourself now, Bridget. I know your father well. He wants more than anything for you to be happy and I know he can see that you love Philip very much."

That evening Papa brought the subject up again and asked me where we were going to live when we were married. "Do you think you will come home to live in Ireland?"

I told him I thought we might settle in Wales. I told him Phil wanted to buy his own pharmacy and run his own business. Papa thought this was a good idea and said, "I wish I'd been my own master instead of working for someone else. I was lucky to hold the post of schoolmaster here for such a long time. My masters, the Education Board, were in Dublin and the only time they troubled me was when the wretched Inspectors arrived and we all know what happened then. I'm glad I'm retired now and can do what I like. Yes, Bridget, encourage Philip to go out on his own. It will be good for you both."

I was pleased that at last Papa seemed to be accepting my situation. I decided to bring up the subject of religion again. "Papa, you mustn't worry about the religious matter. I realise there is a problem but I'll handle this as best I can. I want our children to be brought up in our faith but Philip must have some say in the matter. He is a Baptist, as I told you. You should be pleased he is a churchgoer and a believer even though in a different faith. That is important to both of us."

Papa replied, "Bridget, you must do what you think is best. Whatever happens you will have our blessing." I was relieved that at last Papa could see things my way and I got up and rushed over to him, throwing my arms round his neck and thanked him for being so understanding. At last I had overcome this hurdle and I could now look forward to the future.

On my fourth day at home a letter arrived for me from Phil. I opened it carefully and read the contents. He told me that a chemist shop had come up for sale in a small town in South Wales. He was going to visit it on Saturday. The owner was keen to sell the business quickly due to ill health. Phil wanted to view the property with me if it was possible on my way home from Ireland. I was taking the night boat on Friday and would be in Cardiff by midday on Saturday. As there wasn't time for me to get a reply to him he suggested we meet at Cardiff station at 2 o'clock. If I didn't arrive in time he would view the property on his own. But he stressed that he preferred us to see it together. I was excited by this news.

I hoped that my boat and train were on time so I could meet Phil in Cardiff. I was pleased that he wanted to include me in the decision-making process. I wondered where the small town was. It must be near Cardiff if we were to see it on Saturday afternoon.

I spent the last days in Ireland walking about the neighbourhood, saying goodbye to old friends and relations. I visited Danny and his family again and told them our plans and they were delighted for us. It was so good to have someone who agreed I was doing the right thing.

On my last day at home the sun was shining brightly. It was a crisp winter day. I decided to visit the old churchyard in Modeshill to see where my dear sister Kate had been buried. Mama came with me. As we walked along the frost frozen muddy roads we talked about the past, present and future. Mama told me that Papa had been very pleased he had been able to afford a proper stone for the grave. I asked Mama why Papa hadn't come with us. She replied, "Well, Bridget, it always brings tears to his eyes to visit the grave. It's better for him to stay at home. He'll find plenty to keep him busy around the farm."

I was surprised how fit Mama was. She was a good walker. I realised that city life had slowed me down. I was able to keep up with her but was amazed at her swift pace. It was nearly three miles to Modeshill and we had plenty to talk about. Mama told me she often worried about Papa and wondered how much longer he could keep the farm going. There were difficult days ahead for them.

We walked down the short hill towards the old church and turned left into the track leading to the graveyard. We let ourselves in through the strong iron gates and Mama led the way up the bank towards the resting place of our family. I was amazed to see that Papa had really gone to town and had provided iron railings around the grave and a large marble headstone with details of my grandparents and my sister. I was glad to see the grave was well tended and it was obvious someone visited it often to maintain it. Mama and I knelt together at the grave and Mama took out her rosary and started reciting her prayers. I bowed my head in silence, listening to Mama and joining her in prayer. I opened my eyes and looked into the distance where I could see Mount Slievenamon. The view was splendid. This was an isolated part of the country with no houses around and only a ruined medieval church. I thought what an ideal spot this was for Kate's last resting place. Tears started to fall down my face as I remembered the good times Kate and I had enjoyed as children. Life had been perfect then.

After a while we returned home. As we walked I asked Mama how Papa had afforded such a lovely headstone and railings. She replied,

"We are not well off, Bridget, but we have always had money put aside for a rainy day. Papa now has a pension of £30 a year from the Education Authorities and we manage on this together with the money you and the others occasionally send us. God has been good to us. We have no complaints." I admired my parents' stoicism.

The time soon came for me to leave Ireland. Mama, Papa and Mary-Anne came with me to the station and we stood on the platform and said our tearful farewells. I'd already wished Mary-Anne all the best for her future in America and Mama and Papa still didn't know of her intentions. Mary-Anne and I had spent several hours talking together about America and I knew she was doing the right thing. There was nothing for her here in Ireland.

So it was with sadness that I boarded my train and as it pulled out of the station I wiped away a tear. I knew the Ireland I was leaving held nothing for me now.

I was glad to be on my way home!

# CHAPTER 56

I arrived in Cardiff in good time to meet Phil. He lost no time in telling me where we were going. We set off on another short train trip to a town called Barry. The chemist shop we were to see was in the village of Cadoxton, near Barry. We were excited at the prospect of viewing what might become our first enterprise and home together.

When we arrived we were surprised to find the shop was more run down than we had expected. The owner, Mr. Jones, had been ill for several years and had lost interest in it. We inspected the shop and the living accommodation upstairs. Phil spent some time looking at the stock in the shop.

When we were alone Phil told me that he had made enquiries and there was no other chemist in the locality so no competition. Mr. Jones was keen to get rid of the business quickly. We were delighted as it seemed to be just the sort of business we could build up from scratch. There was a possibility we could get it at a knockdown price.

I took particular interest in the flat above the shop. There was a small kitchen, a living room, two bedrooms, a small box room and no bathroom. I tried to imagine it empty without Mr. Jones' old furnishings. The whole place needed a lick of paint. With a little bit of attention it was an ideal first home for us. I had visions of pretty curtains at the windows and rugs on the floors. I didn't know how much money we had for furniture but this didn't worry me. If the worst came to the worst we could always buy second hand. I was pleased with all I saw and made my way downstairs. Phil was concluding his discussions with Mr. Jones and I could tell they had reached an amicable agreement.

We said goodbye to Mr. Jones, walked to a nearby park, and sat on a bench to discuss what we had seen. Phil was delighted. He had agreed a price that took into account the fact that the business was neglected. There was little or no goodwill left to purchase and it was a case of building the business up from scratch. It was just the opening Phil had been hoping for and he had saved enough money to pay for it. He had only had a cursory look around upstairs and asked me what I thought. I told him it needed a new coat of paint. Then I tentatively asked if we had enough money left over for furniture.

There was a pause and he said, "I was hoping, Bridget, you might have a few pounds put by to help out with this."

"Of course I can help, but I only have enough to buy second hand."

"That's fine," he agreed. "But as soon as we start to make a profit we will buy some nice new items."

We were both so happy with the outcome of the day that we started to laugh and fell into each other's arms in joy.

We made our way back to the station and thence to London. On our way home Phil impressed on me how difficult things might be in the first few months or even for a year or so. He would have to work hard to build the business up but he was determined to succeed.

I told Phil about my trip home and about William Huggins, the old farmer. We had many a laugh about this and he said, "I'm glad you chose me, Bridget!"

To which I replied, "So am I!"

I told Phil my parents had aged a lot since I had left home when I was only 18 and I wondered if I had seen them for the last time. Phil said that as soon as we were on our feet we would save up for a visit to Ireland together.

Then he told me about his parents. "My mother is an angel," he said. "But my father is a bit of a brute. He's only interested in himself and he treats my mother like a housekeeper. I wish there was something I could do about it. Maybe when we are living nearer we can have my mother to stay for a short holiday. I know you will love her, Bridget."

We didn't take long to arrange our wedding. The wedding date was set for March 28th 1907. My good friend Miriam Murphy from the nursing home who had pointed us in the direction of the church in Putney agreed to be a sponsor together with her husband Frank. Miriam and Frank were a lovely couple and I was glad that Phil warmed to them quickly. In the few weeks before the wedding Frank was a great help to Phil and told him all about the customs of the Catholic Church and what he was expected to do at the ceremony. Before the wedding I had a meeting with the Priest who asked me to promise to do all in my power to have our children baptised and raised in the Catholic faith. I agreed to do all I could to achieve this but I knew I was unlikely to succeed. I didn't tell him about the arrangement I had with Phil.

March soon arrived and we were walking up the aisle as man and wife. It was a quiet occasion. None of our parents were able to be there. Only Miriam and Frank were with us.

After the wedding I moved into Phil's flat in Fulham. I still worked at the nursing home. Whenever we weren't working we took time to see the sights of London. One day we went up to Westminster to see the Abbey and the Houses of Parliament. The suffragette movement had taken hold and the lengths these women went to amazed me. There was a demonstration taking place as we walked by. The most important objective in their lives was to obtain the vote for women. I admired them for their courage but I was not likely to join their ranks.

# CHAPTER 57

I decided to work until we moved down to South Wales. Many women gave up work as soon as they were married and concentrated their efforts on the family and the home but my income was important to us especially in the days ahead. We only had a small flat and I could tidy and clean it in an hour and would have nothing to do for the rest of the day if I was at home all day.

Less than two months after our wedding I received the devastating news from Ireland that dear Mama had died. I was heartbroken and couldn't believe the news. I cried more about Mama's passing than I did about my sister Kate's death. Life was so cruel. It seemed that just as I was finding happiness in my life something happened to spoil things.

My grief was intense and Phil didn't know how to console me. Poor Phil, he did his best but he had to go to work every day and he didn't like leaving me alone. I had taken a few days off work when the news reached me but I was soon back at work. Keeping busy took my mind off my troubles. Before I returned to work I wrote a long letter to my brother Tom. I told him how saddened I was that I couldn't be at home to grieve with the family. I told him I was depressed and feeling low. It was difficult to convey my true feelings but I explained to him I felt a traitor not to be at home at these difficult times. I ended the letter with the words, *'Please write to me Tom and tell me everything. Did Mama suffer much? How is Papa taking things? Please, please write soon.'* When Phil came home from work that evening he decided to send a letter of condolence to Papa. I was glad of this and the following day I posted our letters.

Returning to work was the best thing I could have done. Phil noticed a change in me immediately. He said, "Bridget, I'm so glad you are back at work. It gives you something to focus on."

Two weeks later I received a long reply from my brother Tom. It arrived on a Saturday. Phil was at work and after breakfast I sat down and read it:

*Sunday evening.*

*My dear sister,*

*Now you are awful to be taking things so to heart. Indeed I'm sure our poor mother would not be happy were she to know the state you are in. You must remember that God's justice does not end in this world. 'Tis a trouble in store for everyone to lose their mother. "Not our will but God's be done." The happy death poor Mother had should be a source of consolation to you. If ever there is a saint in heaven 'tis Mother. Now we are not as badly off as you imagine. Poor Baby Ann is as good as fair. And Father is now well again.*

*The first few days were the worst. You should see poor Baby Ann, how kind she is to Father. We have Ellen Snell and she does all the work with Bill Tobin. I go home every night and Aunt Mary remains about. Now don't knock yourself about. I have written to America. Poor Dick. Only that morning a letter came from him to his dear mother. Well, Bridgie, Phil's letter was a true source of consolation. Thank him from me.*

*Our poor mother never enjoyed better health than she did during the past few months. And delighted me by looking so good. I was home as usual on Saturday night and remained with her playing the violin and singing until 11 o' clock. We spoke of you in particular. Poor woman how she loved us all. In the morning (Sunday) she called me at 7 to go to Callan. She intended to go to Mass that day. But the rain prevented her. When cooking the dinner she took a pain in her left side and was taken to bed. Tom Docherty went immediately for the Priest and Doctor Delaney. During Sunday night she suffered much from rupture of the bowels. The Dr. did all he could to relieve her and succeeded. On Monday she was quiet and unaltered in manner and remained praying with Fr. Lanigan. Kate Corcoran and all the friends were with her. And poor Mrs. Docherty never went to bed for 4 nights. In the evening she slept but she knew perfectly well her end was drawing on. She called you three times and I believe her last words were "God bless Bridgie."*

*She passed away with a smile, so easy that "we thought her dying when she slept and sleeping when she died."*

*Yes, Bridgie, you are right. Her life was a short and sad one but she looked forward with contentment to the brightness of that light which shines on the Father at the dark time of our death. So happy did she appear that if one solemn wish uttered over her could bring her back to this wicked world again, I would be the last to utter it.*

*At the wake everybody for miles around turned up and Kate Corcoran and Mrs Bryan etc. saw everything alright. Her funeral was splendid. Father left everything in my hands – you know what that means. I shall post you one of the local papers during the week so you can see for yourself who attended. 74 cars conveyed her, and the old church in Modeshill received within its quiet shade all that was mortal of the poor woman. I know 'tis hard on you to hear the impulses of nature but remember that too much fretting serves no useful end. I am sure a few prayers such as you would utter would a thousand times be better.*

*I will be sorry to get such a letter from you again. Everything belonging to poor Mother is yours and will remain locked away by Baby Ann until you come home to dispose of them, as you will. Dick's little bird she cared for to the end and while the noble heart of poor Mother lay still during the wake the flutter of the little bird in its cage drew many a tear from the kind neighbours' eyes.*

*We had two Masses the morning of the funeral and the priests remained and offered a lengthened service by the grave. Scarcely one from the surrounding parishes was missing from that grave which received into its bosom one of the best mothers an Irish boy can want. Wreaths have been forwarded to me from "the past Students of De La Salle Literary Society", from "Callan Dramatic Club", "Kilkenny Teachers' Association" and I had one to place on the grave from her loving children.*

*Goodbye now darling for a few days. Don't you or Phil fret. We shall meet again one day in the far! far! Better land where the trials and tribulations of this*

*little earthy world will haunt us no longer.*
  *From your fond brother, Tom.*


The letter brought tears to my eyes and at the same time it brought consolation. Dear Tom, he had done all he could to acquaint me with the happenings of the sad event and I felt from his letter that I had joined in the wake and the mourning. It gave me great comfort and the mention of his letter to America reminded me how much worse it must be for poor Maggie, Dick, Tom and Pat. I remembered how bad things had been for me when my sister Kate had died. They must be feeling like that now. It wasn't so bad for me. After all I was within travelling distance of Ireland and hopefully I could soon make another visit.

When Phil came home that evening I had his supper prepared. After supper we sat down by our fireside and I showed him Tom's letter. I think it touched him as it had done me and he was glad he had written to Papa.

Spring soon came and we enjoyed London. We walked in the parks and visited the museums. Life couldn't have been better. But there had been a hitch in the sale of the shop in Barry. The owner had fallen ill again and hadn't visited his solicitor to tie up the loose ends. We wondered if the shop would ever be ours. We spent many hours talking about it and planning our future. Phil said I could help him in the shop. He envisaged setting up a first aid centre where I could treat minor cuts and bruises. I was excited about the changes to come in our life.

Then in July I began to feel unwell. Before going to work in the mornings I felt dreadful and was sick on several occasions. Phil was very concerned and ordered me to the doctor. Imagine our surprise when we heard the news that I was expecting our first child. We were overjoyed. I wrote home and told Papa the good news. He was to be a grandfather again! Phil did the same and told his parents the good news. It would be their first grandchild.

# CHAPTER 58

I had to take things easy after my visit to the doctor. I continued working but for less hours. It was summer and when the sickness went I felt really well and was able to work for longer periods of time. Our baby wasn't due until the following February.

The shop had still not materialised but we were managing to save from our wages and put away money each week. Phil was pleased about this but not so happy about the delay. One weekend he decided to go down to Barry and sort things out. I didn't go with him and spent a restful weekend at home. Phil also took the opportunity to visit his parents.

While he was away I had a relaxing time. Miriam and Frank came round and spent Saturday evening with me. I was glad of their company. They were planning to return to Ireland. They had saved enough money to buy a small house and looked forward to the future. They hoped to be quite near to Islands and agreed to call on Papa when they had settled.

When Phil returned he told me his news. Mr. Jones had suffered another stroke and had lost movement in his limbs. Also, his sight had become impaired and it wasn't certain when he could sign the documents. Phil had viewed the shop and flat again and decided to renegotiate the price in view of the deterioration. He suggested that for every month the sale dragged on there should be a further reduction in price. This might have the effect of speeding up the sale.

Phil laughed when he told me this, saying, "If we hang on long enough, Bridget, we might get it for nothing." I was amazed at this but then realised he was joking. The price was realistic, bearing in mind the state of the premises.

I asked, "When do you think we will be able to move in, Phil?"

He replied that it could be November or December if we were lucky.

Time dragged on and we still heard nothing about the completion of the sale. When Christmas came I gave up work as I was nearing my time and the baby was due soon. We spent Christmas with Frank and Miriam who told us they were leaving London in March.

We had a quiet New Year. Phil gave his notice in at work. One day when Phil was still at work I was out shopping and was drawn to another newspaper headline in a shop: *"Second Trial for murderer Harry Thaw begins..."* I bought this and followed details of this second trial over the next few weeks. Eventually Harry Thaw, Evelyn's husband, was found not guilty by reason of insanity and was committed to a mental institution for life. I wondered how Evelyn was coping with this ordeal. I would probably never hear of her again.

In early February Phil went down to Wales to complete the purchase of our first home and business. It really couldn't have come at a worse time, as I was due to give birth at any time. After collecting the keys Phil had decided to stay down in Wales, living in the flat above the shop. He said he expected to return in time for the birth of our baby. But, I went into labour the day after he left and I was unable to contact him. The only means of communication was by telegram or letter. A letter wouldn't reach him in time and I didn't think we could afford the expense of a telegram. My pains started on the 11th February late at night. Luckily I had an easy labour. Our first son David was born the next morning – the 12th Feb 1908. I was lucky that the birth had been so easy.

I was sad that Phil hadn't been at home for the birth but he was due back in a few days' time. When David was just three days old I was at home resting and there was a knock on the door. It was the Priest from Putney. Miriam had told him why I wasn't at Mass and this was a courtesy call to see if I needed anything. I invited him in and he went straight to David's crib and said, "What a lovely baby!" When are you having him christened?" I was taken aback and hadn't expected this. I couldn't tell him about my agreement with Phil.

I hesitated before I replied and said, "We're moving down to South Wales in a few days and as my husband is not here I think it's a good idea to wait until he comes back. He might want to have him christened in Wales."

He was adamant that I should bring David to his church at the first opportunity and he would perform the christening immediately. He would not take "No" for an answer and stressed the importance of acting quickly. He went into a long rant about how easy it was for young ones to pick up diseases. He said how terrible it would be if the poor wee thing passed away and hadn't been accepted into the church. I knew from my experience at home in Ireland that babies were always taken to the church the day after their birth so I was not surprised. I was very worried about breaking my promise to Phil. The Priest left after alarming me and I was disturbed for the rest of the day. In the evening Miriam called round to see if there was anything she could do to help and I told her about my worries. She was a Catholic and unfortunately for me she agreed with the Priest. I was at very low ebb. I hardly slept that night and was torn between my faith and my husband. But, Miriam came the next morning to escort me to church. I plucked up courage and refused to go. I could not renege on my promise to Phil.

Phil returned a week later and could not wait to see baby David. I had posted a letter to him so he wasn't surprised that I had given birth early. He was delighted with David and said he couldn't wait to see us settled in our new home. I had everything packed ready for the move. Fortunately, we didn't have any furniture to move, just our personal possessions. Frank and Miriam saw us off at Paddington

Station and it was with sadness that we waved them goodbye. But we promised to keep in touch, at the same time wishing them luck with their future move.

# CHAPTER 59

We arrived in Barry late at night. Baby David had slept for most of the journey and had been no trouble. "You're a perfect mother, Bridget," said Phil. "I don't know how you manage."

I replied, "Don't forget. Phil, I'm one of eight children. I helped a lot with the young ones in the family. At the hospital in Yonkers I spent some time on the children's ward. I've been used to young children and babies all my life."

We took a cab from the station to our new home in Cadoxton village, just outside the town of Barry. Phil unlocked the front door and took us inside. He showed me the improvements he had made in the last two weeks. The whole of the shop area downstairs had been re-painted and had new shelves and a new counter. I asked Phil how he had managed to get all this done so quickly. "It was easy to find a painter who didn't charge too much for the job. The shelves were put up by a local carpenter," he said.

I asked, "Where did this lovely counter come from?"

"Well," said Phil, "there was an auction in town last week. The counter was a bargain because no one else was bidding for it. I bought some other furniture for us, too. Come upstairs and have a look."

We went upstairs to our rooms above the shop. Phil led me into the sitting room. It was warm and cosy with a sofa and two easy chairs. "It's wonderful," I exclaimed. "This is our first real home together. Phil, you've done wonders in such a short time."

Phil smiled and replied, "All it needs now is a rug on the floor and some curtains at the window. We'll buy a rug next week. Do you think you can make the curtains?"

I wasn't sure about this and replied, "Sewing is not my forte but I'll try."

Phil said, "Well, you can't be good at everything. You have the baby to care for; perhaps we can find a seamstress who will help. After all, I had help with the painting. We'll ask around. I'm sure we'll find someone."

Phil took me to the bedroom and showed me the large double bed he had bought at the auction. He had even purchased the bed linen from a local shop and had made the bed up. A small cot stood in the corner for David. I was very impressed at his efforts and knew from that moment that we had a good life ahead of us. Phil showed me the other rooms which were empty and he remarked, "Plenty of room for expansion." We both laughed.

I put David to bed while Phil made a cup of tea. We'd eaten sandwiches on the train and weren't hungry so decided to have an early night. We made our way to bed for the first night in our first real home.

# CHAPTER 60

Life in Cadoxton was strange at first. When I woke that first morning the sun was streaming in through our bedroom window. It was so quiet after the hustle and bustle of London. It was early but I was eager to get up and explore our new surroundings.

We had a hearty breakfast to make up for our lack of food the previous day and then went downstairs to the shop. Phil told me all his plans. He was waiting for his first delivery of drugs, pills and potions so he could start in business. But he didn't expect these to arrive for a few days so we decided to take time to explore the surrounding area.

Our first walk took us down Vere Street. This road was a fairly long slope that led down to the bottom end of the village. Our shop was in Church Road at the top of Vere Street. In Vere Street there were houses and shop fronts. There was a butcher, a dairy, a grocer and a cobbler. But most important of all there was no chemist or pharmacist in Cadoxton so no competition for us.

As usual Phil was an encyclopaedia of knowledge. He told me that our village was named after St. Cadoc, a Welsh saint.

Phil stopped and spoke with one or two people and told them about his plans. They complained that the nearest chemist was in Barry and they had to go into town for their medicines and prescriptions. Phil lost no time in telling them we hoped to be open in a week and he was looking forward to helping them. We seemed to be well received and we returned home feeling very satisfied.

Three days later, the supplies arrived. While David slept in the afternoon I helped Phil in the shop. We displayed all the items on the shelves and some were locked away for safekeeping.

Phil and I sat in the chairs we had provided for the customers and started talking. He reminded me that I could help some customers in ways that he couldn't. He went on to explain, "Bridget, there will be many people who will come in for bandages, plasters and similar items when they have had a small accident." He continued, "As a trained nurse you'll be able to help them. It won't be long before the whole neighbourhood will look on this as a pharmacy and also a clinic." I was delighted and realised my help in our new venture was going to prove invaluable.

Phil asked me if I thought we needed a licence but I told him I was a fully qualified nurse so no one could question my competence. I said, "In any event, Phil, if anyone comes in with a problem I am unable to solve I'll send them straight to hospital or to a doctor." Phil was satisfied with this reply. We were both excited with this new plan.

The following week we opened the shop. Business was slow at first but in the coming weeks word soon spread and our life became busy. We enjoyed helping people and time passed quickly. Phil was often asked for advice on medical conditions and reluctantly had to refer people to the doctor. He advised people when he could, but he didn't take risks with problems outside his sphere of experience or knowledge. I was kept quite busy bandaging bad cuts, applying lotions to bruises and treating burns. Together we became well known and respected in the neighbourhood.

Our whole life revolved around the shop. We had bought a pram for baby David and I took him out for walks every day, come rain or shine. He was soon sitting up and starting to talk. I remember his first word – "Mama" said hesitantly but once he started talking he moved forward quickly.

In the late afternoons I prepared our evening meal. David sat in his high chair playing with his spoon and teething ring but as soon as he heard Phil locking up the shop and coming upstairs he always got very excited. He loved his father. Then one day as Phil came through the door David threw up his arms and welcomed him with the word "Dada". Phil was delighted. He thought the world of his son.

When we had been settled for about six weeks, I told Phil I was anxious to meet his family and I was sure they wanted to see their grandson. Phil agreed we should visit them soon. One Sunday we set out to see them. They lived in the small village of Nantymoel which was about thirty miles away but it took a long time to get there. We took a train part of the way and then a cab but the roads weren't good and I realised now why Phil had been reluctant to make this journey. I knew he was fond of his mother and it had been quite some time since he'd seen her. She wrote to us regularly and Phil was always dutiful in writing back. I wasn't able to read her letters as her only language was Welsh. Phil always translated them for me. I was anxious as we drew nearer to his home and wondered how we would communicate.

At last we arrived. I had never visited a Welsh valley before and was surprised with the bleakness all around. There was a large coalmine in the valley and nearly everyone who lived there worked in the pit. Behind the mine were huge hills of grey slag. Phil explained that this was the waste material after the coal had been extracted. Before we reached his home he told me his father was a fireman at the pit. He had worked his way up from being a miner in the early days. I knew Phil was proud of his father's achievements but he didn't love him as much as he loved his mother. As we drew near the house I couldn't contain my excitement.

We knocked at the door and a small, but neatly dressed lady came out to greet us. She and Phil embraced one another and I guessed this was his mother. They spoke together in Welsh and I had no idea what they were saying. Then Phil turned round and ushered me towards his mother and introduced us. Hesitatingly, I said, "Hello. I'm very pleased to meet you." She replied in Welsh.

We went inside and they made a great fuss of baby David. I sat back and listened, slightly amused because I couldn't understand a word they were saying. I felt left out but I didn't mind. I could tell that Phil and his mother were very fond of each other and she was very pleased to see him after such a long time. Phil told me later that she liked me and was pleased we were so happy. So, I received the seal of approval!

I wondered where Phil's father was but didn't have long to wait as he soon arrived. He had been to chapel. He was a large man and had a loud voice. He made a great fuss of David and before long was trying to teach him to call him "Tadci" which is Welsh for grandpa. Then Phil's mother joined in and announced that she was to be called "Mamgi" which is Welsh for grandma. This wasn't very successful as David only had one or two words in English.

I had another surprise to come. Phil's brother Tom arrived, closely followed by Phil's stepsister Kate.

Even though I had no idea what they were all talking about I had to admit that I rather liked this family and felt part of them straight away. I was very happy. I wondered if they expected me to learn Welsh.

The day went by quickly and soon it was time for us to leave. The whole family stood on the doorstep waving us goodbye as we set off on our way home.

I knew that Phil was pleased with the visit to his family. I enjoyed the trip but I realised there was always going to be a language barrier. I thought about this as we travelled home and I wondered if I could ever converse with them. As far as Phil was concerned this wasn't a problem He was happy he'd seen his family again and he enjoyed introducing David and me to them.

We were soon back in the daily routine again. One thing continued to worry me. Phil had still hadn't done anything about David's baptism. This was on my mind all the time but I didn't want to cause trouble by mentioning it again. I decided our life was too good for us to fall out over this so I said nothing. Looking back, I'm sorry I didn't have the courage to speak up. But I didn't want to spoil our near perfect life. My conscience nagged me quite regularly but I still said nothing. I continued to go to my church every Sunday and David stayed at home with Phil. At church I saw all the other parents with their children and I longed to have David and Phil with me. But I knew it wasn't to be. The worst thing of all was that Phil had stopped going to his chapel so he had never taken David there. I kept putting this out of my mind.

Not many weeks later I wasn't feeling well and could think of no reason to be so off-colour. Then the penny dropped and I realised what was wrong with me. I went to the doctor and he pronounced I was pregnant again. I lost no time in telling Phil and he was delighted. "You'll have to take care of yourself now, Bridget," he said. "You might not be able to help me in the shop as much as you have." But having had one baby I knew I was going to be all right and hoped to lead a normal life.

As time went on we realised how many poor people there were in the village who couldn't afford to see a doctor. The more we came to know our new neighbours, the more we realised what terrible and overcrowded conditions they lived in. Some households had 3 or 4 children sleeping in one bed, which reminded me of my own childhood back in Ireland. Some families didn't even have beds and slept on rugs and used wooden tea chests for furniture which they had bought very cheaply or found discarded on waste ground. I began to realise how lucky we were.

I became more and more helpful to Phil in the shop and was able to recognise many of the maladies. The doctors must have noticed that not so many people were seeing them but they knew these poor people couldn't pay their bills, so there was no real conflict of interest. Many were out of work and lived on the breadline. I knew Phil often supplied medicines at cost and we made no profit. But we had great satisfaction helping these poor souls. We were gaining quite a reputation in the neighbourhood.

The shop was now thriving. Phil decided we should employ a

woman to help in the flat above. We interviewed several and were lucky to find Edith who proved to be a treasure. She was wonderful with David, loved housework and was a good cook. She came early every morning and started her day by washing up the breakfast dishes. Then she cleaned the flat. This gave me some time with David before I went down to the shop. She took David out for a walk in his pram every day and I was able to spend more time in the shop with Phil. Edith cooked lunch for us every day and we shut up shop for our lunch hour. After lunch Phil always had a nap before going back to work. Some afternoons I went out shopping and took David in his pram and on other days, particularly in the wet and wintry weather, I stayed indoors and turned my hand to knitting. It wasn't unusual to hear Phil calling up from downstairs, "Bridget, can you come here a minute?" And so I would go downstairs to help with another problem. I must have been quite fit as a result of going up and down those stairs so many times. I was hardly aware that I was pregnant.

Edith went home every day at about half past four and always left our evening meal in the oven for us. Sometimes we ate early and had time to walk in the park with David. We lived a busy but happy and contented life.

# CHAPTER 61

My second baby was due to born at Christmas so we prepared early in case things happened sooner. Christmas soon came and David was very excited. This was our first Christmas in our own home. David woke early in the morning searching around his cot to see what Father Christmas had brought him. He soon found his stocking and was delighted with the small presents in it.

Then, on December 29th, our first daughter was born. We decided to call her Mary after Mama and I lost no time in taking her to church to be baptised. Phil didn't come with me. He stayed home to look after David. He knew I was still uneasy about David not being baptised but this was something we didn't talk about.

Since we had moved to Wales I had corresponded regularly with my family in Ireland and New York. When the children were settled in bed at night Phil read his books, magazines and newspaper and I sat at the table writing yet another letter. I wrote often to my brother Tom who was now living in Callan, in County Kilkenny, and to Papa who was coping better than we expected since Mama died. I also kept in touch with my sisters Maggie and Mary-Anne. Mary-Anne had now emigrated to America. I didn't write to my brothers but Maggie often gave me news of them. Maggie was still working and living at the hotel and Mary-Anne had met the love of her life. He was a journalist called Sydney Richardson and they were soon to be married. They intended to move to Washington and I eagerly awaited news of the wedding.

Then, in January 1910, a letter arrived from Ireland with sad news. It was from Tom. My dear Papa had died. I was very upset and Phil had trouble consoling me. Now that both Mama and Papa had died I felt a loss that was difficult to describe. Phil was very understanding and tried to tell me that now we had children of our own we should be looking forward, not back. He said we should be content with our family. He had great expectations for us and was looking forward to having a large family. I was glad he felt like this but I wondered if we could cope with a large family in our small flat. We were well off by most people's standards and lucky to have a thriving business. All these words failed to help me in my grief.

That night I cried myself to sleep thinking of my poor Papa. I was quite despondent next day and very quiet. It wasn't like me to be so quiet. I stayed upstairs for most of the morning. When Phil came up for his lunch he said, "I've been thinking, Bridget. We haven't had a break for some time. Let's go away for a few days. We've put some money aside so we can afford to shut up shop for a few days." I was taken aback as this was the last thing I expected. It wasn't like Phil to leave his business unattended.

I replied, "What about our customers? Where will they go for help when they are ill?"

Phil laughed and said, "Bridget, you are an enigma. I'll never understand you. I thought you were going to jump at the idea."

I said nothing for a few minutes and then asked, "Where will we go?"

Phil said, "Why to Ireland of course! We'll be too late for your father's funeral but it will be good for you to go home. Besides, I've never seen your home and this might be the last opportunity. Yes, Bridget, we must go. David is nearly two years old now and he will enjoy the trip."

I'd only just got over the trauma of the birth of Mary and I wondered if I was well enough to travel. I was also worried that Mary was too young to come. She was only a few weeks old. I wondered if

Phil had thought of this. But he had and said we should leave her at home in the care of Edith. It took me some time to come to terms with leaving my new baby behind and going off on a holiday. But this was different. My dear Papa had died. It might be the only chance I had to pay my last respects to him.

I sat still for several more minutes then I jumped up and threw my arms around Phil and kissed him. "Thank you. Thank you," I said. "I can think of nothing better. Edith is wonderful with children and will look after Mary as if she is her own. It'll do us all good to get away and I know you will enjoy the trip too."

"Well then, that's settled," said Phil. "As soon as we've had lunch I'll go and enquire about train and ferry times. Will you look after the shop, Bridget, while I am out?"

"Of course," I said.

Two days later, leaving baby Mary behind in the care of Edith, we set off on our first family holiday. We caught the train to the port and then the ferry to Ireland. It was a lengthy journey but it was a long time since we had enjoyed a break. In spite of our tiredness we benefited from the change in our daily routine.

Before we left home Phil left a note on the shop door: *"Closed for a few days, due to family bereavement. We apologise for any inconvenience to our valued customers."* It also gave details of a chemist in Barry town that was open while we were away.

# CHAPTER 62

I was looking forward to seeing Phil's reaction to my home and homeland. It was early morning and dark when we disembarked in Ireland and boarded the train for Kilkenny where my brother Tom was going to meet us. As the train drew towards the end of our journey daybreak came and Phil was able to see the countryside. Unfortunately, it was winter and things looked bleak and bare. But the beauty of the hills reminded Phil of Wales and he liked what he saw.

Since leaving Nice I realised Phil enjoyed travelling and going to new places. It was good to see him relaxing as we travelled. He was also able to spend more time with David and this was good for both of them and for me of course! But I felt that only part of me was there. It had been strange leaving baby Mary behind.

We arrived a few days after Papa's funeral. As the train drew into the station I could see Tom standing on the platform. When the train stopped I left Phil with David and rushed over to meet him. We threw our arms around each other and hugged with tears running down our cheeks. It was so good to meet my young brother again. He was, as Papa had told me in one of his letters, quite the gentleman. I was proud to introduce him to Phil. It was only three years since we had seen each other but we both seemed to have grown up in that time.

We were soon in the trap with the pony taking us on our way towards Islands. Tom and I couldn't stop talking. First, Tom told me about poor old Papa. He had deteriorated rapidly after Mama's passing and had withdrawn into himself. He rarely went out and the house and the farm had fallen into disrepair. Tom told me he was surprised at the number of people who had turned out for the Mass and funeral. He said, "Of course, so many people remembered him in his prime and many people came from surrounding villages and had once been his pupils. In spite of all his odd ways he was respected in the neighbourhood and hundreds of youngsters had passed through his schoolroom."

As we passed along the way Tom pointed out places of interest to Phil. I could tell they were going to get on well together.

As we drew nearer to Islands Tom said, "Bridgie, you must let me know when you want to go up to Modeshill to the churchyard. I know you will be anxious to visit the grave."

I hadn't given any thought to where we would be staying. Like all men Tom didn't think it important to tell us these arrangements. I asked him, "Are we to stay at Islands, Tom?"

"Yes, of course," he replied. He said he was still living in the house. He had arranged for Ellen Tobin's daughter, Joanna, to come in and make up the beds for us in the spare room. He said, "She has made up the cot for David."

I laughed and said, "That's wonderful. Just to think, Tom, all of us have slept in that cot and probably generations before us. First it was Kate, then Maggie, then me and then Jack and all you boys. Now it is baby David's turn!" Somehow, the fact that David was to sleep in "our" cot gave a sense of continuity to our lives. Coming home to Ireland at this time was good for me.

We soon settled in at Islands. Ellen Tobin's daughter Joanna had met us when we arrived and she had a fire going in the kitchen. She had prepared a good old Irish stew for our evening meal and I was glad that on that first day I didn't have to do any cooking..

Joanna took me upstairs and showed us the sleeping arrangements. It was strange coming into the empty house that had once been full of all the sounds of family life and the laughter of children.

258

Somehow, it seemed so drab and colourless now. The lace curtains at the windows were dirty and worn. The rugs on the floor were tattered and torn. But the house itself was clean and for this I was thankful to Joanna. I said, "Joanna, you must have had a long hard job to get the house clean for the wake and the funeral."

Joanna said, "Och, that's nothing. It's been a pleasure and Mr. Tom has been very good to me. Sure, he paid me for doing it and then sent me home with eggs fresh from the chickens." Joanna was a good girl and I complimented her on the lovely clean sheets on the beds. I made a mental note to give her a present before we left.

Whilst we were upstairs, Tom took Phil outside and gave him a short tour. I was pleased they were getting on so well. Joanna decided it was time to go home but said she would be back in the morning to see if there was anything we needed. I thanked her and waved her goodbye.

David was now nearly two years old and into everything. He knew Phil was outside and stood at the back door saying, "Want Dada, want Dada." I decided to go out with him to find the men. David ran out into the backyard in front of me. He was happy to be free at last. The poor wee soul had been cramped up in a boat, a train and then a pony and trap for so long. He could see Phil and Tom in the distance and he ran to meet them.

Together we showed Phil round the outbuildings, the cow house, the dairy, the pigsty and all the rest. There was a cold, raw January north wind blowing so we soon decided to go inside and settle down.

After showing us round Tom had other things to do and waved goodbye as he went off. We went inside and settled down in the kitchen. I couldn't believe how bare the house was. It wasn't easy to get comfortable and I remembered my childhood when this kitchen had seemed so warm and inviting. Now it was soulless without a family and we seemed to rattle around inside it, just the three of us.

I set about getting our supper ready and was surprised to hear a knock at the back door. I turned and there stood my brother Pat. I was so surprised to see him. We flung our arms around each other. We were both speechless for a few seconds. He said, "Bridgie you're looking bonny."

Tom hadn't mentioned Pat to us and I hadn't heard anything from Pat since he had returned from America. His visit took me by surprise. I introduced him to Phil and we sat down together round the fire I asked him, "Are you living nearby?"

"It's a long story, Bridgie," he said. "If you're not in a hurry I'll tell you everything." I told him we were about to have our supper so he decided to join us and over the meal he started to tell us what he had been doing. He had come home from New York about a year ago and had lived in Islands for a while with Mama and Papa but moved out to marry his girlfriend just a week before Papa died. He said he was very happy but had been saddened that Papa had died just seven days after his marriage. He told me about his new wife, Anne. After the wedding they had gone to live with her father at Shangarry just a couple of miles away. His father-in-law, Richard Hayden, was a retired blacksmith and a widower. I asked him if he had seen much of Tom since being home and he looked very sheepish and said, "Tom and I don't get on. We never have and when he found out the reason for me returning home he disowned me and we never speak. I'm afraid I'm the black sheep of the family."

I was surprised and said, "Pat, why did you come home from America?"

There was a long silence. He replied, "At the risk of you disowning me I'll tell you. I did something which I'm ashamed of. When I went to New York I was young, just seventeen, and I thought I knew it all. I was confident and wanted to make my life there. But I took some shortcuts. The worst one was that I applied for American citizenship but I lied on the application form. You have to live in the States for 5 years before they will consider you and I had only been there 3 years. To the end of my days I'll regret telling them I had been there 5 years. It took them a long time to reply but I wasn't worried as I didn't think they were going to check up on this. Then I had a letter from them warning me that if I had been untruthful I would be taken to court and charged with Perjury which could entail a prison sentence. You can imagine how I felt. I was terrified. I didn't dare tell Jack or Dick and I decided to run away. I went straight to the Shipping Office and signed on for the next boat home, which fortunately was due to leave in a couple of days. Then I just had to keep my head down and hope I could make my escape."

I was amazed at this story and even more amazed that this was the first I'd heard of it. "You are a naughty boy, Pat," I scolded him. "But I'm glad to hear that you know the error of your ways. Remember what Mama used to say to us when we were children 'Oh what a tangled web we weave when first we practice to deceive'."

"I know," he said. "I often think of dear Mama and her wise sayings. Do you remember her saying to us, 'Is that the truth you're telling me or is that a black spot I see on your tongue?'"

We laughed at these memories. I was prepared to give Pat the benefit of the doubt and forgive him. He seemed to be happily settled and I thought he wasn't likely to do anything like this again to spoil his happiness. But, I could tell that Phil, who had sat quietly listening to all this was not quite so forgiving.

Pat went home before Tom returned and we saw him off, promising to visit him in Shangarry before we left for home.

After supper Phil washed David and put him to bed and I tidied up the kitchen and washed the dishes. We still had to get our water from the pump and this was something I had forgotten. Joanna had left jugs of water ready for us so we didn't have to go to the pump until morning. I looked forward to the next day when I could show the pump to David and Phil.

When Pat had gone Phil settled himself beside the fire in the kitchen in Papa's old chair. Before it got dark I wandered out and up the hill behind the house to our old oak tree. Dusk was falling fast but the moon lit up the countryside for me. This trip down memory lane brought back some wonderful memories. I recalled the days I had spent there with the gang of boys and the tree house and the rope tied to the strongest branch, which we used to haul ourselves up. For several minutes I was transported back to my youth. I sat there in the moonlight with recollections, eventually returning home with a warm, comfortable feeling.

Phil had found two old oil lamps and had lit them. The light brought comfort to the bare kitchen. As we sat by the fire I told Phil how, as youngsters, we had all prayed before going to bed and pointed out the rush mats, which had been so rough on our young knees. Tom came home quite late but we still had time to reminisce about the past.

We were very tired and turned in early that night. The bedroom seemed very cold at first and we piled extra blankets on the bed and on David. Despite the raw cold we were soon asleep.

We all slept well and were up early next day. Tom was up before us and had left early to go to his teaching job. David was anxious to go outside and explore the surroundings but I insisted we had breakfast together. Joanna had left some fresh milk in a jug on the cold stone and this had kept well overnight so David was able to have a good drink of milk. I made porridge for us and then we found Joanna's soda bread, which we had with jam. Although the food in the cupboard was sparse there was enough for a few days and I was grateful Joanna had sorted this out for us before we arrived. I explained to Phil it was a long walk to the shop. We could have taken the donkey and cart but neither of us felt like harnessing the animal at that moment.

Over breakfast we talked about our plans for the day. I wanted to go up to Modeshill to the churchyard and Phil decided to go with me. We found an old pram in one of the sheds and Phil cleaned it down. It was quite a long walk to Modeshill so we put David in the pram and covered him with a warm blanket. We left a note on the kitchen table to tell anyone who called where we were and what time to expect us back. As we stepped out of the back door I remembered there was no need to lock our doors in the country and when I thought about it there really wasn't much of value in the house anyway.

We set off and made our way up the little road and over the bridge that crossed the Kings River. We stopped and looked into the river and I told Phil that in days gone by when the river was flowing fast the boys had been able to catch trout there. Nothing tasted better than fresh river trout. But now the river was slow moving and even though the water was clear we couldn't see any fish.

I had forgotten how bad the roads were. We had taken everything for granted in our youth, but after my travels abroad I saw things with a different eye. Now, in the winter, the roads were very bad, with puddles and ruts. We made our way along the road and soon came the old school at Mohober where Papa had taught. It was holiday time and the school was closed. There was no one about so we went in through the gate and looked through the windows. The classroom which had seemed so big when I was a child looked small and dingy. Phil said it reminded him of the village school he had attended in Wales.

Eventually, we came to Modeshill. As we turned the corner and walked up the slope to the church gates, Phil said, "The church is in ruins. It must be very old. How long is it since they had services here?"

I replied, "I don't know, Phil. It's always been in ruins since I've known it. It is part of Mullinahone parish and the church services are held there and then the coffins are brought here for burial.

"Is your sister Kate buried here as well?" asked Phil.

"Yes, my grandparents, my parents and my sister Kate are all in the same grave." We found the grave and I placed on it some greenery I had gathered in the hedgerows on our way. I dropped to my knees and automatically took out my rosary and began my devotions. Phil stood quietly beside me whilst I said my prayers.

When I had finished I stood up feeling much better. The power of prayer is wonderful and I felt I had at last said goodbye to my mother and father and once again to my sister Kate. I straightened my skirt and brushed off the dirt. I looked away into the distance towards Mount Slievenamon. It was a cold, crisp, clear, winter day and the mountain looked beautiful. I said to Phil, "Sure now, isn't that a wonderful view?"

"It certainly is. It's so peaceful here. I think this visit has helped you a lot, Bridget."

"Yes, Phil, I feel I've done my duty to the family." As we looked at the mountain in the distance I told him of the trip that Danny and I had made to the mountain all those years ago.

We made our way back home through the lanes. David had slept for most of the morning. The country air was good for him. When we were nearly home we took him out of the pram and let him toddle the rest of the way. We went in through the back door and there was Joanna in the kitchen cooking our dinner for us. She had laid the table and everything was ready for us to sit down and eat. "You are a treasure, Joanna," I said. "You make me feel so much at home."

"Good," she replied. "Sure, think nothing of it. My mother worked for your mother and now I'm doing the same for you. If you have all you need I'll be off and I'll see you again in the morning." Phil had taken a liking to Joanna and went to the back door to see her out.

When he came back he said, "She's a lovely girl. We must buy her a present or give her some money before we go home." I agreed and thought she would prefer money.

David was eating well and had lovely rosy cheeks from the fresh country air. After dinner Phil took David upstairs so he could have a short nap and I cleared away the dishes.

When Phil came down he asked, "Is there anything I can do, Bridget?"

I suggested that as we were running out of water we should take a trip to the pump. This we did and as we walked we talked. We decided that later we would harness the donkey and go for a tip to the village. I said to him, "There's not a lot to see, but it will show you the surroundings I grew up in." I was keen to do this, and hoped we might bump into old friends on the way. I wondered if I would see Danny Murphy and his family.

We returned with our buckets full of fresh water. We put them in the kitchen and I covered them with the muslin covers that I remember Mama making many years before.

Then we went out to the stable to get the donkey. We were standing wondering how to harness the donkey when Tom arrived home. He laughed at our predicament and said, "You can tell, Bridgie, it's a long time since you were on a farm!" We all laughed but we were glad to see him, as he could help us. But he said, "Bridgie there are some things in the house which I think we ought to go through. There isn't a lot so it won't take long." I hadn't been looking forward to this but knew it had to be done so we returned to the house.

Tom and I went into the house and Tom said, "Bridget, when Mama died I put her things on one side for you. She wanted you to have them. There isn't much but I think we should look at them now." Tom knelt to get a box out of the sideboard. We put the box on the table and opened it. Poor Mama, she had such a hard life bringing up a large family. She also had Papa's moods to contend with. There had never been much money to spare in the family and I wasn't surprised that she had left so few things. It made me sad to see so little for a life that had meant so much to all of us.

The box contained her prayer book, her rosaries, a brooch that I had sent to her from America, one or two fine hair combs and her picture of the Virgin Mary that used to hang above her bed. There were a few other things like knitting needles, crochet hooks, cottons and sewing needles. Also there was a lovely silver thimble. I tried it on and it fitted me perfectly. This, together with the picture, reminded me of her most. I was going to treasure these in future. I also decided to keep the prayer book and the rosaries.

Tom then asked me all about Maggie and her marriage. We hadn't had a chance to talk like this the last time I had come home. He was sorry to hear about Maggie's situation but agreed it was good that Mama and Papa never knew the full truth about the split in their marriage. "'Tis a strange world," said Tom. "We never thought Maggie was the marrying type but she married almost as soon as she arrived in America. John was her first boyfriend and maybe she should have enjoyed life before settling down with him. If she had, she might have found a worthier husband."

We re-joined Phil and David outside and Tom helped us get the donkey and cart ready for our journey. We laughed as we struggled with the harness and as soon as it was ready Phil picked David up and sat him on the donkey's back. David loved this and started shouting, "Giddy up, giddy up!" Much to his disappointment old Ned didn't even move a hoof, which caused more amusement. We put David in the cart and climbed in beside him.

# CHAPTER 63

Our last few days in Ireland passed quickly. During that week we met up with Danny Murphy and his family and spent a lovely evening with them. Phil got on well with Danny and I was pleased. Danny was looking a lot older, as I expect I was too, but he still had that old sparkle in his eye and it was grand to see him again.

We also visited Pat and met his new wife Anne and his father-in-law. They had a good home at Shangarry and were turning the old forge into a shop where they hoped to sell local produce to their neighbours. I was glad that Pat was well settled. Anne seemed to be a calming influence on him and they were happy.

The last few nights were very cold. Each morning it looked as if it was going to snow and the puddles in the lane were iced over. We had built up a good fire in the kitchen and warmed ourselves around this before going to bed each night. The house had become cold and damp since Papa had been living in it alone. He didn't bother with lighting the fire every day. I remembered the days of our childhood when Mama kept the fire going in the kitchen night and day, in winter and summer. How warm and snug it was in those days gone by.

Our last day soon arrived and Tom took us to the station. We chatted on the way and Tom told me he wasn't in touch with the rest of the family. I told him what I knew about them. Dick was now working as a shipping clerk for a railroad company but hoped soon to be joining the New York Fire Brigade and John was working as a butcher. We both wondered how Mary-Anne was getting on. Still, no mention was made of Pat and I wondered how Tom could disown a brother, particularly one who lived so near him. But Tom was glad to hear news of the rest of the family and I thought he was sad he had lost touch with them.

So our time in Ireland came to an end. We'd enjoyed our stay and the few days' rest had been good for us. I was sad to wave Tom goodbye at the station but he promised to visit us in Wales one day. I wondered how long it would be before we met again. "Keep in touch," he said as the train pulled away from the platform.

# CHAPTER 64

In no time at all we were safely ensconced back in our home in Cadoxton. When we arrived I rushed upstairs and Edith was there to meet us. She took me straight into the bedroom and there was wee baby Mary fast asleep in David's old cot. The sight of her brought tears to my eyes. "Has she been all right?" I asked. "I shouldn't have left the poor wee thing. She's so young."

Edith said, "She's been fine, Mrs. Richards. She's no trouble at all. They always say the second baby is easier than the first. Don't you go worrying yourself now. She's far too young to know you didn't take her with you." Edith was pleased to see us home again and said how well we all looked.

Phil found a pile of post waiting for him. He was keen to open up the shop the next day. As soon as we arrived home he took the notice off the door and replaced it with one that said: *Opening again tomorrow, Wednesday. We are sorry for any inconvenience caused by our absence.*

Edith had prepared a meal for us and we were glad of this after our long journey. We'd eaten well in Ireland but it was good to be eating in our own home again. David was very tired and didn't eat much. As soon as he'd finished his milk we put him to bed. Phil had become quite a dab hand at looking after his son. It had been good for them both to have time together. We were soon in bed ourselves and glad to be back in our own bed.

Our absence hadn't caused too much difficulty for our customers. One or two people came in and said they had missed us but we were soon back to normal.

The children were growing fast. It was time for us to find a school for David. We talked about this one evening and decided to register him at the local school in Cadoxton.

The next few years passed peacefully. We were still working hard to build up the business. One night Phil said he thought the business had reached saturation point. I asked him what he meant and he explained that we had captured all the local business and there was probably no way of increasing our income further. The only way to do this was to acquire another shop. We knew we couldn't give the same personal service if we did this so we decided against it. We weren't badly off at all. Even though the shop brought good returns I knew Phil wanted more. He often told me he envisaged us having more children and bringing up a large family in a big house. This seemed to be light-years away so I didn't dwell on it. I knew Phil was ambitious and I wondered what the next few years would bring.

The town of Barry had grown rapidly over the past few years. The docks had been expanded and they were always busy. Coal was brought by train from the Welsh valleys and exported from the docks. More and more people were moving into the area to find jobs. As more and more houses were built to house the dock workers our little village of Cadoxton was swallowed up and soon became part of Barry town. Phil believed there might be room for more chemists as a result of the rapid expansion of the population.

# CHAPTER 65

It was early in 1914 and David was happy at the local school. He was six years old and had started to read. We both enjoyed helping him and Phil took great pleasure in teaching him to count. David was quick to learn. Mary was due to join David at school soon. As the children grew up I was able to spend more time with Phil in the shop. People were coming in quite often for treatment of cuts, bruises, and sprains and also for advice on their minor ailments. Phil was sure my presence helped the business to grow.

One day, I had a letter from my youngest sister Mary-Anne now in New York. I was delighted to hear that she was getting married and hoped to pay a visit to England with her new husband. I was so excited and couldn't wait to give the news to Phil. We discussed her visit over supper and decided the young married couple should stay with us – even though it was going to be a bit of a squeeze. I wrote back to Mary-Anne at once and told her how much I was looking forward to her visit and I invited her and her new husband Stewart to stay with us. I was longing to see them. When Mary-Anne wrote back she gave me details of their trip and thanked me for the invite to stay but said they had already booked into a hotel in Cardiff. She had planned to have 2 or 3 days with us.

Three weeks later they arrived. Phil and I went into Cardiff to meet them from their train which had brought them down from Liverpool Docks. They were tired from the journey but invited us back to their hotel where we spent several hours catching up on news. Phil got on well with Stewart who told him they were going to visit his old home in Scotland before returning to America. Later it turned out that they loved Wales so much they decided to stay longer in Cardiff. Their visit lasted for ten days and they didn't go to Scotland. We had plenty of time together. Whilst they were with us a letter arrived in Barry from Ireland addressed to Mary-Anne. They weren't visiting Ireland because of the political unrest there so I was anxious to know who had written to her. It had a Dublin post-mark and I was very curious.

When they arrived I handed her the letter and watched her as she opened it and read it. "Why, Bridgie, guess who it's from?"

I couldn't guess and said, "Tell me, I'm dying to know."

"It's from our nephew, Kate's son, John Cleary. Isn't this wonderful? I'm so sorry we won't be going over there. It's quite a sad letter really. Here, you read it. What do you think?"

She handed me the letter and I read it carefully. It went as follows:

*21 Upper Leeson Street, Dublin. Dated 30th June 1914.*

*My Dear Aunt Marion* (everyone now called Mary-Anne, Marion)

*I was delighted some time ago when I heard you were back in England and would have written sooner to welcome you home but I did not know your new name. I am sure you are anxious to see your old native place and the friends of your school days. The changes since you left the dear old Islands are many indeed and there are some new faces to take the place of the old. All of us have left Galbally, except Father, and I am going down to Carrick-on-Suir on Saturday, July 12th and will probably remain until the first days of August. I feel in want of a holiday after the long term in the city. Needless to say I should like to see you very much after so many years. Aunt Bridgie and her children I should like to see also as I have never seen them since before you went to America. Babyanne has grown into a great big girl. I think she has beaten Madgie in this respect. They are both going into the Convent in Carrick and will have a good opportunity of acquiring some knowledge likely to help them in the future. Your other little nieces are four great strong healthy little rogues. I am very fond of them and naturally they are very much attached to me. My new mother has a great many friends and they are all without exception very kind to me. The loneliness of my childhood is thus compensated for to a certain extent and I feel myself rather strong and confident with regard to the future. I was glad when I heard you were married, as a husband's love is always the best kind of love to have. Do you know, Aunt dear that I have upwards of a dozen Uncles and Aunts married? How glad I should be to have such a number of friends! The weather here is very fine and I hope it will be the same when I go on the holidays. Write to me soon and let me know when you are likely to be back in Ireland. Everyone would be glad to see you in Cregg and I am sure you would like the place. I can't very well recall your features to my memory but I know you had that nice white soft creamy skin — something like what is to be seen here in Grafton Street every evening with the exception that you used no powder nor paint.*

*I hope Aunt Bridgie and husband and her children are very well. I don't know anything about your own husband but hope he is fond of you and good to you, as anyone should be of a dear, nice girl like you. I am delighted at the idea of an Aunt as young as you. I'll bet we are more like brother and sister but it is so long since I have seen you that your personality has almost faded away. However, I hope to have a chance before your return of renewing an old acquaintance, for I should regard you as being the nearest link to my mother. Just fancy it is eight years since I have seen any female relative of my mother's. 'Tis getting late Aunt dear so I shall say*

> *Goodbye and remain*
> > *Your affectionate nephew*
> > *JACK.*

*P.S. Have I any more little cousins?*

Marion and I just sat looking at one another. We were both saddened by Jack's letter. In fact it brought tears to our eyes. We pictured our dear sister Kate's eldest son, sitting in a lonely room in Dublin, writing this long letter to his "own mother's family". He was only 19 years old and he sounded so much older in his letter. He seemed to be looking for a family or someone to call his own.

Jack's letter brought us back to reality. We talked about our ages. I was now 34, Marion was 26 and Jack Cleary was 19. I was married with two children, Marion was just married and Jack was obviously longing to have a family of his own one day. This led us to talking about the rest of the family again. Marion had brought news of my brothers from New York. Jack was working hard and courting, whilst Dick was now with the New York Fire Brigade. We both wondered how Maggie was managing. She always tried to put a brave face on things. We knew she wasn't as happy as we were. Poor Maggie!

After a wonderful ten days we said goodbye to Marion and Sid. I had mixed feelings as we waved them off at Cardiff station. I had enjoyed their visit and I wondered if we would ever meet again.

I worried about Marion until I knew she had arrived safely home. It was only two years since the wonderful ship the *Titanic* had hit an iceberg in the Atlantic and had sunk with the loss of many lives. But all was well and a letter arrived three weeks later saying they had arrived safely home and the sea crossing had been a good one.

Things soon returned to normal and we were sitting quietly one evening and Phil was reading his newspaper. The children were in bed. Phil said, "The situation in Europe is getting very grave. The pundits are suggesting we might soon be at war with Germany." As I rarely read the papers Phil kept me up to date with the news. There was trouble in Ireland too, with the Home Rule Bill. As days passed by, it became more and more obvious the Government were not going to put up with the threatened German invasion of Belgium. We were all very worried.

On August 3rd 1914 Phil set off as usual to the bank to pay in our takings for the day. He returned and said the bank was closed. All banks had closed by order of the Government. Things were looking bad. Then, we heard that Germany had declared war on France. The next day, August the 4th, it was announced that Britain had entered the war in Europe. Germany had invaded Belgium and we couldn't stand aside.

At the start of the war many young lads decided to do their duty and sign up as soldiers. We knew many young men who were sent off to the battlefields of Europe. It was a worrying time. There was even talk of conscription into the army. This worried me and I asked Phil if he was likely to be conscripted. He told me some occupations were considered to be important to the nation and were called "reserved" occupations. People in such occupations weren't being called up. Doctors, nurses, policemen and people like that were unlikely to be conscripted. I asked him if chemists came into the same category and he said he thought this was a borderline case and he didn't really know the answer. But he did think the younger men were being called up first. Phil was just short of his 33$^{rd}$ birthday so for the moment we could relax. It was also rumoured in these early days that married men might also be exempted. I couldn't imagine life if Phil had to go to war.

Everyone who came into the shop talked about the dark days that lay ahead. Most people had someone in their family who had joined up. The mood was gloomy. We hadn't sent boys to war since the Boer War at the start of the century and many young boys still in their teens were signing up. I prayed every night for a quick end to the war and for the safe return of all our soldiers. But the future looked bleak and some people thought the war might drag on for months.

As the war progressed I noticed Phil was becoming moody. So, one evening as we sat by the fire I asked him what was troubling him. He poured his heart out to me. "I want to do something useful," he said. "I want to feel I am making a greater contribution to the world." I was surprised at this outburst as there had been no hint of this before.

I asked, "Phil, don't tell me you want to go to war. Don't you think you are helping people by providing them with their medicines?"

He replied, "I want to do more than that. There is so much suffering now and I don't feel I am playing my part."

275

"What more can you do?" I asked. I really was afraid that he wanted to go to war and fight for his country. He said it was difficult to explain. Then he reached out for his latest edition of The Pharmaceutical Journal and pointed to an article. It was headed "Shortage of Doctors". I read it and it described the shortage of medical practitioners as many doctors had gone off to war. It went on to say that pharmacists were eligible to train as doctors. So that was it!

I knew immediately what was on his mind. "Do you really want to become a doctor, Phil?" I asked.

He replied, "Yes, with all my heart. It is my deepest ambition. I want to help people more than I do now." I was so taken aback by this revelation that I couldn't speak. We sat in silence for several minutes. Then, I got up and made a cup of tea. When I returned with the tea Phil moved across the room and sat next to me and, taking my hand into his palms, he said, "Bridget, do you understand?" I couldn't reply. This was like a bolt from the blue.

After a while I said, "Phil, of course I understand. This was how I felt before I took up nursing but how will we manage if you decide to go ahead with this?"

He said, "I don't know but I'm sure if we are careful it will be possible. We can employ a manager in the shop and you can keep an eye on things while I am studying. I might have to go away to study but I am sure you will cope."

I asked, "Where do you think you will go?" Phil didn't know but said it could be Cardiff or even London. "Well," I said, "let's go to bed and sleep on it and talk again in the morning." I slept only fitfully that night. The thought of looking after the family and running the shop was daunting. I was sure I could manage but I thought I needed plenty of help. I tossed and turned for several hours, eventually falling into a deep sleep.

The next morning I didn't feel well. I thought it must be caused by lack of sleep but then I was violently sick. I didn't think I had eaten anything to cause this and I had a sinking feeling that I might be pregnant again. Sure enough I was and this only added to the pressure I felt since Phil's revelations the previous evening.

Phil was delighted we were to have another child but it was a while before I got used to the idea. "You'll have to have more help, Bridget. Do you think that Edith can come in for a few extra hours every day?" I said I would ask her.

The subject of Phil becoming a doctor was raised again quite soon and Phil asked me if I had any further thoughts.

I replied, "Yes, I have, Phil. Things won't be easy for me but I remember my dear old Mama's favourite saying. It was 'Follow your heart' and I think you should do that. If you really want to be a doctor I am right behind you and will do all I can to help. I remember my own feelings when I wanted to be a nurse and I understand how you feel." Phil was over the moon to hear this and gave me a great big hug and a kiss!

So, Phil initiated enquiries and there followed a long drawn out period of almost a year with letters backwards and forwards.

In January 1915 I was heavily pregnant. Edith moved in with us just a week before the baby was due. She was wonderful with David and Mary and we knew we could rely on her for help. Phil gave her a long lecture on the signs of imminent birth so she was well versed in what she had to do if he was out when I went into labour. I knew the midwife well so I wasn't worried about the birth. My only worry was that our rooms were cramped and Edith had to sleep in the same room as the children. But she didn't seem to mind this.

Then on January 28th the big day came and another baby boy made his way into the world. Phil and I had decided to call him Leslie. As time went on I was very worried that Leslie hadn't been baptised like poor little David. I decided to stand by the agreement I had made with Phil and wait for him to do something. Time went by and nothing happened. If the past was anything to go by it never was going to happen. This nagged on my mind and I couldn't help worrying about it.

Then, one day, the unimaginable happened. Phil was away for the day in Cardiff at a meeting. Our local Priest had heard we had another baby and called to see me. He was most insistent that I should take Leslie along to church as soon as possible and have him christened. I realised what a difficult situation I was in. I was at low ebb after the birth and I allowed myself to be talked into it. I couldn't think of a reason for not doing what he asked. I couldn't tell him about the agreement Phil and I had made as the Church were totally against such arrangements. I didn't tell Phil about the Priest's visit but I confided instead in Edith. She understood my predicament as she, too, was a Catholic.

The following day I took baby Leslie along to church to be christened. It was not until we arrived home that I started to worry about how I was going to tell Phil. Fortunately, the Priest didn't know that David hadn't been christened or he would have insisted on that too.

Time passed and I still hadn't told Phil about the Priest's visit. Then, one Sunday I dressed for church as usual and Mary and Leslie were ready to go with me. Off we went and still Phil didn't realise what had happened. David always stayed at home with Phil on Sundays. As we left Phil was reading the Sunday newspaper and he didn't notice Leslie was with us. After church we returned home and Edith had lunch ready for us. Still Phil didn't notice what had happened.

But the following Sunday was different. I got the children ready and as we were leaving David asked, "Why can't I come too?" David realised he was being left out and ran complaining to Phil.

Phil asked me, "Why are you taking Leslie with you, Bridget?" I was stunned and couldn't think of a reply.

After a few minutes I said, "Well, you won't get David baptised in your church so I've had Leslie done in our church. The Priest came to visit me a couple of weeks ago and encouraged me to take him along." Phil's face turned white and I could see he was very annoyed.

"You've broken trust with me, Bridget," was all he could say. Then he picked David up and went back into the sitting room, slamming the door behind him.

Edith came to comfort me. "Don't take on so. Isn't it best that you have at least two of them going to church with you?" By this time I was sobbing, as I knew I had let Phil down and I hadn't even apologised. But, at the same time, I was angry that Phil hadn't kept his part of the bargain. Edith suggested I should dry my eyes and go to church and talk things over when I got back.

When we returned from church Phil and David were nowhere to be seen. Edith met me at the top of the stairs and told me they had gone out about 15 minutes after me and hadn't said where they were going.

I was very worried as this was unusual behaviour. I didn't know what to do. Edith made us a cup of tea and we sat and waited in the sitting room. About an hour later they arrived home. David came bouncing up the stairs with a big grin on his face. "Mama, what do you think? Dada and I have been to church."

I couldn't believe what I was hearing. I was so pleased and relieved.

When Phil came in I said, "David says you've been to church. I'm so glad." Phil said nothing and to my surprise didn't talk to me for the rest of the day. This was a side of him I hadn't seen before and I was taken aback. He continued to talk to the children as if nothing had happened but he treated me as if I didn't exist. I was so unhappy. I knew I had broken his trust and I wondered how long it would be before things returned to normal. The only good thing to come of this was that he had kept his side of our agreement by taking David to church. Where it was all going to end?

# CHAPTER 66

It was about ten days before Phil spoke to me again.

He said he had given the matter of becoming a doctor a lot of thought. He'd decided to go away to train as a doctor and as far as he was concerned I could do what I liked with the children when he was away.

There was a bad atmosphere in the family, which wasn't good for the children. I was desperately sorry for what I'd done but I still hadn't apologised to Phil. I knew this would help the situation but he was in such a black mood I found it difficult to talk to him. He continued to ignore me but still expected me to help in the shop and we didn't talk unless it was absolutely necessary.

I decided that enough was enough. So, one evening I tackled Phil about things. We'd finished supper and we were in the sitting room. I said, "Phil, I'm desperately unhappy and I wish I knew what I could do to break this terrible atmosphere between us." Phil looked up from his paper and said nothing. Then I said, "I am truly sorry for what I have done and I wish we could go back and start again. Please forgive me."

Phil looked at me and put his paper down. He replied, "That's the first time you've said sorry, Bridget. I've been waiting for your apology. You broke the trust between us and it will be difficult to mend things but I'm willing to try."

All I could say was, "Thank you." I breathed a sigh of relief and hoped for better things in future. I didn't dare mention he had broken trust with me!

We went to bed and next morning things seemed to be almost back to normal again. Phil announced he had planned a visit to his parents again so they could see baby Les. The journey would be more difficult this time with three children in tow.

Phil's family were pleased to see us and again I felt left out of things as they all gabbled away in Welsh. The children delighted in calling their grandparents Tadci and Mamgi. David and Mary both loved going to Nantymoel and they were spoilt by their grandparents. Even though they spoke a different language it was amazing how the children were able to converse with their grandparents. After a long day it was time to go home. We were all exhausted when we finally arrived back in Cadoxton.

The next morning at breakfast Phil said he didn't fancy that journey again with three children. I suggested that in future we should invite his mother to stay. If the children all slept in the second bedroom she could have a bed in the third room. It was small but there was room in there for a bed and chest of drawers. Phil was delighted and we set about moving the furniture round. He wrote to his mother and invited her to stay later in the year when the weather was warmer. I knew Phil preferred his mother coming rather than his father. There always seemed to be a barrier between him and his father.

Then Phil told me he had decided to buy a motorbike. I was surprised at this and asked him how much they cost and he replied, "About 100 guineas." I was worried at the expense but Phil explained he could use it to offer a delivery service for medicines. Eventually the day came when Phil became the proud owner of his first motorbike. I was pleased to see it had a sidecar big enough for a passenger or even for two small children. Then he had another idea, he decided to go and collect his mother when the time came for her to stay with us.

Every day we were getting news of the war on the radio and in the newspapers. We were horrified to hear in May of that year that the British liner Lusitania was sunk by a German U-Boat with the loss of over a thousand British and American civilian lives. I was so glad that none of my family was travelling but having crossed the Atlantic twice in my short life I realised what a horrific event this was. Phil said the loss of American lives might bring the Americans into the war which might help to shorten the war.

Phil's mother didn't come to stay with us that year. She kept making excuses. We weren't sure why she was reluctant to visit us. I wondered if she was frightened of the motorbike. Phil explained to me that she had never travelled far. Her longest journey had been when they moved to Nantymoel from Llanelli when his father took up a job with the Ocean Coal Company. Since then she had only made infrequent visits back to Llanelli to see her family. Her family visited her quite often so her trips to Llanelli were few and far between. I began to understand why she hadn't come to us yet. I thought about my own parents. Mama and Papa had rarely left home. In fact I could never remember either of them going away. Phil was good to his parents and continued to visit them regularly, usually on his own, always taking them something they appreciated such as butter or fresh eggs which he bought on his way there.

The following year, 1916, Phil's mother came to visit us in the summer. Phil went to collect her and she travelled with him in his sidecar. She was in a state of nervous exhaustion when she arrived. The motorbike had really frightened her. She had never travelled at such speeds before. It took nearly three days for her to settle after the journey.

The good thing about her visiting us that year was that "British summertime" had been introduced and we put our clocks forward one hour to increase daylight. While she was with us we enjoyed long hot days and we made several trips to the beach with the children. Leslie was now walking and the children were easier to manage.

Phil's mother worried about her eldest son, Tom, who had joined the army. News of the war was not good and it seemed that it was never going to end. The Germans were using airships (called

Zeppelins) to bomb England. They targeted London docks and channel ports on the east coast of England. Fortunately, Barry was too far west and hadn't been targeted.

Phil's mother still only spoke in her native Welsh language. It was always difficult for me to understand what she wanted. One day, during her brief stay with us, I heard her calling out in her bedroom. I went to see what the trouble was. She looked very upset and was saying, "Piche, piche," and kept repeating these words.

I tried to understand her in vain so I ran down to the shop and asked Phil, "What does piche mean?" He looked puzzled and then laughed. He replied, "It means petticoat. Why do you want to know?" I told him his mother was beside herself upstairs and kept repeating this word. He was amused and asked me to look after the shop while he went up to sort things out.

Phil came back, laughing, "Bridget, she put her petticoat under the mattress last night and forgot where it was and couldn't find it." Later that night when everyone was in bed Phil said, "You've learnt one word of Welsh, Bridget. Who knows, by the time Mother goes home you might be able to string a sentence together." I laughed and said there wasn't much hope of that. I was far too busy to learn another language. But when we went to bed that night I kissed Phil, saying as I did so, "Nostad!" which is Welsh for goodnight.

Phil's mother spent a whole week with us. I think she enjoyed her visit and I told Phil to tell her she must come again. David and Mary had both picked up several Welsh phrases during the visit but none of us understood what Phil and his mother talked about in the evenings. They gabbled away and I was somewhat relieved I didn't have to keep up a polite conversation.

At the end of the week Phil took his mother home in the motorbike's sidecar and David went too. I don't know how we'd managed that journey before we had the motorbike.

# CHAPTER 67

During the war the absence of so many men who were away in the army led to many job vacancies. Women had to take on different roles. They soon became adept as head of the household, handling the budget, disciplining the children and dealing with doctors and teachers and others. It was surprising how quickly the women learnt. Many women went out to work, doing the work their husbands had done before.

I often thought about returning to nursing. Phil valued my help in the shop so I was reluctant to raise the matter with him. One evening he read to me from the local newspaper that young men were coming home with horrendous wounds and there wasn't enough room for them in the larger hospitals. The Red Cross and St. John Ambulance Brigade were taking over buildings as hospitals and recruiting voluntary help to run them. Phil asked me, "Have you ever thought of becoming a volunteer nurse, Bridget?" I told him the thought had crossed my mind but I had dismissed it as he needed my help in the shop. He said this wasn't a problem so, the next week, I signed on. As a result I spent two days every week helping in St. John's Hospital on Barry Island. All the nurses were volunteers. Other helpers joined the Voluntary Aid Association or the VAD as it was called.

This interlude in my life helped me in many ways. It was good for me to do something outside the family sphere and I left the children in the care of Edith when I was at the hospital. Phil was wonderful and always took me to and from work on his bike. Once again I felt I was doing something worthwhile for society.

The young men who passed through our hands in hospital were wonderfully courageous. Some of them had suffered terrible burns and had lost their handsome looks. Others had legs or arms amputated. But they were all cheerful and it was a tonic to see how they bore their troubles with a smile.

Then, in 1917 Phil heard from London about training to be a doctor. He was offered a place in the next term's intake of medical students at St. Bart's Hospital in London. We sat down that evening when the children were settled in bed and discussed the letter. He was invited to join a specially designed course for pharmacists. This course was shorter than the normal medical students' course. It lasted four years but he would be able to come home for the Easter, summer and winter holidays. However, in the last year he was expected to spend some time during his holidays working in the hospital to gain experience. At first, this seemed daunting. I was suddenly aware that Phil was going to be away for considerable lengths of time and our family and home would be my total responsibility. Even though we would have a manager in the shop Phil impressed on me that it would be my responsibility. He impressed on me that my help was needed in ordering stock, looking after the accounts and doing some first aid when required. So it looked as if I was going to be very busy.

Phil was to study at London University as well as learning practical work at St. Bartholomew's Hospital. I had hoped he would study at Cardiff but that wasn't to be. I agreed with Phil that he must accept this offer. It was a wonderful opportunity for him to achieve his ambitions. I had some reservations but I managed to put these to the back of my mind.

Phil was now nearly 37 years old and he would be over 40 by the time he qualified as a doctor.

We interviewed several young men for the manager's post. Eventually, we settled on a young man from West Wales. His name was Hugh Jones. He was just 28 years old. We both liked him immediately. He started with us two weeks before Phil went to London.

It was surprising how much there was to do before Phil finally left for London. We had to organise a separate bank account for him for his use in London. Phil was confident in leaving me in charge of the shop's accounts and he trusted Hugh who in his first two weeks had already been a great help.

The children didn't understand what was happening. They wondered why their father was moving out and I had a lot of explaining to do. They were going to miss Phil.

So, the day came when Phil had to go. It was with a heavy heart that I waved him off on the train. But I put on a brave face as I knew how much he wanted this. He promised to write to us soon. Tears fell down my cheeks as I waved him goodbye. He was entering another world and we were being left behind.

But Phil wasn't the sort to forget his family and wrote to us regularly. I looked forward to his letters each week and I always read them to the children.

# CHAPTER 68

In 1918 the great 'flu pandemic was sweeping across Europe and arrived in England. Hundreds of people were ill and London was badly hit. To my surprise Phil arrived home late one evening looking very ill. He had travelled down by train and wasn't only ill but also worn out by the journey. I was extremely worried and suggested I call the doctor. "No," said Phil. "There's no need. I have this wretched 'flu and bed is the best place for me. Please just keep me supplied with plenty of drinks. I have a high temperature and I must fight my way through this. But it's important that I keep away from the children. You must explain to them how important this is."

I didn't argue with him and hurried to make him a hot drink. Then I set about boiling water for the stone hot water bottle to warm his bed. He insisted on sleeping in the spare room away from us all. He repeated that the children must stay away from him until he was well again. I was very worried.

I was surprised the hospital had sent him home but he explained to me that home was the best place to be. The hospital was running out of bed space as so many people were ill. The next morning I wrote a hurried note to Phil's mother telling her what had happened. I had to write in English and I knew Tom would translate it for her. Two days later she arrived unexpectedly. Phil's brother Tom, who had been invalided out of the army brought her. She announced in Welsh (translated by Tom) that she had come to look after Phil. As soon as she was settled Tom went home. In the following days even though we couldn't converse she was a great help to me. It was so important to keep the children away from Phil so her presence at his bedside made this job easier. She had no fear of catching the illness herself. There was no doubt in my mind that she loved Phil dearly and he was the favourite of her two sons. We had several very worrying days and nights but it was a great relief when Phil turned the corner and started to get better. We were so lucky because hundreds of thousands of people had died in this pandemic. We read in the papers that the figures worldwide ran into millions.

While Phil was at home we received the welcome news that the War had ended. There was rejoicing in the streets and flags were flown from all the houses. A street party was held in Vere Street and Edith and I took the children to this. It was a joyous moment. We had two things to celebrate – the end of the War and Phil's return to good health.

Three weeks later Phil returned to London to resume his studies. He had weathered the storm.

We were very busy in the shop. Hundreds of people had gone down with the 'flu. There wasn't much we could do for them but many came for advice. The best advice we could give was that they should go to bed, keep warm and have plenty to drink. Some of them bought cough linctuses and tonics, even though we advised them these might not help.

We were living in a strange world. At the end of 1918 and well into 1919 as men were returning from war they were finding their role in the home was never to be the same again. They arrived to find their wives in charge of the household. But there was plenty of work for them. Even though the country had been at war the state of the economy was good.

Every day in Barry hundreds of tons of coal were brought in by train from the mines in the valleys. The trains went directly to the docks where the coal was loaded onto ships. This trade provided plenty of work for the men. The town seemed to be growing at an alarming rate as more and more families flocked to the district to find work.

Now the War was over it was an exciting time. There were still shortages in the shops but things were gradually returning to normal.

It was a time of great optimism. We read in the newspapers about the first transatlantic aeroplane flight by two men called John Alcock and Arthur Brown. I couldn't believe that an aeroplane could attempt this feat. I thought back to that time, 20 years ago, when my journey across the Atlantic had taken me seven whole days. This flight had taken less than 24 hours to complete.

# CHAPTER 69

The next few years went by quickly and eventually Phil finished his studies. He returned home and anxiously awaited the result of his final examinations. Two weeks later a letter arrived with a London postmark. I knew he was apprehensive and when the children had gone to school we sat down and opened the envelope. I knew immediately from Phil's face that he had passed his exams. He had a big smile on his face. He was now a qualified doctor. He read his results to me.

We were both elated. We hadn't realised until now the enormity of his success. It was going to be life changing for us. We would have more money at our disposal and now had to plan our future. The whole pattern of our lives would change.

When the children were safely tucked up in bed that evening we discussed our future plans over a leisurely supper. Phil opened a bottle of wine – a very rare thing for us in those days. But as Phil said, "We have a lot to celebrate. It's not every day we have such good news." Then he made a toast. "To our future, Bridget," he said. "Thank you for being such a stalwart over these last few years. I couldn't have done this without your help." I was somewhat overcome by this. I hadn't realised until now what an effort it had been. I thanked Phil and we started to think about our future.

I hoped there would be work for Phil in Barry and we wouldn't have to move away to another town. We were settled in Barry and a move would be unsettling for us all. But before going to London Phil had made enquiries about working in Barry as a doctor. Two doctors had suggested he come and see them when he was qualified. He decided to approach them both to see how the land lay. Hopefully, one of them was going to offer him employment.

The next day Phil came home with the offer of work with Dr. Griffiths, a well-known doctor in Barry town. Phil was even more delighted because the doctor had hinted that if things worked out well there could be a partnership in future. This was something we hadn't expected and the future looked rosy.

Phil decided to sell the shop. He thought Hugh might be interested in buying it. Hugh had been a great help to us when Phil was away and I thought this was a good idea. It meant we had to move out of the flat and find somewhere else to live. I was pleased to hear this as the flat had become very cramped with three young children and the thought of a new home filled me with delight.

Phil started work almost immediately and I cannot describe the fulfilment his work gave him. I knew what it meant to him to be helping people because this was how I felt when I started nursing. It brought back memories of my work in New York.

Phil's new job took up many hours but in spite of the long days he was a very happy man. He came home tired but never failed to give some time to the children. In the evenings over our meal he told me about his day, describing to me the patients he had seen and telling me about their maladies. There were many sick people and he was kept very busy.

Hugh was delighted with the chance to buy the business and made an offer we couldn't refuse. This offer included the living quarters above the shop. We didn't want to move far as the children were well settled in their schools and Phil's work covered our end of town, leaving Dr. Griffiths to cover the other end.

Phil placed the sale of the business in the hands of our solicitor. One day he came home with a beaming smile on his face. It was early summer and he suggested we should take a walk that evening and take the children with us. "I want to show you something," he said. I was very curious. We finished our evening meal in double quick time and were soon out walking with the children. Phil guided us up one road then down another and I wondered what he was so excited about. I hadn't long to wait for he stood on one side of the road and pointed to the house opposite. It was fairly new, about five years old, detached and built of red brick and three storeys high. It had a lovely front door with a polished brass letterbox. There was a side gate to the left that led into the garden. I looked at Phil and asked him why we had come to see this house. "Bridget, my love, this house is for sale. I have fallen for it and I intend to buy it for us."

I stammered, "But Phil, we can't afford a house as grand as this. It's so big. It must cost a fortune."

"Don't worry about that, Bridget," Phil replied. "Have you forgotten that we are selling the business? We will have to take a small mortgage but as soon as we have finalised the shop sale we will have a good deposit for this." I was staggered. After living for years in the cramped quarters above the shop this seemed a luxury. I suddenly realised all the hard work had been worthwhile and I was delighted.

Phil arranged with the agent for us to view the house a day later. I was even more pleased when I saw the inside. To the left of the front door was a large lounge. Beyond this a dining room and a passageway led to the large breakfast room. In this room there was a lovely coal-fired range for cooking. Beyond was a small scullery. Then we were shown a door that led to the cellar. The agent explained that the owner was a ship's captain and the house had been built for him and his family. He was retiring and returning to East Anglia where he had originally come from. He had called the house "East Anglia" and had expected to retire here but his wife hadn't settled and wanted to return to her roots.

He was anxious for a quick sale. The agent explained to us that the cellar was used for water storage. The captain had obtained steel plates from a battle ship which was being dismantled in Barry Docks, and the cellar was lined with these plates and was completely watertight. Whenever the water level in the tank fell below a certain level the Water Company came and re-filled it. A long discussion followed about water supplies and I was pleased to hear that treks to the pump would be a thing of the past.

Then we were taken out into the garden. Doors from the dining room led on to a terrace, which was covered in terracotta tiles. It was very pleasant and overlooked a small lawn and apple trees. A stone wall bordered this area and we were taken through an archway in the wall to the rest of the garden, which was about 250 feet long and quite wide. It was amazing and the view from the end of the garden was wonderful. This end of the garden was on a large rock outcrop and it looked down over a large area of the town.

We walked back through the gate and were shown the outbuildings consisting of a laundry area, above which was a greenhouse and next to this, another greenhouse. But there was more to come. A gate in the back wall led to a further garden area beyond which was the door to a large garage which opened on to the main road.

We were amazed at the extent of the gardens and outbuildings. Phil said, "Come on, Bridget, we haven't seen upstairs yet." So we went inside and mounted the stairs. On the first floor there were four bedrooms, all of them a good size and a bathroom. Then we mounted the next staircase to find three small attic rooms on the top floor.

"So there you have it," said the agent. "Three reception rooms, seven bedrooms, a bathroom, a kitchen, a scullery, a cellar full of fresh water not to mention the gardens and the outbuildings. What do you think?"

Without even asking me what I thought Phil said we were very interested and the following day he made an offer for the house. It was accepted almost immediately. We couldn't believe our luck. I thought I was going to get lost in such a large place and worried about all the housework, not to mention the extra furniture needed. But Phil put my mind at rest. He was sure Edith would come with us and if necessary we could get more help, possibly a live-in maid, who could sleep in one of the small attic bedrooms.

Finally, three months later the sale of the shop was complete and we moved to "East Anglia".

On the day of our move to "East Anglia" Edith took the children home with her so Phil and I were free to oversee the move. The children were excited to be going with Edith and even more excited when they knew that afterwards they were going home to a new house.

Phil and I were up early on the day of the move. Phil had arranged for one of his patients to move things for us in his horse and cart. We didn't have much furniture and I realised how empty the new house was going to feel, even with our belongings installed. I had spent days packing bedding, crockery and other loose items in boxes and these were marked with their destinations, such as "kitchen", "dining room" and "bedroom 1". The whole day went very smoothly and we were soon in our new home. The old sea captain and his wife had sold us their carpets and curtains for a small sum so I didn't have those to worry about.

Edith arrived with the children just as George was leaving with his horse and cart and they ran to the door shouting, "Mama, can we come in?"

They were soon inside and with Edith had a tour of the house, conducted by Phil. David couldn't contain himself. "It's so big," he kept saying. Mary was quiet and kept asking me where she was going to sleep.

Leslie loved the garden and said, "Can we have a dog now?"

I had forgotten what it was like to go out of your own back door into a real garden. This was so different from the back yard at the shop. I told the children about life back home in Ireland and about the animals we kept. Edith made herself busy in the kitchen unpacking the pots and pans and crockery.

Then, we made up the beds ready for the night. Sleep came quickly that night, for all of us.

# CHAPTER 70

Life soon settled into a routine. Phil was up early each morning and out on his motorbike to hold the surgery. Edith came every day as usual and we now had a maid to help us with the housework. Her name was Joan Collins and she was very good with the children. All three children were now at school and had to be taken there every day.

I really don't know where the time went. I was lucky to have the help of Edith and Joan. My time was taken up with so many things. I always looked forward to the weekends when Phil wasn't working. But he only had one weekend in four off. So these weekends were eagerly awaited not only by me but also by the children. We then had time together as a family. These were precious times.

Phil had taken on a gardener called Wally. Many hours were spent planning the garden. It wasn't long before we were growing all our own vegetables and Phil had other ideas about growing soft fruit and planting apple and pear trees.

One morning I wasn't feeling well and felt so bad I didn't want to get up. But I hauled myself out of bed and made my way to the bathroom. I was violently sick and felt off colour for the rest of the day. When Phil came home he noticed my pale face and asked what the trouble was. I told him how unwell I felt and he decided I should see Dr. Griffiths, his partner, if I didn't improve. The next day, I was unwell again and I realised I was pregnant again. I was to have a long and difficult pregnancy and I spent many days during the following months just sitting down unable to do much.

I felt guilty that the house wasn't receiving proper attention. By now, I should have organised it and I should have purchased more furniture. But it stayed as it was on the day we moved in. I felt guilty because Phil was holding down a demanding job and still managed to organise the garden and I couldn't even sort out the house.

On the 31st March 1920 I gave birth to a beautiful baby daughter. Mary was thrilled to have a little sister and made a great fuss of her. Phil was delighted and so, too, were David and Leslie.

Of course, she was to be a Catholic and this time there was no disagreement. I was thankful Phil didn't disagree. But troubles lay ahead because Phil still didn't take David to church regularly. Every Sunday I went to mass with Mary, Leslie and baby Esme. David stayed at home and I know he felt left out. I asked Joan what he did when we weren't there and she said, "It varies, ma'am, sometimes he stays indoors and reads and other times he goes out and loses himself in the garden. He seems to be quite a lonely boy, but I think he is happy in his own company." Joan knew I worried about David.

Edith and Joan both loved helping me with the new baby. I soon found I had time on my hands as between them they did the housework and some of the cooking. Phil was kept very busy with surgeries and home visits. He was often called out at night to mothers giving birth to babies in their homes. He said he liked the mothers to have their babies at night because he had more time to give them his full attention. Phil was a man full of love and the care he gave to his patients was no less than that which he gave to his own family.

Phil had a saying, "cast your bread upon the waters and it will come back to you." I realised he must have learnt this as a young boy when at chapel with his parents and he never forgot it. His patients were lucky to have him as their doctor.

We had been living in "East Anglia" for two years when Phil came home one day and said there was something he wanted to discuss with me. We packed the children off to bed and settled in the sitting room. I wondered what was coming! "Bridget," Phil said, "I have some good news for you." I was anxious to hear what Phil had to tell me and I sat back and listened. He continued, "I've been working for Dr. Griffiths for two years now and this morning he said he wanted to have a talk with me. The long and the short of it is he has offered me a partnership in the practice."

I was delighted and jumped up and gave Phil a big hug and a kiss. "That's wonderful," I said. "You have proved yourself, Phil. You have worked hard and you deserve this."

Phil went on, "It's not quite as straightforward as it might seem."

"Why ever not?" I asked.

"Well, Dr. Griffiths wants us to live in the house in town where we have the surgery.

"Oh Phil," I said. "Just when we are getting settled here. We'll have to move, will we?"

"I've been thinking it through," said Phil who had pondered over this all day. "We don't have to sell our house. We can rent it to a good tenant. Then, when the practice is established in a year or two we can move back. What do you think, Bridget?"

I was amazed. But I had mixed feelings about the whole idea. I was delighted for Phil but, at the same time, I didn't want to leave our lovely home. Phil assured me he had thought the whole matter through. He told me he expected a salary increase. He even talked about sending the children away to boarding school for a better education. I wasn't happy about this but, as it was way off in the future decided this wasn't the time to discuss it. Instead I concentrated on the pending move. I was insistent that I should visit this new house to see what the living conditions were like before we agreed to move. Phil was pleased with my positive attitude and arranged for us to visit the house.

We were up early in the morning and after the children had all left for school, I climbed into the sidecar of the motorbike and off we went to the centre of town to inspect our new home. The house was called "Ravenscourt" and was only a few years old. I was pleased with what I saw. There was plenty of space for the family. It was right in the centre of town and was very close to the shops. Another bonus was that it was only a short walk from my church. Phil could see I was pleased and after inspecting the house we went out into the back garden. The garden was small but there was enough room for a washing line and a small area of grass and a vegetable patch. I was pleased but I hoped we would be able to move back to our own home in the not too distant future.

We found tenants quite quickly for our house. "East Anglia" was let on a 5-year lease until 1927. So our move back home was 5 years away. This gave Phil plenty of time to establish himself as a partner in the practice.

We moved to Ravenscourt very quickly. We soon had a telephone installed and Phil talked about buying a car. I felt that life couldn't be better. He had seen a car he was keen to buy and one day turned up in it. It was an Overland de Luxe and it had a hood which could be taken down in fine weather. David and Leslie rushed out to see it and had a ride round the block with Phil. The boys were thrilled with it and couldn't stop talking about it. David asked Phil what the number on the front – UH15 – meant. Phil explained to him that this was the registration number. In the coming days we had some lovely family trips in the car.

Then we had a telephone installed. It must have been one of the first in Barry. Our telephone number was BARRY 15.

Hardly any patients had phones to call us but it was most useful when Phil had to phone out to hospitals.

It was 1922 and all the talk was about the new age we were entering. It was the time of the "flapper girls", the Charleston dance and many other new things – not that we saw any of this in Barry, but we read about them in newspapers.

A wind of change was sweeping through society. We also read about the new fashions. The flapper girls had slim bodies, short skirts and exposed knees. They had short hair and lots of make-up. There was a new independence and almost defiance in young women. They were even known to smoke in public. These young women thought they had a new freedom.

This social change was accompanied by a change in political status. In 1918, women over 30 were given the vote, and a few years later everyone over 21 was enfranchised. Phil said women and politics would never be the same again!

Life was changing in the home too. Many new tools became available to make life easier. We were fortunate to have a good electricity supply, which these new devices needed. We soon had a vacuum cleaner, a toaster and an electric iron and an electric kettle. I still preferred to boil up a kettle of water on the stove for a fresh cuppa! This was a reminder of the good old days at home in Ireland.

As my church, St. Helen's, was only a short walk from our new home I was able to take part in more of the social activities. I don't know whether Phil approved, but he never complained. Gradually I became quite involved in the church.

# CHAPTER 71

My health had deteriorated since the birth of little Esme and I was finding it harder and harder to cope with everyday tasks. Dr. Griffiths suggested to Phil that we should send David, Mary and Leslie away to school to make life easier for me. Everyone thought boarding school was character forming for children. I didn't like the idea and thought the children were too young to go away. But Phil reminded me that my brother Tom had gone away to school in Waterford. He said, "It was good for Tom and I think it will be good for David." I said I would think about it.

After a lot of thought I eventually resigned myself to the idea of boarding school. I realised it gave David the opportunity to meet other boys from varying backgrounds. I remembered how much my brother Tom had benefited from this. One day I told Phil that I agreed to send David to school but I didn't want Mary or Leslie to go until we knew how it affected David. I thought they were too young to go away. Phil lost no time in making enquiries and the following autumn David went away to Kings College in Taunton over in Somerset. It was a long way for him to go and Phil took him there on the train. I went to see them off at the station remembering the many times in my life when I had waved goodbye to loved ones at railway stations. I really hated to see him go but I'd convinced myself that it was going to be good for him. Only time would tell.

Having only three children at home made life much easier but I really did miss David. Phil consoled me by saying it was only 6 weeks before the half-term holiday. I wondered if Mama had felt like this when young Tom had gone off to school in Waterford.

It was amazing how good the boarding school was for David. He came home at half term and he had grown into quite a little gentleman. I was glad he was enjoying his time there. He proudly showed us a photograph of his class taken outside the school building which was very impressive.

Phil was still considering sending Mary away to school. We discussed it many times and I insisted she should attend a Catholic school. We heard about a good convent boarding school for girls in Bristol. So, eventually we took Mary to La Retraite College in Bristol. Mary didn't want to leave home but Phil persuaded her she was going to love it. She was jealous of Esme and Les staying at home and getting all the attention when she and David were away. But it didn't take long for her to settle at school.

With the two older children off my hands I had a much easier time. It wasn't long before Esme was old enough to go to school. I enrolled her at the little school attached to our church so in the early days I walked her there and back every day. After I'd left her at the school gates I often went into the church and said a few prayers, thanking God for the good life we enjoyed.

The school holidays always came round quickly. The children had for some time been asking us to buy them a pet. They really wanted a dog. One day Phil came home and said he had a surprise for them. He had come in the back way and he took them out into the back garden. There in the garden was a little Airedale terrier puppy. They named him Buster and they loved him. Esme loved taking him to the park for walks and she felt quite grown up with her little dog on a lead.

We were now able to think about taking a summer holiday and Phil arranged for us to stay on a farm in Pembrokeshire for three weeks. Phil continued to work but joined us at weekends. Phil was still worrying about my health and when he came to see us on the second weekend he was pleased to see how well I was looking. I felt much better for the change of air and the children had a marvellous time.

David and Mary went back to school in the autumn that year and Phil and I often talked about taking a trip to Ireland. My brother Tom had invited us to stay several times but I had always put this off because of the troubles in Ireland. In 1925 we realised Ireland seemed to be peaceful again and I longed for that trip. Phil was very busy and suggested I should go and take Leslie and Esme with me during term time while David and Mary were away.

Arrangements were made and one fine day we set off. Phil took us to the station and we had a long train ride to West Wales where we caught the ferry at Fishguard. The children were exhausted when we arrived at the boat. I was thankful Phil had booked a cabin for us. Leslie insisted on having the top bunk and I squeezed into the bottom bunk with Esme. Poor little soul! She was only five years old and quite done in. We all slept well and managed to get a quick breakfast before the boat docked. A train was waiting at the dockside and we climbed in. Esme said, "Not another train ride!" Leslie and I burst out laughing but the poor little scrap didn't think it funny at all.

Tom met us at Kilkenny station. I hadn't seen him for about 14 years and he had grown into a fine gentleman. I embraced him and then introduced him to the children. Young Esme was sitting on a suitcase and crying, "I want to go home," and sobbing her little heart out.

I picked her up and said to Tom, "She is exhausted by all the travelling." We were soon in Tom's smart pony and trap and this seemed to calm Esme down. When we arrived in Callan Tom introduced us to his wife, Anne. She made us very welcome and I was delighted that the children took to her immediately. Then we were introduced to Tom's children – Richard, Michael and baby Mary. Leslie and Esme were meeting their cousins for the first time and wondered why they hadn't met these relations before. The children all got on well together.

We planned to stay for a week. I wanted to visit our house at Islands again and also to visit the family grave.

We went to bed early on that first night. We were exhausted but after a good night's sleep we were all refreshed and I was eager to see my old haunts. Our first trip was out to Islands to see the old house. It looked even smaller than the last time I had visited. New people had bought it and it had a fresh lick of paint so it looked better than I ever remembered it. Leslie was old enough to be interested in all we saw but Esme was too young to be concerned. Tom said he knew the new owners and knocked at the front door hoping that we could go in and have a look round again. But we were not in luck. They weren't in. Tom said, "Come on, Bridgie, let's go round the back and have a peep there." So we all crept into the back yard and then we went for a walk up to the field where we had all played those many years ago. It was lovely to be back. The air was fresh and, as we walked up the hill together, we re-lived some of the things we had done there as youngsters. It was a lovely day and I was so glad I had made the journey.

Over the next few days, we met up with old neighbours and friends. I visited Danny Murphy and his wife. We had lost touch over the years but I was amazed to hear they had seven children. Even though we never communicated with one another our old friendship blossomed quickly again. It was as if we had never been apart. We were old friends and there was always something special between us.

We also visited my brother Pat and his wife Anne in Shangarry. Tom wasn't keen for us to go there – there was still some sort of feud between the brothers. I didn't want this to get in the way of my friendship with Pat and put Tom's concerns to one side. Pat and Anne now had three young children; Richard was 13, Mary 11 and George 8 years old – more cousins for Leslie and Esme.

But I was saddened when I heard that Pat's children weren't all in good health. Little Mary was fine and bonny but Richard had something wrong with his back and legs and was almost a cripple.

And young George suffered from fits. Pat seemed unconcerned by his children's ailments, saying, "Sure, they're both fine. They've never known anything else and they're both happy boys." Anne kept very quiet and spent most of the time in the kitchen making tea for us.

The children all got on well together. Leslie was the same age as George who wanted to teach him hurling. Esme wasn't to be left out and was running up and down the field trying to keep up with them. It was soon time to say goodbye and I wondered when we might see them again. On the way back Leslie said to me, "I think Mary is beautiful and I think I'll marry her one day!"

The week in Ireland went by very quickly. When the children were in bed at night Tom and his wife told me how things were settling down again after the troubles. They had been through a bad time when Ireland was fighting for Home Rule. For years many Irish had seen the British as their enemies but things were different in the south now Ireland had gained independence from Britain. Everyone was looking forward to a brighter future.

Before we left for home at the end of the week, I paid another visit to our family grave in Modeshill. Once again I knelt beside the grave and offered up my prayers, remembering my grandparents, Mama and Papa and my dear sister Kate.

Too soon it was time to go. At the end of the week, I said goodbye to Tom and to my dear old Ireland. It had been a good trip and I was glad we had made it.

# CHAPTER 72

In spite of my trip to Ireland I was still not feeling well. Phil decided it was now time for Leslie to go away to school. We didn't want him to go to the same school as David. Phil thought it better for them to make their own way and he had heard about Epsom College in Surrey. He made the usual enquiries. It was a long way for him to go but I reluctantly agreed, knowing how much easier life was going to be with three children away at school. But Leslie didn't stay long at the school. He was most unhappy and complained that the older boys bullied him. We brought him home after just one term and sent him to a day school in nearby Penarth. He liked the new school.

Phil always held his surgery in the morning and afterwards he and Dr. Griffiths met in our breakfast room over a cup of coffee to discuss various patients. Each day they made up lists of the patients who needed visits. After coffee they each went their own way with their lists. Phil returned every day for his lunch and always took a nap in his chair before setting off again for the afternoon visits. One day he came home unexpectedly early and found me lying down upstairs. I often had a rest during the afternoon. He was concerned immediately about my health, saying that I was too young to need a rest during the day. I had been worried myself about my health for some time but I didn't want to worry Phil, as there didn't seem to be any reason for my condition. Phil took my temperature, which was normal, and did various checks, feeling my pulse and listening to my chest. He couldn't find anything wrong with me but suggested I should see a consultant. I duly attended the hospital in Cardiff to see the top man.

Once again, no reason could be found for my tiredness and lethargy. I knew Phil was still worried but he was pleased to have the all-clear from the consultant.

My activities at the church took up much of my time and while there I seemed to forget my ill health. I joined the Ladies Sewing Guild. We were a friendly crowd and sewing wasn't our only activity. We raised money for charity and we helped those in the community less fortunate than ourselves. My interests grew as the years passed and eventually I was elected President of the Sewing Guild. How strange – from the young girl in New York who couldn't stand sewing to the President of our local guild! I took my duties seriously and these interests took my mind off my failing health.

One day Phil picked up the local paper and said, "Have you seen this, Bridget? You're mentioned in the local paper. It says, '*the President of the Ladies Guild, Mrs. B. Richards, presented the new Bishop with a beautiful clock, the gift of the members of the Guild to mark the esteem in which they hold their much beloved Bishop. The Bishop thanked the ladies for their kind and generous gift, which he would always appreciate. He wished the Guild to continue in their efforts to help the Parish and hoped they would always have success.'*"

When Phil finished reading he put the paper down and came over to me and gave me a kiss, saying, "I'm proud of you, Bridget, in spite of your ill health you are making an important contribution to society."

In 1927 my health took a turn for the worse again and I returned to see the consultant in Cardiff. Phil came with me and we were told that the problem was with my kidneys, but the doctor wasn't able to say exactly what the trouble was and couldn't provide a cure. He suggested plenty of rest and I was to see him again in a month's time.

Phil arrived home one day to tell me the people who had been living in our house were about to vacate it. Five years had passed by very quickly. Although we had been happy in "Ravenscourt" I was pleased we were moving back to "East Anglia".

We settled down happily in our old home and life was much easier for me as we had a live-in maid. I was able to relax knowing there was always someone there to help me.

The children were all leading busy lives. They had many good times. There was a new cinema not far away and Esme loved the new film "Felix the Cat" and wanted to see it more than once. I decided once was enough. We only allowed the children to go to the cinema about once a month although other children went several times. David loved going to the cinema and I was surprised when he told me the programme consisted of a newsreel, a feature film, a second film, followed by adverts and cartoons. It seemed to be very good value for money. The cinema sold sweets to the children and we always gave Esme a halfpenny to take with her so she could buy sherbet. David and Leslie bought gobstoppers and candies!

The children were always getting up to some mischief or other. Little Esme had a teddy bear called Moco. One day Leslie stole the teddy from her and cut it up into little pieces. Esme was distraught and cried for hours. Phil was cross with Leslie and he was duly punished.

David had left school and was soon to go to Cardiff where he had obtained a place in the medical school attached to Cardiff Royal Infirmary and the university. He was following in his father's footsteps. Mary was still at school and they were both enjoying the summer holidays. They both had friends locally and spent much time with them. They often went swimming and spent a lot of time on the beach.

One day David came home and told me he had been to see a new film in Cardiff. It was called "The Jazz Singer". He raved over it. It was the first film to have fully synchronised sound. David was very musical and could play the piano by ear. Films were in fashion and a new children's film came to Barry. It was called "Mickey Mouse". Esme loved it.

Then one day at the church I saw a poster on the notice board about a forthcoming pilgrimage to Lourdes. I had read a lot about Lourdes and I knew many miracle cures had taken place there. My medical training told me this wasn't really possible and I knew that Phil, as a doctor, thought the same. I wondered if I should try and make this trip. If the doctors couldn't cure me then my faith might help to make things easier for me. It was a long shot but for the moment I decided not to say anything about it.

Since Phil had been in practice with Dr. Griffiths life had been much easier for us, in spite of my deteriorating health. Phil had made several friends locally and had started to play golf when he had time off. He always brought his friends home after a round of golf and I prepared supper for them. We all became very friendly and after supper we played cards and had a social drink together. Griff Jenkins and Nash Jones became firm friends of ours. Griff was a confirmed bachelor and Nash was married. He often brought his wife Molly with him when they stayed for supper.

Griff and I became great pals. He was a very understanding man and I often poured my heart out to him. I told him about our religious difficulties and he knew about my illness. When I told him about the forthcoming pilgrimage to Lourdes he seemed to be in favour of it. He encouraged me to go if I could manage it. Phil, however, was against the idea when I mentioned it to him.

I read more about Lourdes from a book I had borrowed from our Priest. Lourdes was in southern France, quite near to the Pyrenees Mountains. In 1858 a peasant girl called Bernadette Soubirous was wandering outside her village when she discovered a cave. Bernadette came from a poor family and at the age of 11 years she contracted cholera. She was 14 years old when she saw her first apparition in the cave of the Virgin Mary. When she explored the cave she discovered a spring. It was at this spring that a number of miracle cures were said to have taken place.

This cave later became known as the Grotto. Here, in the cave the apparition said to her, "I am the immaculate conception." One day the apparition told her to tell her Priest that people were to come to the cave in procession. The church listened to her but remained indifferent, believing her to be rather strange. Rumours soon spread of the apparition of "Our Lady" at Lourdes. Bernadette didn't have anything to do with the cave as in later years she became a nun and died at the age of 35.

But in 1862 the local Bishop acknowledged the apparitions and authorised the building of a shrine. Then a railway line was built linking the town of Lourdes by rail to the rest of France and Europe.

Now, some 60 years later it was a place of pilgrimage for Catholics from all over the world. There was the story of a young man who had been badly injured in the Great War. He was a young Irish man who had fought at Gallipoli. He had been injured by machine gun fire and was wounded in the head and he had two bullet wounds in the chest. He was in a bad state and the surgeons wanted to amputate one of his arms. He refused. He suffered from fits and became incontinent. Both his legs were paralysed. In 1920 his skull had been trepanned and a silver plate inserted to protect his brain. His condition worsened and he was confined to a wheelchair. He was admitted to a home for Incurables. He was a Catholic and wanted to go to Lourdes. His carers didn't want him to go but he persevered and he nearly died on the journey. He arrived safely and went to the procession of the Blessed Sacrament in front of the Basilica.

The stretcher-bearers took him to the baths several times. The water from the spring flowed into the baths and was said to have curative elements. The Archbishop of Rheims passed in front of him and at that moment he realised that for the first time in 8 years he was able to move his arm. He tried to get up from the stretcher and the brancardiers (volunteer stretcher-bearers) thought he was hysterical and sedated him. When he arrived back at the hospital he was able to walk several steps. His reflexes had been restored. The next morning he got up from bed and went to the Grotto where he prayed. A crowd gathered and news soon spread of this miracle cure. Before he left Lourdes the doctors examined him and they pronounced him fit and well.

I was very interested to read about this young man. But I knew cases like this were very rare. I decided there and then to go on the pilgrimage although I didn't expect a cure. I was going for spiritual healing, to help me persevere with my life. I knew it was going to be difficult to persuade Phil. I knew he would never understand the fulfilment this journey would give me.

I talked to Griff and explained my plans to him and told him I expected difficulties when I told Phil. Griff was very supportive and told me I should go ahead with my plans. So, one evening I mentioned my desires to Phil again. As expected, he wasn't keen on the idea. But he didn't say I couldn't go and so from then on I continually nagged him until eventually he gave in.

The day of my departure to France came quickly once the decision had been made. I was pleased when I realised the trip had been organised by none other than Bishop Vaughan who had been our Parish Priest some years ago. Phil took me to Cardiff and from there I took the train to London where the pilgrims met at Southwark. From London we took the train to Dover. The train sped through the Kent countryside and as we passed Canterbury we could see the Cathedral spire in the distance. Then we took the boat to France. Several hours after leaving London we arrived on French soil at Boulogne. It took some hours for all the sick to be transferred from the boat to the train.

We began our long journey through the French countryside. Phil and I had made this journey in the opposite direction on our return from Nice. Some of the places we passed through I remembered from that journey so long ago.

Early in the morning and still on the train we woke to the sound of prayers from loudspeakers. I noticed that many of the pilgrims were Irish. I had forgotten how religious the Irish were. They sang a lot on the journey – national songs and hymns.

There were many sick and ill people on the train. By comparison I felt quite well and healthy. There were people suffering from incurable illnesses and I noticed many old soldiers who had been injured in the Great War. They made a sad sight, with their amputated limbs, shell shock and general debility. This pilgrimage demanded a great effort from those who were brave enough to embark on it.

The pilgrimage also demanded spiritual preparation but this wasn't as difficult as the physical effort. We were all given a badge to wear. The badge had a figure representing the Virgin Mary in the centre. I wore this with pride. We were told that it distinguished the sick from the helpers.

Eventually we arrived at our destination. I went straight to my hotel – the Grand Hotel de la Chapelle du Parc. I was amazed to find the proprietor's name was Soubirous and that he was a relative of Bernadette Soubirous. He acquainted himself with all the pilgrims and his welcome made us feel at home. After our long journey we retired to our rooms to rest. I slept like I have never slept before. It was very quiet there and I slept for a full 14 hours. When I rose the next day I felt refreshed and was ready to take to the waters.

After breakfast I joined a party visiting the famous Grotto. We stood in a steadily moving queue of pilgrims making their way in the same direction. As I arrived at the grotto I saw the stone was black and shiny. Pilgrims were walking round the edge of the cave. Some were running their hands over the stone. Others were touching the stone with their rosaries. With the others I knelt and kissed the stone.

We all prayed for relief from our illnesses. Very few pilgrims expected a cure. We all hoped and prayed for a miracle but most of us recognised this was a spiritual journey. We were seeking composure and serenity. We expected to achieve great blessings from that alone.

The statue of "Our Lady" occupied a niche in the rock. It was carved from marble. The original spring was now piped underground and the water was channelled to the Baths where the pilgrims bathed each day.

Every day we followed the same routine. In the morning the sick bathed in the Baths. In the afternoon we joined the procession of the Blessed Sacrament. This procession was very emotional and ended with the blessing of the sick. In the evenings we joined a torchlight procession. Thousands of pilgrims were singing the Ave Maria and carrying candles. It was a sight to behold and very emotional. The water in the Baths was very cold early in the morning but warmed up during the day so I delayed my visits as long as possible. At the far end of the Baths was a statue of the Madonna and a card for prayers. The stretcher-bearers lowered the immobile into the water.

After two days we had a free day. I took the opportunity to visit the Pyrenees. This was a wonderful trip and I made friends with several pilgrims during the day. That evening, May 20th, 1928, I sat down and penned a letter to my friend Griff at home. It went as follows:

*My dear Griff,*

*You would be astonished if I could fully describe all that I have seen since I arrived here. The hours of devotion are numerous and between the Acts I think of you. This sounds nearly like a love letter Griff. But you know me well enough and will allow for my respectful familiarity. It is truly written from my heart. I stood the journey well Griff. I have had not a moment's uncomfortableness during the trip.*

*There are a large number of pilgrims and the torch light procession is very wonderful and when one sees people so fervent and faithful one has to realise that there is some great power behind it all. The churches are magnificent and the architecture fine. The weather is cold and wet and I'm glad I brought some warm clothes.*

*The Archbishop of Cardiff leads the pilgrimage with Bishop Vaughan and the Bishop of Brentwood. I shall be glad to get home and I am longing to see my family again. There is no place like home.*

*Phil is coming to Lourdes someday. I should like him to see it and the children too. How is Nash? Remember me to him. I will send him a card from Paris. Everyone seems so good here and the absence of smoking is remarkable.*

*Cheerio*

*Yours very sincerely B.M. Richards*

I posted the letter and returned to the hotel. I wondered what made me write such a letter. After all, I had only sent short postcards to Phil and the children. I found peace in this place and I wrote to the only person who had encouraged me to come here. It was a strange feeling. As I lay in bed that night my thoughts went back to my youth in Ireland and then over my life. I had really only had two firm boyfriends. First there was Danny Murphy, then Phil and now in my latter years I had met Griff. I always thought of myself as a "one-man" woman but I realised that each of my friends had comforted me in different ways. Danny had been the sweetheart of my youth, Phil was my lifetime partner and now Griff was my soulmate. I loved them all in different ways. Life was strange.

Eventually our week at Lourdes was over and one of the last ceremonies before departure was the Mass and the anointing of the sick. This was a reminder to us of Eternal Life and a reminder of Bernadette's message. She said, "There is no promise of happiness in this world." This was a sobering thought. Suffering now had a meaning for us and we were strengthened. We believed what we were told, "that the sick had been chosen to suffer for the healthy".

On my way home, I broke the journey in Paris and as promised sent a card to Nash. I only spent one night there, as I was anxious to return home.

I was tired when I arrived back in Cardiff. Phil met me at the station and asked how I was feeling. I told him I was exhausted from the journey but spiritually refreshed. I had gained a new energy to continue my life. And so life continued.

Our children were happy. David was now studying medicine and Leslie hoped to follow him. We discussed the merits of sending Esme away to school but in then end decided against it and she went to the Barry County School. Mary decided she wanted to be a nurse and she also went to Cardiff to train at Cardiff Infirmary.

Phil was earning a good living as a doctor. He was a kind and considerate person. He knew that many of his patients were poor and couldn't afford to pay his bills. He told me once that he could tell by the condition of their shoes whether they were able to afford his bill. I know there were some people he didn't charge for his services. He was well liked in the town. We never suffered by not charging fees to everyone.

In general, times were hard for many people. In America there was mass unemployment and things were bad in Britain too. Then in October 1929 we heard about the Wall Street crash in New York. It made headlines in all the papers. The crash of the stock market was followed by a great depression. People were worried as the same was expected to happen in Britain. I worried about my brothers and sisters in New York and hoped they were not out of work.

As the next three years progressed I grew more unwell but I soldiered on, remembering the blessings I had received in France. But things had to end for me and my illness took a turn for the worse. In the spring of 1931 I took to my bed. Phil looked after me and engaged a night nurse to be with me at this difficult time. The consultant came from Cardiff and Phil asked Dr. Griffiths to examine me too.

I realised the writing was on the wall. Then I was told that I had Bright's disease – a disease of the kidneys, for which there was no cure. Phil sat by my bed and talked me through the difficult hours.

I was glad the children were settled and my only worry was little Esme. I said to Phil, "Look after the children for me and make sure Esme says her prayers."

Phil was desperately sad and felt useless and frustrated as there was little he could do to help. He said, "Hush now, try and get some rest. Please don't talk like that."

I replied, "Phil, I am ready to go. I will miss you and the children but you mustn't mourn for too long. I hope you can find a good woman to look after you all." Phil hated me talking like this. He didn't realise how much my faith helped me in my last days. That night Esme came to see me and kissed me goodnight.

*Bridget passed peacefully away that night. She died in the knowledge that she had lived a good life and that Phil would take care of her children.*

# AFTERWORD

*Dear Reader,*

I hope you enjoyed reading *First to Go*. I would like to tell you a little more about the book.

Two years after Bridget's death Philip married an old family friend, Edith Anne Hughes. Edith was a domestic science teacher at a local school and had been a nurse with Bridget at the hospital during the First World War. She took over the household and Bridget's children always called her "Auntie".

Philip and Edith were married in Llandaff Cathedral in Cardiff. Edith was of the Anglican faith and Philip was still a Baptist. Two years later Philip's first grandson (David's son) Alun was born in London and a year later I was born in Cardiff. It is strange and amazing that Philip arranged for his two grandchildren to be christened at Llancarvan Parish Church in the vale of Glamorgan in the Anglican faith. It is also amazing that both Alan and I were christened with the middle names "Frisby" in memory of our grandmother. This naming custom was followed in later years for my sister Anne and my brother Peter. I do not know whether this was Philip's idea or my father's. But, for whatever reason, whether it was because of Philip's remorse or David's love of his mother, we were christened in memory of our grandmother who we would never know.

So, I grew up always wondering why I had this strange middle name. My father told me it was in memory of his mother, Bridget Frisby, who had died young. I always wondered about Bridget. What was she like? Did I look like her? Much later in life I decided to find out more about the Frisby family. I contacted my father's sister, my Aunty Esme, who told me all about her mother. Esme was only 11 years old when Bridget died.

All the anecdotes she related to me are contained in *First to Go*. In 1991 I went with Esme to Ireland to find out more about the Frisby family. Our first stop was at the National Archives in Dublin and I am grateful to the staff for the help they gave us. There we saw the original documents of the 1901 Ireland Census. It listed the family still living at Islands and was signed by my great grandfather, Richard Frisby. It also listed all the outbuildings, the cow house, the calf house, the dairy, the piggery, the fowl house, the shed and the stable.

In the Archives we also found the education records for Mohober School and read with interest the examiner's reports over the years. It is easy to see from these how unsettling they were for Richard.

We visited the National Library of Ireland and here I record my thanks to the staff who helped us. We browsed the microfilm of Catholic Parish Records but this was going to be a long job so we decided to take a short cut and visit the Parish Priest in Ballingarry to see if we could find out more about the family. Whilst in the library we viewed various records in search of our Frisby ancestors. We found two in the 17th century, Francis and William.

The book *A Dictionary of Irish Surnames* by Edward MacLysaght recorded the name Frisby first appearing in Ireland in County Kilkenny in the 17th century. We were unable to link our family back to the 17th century as Irish records before 1800 are almost non-existent – unless your ancestor was someone of renown.

We made our way to County Tipperary. We visited the old family house at Islands and the present occupants, Irene and Peter Waring, invited us in and showed us around. An extension had been built in recent years but the rooms our ancestors had lived in still existed and it was a strange to stand in one of the bedrooms and realise this was where my grandmother had been born.

This was a very moving visit. We noticed the thick walls and how small the windows were.

As we left the house at Islands my aunt and I felt we had been taken back to another era. We imagined life as it had been in previous centuries, without gas, electricity, or a water supply. We were grateful to Peter and Irene for allowing us this insight into our family's past and we understood better what life must have been like for Bridget, her parents and siblings.

I was in touch with the Warings a few years later when a book on the history of Mohober School was being compiled. I was able to supply them with details of the history of the school which I had obtained from the Archives in Dublin on a previous visit. When the book was published it contained the article I had written and a photograph of my great grandfather, Richard Frisby who had been schoolmaster at Mohober for nearly 40 years.

Next we visited the school at Mohober and Miss Lahert, the teacher in charge, welcomed us and showed us round the small ancient building. She pulled out some old books – school registers. Imagine our surprise when we saw the names of Bridget and her siblings listed among the pupils. Again a strange feeling as we realised that the handwriting was that of Bridget's father, Richard.

The following day we visited Father Philip Morris, the Parish Priest at Ballingarry. He welcomed us and pulled out his old records. Imagine our surprise when we left with details of four generations of our family back to a christening in 1815 – and the parents of this child were listed and this took us back to 1790. Four generations of the family had lived in the house at Islands.

What an amazing journey we had.

Following this I have made several trips to Ireland almost once a year. I visited many places. The newspaper collection at Thurles Library had helpful obituaries and articles. I did so much research that I was able to contact other Frisby families. Sister Hannah Frisby of Callan provided me with details of the Kilkenny Frisbys and I am grateful to her, not only for the information she gave me, but for all the hospitality. Hannah has been a good friend over the years and on every visit to Ireland has helped me with my research. We have spent many times visiting graveyards and other places of interest.

My research was also conducted through the website Ancestry.com. From this I was able to trace the whereabouts of Bridget's brothers' families in New York. John and his descendants had stayed in New York. Richard, when he left the New York Fire Brigade, had retired to a lakeside home in New Jersey but his descendants are still in New York today. I am in touch with three descendants of Bridget's brothers in New York.

The letters I have transcribed in the book actually exist. Written over 100 years ago, they are an insight into the minds of the writers. They have helped me enormously to understand the character of the family.

I hope you enjoyed reading this story.

*Pam Skelton*

*Copy of the Mohober school register showing Bridget's brothers, Thomas, Patrick and Richard (about 1895)*

*Part of Tom's letter to Bridget after the death of their mother in 1907*
*(My Dear sister)*

GRAND HOTEL DE LA CHAPELLE
ET DU PARC

É-SOUBIROUS
PROPRIÉTAIRE

LOURDES

CENSEUR

LÉPHONE : 10

Com. Lourdes 276

*May. 20 14 1928*

*From letter sent by Bridget from Lourdes in 1928*

*Philip Richards aged 18*

*Bridget Frisby in 1904, aged 25*

*Bridget & Philip in 1910 with David*

*The house at Islands, Tipperary in about 1905.*
*From left to right, John Cleary, Richard Frisby, Bab-Ann Cleary,*
*Mary Frisby & Mary-Ann Frisby*

*Richard Frisby, Bridget's father – about 1900*

*Philip & David on Ned at Islands in 1910*

*David & Mary*

*David & Mary with their Welsh grandparents*

*Philip & Bridget with Leslie (top), David & Mary*

*Bridget – about 1910*

*Esme at 18-years-old*

*"East Anglia" – as it is today*

# BIBLIOGRAPHY

## BOOKS

1. *The Crime of the Century* by Charles River Editors
2. *Ragtime* by E.L. Doctorow, Random House, Inc., 1974
3. *The Murder of Stanford White* by Gerald Langford, The Bobbs-Merrill Company, Inc., 1962.
4. *The Architect of Desire* by Suzannah Lessard, Bantam Doubleday Dell, 1996.
5. *Evelyn Nesbit and Stanford White* by Michael Macdonald Mooney, William Morrow and Company, Inc., 1976.
6. *The Girl in the Red Velvet Swing* by Charles Samuels (New York: Gold Medal Books, 1953, re-printed Mattituck: Aeonian Press ND)

## FILM

"THE GIRL IN THE RED VELVET SWING", 1955, 20th Century Fox, 109 min. Joan Collins stars as Gibson-girl Evelyn Nesbit, whose fatal charms led to the murder of architect Stanford White.

## INTERNET

1. Ancestry.co.uk – the genealogical website with millions of records
2. Wikipedia – the Internet's free encyclopaedia
3. Encarta – Microsoft Encarta was a digital multimedia encyclopaedia published by Microsoft Corporation from 1993 to 2009.
4. LIBRARY OF CONGRESS (USA) Newspaper Reading Room website: https://www.loc.gov/rr/news/topics (Various newspapers reporting the trial of Harry Thaw/Stanford White murder/Evelyn Nesbit. 1906/7/8. This website has a cornucopia of newspaper articles. Website: Evelynnesbit.com

# ACKNOWLEDGEMENTS

My biggest thanks go to my Aunt Esme (RIP) who told me all she knew about her mother's life. Without her this story would not have been told.

Secondly my thanks Peter and Irene Waring at Islands, Tipperary, for welcoming us into their home and subsequently incorporating details of Richard Frisby in the book telling the history of Mohober School.

In Ireland I had much help from Sister Hannah Frisby in Callan, County Kilkenny, who came from another branch of the Frisby family. She and I spent many hours travelling around in Counties Kilkenny and Tipperary piecing together details of Frisby ancestry. Thank you, Hannah – I won't be dragging you round any more gravestones. And I must not forget Sister Magdalena Frisby (RIP) in Dublin who told me all about her branch of the family.

The genealogical records of Ancestry.com have been invaluable and enabled me to find the whereabouts of Bridget's siblings in New York and I was able to trace their descendants, still living in New York today.

Thanks also to the staff at the National Archives in Dublin and the National Library in Dublin whose staff always gave of their time willingly.

Thank you to Philip Morris, parish priest at Ballingarry, County Tipperary for providing details of 4 generations of the Frisby family who all lived in the house at Islands

Thank you also to Miss Lahert, teacher at Mohober National school who invited us into the old school building and showed us the registers of pupils which included several Frisby children.

The staff at Thurles Library, county Tipperary were helpful in providing access to old Irish newspapers.

Thanks to my sister Anne who came with me to Cardiff Central Library to search for articles and obituaries in old copies of the newspaper Barry & District News.

Thank you to my friends Anne Chidgey and Ann Morgan who read the original manuscript and gave me some valuable comments.

Finally, I could not have written the book without the support of my husband – thank you, Michael.

This has been a long journey but it has resulted in a memoir of my grandmother who I never knew. This story is based on true facts but for the sake of the story it has been embellished. I researched historical events and any historical error is entirely mine.

# ABOUT THE AUTHOR

Pam was born in Cardiff but spent most of her early life in Bristol where she was educated at the Red Maids School. After leaving school she did not follow any usual career path but after a short spell at a commercial college she took a secretarial job and later managed to achieve success in business in London as firstly an Export Manager then as a Company Director. The rest of her working life was spent in business back in Bristol with her husband Michael. Pam and Michael have one son, David. On her retirement Pam took up various hobbies – golf, genealogy, travel and bridge. Her love of genealogy led her to discover much about her family, on which this novel is based.

Printed in Great Britain
by Amazon